Women of Wonder

THE CONTEMPORARY YEARS

WITHDRAWN

Women of

Science Fiction by Women

A HARVEST ORIGINAL ★ HARCOURT BRACE & COMPANY

Wonder

THE CONTEMPORARY YEARS

from the 1970s to the 1990s

Edited and with an introduction and notes by

PAMELA SARGENT

San Diego New York London

Copyright © 1995 by Pamela Sargent

All rights reserved. No part of this publication may be reproduced or transmitted in any form or by any means, electronic or mechanical, including photocopy, recording, or any information storage and retrieval system, without permission in writing from the publisher.

Requests for permission to make copies of any part of the work should be mailed to: Permissions Department, Harcourt Brace & Company, 6277 Sea Harbor Drive, Orlando, Florida 32887-6777.

Library of Congress Cataloging-in-Publication Data
Women of wonder, the contemporary years: science fiction by women from the 1970s to the 1990s/edited and with an introduction and notes by Pamela Sargent.—1st ed.
p. cm.
"A Harvest original."
Includes bibliographical references.
ISBN 0-15-600033-4
1. Science fiction, American—Women authors. 2. Women—Social life and customs—Fiction. 3. American fiction—20th century.
I. Sargent, Pamela.
PS648.S3W643 1994
813'.08762089287—dc20 94-39228

DECATUR PUBLIC LIBRARY
OCT 15 1995
DECATUR, ILLINOIS

Text set in Primer
Designed by Kaelin Chappell
Printed in the United States of America
First edition
A B C D E

Permissions acknowledgments appear on pages 421–22, which constitute a continuation of the copyright page.

Contents

Acknowledgments

I would like to thank the following people:

Richard Curtis, Joseph Elder, Anne Freedgood, David Garnett, Martin H. Greenberg, Virginia Kidd, John Radziewicz, Shirley Sargent, Ian Watson, and Janeen Webb.

I am also extremely grateful to my editors, Michael Kandel and Christa Malone, for their counsel and their patience.

Vonda N. McIntyre deserves thanks for helping to guide the first *Women of Wonder* anthology to its original publisher.

Special thanks are owed to Jack Dann for his brainstorming, and most especially to George Zebrowski, whose moral support, editorial advice, and library were invaluable.

I also owe much to the late Janet Kafka, who offered me the chance to edit my first anthology twenty years ago, and who was the kind of editor all writers hope to have.

Introduction

PAMELA SARGENT

In March of 1991, science fiction and fantasy writer Pat Murphy announced the establishment of a new award for science fiction that imaginatively examines gender roles, the James Tiptree Jr., Award. (Tiptree died in 1987, at the age of seventy-one.) Murphy was assisted in the planning of this award by another writer, Karen Joy Fowler, and had the approval of the Tiptree estate.

When James Tiptree, Jr., revealed in 1977 that she was a woman named Alice Sheldon, the news came as a great surprise to most of the science fiction community. Her writing, despite its obvious sympathy and compassion for women, had seemed so male to many readers. For an award designed to honor the kind of science fiction that explores and expands the roles of women and men, the Tiptree name seemed an eminently suitable choice. In addition, as Pat Murphy pointed out, science fiction already had several awards named after men, among them the Hugo Award (named for Hugo Gernsback), the Theodore Sturgeon Award (given annually to an outstanding work of fantastic short fiction), the John W. Campbell Awards for Best Novel and for Best New Writer (named after the influential editor of *Astounding* and *Analog*), the Arthur C. Clarke Award (for the best science fiction novel of the year published in England), and the Philip K. Dick Award (for the best science fiction or fantasy book first published in paperback). It was time for an award to be named after a female writer, and the fact that the name was a female writer's male pseudonym added a nice touch of irony. The Tiptree Award has been given annually since 1992, financed largely by such typically female fund-raising activities as bake sales and the selling of cookbooks.

The Tiptree Award calls attention to works that fulfill one of the main purposes of science fiction: freeing the reader, at least temporarily, from the social and sexual assumptions of our culture. As Joanna Russ has stated:

> The myths of science fiction run along the lines of exploring a new world conceptually (not necessarily physically), creating needed physical or social machinery, assessing the consequences of technological or other changes, and so on. These are not stories about men *qua* Man and women *qua* Woman; they are myths of human intelligence and human adaptability. They not only ignore gender roles but—at least theoretically—are not culture-bound. Some of the most fascinating characters in science fiction are not human.[1]

By 1991, the effect of the women's movement on science fiction had faded in the minds of many. There was a need by then for an award that specifically honored and called attention to works that dealt imaginatively and inventively with gender roles. Some of the writers who had created a stir in the '70s were being forgotten. Women were still writing science fiction and winning acclaim for their work; indeed, some of the most honored, accomplished, and important writers in the field were women, so no one could say that the field excluded women or that they had no audience. The situation was more complicated and ambiguous than that.

On the surface, it seemed that women writers were finally being accepted, with their gender being irrelevant. In 1980, Joan D. Vinge's popular novel *The Snow Queen* was published; this novel about the ruler of the planet Tiamat and her cloned daughter won a Hugo Award and the praise of Arthur C. Clarke. A year later, Julian May returned to science fiction, after almost three decades away from the field, with her novel *The Many-Colored Land* (1981). Ursula K. Le Guin had become as important an influence on the genre as Arthur C. Clarke, Isaac Asimov, and Robert A. Heinlein. Anne McCaffrey had reached the best-seller lists; C. J. Cherryh and Tanith Lee were developing into two of science fiction's most prolific writers. Cherryh's "Cassandra" (1978) is a moving portrayal of a woman gifted—or cursed—with precognition. Lee, one of the field's most versatile writers, is represented here by "The Thaw" (1979), which tells of a woman who must deal with a cryonically preserved ancestor who is revived. In the late '70s and early '80s, it seemed that women in science fiction had overcome all gender barriers and that even more of them would enter and be welcomed in the field.

To a great extent, this is what happened. But in the late '70s, the

[1] Joanna Russ, "What Can a Heroine Do, or Why Women Can't Write," *Images of Women in Fiction: Feminist Perspectives,* edited by Susan K. Cornillon (Bowling Green, Ohio: Bowling Green University Popular Press, 1973), 4.

most widely popular event in science fiction was not the publication of a written work but the release of a motion picture, *Star Wars*, which derived its plot, characters, and settings largely from old pulp-magazine science fiction. Indeed, there is only one important female character in *Star Wars*. This movie, diverting entertainment that it is, had a significant effect on written science fiction.

The late '70s also saw the growth of conservatism in both the U.S. and Britain, which affected the genre as well. Publishers, influenced partly by *Star Wars*, were confronted with the fact that there was a much wider audience for traditional adventure stories than for innovative fiction. They became increasingly hostile to literary experimentation in science fiction, thus limiting the range of innovations in the field and the varieties of work available to readers. A conservative political climate that encouraged tradition brought more people to view feminism as a step in the wrong direction, even as an aberration.

To discuss any literature, especially one as rooted in popular culture as science fiction, without taking market forces and the general cultural climate into consideration is a mistake. Science fiction derives from both the utopian literary tradition and pulp adventure fiction. Writers have used the tropes of the genre both to write serious literary work and to spin yarns. Some have argued convincingly that the television series (and later movie series) *Star Trek*, which won the devotion of many female fans (partly because *Star Trek* makes an effort to give women, as well as people of different races and backgrounds, important roles in its imagined future), may have attracted more women to science fiction than did the women's movement.

Some science fiction succeeds in removing readers from their own culture, but some is simply our world or our past in disguise. There has always been a tension between the more intellectual purposes of the genre (the questioning of our society's assumptions) and what many readers seek in it (escapism that is diverting without being disturbing). Not surprisingly, the escapist variety of science fiction is the more popular and is almost always more commercially successful. It is what most people unfamiliar with science fiction think of as science fiction, even though the more ambitious variety is in time pillaged to feed the commercial mills. Increasingly, the late '70s saw less room on publishers' lists for work that wasn't popular entertainment or written by the genre's best-known authors.

The '80s, for women in the science fiction community as well as for their sisters in other spheres, was an ambiguous decade. Women were writing and publishing science fiction with regularity, but more were consciously or unconsciously trying to avoid the label of "feminist," a term that had fallen into disrepute. Some people could be heard questioning whether or not the science fiction that women were writing was in fact "real" science fiction. In this context, the '70s no longer seemed such an innovative period for the genre. The contributions of women during that time, when not ignored, came in for some criticism. The writer Charles Platt typifies this attitude toward the '70s:

> Thus from the New Wave, via the *Dangerous Visions* series, thence Damon Knight's *Orbit* anthologies and Milford writing workshops, evolved a generation who used the props of science fiction (aliens, time travel, starships) without any real interest in plausibility as their predecessors had known it. A new "soft" science fiction emerged, largely written by women: Joan Vinge, Vonda McIntyre, Ursula Le Guin, Joanna Russ, Kate Wilhelm, Carol Emshwiller. Their concern for human values was admirable, but they eroded science fiction's one great strength that had distinguished it from all other fantastic literature: its implicit claim that events described could actually come true.[2]

This statement of Platt's, I would argue, actually demonstrates some progress. Once women were discouraged from being members of the science fiction community, and now they are influential enough to be blamed for the decline of the field. One wonders, however, why Platt aimed his criticism specifically at women when many men writing science fiction were vulnerable to the same charges.

Another view of the '70s, offered by writer Bruce Sterling, is unambiguous: "I found most science fiction in the 1970s to be unreadably dull . . . the vast majority of published science fiction, then as now, is hollow pop entertainment. . . ."[3] He did not single out women writers for blame, but one might ask how the highly talented Sterling, who published his own earliest novels during the '70s, could have such a poor impression of a decade in which accomplished science fiction was published by Samuel R. Delany, J. G. Ballard, Ursula K. Le Guin, Brian Aldiss, Thomas M. Disch, Kate Wilhelm, Harlan Ellison, Robert Silverberg, Octavia E. Butler, Joanna Russ, and Gene Wolfe.

Maybe it's just that newcomers wanting to make a name for themselves find it to their advantage to sweep away the past, to call earlier

[2] Charles Platt, "The RAPE of Science Fiction," *Science Fiction Eye,* 1, no. 5 (July 1989), 44.

[3] Bruce Sterling, *Aurora SF* 10, no. 2 (Summer 1990), 7.

accomplishments insignificant, or to demonstrate that all progress leads to them. Maybe it's only a sign that Americans in particular have a propensity for cultural and historical amnesia. But the publishing atmosphere and the political climate later on surely had an effect on how the science fiction of the '70s (and that decade in general) was viewed by some of those looking back.

A backlash had developed. Much of the innovative writing of the '70s, including that by women, was neglected or had been forgotten. One could be left with the impression, if one had not been actively involved in science fiction during the '70s, that the science fiction of that decade was as dull as Sterling imagines it to be.

In fact, what was happening during the '70s mirrored some of the divisions that marked the genre in previous decades. Jules Verne centered his books around feats of technology and engineering (although he offered some sociological and political criticism as well), while H. G. Wells became more utopian in his works. The exotic pulp adventures of the magazines of the '30s, with their lengthy descriptions and expository passages, were displaced during the '40s by crisply written science fiction rooted in realism; Robert Heinlein was perhaps the most influential of those new '40s writers. During the '50s, more writers were coming to use the genre as a vehicle for sociological extrapolation and for satire. The '60s saw a debate between more traditional writers and the advocates of literary experimentation. During the '70s, the questions raised by the women's movement offered new opportunities to imagine worlds that did not take our world's deeply rooted assumptions about the sexes for granted.

All of these divisions and disputes served the purpose of shaking up the genre, keeping the best writers from becoming too complacent and bringing new writers into the field. Some ignored such disputes and went on writing as they always had; others became partisans of one side or another; still others were influenced by the new approaches and adapted them to their own fiction without abandoning all of their former techniques. To its benefit, the genre tended to assimilate what was useful.

It is in this context that one might begin to understand the worries expressed by Charles Platt. He expresses a concern for science fiction's realistic tradition when he claims that the only feature distinguishing science fiction from other fiction is its plausibility. Isaac Asimov offers as a definition of science fiction that it is fiction about the human impact of science and technology. Lose that as science fiction's center, one might argue, and nothing distinguishes it from any other kind of fantastic fiction; it becomes simply another kind of fantasy. Whether one agrees with this assertion or not, it is still difficult to understand why Platt directs his reproach at women writers unless he is simply looking for scapegoats. It's especially strange when some of the women on Platt's list, Kate Wilhelm and Vonda McIntyre in particular, write work that aims at realism and plausibility.

Bruce Sterling's misgivings are also understandable as an expression of concern for realism and well-developed ideas. Looking at what much science fiction appeared to be, namely "hollow pop entertainment" (as, in fact, a lot of published science fiction has been during every period of the genre's history), he concludes that the science fiction of the '70s was "dull." That the women's movement had had an effect on the best writing in the field (and, later on, even on some of the "pop entertainment") escapes him. He is not alone in his view of the '70s: Others have expressed similar attitudes, as though excising certain kinds of writing from the genre's history altogether. Whatever view one holds of the '60s New Wave, or other past movements in science fiction, few commentators would forget or deny that they existed. Yet the '70s, to some, seems a time when science fiction was unexceptional and nothing innovative was taking place. This is demonstrably untrue.

The 1980s were to be a time for another debate among science fiction writers. The momentum of the '70s had been lost, old-fashioned commercial science fiction was rising in popularity, and although women writers were even more important to the genre than before, the women's movement had fallen on hard times. As it happened, the most distinctive literary movement in science fiction during the '80s would turn out to be cyberpunk science fiction, a form dominated by men.

At the beginning of the 1980s, women still represented a minority of writers in the field, but they were no longer a minor voice. An impressive number of them were to become some of the most important new writers of science fiction.

Connie Willis, who had published her first story in 1971, began winning attention and awards for her short fiction in the '80s. Among her most popular stories are "Fire Watch" (1982); "A Letter from the Clearys" (1982); "The Last of the Winnebagos" (1988); "At the Rialto" (1989), a story using theoretical physics as a metaphor; and "Even the Queen" (1992), a humorous tale about menstruation. She is a versatile writer whose accessible prose and feeling for her characters draw the reader into her complexly plotted stories. She is also the author of two novels, *Lincoln's Dreams* (1987) and *Doomsday Book* (1992), a novel of time travel set in fourteenth-century England.

Willis has the distinction of being the only writer ever to be honored with Nebula Awards in all four categories of fiction for which the award is given. In fact, she has won more awards than almost any writer in the genre. Yet a recent reviewer of her work remarks about her: "Willis is so good at characterization that the mild SF elements [in her stories] seem like no more than an excuse for it, and so the stories feel more like mainstream than SF. . . . [S]he's a great writer, but not, for my part, a great *SF* writer."[4]

This reviewer, I suspect, would have made the same charge against a man writing science fiction stories that seemed insufficiently science-fictional. This particular case isn't one of a woman being singled out for blame because she is a woman. But what is interesting about the charge is that it echoes one that has been made against several women writers in the genre and that is less often made against men when they write the same sort of story.

In fact, Connie Willis presents an excellent example of one of the directions in which science fiction has traveled in recent years. The science-fictional ideas and details in her stories are often more metaphorical than realistic (although she has also proven her talent at more traditional science fiction), while her writing and characterization are skilled enough to lead the reviewer previously quoted to think that they overwhelm the science-fictional elements in her work.

One can argue about whether or not science fiction should go in this direction. Some insist that the ideas in a story be on the same level, and as well developed, as the writing, and that a well-written story with a weak or almost nonexistent idea still fails as science fiction. But a number of writers have taken Willis's more literary road, and they have had predecessors along this path. In a recent essay, Willis acknowledged her debt to earlier writers who stretched science fiction's boundaries: "Shirley Jackson's and Mildred Clingerman's and Kit Reed's and Margaret St. Clair's stories (along with Damon Knight's and Jerome Bixby's and Theodore Sturgeon's) influenced me."[5] (In her essay, she also deplores the fact that so many of science fiction's women writers have been neglected, but perhaps that should not have surprised her. Some of these writers were also seen as being insufficiently science-fictional.) Clearly more readers, given Willis's awards

[4] Moshe Feder, "On Books," *Asimov's Science Fiction* 18, no. 6 (May 1994), 169–70.

[5] Connie Willis, "The Women SF Doesn't See," *Isaac Asimov's Science Fiction Magazine* 16, no. 11 (October 1992), p. 8.

and popularity, are prepared to overlook traditional strictures on what science fiction "should" be.

Karen Joy Fowler, who was hailed almost immediately after the publication of her first stories as an important new voice and whose first collection of short fiction, *Artificial Things* (1986), was widely praised, often approaches her material obliquely. Some of her stories seem to straddle the border between science fiction and magic realism. She is represented here by "Game Night at the Fox and Goose" (1989), a story that plays with the notion of alternative history. Her first novel, *Sarah Canary* (1991), bewildered some science fiction readers, perhaps because they could not see how a novel set in the late 1800s, with a mysterious central character who remains an enigma even at the end of the book, could be science fiction. Other readers had no problem. Critic John Clute said about the book:

> Karen Joy Fowler's *Sarah Canary* . . . traces with steely smiling delicacy the ways in which it might be possible to understand, and to misconstrue, a speechless but birdlike female creature as she drifts through the Pacific Northwest, gathering 'round her a congeries of other outcasts: a Chinese, a suffragette, an Indian, an idiot. As far as the male imperial mind is concerned, they are all outside the pale, and must be coerced into being "understood." Sarah Canary herself may, in fact, be a "true" alien. As far as most SF readers are concerned, she almost certainly is. As far as the book is concerned, she is certainly "Other."[6]

To ask this novel to explain its "alien" in a manner common to more conventional science fiction is to miss the point. One might as well ask characters in an opera to talk instead of sing.

Pat Murphy began publishing both science fiction and fantasy in the late '70s. She won Nebula Awards for her novel *The Falling Woman* (1986) and for her novelette "Rachel in Love" (1987), the story of a chimpanzee with imprinted human thoughts and memories. Her collection of short fiction, *Points of Departure* (1990), and her third published novel, *The City, Not Long After* (1989), which is set in a near-future San Francisco, show a writer whose work often pushes beyond the traditional boundaries of science fiction, and, in fact, Murphy has had to endure accusations of not being a "real" science fiction writer. Despite the scientific theme in her story "Rachel in Love," one

[6] John Clute, "Is Science Fiction Out to Lunch? Some Thoughts on the Year 1992," in *Nebula Awards 28*, edited by James Morrow (San Diego: Harcourt Brace, 1994), 7.

critic contended that there was nothing in it, apart from one detail, that was at all science-fictional. Theodore Sturgeon has defined a science fiction story as one that could not have been told without the science-fictional elements; by this criterion, "Rachel in Love" is clearly science fiction.

Murphy herself related the following anecdote about another reaction to her work:

> I was at a dinner. . . . The writer sitting beside me started talking about *The Falling Woman*. He asked me, quite politely, if I minded if he pointed out a problem with the book. I said, "Sure, I'd like to hear it."
>
> And he said, "There are no strong male characters anywhere in it."
>
> Now I found it interesting that he perceived this as a problem. I've never heard anyone criticize *Moby Dick* on the grounds that it has no strong female characters—no female characters at all, except for a couple of whales with bit parts.
>
> . . . [T]he writer was interpreting my work according to an underlying set of expectations and assumptions. . . . A good novel has strong male characters. So of course the absence of such characters was a problem.[7]

Lisa Goldstein, whose first novel, *The Red Magician,* was published in 1982, is, like Murphy, a writer who moves easily between science fiction and fantasy. Among her novels are *The Dream Years* (1985), set in Paris during the 1920s and the late 1960s; *A Mask for the General* (1987), a story of a future dictator and those resisting him; and *Tourists* (1989), in which some American travelers find themselves in a mysterious country. Her story "Midnight News" (1990) takes a character belonging to that often-ignored category of people, old women, and makes her the most important person in the world.

Nancy Kress, whose earliest novels were fantasies, moved to science fiction in her novel *An Alien Light* (1988). Most of her work is solidly realistic and rooted in plausibility. In the novel *Brain Rose* (1990), the novella "Beggars in Spain" (1991), and much of her short fiction, Kress demonstrates her ability to combine speculation about possible biological advances with a consideration of the ethical issues such advances might raise. Compared with Willis, Fowler, Murphy, and Goldstein,

[7] Pat Murphy, "Illusion and Expectation," *The Bakery Men Don't See* (Madison, Wis.: SF^3, 1991), 8.

Kress probably adheres most closely to the "traditional" realistic strictures of science fiction, but she does not sacrifice strong characterization and literary grace to do so. In "And Wild for to Hold" (1991), she makes the historical figure of Anne Boleyn her central character, then thrusts her into an alternative history.

What these five writers have in common with one another, and with other writers of science fiction in recent years, is that they have pushed beyond the conventional limitations of the form. Their writing styles are diverse and vary widely, as do their subjects. They can take certain assumptions, such as female characters engaged in a variety of pursuits, for granted, as their predecessors could not. They can also be seen simply as writers and not as the "special cases" their predecessors were often perceived to be.

Other writers also pushing at science fiction's perceived limitations were grouped (sometimes willingly, sometimes not) under the label of "cyberpunks." What is cyberpunk science fiction? John Kessel, a writer of science fiction who is also a perceptive observer of the genre, offers one explanation:

> The movement can be described as a fusion of high-tech ambience . . . with a countercultural, third world, or even cheerfully nihilistic denial of middle-class American values. . . .
>
> Like rock music's punks, who went back to the crude instrumentation and energy of 1950s rock and roll, injecting it with a contemporary political (or antipolitical) message, the cyberpunks returned to the technological SF of the 1940s and 1950s, of Isaac Asimov and Robert A. Heinlein, but with a radical sensibility.[8]

Some of the most interesting of the new writers of the '80s had soon divided themselves (or were divided by others) into two groups, cyberpunk writers and those described as the "new humanists." The differences between the two groups are delineated by writer Michael Swanwick in his essay "A User's Guide to the Postmoderns," a term he applies to both groups:

> The first group, the humanists, produce literate, often consciously literary fiction, focusing on human characters who are generally seen as frail and fallible, and using the genre to explore large philosophical questions, sometimes religious in nature. . . .
>
> The other group has been tagged the cyberpunks. . . . Their fic-

[8] John Kessel, "Cyberpunk," *The New Encyclopedia of Science Fiction,* edited by James Gunn (New York: Viking, 1988), 116.

> tion is characterized by a fully realized high-tech future, "crammed" prose, punk attitudes including antagonism to authority, and bright inventive details.[9]

The book generally claimed as the earliest cyberpunk novel is William Gibson's *Neuromancer* (1984), while writer Bruce Sterling soon became the movement's chief advocate. Other writers who have been associated with cyberpunk science fiction, to a greater or lesser degree, are K. W. Jeter, Rudy Rucker, Marc Laidlaw, Greg Bear, Paul Di Filippo, Lewis Shiner, John Shirley, and Pat Cadigan. In other words, this particular movement resembles earlier science fiction not only in its embrace of technology but also in being dominated by men.

During the '80s, Pat Cadigan was the only female writer to be grouped with the cyberpunks. Her novels *Mindplayers* (1987), *Fools* (1992), and *Synners* (1991)—which won the Arthur C. Clarke Award—and most of her short stories share the streetwise sensibility and fascination with technology characteristic of the cyberpunks. Her hard and savvy women characters are taken for granted, not seen as unusual; her writing is strong and direct. A fine example of her art is the story "Angel" (1987), with its tough yet vulnerable narrator. It is interesting to note that the talented Cadigan, in relation to the cyberpunk school, occupied a place analogous to the one that earlier women science fiction writers such as Leigh Brackett did in the field as a whole. She was the exception, the woman who could write as well, and in the same manner, as the men did.

The cyberpunk writers shook up science fiction—definitely a worthwhile end—and opened the field to new ways of looking at the future. The traditional infatuation with technology was still there, without the conventional baggage and genre clichés. But most of the female characters in cyberpunk fiction occupied secondary or standard roles—a standard role in this context often being a leather-clad dominatrix, a sex object, a whore, or a victim, as opposed to being a housewife. (There were exceptions, among them the protagonist in Bruce Sterling's *Islands in the Net* [1988], but not many.) The noisiest new movement in science fiction ended up, however unintentionally, largely devoid of women.

While a few cyberpunk and new humanist science fiction writers were issuing manifestos, others, many of them women, were contributing

[9] Michael Swanwick, "A User's Guide to the Postmoderns," *Isaac Asimov's Science Fiction Magazine* 10, no. 8 (August 1986), 24.

to the body of utopian science fiction. Among them were Joan Slonczewski, Margaret Atwood, Suzette Haden Elgin, and Sheri S. Tepper.

Joan Slonczewski's *The Door into Ocean* (1986), winner of the John W. Campbell Award, drew on the author's training as a biologist to depict a pacifist female society and a more aggressive masculine culture. In a sense, Slonczewski's novel can be seen as a response to Frank Herbert's *Dune* (1965). If Herbert's desert world of Arrakis breeds warriors, Slonczewski's ocean world of Shora has produced pacifists.

Margaret Atwood, a writer not usually associated with science fiction, wrote *The Handmaid's Tale* (1985), a dystopia about a future in which women have no legal rights and are restricted to rigid roles. Disturbingly, many of these women assist in their own repression. This novel won acclaim both inside and outside the genre and was honored with the first Arthur C. Clarke Award.

Ursula K. Le Guin's innovative *Always Coming Home* (1985), which could almost serve as a guidebook to the world it shows, models its fictional future on tribal societies of the past. This novel rejects conventional narrative and, instead, gives the reader tales, poetry, drawings, reports, a short narrative, even music (on a tape cassette included with the book) of the Kesh, Le Guin's imagined matriarchal society.

Suzette Haden Elgin, who won earlier praise for her story "For the Sake of Grace" (1969), in which a brilliant young woman on a male-dominated world must take a great risk for the chance at an education, continued to write throughout the '70s. During the '80s, she published her most influential novels, *Native Tongue* (1984) and *Native Tongue II: The Judas Rose* (1987). In these novels, women living in a future in which they have no rights develop their own language, Láadan. Although they have no legal rights, they are still valued as Earth's translators and interpreters in dealing with alien civilizations. (Elgin's invented language of Láadan has since taken on a life of its own, with fans of the novels contributing to its development.)

Sheri S. Tepper has a strong didactic streak in her work, and has become an important science fiction novelist. Although her first novel was not published until the early '80s, she had been writing for some time before then. In *The Gate to Women's Country* (1988), she depicts a world where men and women, with few exceptions, live entirely separate lives. She followed this book with a trilogy of novels, *Grass* (1989), *Raising the Stones* (1990), and *Sideshow* (1992), in which overpopulation and fundamentalist religion are soundly criticized within the tale of settlers on an alien world.

All these works confront the relationships between men and women and the ways in which different societies might alter them. They are not sterile blueprints for ideal societies, novels heavily burdened by messages, or polemics where an author's outrage has overwhelmed her story; they are passionately felt stories that move and involve the reader while seeking to address important issues. In recent years, women writers in science fiction have been largely responsible for keeping the utopian tradition alive, as these novels demonstrate.

A necessarily incomplete list of other women writers who contributed to science fiction during the '80s includes Kim Antieau, Jayge Carr, Jo Clayton, Storm Constantine, Grania Davis, Diane Duane, M. J. Engh, Zoë Fairbairns, Cynthia Felice, Esther Friesner, Mary Gentle, Molly Gloss, Eileen Gunn, Gwyneth Jones, Leigh Kennedy, Lee Killough, R. A. MacAvoy, Ann Maxwell, Ardath Mayhar, R. M. Meluch, Rachel Pollack, Elizabeth Ann Scarborough, Jody Scott, Susan Shwartz, Nancy Springer, S. C. Sykes, Sydney J. Van Scyoc, Sharon Webb, Cherry Wilder, M. K. Wren, and Jane Yolen.

Two eminently worthwhile anthologies of science fiction by women published during that decade are *Isaac Asimov's Space of Her Own* (1984), edited by Shawna McCarthy (a book that includes stories by women that were published in *Isaac Asimov's Science Fiction Magazine*), and *Despatches from the Frontiers of the Female Mind* (1985), edited by Jen Green and Sarah Lefanu.

While some women were extending the boundaries of science fiction, others were succeeding as writers of more conventional narratives. Lois McMaster Bujold, who published her first novel, *Shards of Honor*, in 1986, was quickly hailed as one of the most entertaining new writers of traditional science fiction adventure. Her books are entertainments but also stories with depth. Miles Vorkosigan, one of her most popular characters, may be a military genius, but he is also a man with physical disabilities. *Falling Free* (1988) is the story of human beings genetically engineered to work in space, people who can function in the weightlessness of space but who would be seriously disabled on Earth.

Bujold, like C. J. Cherryh, is as popular among male science fiction readers as among women. This does not mean that readers of adventure science fiction, hard science fiction, or military science fiction in particular welcome books by women even now. There is some anecdotal evidence that a few editors are reluctant to publish hard or military science fiction by writers whose by-lines are clearly female. This may mean only that these particular subgenres of science fiction are often treated by publishers as popular fiction for men, much in the same manner as romance novels, with their almost exclusively female by-lines, are seen as popular fiction for women. But it is also a sign that there is still some separatism within the genre as a whole.

In the meantime, the late '80s and early '90s have seen the increasing popularity of large sagas that are superficially science fiction or fantasy but also resemble, in their packaging and subject matter, romantic historical novels. Most of the readers of such sagas are assumed to be women; the same, judging by their by-lines, is true of those who write these books, which are often centered around a love story of some kind. This may be an economic advance for the women who write them—the books are fairly popular—but the rise of a subgenre of "women's" science fiction is an ambiguous trend at best.

The fragmentation of the genre into cyberpunk, new humanism, romantic sagas, military technothrillers, magic realism, postmodernism, and other approaches mirrors what in a broader literary context has been called the "Balkanization of literature." There is no longer a common literary culture that all writers can be assumed to share or an accepted canon of classics, and this is true of science fiction as well. We live in a world where old systems have been shattered, conflicts are both closer to home and increasingly bitter, and old certainties have vanished. It is not surprising that science fiction, like many nations, is also fragmenting into widely differing styles, approaches, techniques, and subgenres, for better or worse. Science fiction, although still far from being a model of diversity (white men and boys are still the majority of writers and readers), has become more diverse than it once was. The proliferation of subgenres means that authors allegedly working in the same genre often have little in common as writers.

What can the term "science fiction" actually mean in such a context? Not much of what is written seems to fit into the mold of hard science fiction, which scientist and writer Gregory Benford has defined as "that which highly prizes fidelity to the physical facts of the universe, while building upon them to realize new fictional worlds. It sticks to the facts—unless some crucial new experiment or discovery changes those—but can play fast and loose with theory as it likes."[10] Benford has expressed a wish that this kind of science fiction remain at the center of the genre as an aspiration, even if it remains "a paradigm more often honored in the breech than not."[11]

Few women have written hard science fiction, and some critics point

[10] Gregory Benford, "A Scientist's Notebook: Imagining the Real," *The Magazine of Fantasy & Science Fiction* 84, no. 1 (January 1993), 47.

[11] Ibid., 59.

to this fact when asserting that women do not write "real" science fiction. Often ignored is the fact that most men who write science fiction don't write this sort of work, either. One cannot write hard science fiction without some understanding of science, and women have traditionally been discouraged from pursuing educations and careers in science. But much of Katherine MacLean's work qualifies as hard science fiction, and more women with backgrounds in the sciences now are writing in the genre. (Jayge Carr is a former NASA physicist, Joan Slonczewski is a research biologist, and Vonda N. McIntyre and Pat Murphy hold degrees in biology; Kate Wilhelm, Nancy Kress, Lois McMaster Bujold, and Maureen F. McHugh are just a few of the writers who have written work that can qualify as hard science fiction.) Some may, in their assessments, unfairly and inaccurately exclude women from this core of the genre because they don't see that some women are writing a subtler kind of hard science fiction.

Isaac Asimov's definition of science fiction as a literature about the human impact of science and technology is certainly less rigid and more inclusive and encompasses many more writers. One critic, Tom Shippey, has described science fiction this way:

> [It] is the steady, cumulative creation of a mindset, and a readership, that is accustomed to change and ready to accept that technological change will inevitably bring social and political change as well. . . .
>
> Science fiction . . . is peopled with acute observers who take a long view. . . . [It] is inherently unpredictable. Its authors are committed (with exceptions) to the belief that unpredictability is as true of the future as it has been in the recent past.[12]

But we are still talking about a literature rooted in realism, and there are writers who don't quite fit into these limits. For some of them, science fiction is essentially another kind of fantasy, the difference being that science fiction draws its symbols from science and technology, while fantasy uses magic and myth as its wellsprings. A story with only a trace of a science-fictional notion can thus qualify as science fiction. To have such a broad definition, one that might allow for almost any kind of fantastic fiction, has the virtue of bringing more writers, and often very gifted ones, into the genre and encouraging others to be more literarily ambitious. But some would argue that this definition ignores, and may even destroy, those features that distinguish

[12] Tom Shippey, "Introduction," *The Oxford Book of Science Fiction Stories,* edited by Tom Shippey (Oxford and New York: Oxford University Press, 1992), xxiv–xxv.

science fiction from other kinds of literature. In this view, there would be no distinctive literature reflecting, however faintly, the spirit of scientific inquiry and the belief that certain tools can give us insights into reality and what the universe in fact is. A reader could no longer assume that certain science-fictional details denoted imagined possible realities; they might be only metaphors, as they are in other kinds of writing.

The debate about what science fiction is and should be is likely to continue, as it has throughout the genre's history. With that in mind, a couple of important points should be made here: It is no longer possible to discuss science fiction without mentioning the women who have contributed to it. Conversely, it is also impossible to give an account of women science fiction writers and their work without discussing the genre as a whole. The topic of women and science fiction is not an ancillary topic anymore, one to be set aside from the history of the literature as a kind of sidebar or footnote; to discuss women and science fiction is, of necessity, to discuss the entire field. Perhaps eventually, if sexism and racism diminish sufficiently, we may finally discuss only *writers*.

The number of women writing science fiction, and influencing the field, has been increasing during the early '90s. The influence of women as editors has also increased. Kristine Kathryn Rusch, who won the John W. Campbell Award for Best New Writer in 1990 for her own writing, edited the small magazine *Pulphouse* for several years before becoming the editor of *The Magazine of Fantasy & Science Fiction*. She joined an impressive list of women who have affected the genre as editors, among them Judith Merril, Cele Goldsmith (editor of *Amazing Stories* during the '60s), Shawna McCarthy (editor of *Isaac Asimov's Science Fiction Magazine* in the early '80s), Ellen Datlow (fiction editor of *Omni Magazine* for over a decade), and science fiction editors at several publishing houses.

Writers actively writing science fiction now include Patricia Anthony, Wilhelmina Baird, Maya Kaathryn Bohnhoff, Emma Bull, Mary Caraker, Susan Casper, Paula Downing, Julia Ecklar, Kate Elliott, Nancy Etchemendy, Sharon Farber, Nancy Farmer, Maggie Flinn, Carolyn Ives Gilman, Karen Haber, Nina Kiriki Hoffman, Janet Kagan, Katharine Eliska Kimbriel, Sonia Orin Lyris, Lisa Mason, Bridget McKenna, Linda Nagata, Michaelene Pendleton, Mary Rosenblum, Michelle Sagara, Melissa Scott, Martha Soukup, Lois Tilton, Mary A. Turzillo, and Deborah Wheeler. (Had I added the names of writers who have written a little science fiction but are primarily fantasy or horror writers, the list would be longer.)

Among the strongest science fiction novels of the early '90s were three that were honored with the James Tiptree Jr., Award. The British writer Gwyneth Jones in her award-winning novel *White Queen* (1991) depicts an alien invasion in which the aliens remain ambiguous. Jones is also known for an earlier novel about a post-holocaust matriarchy, *Divine Endurance* (1984). Eleanor Arnason, who has been publishing science fiction since the '70s, was honored for *A Woman of the Iron People* (1991), which manages the difficult tasks of showing a detailed alien culture in which the sexes are almost completely separated, revealing the dilemmas of the human anthropologists studying their world, and creating a socialistic future Earth that is a convincing extrapolation, even in our current conservative political climate. Maureen F. McHugh, one of the most promising new writers of science fiction, won the Tiptree Award for *China Mountain Zhang* (1992), in which her central character is a homosexual man in a homophobic society. McHugh extrapolates her imagined science and technology in the context of a future world dominated by China—a difficult job for a Western writer.

The future of science fiction, and of science fiction written by women, should be extremely bright. Unfortunately, a number of factors now threaten the genre as a whole.

One is a publishing industry increasingly devoted to the production of best-sellers or "brand-name" books. Within science fiction, this has resulted in great popularity and large sales for the best-known writers of science fiction, among them Arthur C. Clarke, Isaac Asimov, Anne McCaffrey, Ursula K. Le Guin, and several others, most of whom are writers of long standing. Other extremely profitable science fiction books are those based on movies and television programs such as *Star Wars* and *Star Trek;* these series often take up much of the shelf space of science fiction sections in bookstores. Other popular books include novels or series in which a lesser-known writer writes a book set in a background created by a well-known writer. Some of these novels are true collaborations, in which the two authors work together, while others are almost entirely written by the lesser-known writer.

Some of these books are better than others, and some serve to attract new readers to the genre, but what they all have in common is that they exist primarily to trade on a famous writer's name or on a trademark. I pointed out earlier that it's a mistake to look at any literature apart from the culture around it. Ironically, for people who have prided themselves on looking forward, authors of science fiction are now being encouraged either to look back and mine the genre's past or to work in backgrounds or imagined worlds developed by others. Newer writers who set their tales in someone else's world have less chance to develop their own. Writing that isn't obviously commercial has a harder time getting published.

More important, we exist in a society where the written and printed word has less and less influence. Various observers have talked about the death of print or the twilight of the written word. One can argue about whether this is too pessimistic a view; most human societies of the past had a large percentage, often a majority, of people who were illiterate. Still, the fact remains that people have many more distractions than they once did, and fewer of those who are literate choose to spend their time with books.

Science fiction once had a large number of adolescents among its readers, many of whom would give up reading such stories in adulthood. Now, the teens who might in other times have been avid readers of science fiction have gaming, computers, television, popular music, and other possible pursuits competing for their attention. Various surveys, including those done by the science fiction trade magazine *Locus* of its subscribers, indicate that the genre's readership is steadily growing older. The most innovative science fiction ideas and the most imaginative scenarios have always been found in print. Movies, television, comics, and other popular forms draw heavily on science fiction but lag behind the printed word in the development of their ideas. It may be that science fiction writers will increasingly have to embrace some of these forms and the more diverse audiences they draw in order to reach more people.

In addition, writers, and women writers in particular, are now contending with what has been called the "post-feminist" era—a misleading term, since it assumes women have already achieved most of their goals. The critic Joan Gordon has written about what this means for science fiction:

> Feminism has reached the stage of denial. Since its detractors have so successfully defined it as a rabid, humorless policing of gender attitudes—a kind of dreaded political correctness—the very people who seem to sympathize with its most sensible aims (equal treatment under the law, for instance) have begun to deny membership. In such a climate, overtly feminist sf as so magnificently practiced by Joanna Russ and Suzy McKee Charnas has been replaced for the most part by a more covert brand. . . . female characters are strong, active, given to non-gender-linked jobs, but although these characters may live as feminists have striven for women to be al-

> lowed to live, their right to live that way is not the central issue of the writing. . . .
>
> [Recent female writers] don't neglect feminist thought: they assume, apply, and subsume it in their texts.[13]

In other words, more science fiction writers are writing almost as if there is no question about the justice of equal rights for women, even though the goals of the women's movement have provoked questions, second thoughts, resentment, and a backlash in some Western nations, while women in much of the world still have no real rights. Constructive as it is to imagine worlds where matters are otherwise and to enable readers to live vicariously in these worlds, maybe there is still a place for the more polemical brand of writing as well. As Joan Gordon goes on to say: "Post-feminism cannot afford to be smug: benign neglect can become malign."

Women, as writers and as editors, have made important contributions to the literature of science fiction. Feminist ideas and concerns have influenced this contribution, although few writers of science fiction, even the most strongly feminist ones, ever toed anything resembling a party line, and at least a few writers would probably deny that they are feminists at all.

Women have unquestionably made advances. It remains to be seen whether these advances are subtle and pervasive, but not yet easily discerned, or are instead ambiguous.

A word about the stories in this anthology and its companion volume, *Women of Wonder, The Classic Years:* My purpose is to present thoughtful, entertaining, well-written science fiction by women in which female characters, human or alien, play important roles. Although some stories are likely to strike the reader as feminist in tone, no ideological ruler was used to measure them for selection. One of my goals is to present stories that reflect the *variety* of different literary paths women have taken in writing science fiction and the varied imaginary worlds they have created. This requires including stories that some may see as pre-feminist, post-feminist, or not feminist at all.

It would have been impossible, even in a much larger volume, to include every accomplished writer. My hope is that the reader will be moved to seek out other stories and books by the writers who appear

[13] Joan Gordon, "Connie Willis's *Doomsday* for Feminism: *Doomsday Book* by Connie Willis," *The New York Review of Science Fiction* 58 (1993), 5.

here and also by those who do not. Intending that no one worthy be overlooked, I have provided a list of recommended reading, with bibliographic information, at the back of each *Women of Wonder* volume. Science fiction, by both women and men, now encompasses such a wide variety of styles and such a diversity of approaches that almost any reader can find at least a few authors to treasure.

In addition to the stories already mentioned, the reader will find Octavia E. Butler's award-winning "Bloodchild" (1984) and Rebecca Ore's "Farming in Virginia" (1993), both of which depict some of science fiction's more memorable aliens. Butler is becoming one of the most important writers in the genre, while Ore is a genuinely different and unique voice. "Webrider" (1985) by Jayge Carr, a writer who deserves more attention than she has been paid, and "Scorched Supper on New Niger" (1980) by Suzy McKee Charnas, which uses African motifs, are detailed and intelligent science fiction adventures. "Bluewater Dreams" (1981) by Sydney J. Van Scyoc is a moving story of a young settler and her alien friend, while my own "Fears" (1984) speculates about the kind of world present-day biological developments might bring about. "The Cabinet of Edgar Allan Poe" (1982) by Angela Carter, one of the major British fantasists, is a meditation on an author whom Brian Aldiss has placed in the pantheon of science fiction's ancestors. In "The Harvest of Wolves" (1984), Mary Gentle offers a glimpse into one small corner of a bleak near-future society. The Australian writer Rosaleen Love wittily plays with both alternative history and the nature of time in "Alexia and Graham Bell" (1986), while Sheila Finch offers an alternative history in "Reichs-Peace" (1986) that uses the notion of a triumphant Nazi Germany and gives it an unexpected twist. Storm Constantine's "Immaculate" (1991) does a riff on popular media, biological science, and artificial intelligence. Judith Moffett's "Tiny Tango" (1989) shows an accomplished writer who is not afraid to provoke and disturb her readers. And Carol Emshwiller, in "Abominable" (1980), views the relationship of women and men in her own original way.

In the past, women may have shown good sense by not being interested in science fiction. Why read a literature in which the future was often made by men for men? Why be interested in worlds that excluded women from any meaningful activities? But in the serious science fiction of the past, and in that being written today, we may find an art that life can imitate.

Cassandra

C. J. CHERRYH

Fires.

They grew unbearable here.

Alis felt for the door of the flat and knew that it would be solid. She could feel the cool metal of the knob amid the flames . . . saw the shadow-stairs through the roiling smoke outside clearly enough to feel her way down them, convincing her senses that they would bear her weight.

Crazy Alis. She made no haste. The fires burned steadily. She passed through them, descended the insubstantial steps to the solid ground —she could not abide the elevator, that closed space with the shadow-floor, that plummeted down and down; she made the ground floor, averted her eyes from the red, heatless flames.

A ghost said good morning to her . . . old man Willis, thin and transparent against the leaping flames. She blinked, bade it good morning in return—did not miss old Willis's shake of the head as she opened the door and left. Noon traffic passed, heedless of the flames, the hulks that blazed in the street, the tumbling brick.

The apartment caved in—black bricks falling into the inferno, Hell amid the green, ghostly trees. Old Willis fled, burning, fell—turned to jerking, blackened flesh—died, daily. Alis no longer cried, hardly flinched. She ignored the horror spilling about her, forced her way through crumbling brick that held no substance, past busy ghosts that could not be troubled in their haste.

Kingsley's Cafe stood, whole, more so than the rest. It was refuge for the afternoon, a feeling of safety. She pushed open the door, heard the tinkle of a lost bell. Shadowy patrons looked, whispered.

Crazy Alis.

The whispers troubled her. She avoided their eyes and their presence, settled in a booth in the corner that bore only traces of the fire.

WAR, the headline in the vendor said in heavy type. She shivered, looked up into Sam Kingsley's wraithlike face.

"Coffee," she said. "Ham sandwich." It was constantly the same. She varied not even the order. Mad Alis. Her affliction supported her. A check came each month, since the hospital had turned her out. Weekly she returned to the clinic, to doctors who now faded like the others. The building burned about them. Smoke rolled down the blue, antiseptic halls. Last week a patient ran—burning—

A rattle of china. Sam set the coffee on the table, came back shortly and brought the sandwich. She bent her head and ate, transparent food on half-broken china, a cracked, fire-smudged cup with a transparent handle. She ate, hungry enough to overcome the horror that had become ordinary. A hundred times seen, the most terrible sights lost their power over her: she no longer cried at shadows. She talked to ghosts and touched them, ate the food that somehow stilled the ache in her belly, wore the same too-large black sweater and worn blue shirt and gray slacks because they were all she had that seemed solid. Nightly she washed them and dried them and put them on the next day, letting others hang in the closet. They were the only solid ones.

She did not tell the doctors these things. A lifetime in and out of hospitals had made her wary of confidences. She knew what to say. Her half-vision let her smile at ghost-faces, cannily manipulate their charts and cards, sitting in the ruins that had begun to smolder by late afternoon. A blackened corpse lay in the hall. She did not flinch when she smiled good-naturedly at the doctor.

They gave her medicines. The medicines stopped the dreams, the siren screams, the running steps in the night past her apartment. They let her sleep in the ghostly bed, high above ruin, with the flames crackling and the voices screaming. She did not speak of these things. Years in hospitals had taught her. She complained only of nightmares, and restlessness, and they let her have more of the red pills.

WAR, the headline blazoned.

The cup rattled and trembled against the saucer as she picked it up. She swallowed the last bit of bread and washed it down with coffee, tried not to look beyond the broken front window, where twisted metal hulks smoked on the street. She stayed, as she did each day, and Sam grudgingly refilled her cup, which she would nurse as far as she could and then she would order another one. She lifted it, savoring the feeling of it, stopping the trembling of her hands.

The bell jingled faintly. A man closed the door, settled at the counter.

Whole, clear in her eyes. She stared at him, startled, heart pounding. He ordered coffee, moved to buy a paper from the vendor, settled again, and let the coffee grow cold while he read the news. She had view only of his back while he read—scuffed brown leather coat, brown hair a little over his collar. At last he drank the cooled coffee all at one draught, shoved money onto the counter, and left the paper lying, headlines turned face down.

A young face, flesh and bone among the ghosts. He ignored them all and went for the door.

Alis thrust herself from her booth.

"Hey!" Sam called at her.

She rummaged in her purse as the bell jingled, flung a bill onto the counter, heedless that it was a five. Fear was coppery in her mouth; he was gone. She fled the café, edged round debris without thinking of it, saw his back disappearing among the ghosts.

She ran, shouldering them, braving the flames—cried out as debris showered painlessly on her, and kept running.

Ghosts turned and stared, shocked—*he* did likewise, and she ran to him, stunned to see the same shock on his face, regarding her.

"What is it?" he asked.

She blinked, dazed to realize he saw her no differently than the others. She could not answer. In irritation he started walking again, and she followed. Tears slid down her face, her breath hard in her throat. People stared. He noticed her presence and walked faster, through debris, through fires. A wall began to fall, and she cried out despite herself.

He jerked about. The dust and the soot rose up as a cloud behind him. His face was distraught and angry. He stared at her as the others did. Mothers drew children away from the scene. A band of youths stared, cold-eyed and laughing.

"Wait," she said. He opened his mouth as if he would curse her; she flinched, and the tears were cold in the heatless wind of the fires. His face twisted in an embarrassed pity. He thrust a hand into his pocket and began to pull out money, hastily, tried to give it to her. She shook her head furiously, trying to stop the tears—stared upward, flinching, as another building fell into flames.

"What's wrong?" he asked her. "What's wrong with you?"

"Please," she said. He looked about at the staring ghosts, then began to walk slowly. She walked with him, nerving herself not to cry out at the ruin, the pale moving figures that wandered through burned shells of buildings, the twisted corpses in the street, where traffic moved.

"What's your name?" he asked. She told him. He gazed at her from time to time as they walked, a frown creasing his brow. He had a face well-worn for youth, a tiny scar beside the mouth. He looked older than she. She felt uncomfortable in the way his eyes traveled over her:

she decided to accept it—to bear with anything that gave her this one solid presence. Against every inclination she reached her hand into the bend of his arm, tightened her fingers on the worn leather. He accepted it.

And after a time he slid his arm behind her and about her waist, and they walked like lovers.

WAR, the headline at the newsstand cried.

He started to turn into a street by Tenn's Hardware. She balked at what she saw there. He paused when he felt it, faced her with his back to the fires of that burning.

"Don't go," she said.

"Where do you want to go?"

She shrugged helplessly, indicated the main street, the other direction.

He talked to her then, as he might talk to a child, humoring her fear. It was pity. Some treated her that way. She recognized it, and took even that.

His name was Jim. He had come into the city yesterday, hitched rides. He was looking for work. He knew no one in the city. She listened to his rambling awkwardness, reading through it. When he was done, she stared at him still, and saw his face contract in dismay at her.

"I'm not crazy," she told him, which was a lie that everyone in Sudbury would have known, only *he* would not, knowing no one. His face was true and solid, and the tiny scar by the mouth made it hard when he was thinking; at another time she would have been terrified of him. Now she was terrified of losing him amid the ghosts.

"It's the war," he said.

She nodded, trying to look at him and not at the fires. His fingers touched her arm, gently. "It's the war," he said again. "It's all crazy. Everyone's crazy."

And then he put his hand on her shoulder and turned her back the other way, toward the park, where green leaves waved over black, skeletal limbs. They walked along the lake, and for the first time in a long time she drew breath and felt a whole, sane presence beside her.

They bought corn and sat on the grass by the lake and flung it to the spectral swans. Wraiths of passersby were few, only enough to keep a feeling of occupancy about the place—old people, mostly, tottering about the deliberate tranquility of their routine despite the headlines.

"Do you see them," she ventured to ask him finally, "all thin and gray?"

He did not understand, did not take her literally, only shrugged. Warily, she abandoned that questioning at once. She rose to her feet and stared at the horizon, where the smoke bannered on the wind.

"Buy you supper?" he asked.

She turned, prepared for this, and managed a shy, desperate smile. "Yes," she said, knowing what else he reckoned to buy with that—willing, and hating herself, and desperately afraid that he would walk away, tonight, tomorrow. She did not know men. She had no idea what she could say or do to prevent his leaving, only that he would when someday he recognized her madness.

Even her parents had not been able to bear with that—visited her only at first in the hospitals, and then only on holidays, and then not at all. She did not know where they were.

There was a neighbor boy who drowned. She had said he would. She had cried for it. All the town said it was she who pushed him.

Crazy Alis.

Fantasizes, the doctors said. Not dangerous.

They let her out. There were special schools, state schools.

And from time to time—hospitals.

Tranquilizers.

She had left the red pills at home. The realization brought sweat to her palms. They gave sleep. They stopped the dreams. She clamped her lips against the panic and made up her mind that she would not need them—not while she was not alone. She slipped her hand into his arm and walked with him, secure and strange, up the steps from the park to the streets.

And stopped.

The fires were out.

Ghost-buildings rose above their jagged and windowless shells. Wraiths moved through masses of debris, almost obscured at times. He tugged her on, but her step faltered, made him look at her strangely and put his arm about her.

"You're shivering," he said. "Cold?"

She shook her head, tried to smile. The fires were out. She tried to take it for a good omen. The nightmare was over. She looked up into his solid, concerned face, and her smile almost became a wild laugh.

"I'm hungry," she said.

They lingered over a dinner in Graben's—he in his battered jacket, she in her sweater that hung at the tails and elbows: the spectral patrons were in far better clothes and stared at them, and they were set in a corner nearest the door, where they would be less visible. There was cracked crystal and broken china on insubstantial tables, and the stars winked coldly in gaping ruin above the wan glittering of the broken chandeliers.

Ruins, cold, peaceful ruin.

Alis looked about her calmly. One could live in ruins, only so the fires were gone.

And there was Jim, who smiled at her without any touch of pity, only a wild, fey desperation that she understood—who spent more than he could afford in Graben's, the inside of which she had never hoped to see—and told her—predictably—that she was beautiful. Others had said it. Vaguely she resented such triteness from him, from him whom she had decided to trust. She smiled sadly when he said it; and gave it up for a frown; and, fearful of offending him with her melancholies, made it a smile again.

Crazy Alis. He would learn and leave tonight if she were not careful. She tried to put on gaiety, tried to laugh.

And then the music stopped in the restaurant, and the noise of the other diners went dead, and the speaker was giving an inane announcement.

Shelters . . . shelters . . . shelters.

Screams broke out. Chairs overturned.

Alis went limp in her chair, felt Jim's cold, solid hand tugging at hers, saw his frightened face mouthing her name as he took her up into his arms, pulled her with him, started running.

The cold air outside hit her, shocked her into sight of the ruins again, wraith figures pelting toward that chaos where the fires had been worst.

And she knew.

"No!" she cried, pulling at his arm. "No!" she insisted, and bodies half-seen buffeted them in a rush to destruction. He yielded to her sudden certainty, gripped her hand, and fled with her against the crowds as the sirens wailed madness through the night—fled with her as she ran her sighted way through the ruin.

And into Kingsley's, where café tables stood abandoned with food still on them, doors ajar, chairs overturned. Back they went into the kitchens and down and down into the cellar, the dark, the cold safety from the flames.

No others found them there. At last the earth shook, too deep for sound. The sirens ceased and did not come on again.

They lay in the dark and clutched each other and shivered, and above them for hours raged the sound of fire, smoke sometimes drifting in to sting their eyes and noses. There was the distant crash of brick, rumblings that shook the ground, that came near, but never touched their refuge.

And in the morning, with the scent of fire still in the air, they crept up into the murky daylight.

The ruins were still and hushed. The ghost-buildings were solid now, mere shells. The wraiths were gone. It was the fires themselves that were strange, some true, some not, playing above dark, cold brick, and most were fading.

Jim swore softly, over and over again, and wept.

When she looked at him she was dry-eyed, for she had done her crying already.

And she listened as he began to talk about food, about leaving the city, the two of them. "All right," she said.

Then clamped her lips, shut her eyes against what she saw in his face. When she opened them it was still true, the sudden transparency, the wash of blood. She trembled, and he shook at her, his ghost-face distraught.

"What's wrong?" he asked. "What's wrong?"

She could not tell him, would not. She remembered the boy who had drowned, remembered the other ghosts. Of a sudden she tore from his hands and ran, dodging the maze of debris that, this morning, was solid.

"Alis!" he cried and came after her.

"No!" she cried suddenly, turning, seeing the unstable wall, the cascading brick. She started back and stopped, unable to force herself. She held out her hands to warn him back, saw them solid.

The brick rumbled, fell. Dust came up, thick for a moment, obscuring everything.

She stood still, hands at her sides, then wiped her sooty face and turned and started walking, keeping to the center of the dead streets.

Overhead, clouds gathered, heavy with rain.

She wandered at peace now, seeing the rain spot the pavement, not yet feeling it.

In time the rain did fall, and the ruins became chill and cold. She visited the dead lake and the burned trees, the ruin of Graben's, out of which she gathered a string of crystal to wear.

She smiled when, a day later, a looter drove her from her food supply. He had a wraith's look, and she laughed from a place he did not dare to climb and told him so.

And recovered her cache later when it came true, and settled among the ruined shells that held no further threat, no other nightmares, with her crystal necklace and tomorrows that were the same as today.

One could live in ruins, only so the fires were gone.

And the ghosts were all in the past, invisible.

The Thaw

TANITH LEE

Ladies first, they said.

That was OK. Then they put a histotrace on the lady in question, and called me.

"No thanks," I said.

"Listen," they said, "you're a generative bloodline descendant of Carla Brice. Aren't you interested, for God's sake? This is a unique moment, a unique experience. She's going to need support, understanding. A contact. Come on. Don't be frigid about it."

"I guess Carla is more frigid than I'm ever likely to be."

They laughed, to keep up the informalities. Then they mentioned the Institute grant I'd receive, just for hanging around and being supportive. To a quasi-unemployed artist, that was temptation and a half. They also reminded me that on this initial bout there wouldn't be much publicity, so later, if I wanted to capitalize as an eyewitness, and providing good old Carla was willing—I had a sudden vision of getting very rich, very quick, and with the minimum of effort, and I succumbed ungracefully.

Which accurately demonstrates my three strongest qualities: laziness, optimism, and blind stupidity. Which in turn sums up the whole story, more or less. And that's probably why I was told to write it down for the archives of the human race. I can't think of a better way to depress and wreck the hopes of frenzied, shackled, bleating humanity.

But to return to Carla. She was, I believe, my great-great-great-great-great grandmother. Give or take a great. Absolute accuracy isn't one of my talents, either. The relevant part is, however, that at thirty-three, Carla had developed the rare heart complaint valu—val—well, she'd developed it. She had a few months, or less, and so she opted, along with seventy other people that year, to undergo Cryogenic Suspension till a cure could be found. Cry Sus had been getting progressively more popular, ever since the 1980s. Remember? It's the freezing method of holding a body in refrigerated stasis, indefinitely preserving thereby flesh, bones, organs, and the rest, perfect and pristine, in a frosty crystal box. (Just stick a tray of water in the freezer and see for yourself.) It may not strike you as cozy anymore, but that's hardly surprising. In 1993, seventy-one persons, of whom four-or-five-or-six-great granny Carla was one, saw it as the only feasible alternative to death. In the following two hundred years, four thousand others copied their example. They froze their malignancies, their unreliable hearts, and their corroding tissues, and as the light faded from their snowed-over eyes, they must have dreamed of waking up in the fabulous future.

Funny thing about the future. Each next second is the future. And now it's the present. And now it's the past.

Those all-together four thousand and ninety-one who deposited their physiognomies in the cold-storage compartments of the world were looking forward to the future. And here it was. And we were it.

And smack in the middle of this future, which I naively called Now, was I, Tacey Brice, a rotten little unskilled artist, painting gimcrack flying saucers for the spacines. There was a big flying saucer sighting boom that year of 2193. Either you recollect that, or you don't. Nearly as big as the historic boom between the 1930s and '90s. Psychologists had told us it was our human inadequacy, searching all over for a father-mother figure to replace God. Besides, we were getting desperate. We'd penetrated our solar system to a limited extent, but without meeting anybody on the way.

That's another weird thing. When you read the speculativia of the 1900s, you can see just how much they expected of us. It was going to be all or nothing. Either the world would become a miracle of rare device with plastisteel igloos balanced on the stratosphere and metal giblets, or we'd have gone out in a blast of radiation. Neither of which had happened. We'd had problems, of course. Over two hundred years, problems occur. There had been the Fission Tragedy, and the World Flood of '14. There'd been the huge pollution clear-ups complete with the rationing that entailed, and one pretty nasty pandemic. They had set us back, that's obvious. But not halted us. So we reached 2193 mostly unscathed, with a whizz-bang technology not quite as whizz, or bang, as prophesied. A place where doors opened when they saw who you were, and with a colony on Mars, but where they hadn't solved the unemployment problem or the geriatric problem. Up in the ether there were about six hundred buzz-whuzzes headed out into nowhere, bleeping information about earth. But we hadn't landed on Alpha Centauri yet. And if the waste-disposal jammed, brother, it jammed. What I'm trying to say (superfluously, because you're ahead of me) is that their future, those four thousand and ninety-one, their future, which was our present, wasn't as spectacular as they'd trusted or feared. Excepting the Salenic Vena-derivative drugs, which had rendered most of the diseases of the 1900s and the 2000s obsolete.

And suddenly, one day, someone had a notion.

"Hey, guys," this someone suggested, "you recall all those sealed frosty boxes the medic centers have? You know, with the on-ice carcinomas and valu-diddums in 'em? Well, don't you think it'd be grand to defrost the lot of them and pump 'em full of health?"

"Crazy," said everybody else, and wet themselves with enthusiasm.

After that, they got the thing organized on a global scale. And first off, not wanting to chance any public mishaps, they intended to unfreeze a single frost box, in relative privacy. Perhaps they put all the names in a hat. Whatever, they picked Carla Brice, or Brr-Ice, if you liked that Newsies' tablotape pun.

And since Carla Brr-Ice might feel a touch extra chilly, coming back to life two hundred years after she's cryonised out of it, they dredged up a bloodline descendant to hold her cold old thirty-three-year hand. And that was Tacey Brr-Ice. Me.

The room below was pink, but the cold pink of strawberry ice cream. There were forty doctors of every gender prowling about in it and round the crystal slab. It put me in mind of a pack of wolves with a carcass they couldn't quite decide when to eat. But then, I was having a nervous attack, up on the spectator gallery where they'd sat me. The countdown had begun two days ago, and I'd been ushered in at noon today. For an hour now, the crystal had been clear. I could see a sort of blob in it, which gradually resolved into a naked woman. Straight off, even with her lying there stiff as a board and utterly defenseless, I could tell she was the sort of lady who scared me dizzy. She was large and well-shaped, with a mane of dark red hair. She was the type that goes outdoor swimming at all seasons, skis, shoots rapids in a canoe, becomes the coordinator of a moon colony. The type that bites. Valu-diddums had got her, but nothing else could have done. Not child, beast, nor man. Certainly not another woman. Oh my. And this was my multiple-great granny that I was about to offer the hand of reassurance.

Another hour, and some dial and click mechanisms down in the strawberry ice room started to dicker. The wolves flew in for the kill. A dead lioness, that was Carla. Then the box rattled and there was a yell. I couldn't see for scrabbling medics.

"What happened?"

The young medic detailed to sit on the spec gallery with me sighed. "I'd say she's opened her eyes."

The young medic was black as space and beautiful as the stars therein. But he didn't give a damn about me. You could see he was in love with Carla the lioness. I was simply a pain he had to put up with for two or three hours, while he stared at the goddess beneath.

But now the medics had drawn off. I thought of the Sleeping Beauty story, and Snow White. Her eyes were open indeed. Coppery brown to tone with the mane. She didn't appear dazed. She appeared contemptuous. Precisely as I'd anticipated. Then the crystal box lid began to rise.

"Jesus," I said.

"Strange you should say that," said the black medic. His own wonderful eyes fixed on Carla, he'd waxed profound and enigmatic. "The manner in which we all still use these outdated religious expletives: *God, Christ, Hell,* long after we've ceased to credit their religious basis as such. The successful completion of this experiment in life-suspense and restoration has a bearing on the same matter," he murmured, his inch-long lashes brushing the plastase pane. "You've read of the controversy regarding this process? It was seen at one era as an infringement of religious faith."

"Oh, yes?"

I kept on staring at him. Infinitely preferable to Carla, with her open eyes, and the solitary bending medic with the supadermic.

"The idea of the soul," said the medic on the gallery. "The immortal part which survives death. But what befalls a soul trapped for years, centuries, in a living yet statically frozen body? In a physical limbo, a living death. You see the problem this would pose for the religious?"

"I—uh—"

"But, of course, today . . ." He spread his hands. "There is no such barrier to lucid thought. The life force, we now know, resides purely in the brain, and thereafter in the motor nerves, the spinal cord, and attendant reflexive centers. There is no *soul.*"

Then he shut up and nearly swooned away, and I realized Carla had met his eye.

I looked, and she was sitting, part reclined against some medic's arm. The medic was telling her where she was and what year it was and how, by this evening, the valu-diddums would be no more than a bad dream, and then she could go out into the amazing new world with her loving descendant, whom she could observe up there on the gallery.

She did spare a glance for me. It lasted about .09 of a mini-instant. I tried to unglue my mouth and flash her a warming welcoming grin, but before I could manage it, she was back to studying the black medic.

At that moment somebody came and whipped me away for celebratory alcohol, and two hours later, when I'd celebrated rather too much, they took me up a plushy corridor to meet Carla, skin to skin.

Actually, she was dressed on this occasion. She'd had a shower and a couple of post-defrosting tests and some shots and the anti-valudiddums stuff. Her hair was smoldering like a fire in a forest. She wore the shiny smock medical centers insisted that you wore, but on her it was like a design original. She'd even had a tan frozen in with her, or maybe it was my dazzled eyes that made her seem all bronzed and glowing. Nobody could look that good, that *healthy*, after two hundred years on ice. And if they did, they shouldn't. Her room was crammed with flowers and bottles of scent and exotic light paintings, courtesy of the Institute. And then they trundled me in.

Not astoundingly, she gazed at me with bored amusement. Like she'd come to the dregs at the bottom of the wine.

"This is Tacey," somebody said, making free with my forename.

Carla spoke, in a voice of maroon velvet.

"Hallo, er, Tacey." Patently, my cognomen was a big mistake. Never mind, she'd overlook it for now. "I gather we are related."

I was drunk, but it wasn't helping.

"I'm your gr—yes, we are, but—" I intelligently blurted. The "but" was going to be a prologue to some nauseating, placatory, crawler's drivel about her gorgeousness and youth. It wasn't necessary, not even to let her know how scared I was. She could tell that easily, plus how I'd shrunk to a shadow in her high-voltage glare. Before I could complete my hiccuping sycophancy, anyway, the medic in charge said: "Tacey is your link, Mz Brice, with civilization as it currently is."

Carla couldn't resist it. She raised one manicured eyebrow, frozen exquisite for two centuries. If Tacey was the link, civilization could take a walk.

"My apartment," I went on blurting, "it's medium, but—"

What was I going to say now? About how all my grant from the Institute I would willingly spend on gowns and perfumes and skis and automatic rifles, or whatever Carla wanted. How I'd move out and she could have the apartment to herself. (She wouldn't like the spacine murals on the walls.)

"It's just a bri—a bridge," I managed. "Till you get acclimatozed—atized."

She watched me as I made a fool of myself, or rather, displayed my true foolishness. Finally I comprehended the message in her copper eyes: Don't bother. That was all: Don't bother. You're a failure, Carla's copper irises informed me, as if I didn't know. Don't make excuses. You can alter nothing. I expect nothing from you. I will stay while I must in your ineffectual vicinity, and you may fly round me and scorch your wings if you like. When I am ready, I shall leave immediately, soaring over your sky like a meteor. You can offer no aid, no interest, no grain I cannot garner for myself.

"How kind of Tacey," Carla's voice said. "Come, darling, and let me kiss you."

Somehow, I'd imagined her still as very cold from the frosty box, but she was blood heat. Ashamed, I let her brush my cheek with her meteoric lips. Perhaps I'd burn.

"I'd say this calls for a toast," said the medic in charge. "But just rose-juice for Mz Brice, I'm afraid, at present."

Carla smiled at him, and I hallucinated a rosebush, thorns too, eviscerated by her teeth. Lions drink blood, not roses.

I got home paralyzed and floundered about trying to change things. In the middle of attempting to re-spray-paint over a wall, I sank on a pillow and slept. Next day I was angry, the way you can only be angry over something against which you are powerless. So damn it. Let her arrive and see space shuttles, mother ships, and whirly bug-eyed monsters all across the plastase. And don't pull the ready-cook out of the alcove to clean the feed-pipes behind it that I hadn't seen for three years. Or dig the plant out of the cooled-water dispenser. Or buy any new garments, blinds, rugs, sheets. And don't conceal the Wage-Increment checks when they skitter down the chute. Or prop up the better spacines I'd illustrated on the table where she won't miss them.

I visited her one more time during the month she stayed at the Institute. I didn't have the courage not to take her anything, although I knew that whatever I offered would be wrong. Actually, I had an impulse to blow my first grant check and my W-I together and buy her a little antique stiletto of Toledo steel. It was blatantly meant to commit murder with, and as I handed it to her I'd bow and say, "For you, Carla. I just know you can find a use for it." But naturally I didn't have the bravura. I bought her a flagon of expensive scent she didn't need and was rewarded by seeing her put it on a shelf with three other identically packaged flagons, each twice the size of mine. She was wearing a reclinerobe of amber silk, and I almost reached for sunglasses. We didn't say much. I tottered from her room, sunburned and peeling. And that night I painted another flying saucer on the wall.

The day she left the Institute, they sent a mobile for me. I was supposed to collect and ride to the apartment with Carla, to make her feel homey. I felt sick.

Before I met her, though, the medic in charge wafted me into his office.

"We're lucky," he said. "Mz Brice is a most independent lady. Her readjustment has been, in fact, remarkable. None of the traumas or rebuttals we've been anxious about. I doubt if most of the other subjects to be revived from Cryogenesis will demonstrate the equivalent rate of success."

"They're really reviving them, then?" I inquired lamely. I was glad to be in here, putting off my fourth congress with inadequacy.

"A month from today. Dependent on the ultimately positive results of our post-resuscitation analysis of Mz Brice. But, as I intimated, I hardly predict any hitch there."

"And how long," I swallowed, "how long do you think Carla will want to stay with me?"

"Well, she seems to have formed quite an attachment for you, Tacey. It's a great compliment, you know, from a woman like that. A proud, volatile spirit. But she needs an anchor for a while. We all need our anchors. Probably, her proximity will benefit you, in return. Don't you agree?"

I didn't answer, and he concluded I was overwhelmed. He started to describe to me that glorious scheduled event, the global link-up, when every single cryogone was to be revived, as simultaneously with each other as they could arrange it. The process would be going out on five channels of the Spatials, visible to us all. Technology triumphant yet again, bringing us a minute or two of transcendental catharsis. I thought about the beautiful black medic and his words on religion. And this is how we replaced it, presumably (when we weren't saucer-sighting), shedding tears sentimentally over four thousand and ninety idiots fumbling out of the deep-freeze.

"One last, small warning," the medic in charge added. "You may notice—or you may not, I can't be positive—the occasional lapse in the behavioral patterns of Mz Brice."

There was a fantasy for me. Carla, *lapsed*.

"In what way?" I asked, miserably enjoying the unlikelihood.

"Mere items. A mood, an aberration—a brief disorientation even. These are to be expected in a woman reclaimed by life after two hundred years, and in a world she is no longer familiar with. As I explained, I looked for much worse and far greater quantity. The odd personality slip is inevitable. You mustn't be alarmed. At such moments the most steadying influence on Mz Brice will be a non-Institutional normalcy of surroundings. And the presence of yourself."

I nearly laughed.

I would have, if the door hadn't opened, and if Carla, in mock red-lynx fur, hadn't stalked into the room.

I didn't even try to create chatter. Alone in the mobile, with the auto driving us along the cool concrete highways, there wasn't any requirement to pretend for the benefit of others. Carla reckoned I was a schmoil, and I duly schmoiled. Mind you, now and again, she put out a silk paw and gave me a playful tap. Like when she asked me where I got my hair *done*. But I just told her about the ready-set parlors and she quit. Then again, she asked a couple of less abstract questions. Did libraries still exist, that was one. The second one was if I slept well.

I went along with everything in a dank stupor. I think I was half kidding myself it was going to be over soon. Then the mobile drove into the auto-lift of my apartment block, the gates gaped, and we got out. As my door recognized me and split wide, it abruptly hit me that Carla and I were going to be hand in glove for some while. A month at least, while the Institute computed its final tests. Maybe more, if Carla had my lazy streak somewhere in her bronze and permasteel frame.

She strode into my apartment and stood flaming among the flying saucers and the wine-ringed furniture. The fake-fur looked as if she'd shot it herself. She was a head taller than I was ever going to be. And then she startled me, about the only way she could right then.

"I'm tired, Tacey," said Carla.

No wisecracks, no vitriol, no stare from Olympus.

She glided to the bedroom. OK. I'd allocated the bed as hers, the couch as mine. She paused, gold digit on the panel that I'd preset to respond to her finger.

"Will you forgive me?" she wondered aloud.

Her voice was soporific. I yawned.

"Sure, Carla."

She stayed behind the closed panels for hours. The day reddened over the city, colors as usual heightened by the weather control that operates a quarter of a mile up. I slumped here and there, unable to eat or rest or read or doodle. I was finding out what it was going to be like, having an apartment and knowing it wasn't mine anymore. Even through a door, Carla dominated.

Around nineteen, I knocked. No reply.

Intimidated, I slunk off. I wouldn't play the septophones, even with the ear-pieces only, even with the volume way down. Might wake Granny. You see, if you could wake her from two hundred years in the freezer, you could certainly wake her after eight hours on a dormadais.

At twenty-four midnight, she still hadn't come out.

Coward, I knocked again, and feebly called: "Night, Carla. See you tomorrow."

On the couch I had nightmares, or nightcarlas to be explicit. Some were very realistic, like the one where the trust bonds Carla's estate had left for her hadn't accumulated after all and she was destitute, and going to remain with me forever and ever. Or there were the comic-strip ones where the fake red-lynx got under the cover and bit me. Or the surreal ones where Carla came floating toward me, clad only in her smoldering hair, and everything caught fire from it, and I kept saying, "Please, Carla, don't set the rug alight. Please, Carla, don't set the couch alight." In the end there was merely a dream where Carla bent over me, hissing something like an anaconda—if they do hiss. She wanted me to stay asleep, apparently, and for some reason I was fighting her, though I was almost comatose. The strange thing in this dream was that Carla's eyes had altered from copper to a brilliant topaz yellow, like the lynx's.

It must have been about four in the morning that I woke up. I think it was the washer unit that woke me. Or it could have been the septophones. Or the waste-disposal. Or the drier. Or any of the several gadgets a modern apartment was equipped with. Because they were all on. It sounded like a madhouse. Looked like one. All the lights were on, too. In the middle of chaos: Carla. She was quite naked, the way I'd seen her at the first, but she had the sort of nakedness that seems like clothes, clean-cut, firm, and flawless. The sort that makes me want to hide inside a stone. She was reminiscent of a sorceress in the midst of her sorcery, the erupting mechanisms sprawling around her in the fierce light. I had a silly thought: *Carla's going nova*. Then she turned and saw me. My mouth felt as if it had been security-sealed, but I got out, "You OK, Carla?"

"I am, darling. Go back to sleep now."

That's the last thing I remember till ten A.M. the next day.

I wondered initially if Carla and the gadgets had been an additional dream. But when I checked the energy-meter I discovered they hadn't.

I was plodding to the ready-cook when Carla emerged from the bedroom in her amber reclinerobe.

She didn't say a word. She just relaxed at the counter and let me be her slave. I got ready to prepare her the large breakfast she outlined. Then I ran her bath. When the water-meter shut off half through, Carla suggested I put in the extra tags to ensure the tub was filled right up.

As she bathed, I sat at the counter and had another nervous attack.

Of course, Carla was predictably curious. Back in 1993, many of our gadgets hadn't been invented, or at least not developed to their present standard. Why not get up in the night and turn everything on? Why did it have to seem sinister? Maybe my sleeping through it practically nonstop was the thing that troubled me. All right. So Carla was a hypnotist. Come to consider, should I run a histotrace myself, in an attempt to learn what Carla was—had been?

But let's face it, what really upset me was the low on the energy-meter, the water-meter taking a third of my week's water tags in one morning. And Carla luxuriously wallowing, leaving me to foot the bill.

Could I say anything? No. I knew she'd immobilize me before I'd begun.

When she came from the bathroom, I asked her did she want to go out. She said no, but I could visit the library, if I would, and pick up this book and tape list she'd called through to them. I checked the call-meter. That was down, too.

"I intend to act the hermit for a while, Tacey," Carla murmured behind me as I guiltily flinched away from the meter. "I don't want to get involved in a furor of publicity. I gather the news of my successful revival will have been leaked today. The tablotapes will be sporting it. But I understand, by the news publishing codes of the '80s, that unless I approach the Newsies voluntarily, they are not permitted to approach me."

"Yes, that's right." I gazed pleadingly into the air. "I guess you wouldn't ever reconsider that, Carla? It could mean a lot of money. That is, not for you to contact the Newsies. But if you'd all—allow me to on your beh—half."

She chuckled like a lioness with her throat full of gazelle. The hair rose on my neck as she slunk closer. When her big, warm, elegant hand curved over my skull, I shuddered.

"No, Tacey. I don't think I'd care for that. I don't need the cash. My estate investments, I hear, are flourishing."

"I was thinking of m—I was thinking of me, Carla. I cou—could use the tags."

The hand slid from my head and batted me lightly. Somehow, I was glad I hadn't given her the Toledo knife after all.

"No, I don't think so. I think it will do you much more good to continue as you are. Now, run along to the library, darling."

I went mainly because I was glad to get away from her. To utter the spineless whining I had, had drained entirely my thin reserves of courage. I was shaking when I reached the auto-lift. I had a wild plan of leaving town, and leaving my apartment with Carla in it, and going to ground. It was more than just inadequacy now. Hunter and hunted. And as I crept through the long grass, her fiery breath was on my heels.

I collected the twenty books and the fifty tapes and paid for the loan. I took them back to the apartment and laid them before my astonishing amber granny. I was too scared even to hide. Much too scared to disobey.

I sat on the sun-patio, though it was the weather control day for rain. Through the plastase panels I heard the tapes educating Carla on every aspect of contemporary life: social, political, economic, geographical, and carnal.

When she summoned me, I fixed lunch. Later, drinks and supper.

Then I was too nervous to go to sleep. I passed out in the bathroom, sitting in the shower cubicle. Had nightcarlas of Carla eating salad. Didn't wake up till ten A.M. Checked. All meters down again.

When I trod on smashed plastase, I thought it was sugar. Then I saw the cooled-water dispenser was in ninety-five bits. Where the plant had been, there was only soil and condensation and trailing roots.

I looked, and everywhere beheld torn-off leaves and tiny clots of earth. There was a leaf by Carla's bedroom. I knocked and my heart knocked to keep my hand company.

But Carla wasn't interested in breakfast, wasn't hungry.

I knew why not. She'd eaten my plant.

You can take a bet I meant to call up the Institute right away. Somehow, I didn't. For one thing, I didn't want to call from the apartment and risk Carla catching me at it. For another, I didn't want to go out and leave her, in case she did something worse. Then again, I was terrified to linger in her vicinity. A *lapse,* the medic in charge had postulated. It was certainly that. Had she done anything like it at the Institute? Somehow I had the idea she hadn't. She'd saved it for me. Out of playful malice.

I dithered for an hour, till I panicked, pressed the call button and spoke the digits. I never heard the door open. She seemed to know exactly when to—*strike;* yes, that *is* the word I want. I sensed her there. She didn't even touch me. I let go the call button.

"Who were you calling?" Carla asked.

"Just a guy I used to pair with," I said, but it came out husky and gulped and quivering.

"Well, go ahead. Don't mind me."

Her maroon voice, bored and amused and indifferent to anything I might do, held me like a steel claw. And I discovered I had to turn around and face her. I had to stare into her eyes.

The scorn in them was killing. I wanted to shrivel and roll under the rug, but I couldn't look away.

"But if you're not going to call anyone, run my bath, darling," Carla said.

I ran her bath.

It was that easy. Of course.

She was magnetic. Irresistible.

I couldn't—

I could *not*—

Partly, it had all become incredible. I couldn't picture myself accusing Carla of houseplant-eating to the medics at the Institute. Who'd believe it? It was nuts. I mean, too nuts even for them. And presently, I left off quite believing it myself.

Nevertheless, somewhere in my brain I kept on replaying those sentences of the medic in charge: *the occasional lapse in the behavioral patterns . . . a mood, an aberration. . . .* And against that, point counterpoint, there kept on playing that phrase the beautiful black medic had reeled off enigmatically as a cultural jest: *But what befalls a soul trapped for years, centuries, in a living yet statically frozen body?*

Meanwhile, by sheer will, by the force of her persona, she'd stopped me calling. And that same thing stopped me talking about her to anybody on the street, sent me tongue-tied to fetch groceries, sent me groveling to conjure meals. It was almost as if it also shoved me asleep when she wanted and brought me awake ditto.

Doesn't time fly when you're having fun?

Twenty days, each more or less resembling each, hurried by. Carla didn't do anything else particularly weird, at least not that I saw or detected. But then, I never woke up nights anymore. And I had an insane theory that the meters had been fiddled, because they weren't low, but they felt as if they should be. I hadn't got any more plants. I missed some packaged paper lingerie, but it turned up under Carla's bed, where I'd kicked it when the bed was mine. Twenty days, twenty-five. The month of Carla's post-resuscitation tests was nearly through. One morning, I was stumbling about like a zombie, cleaning the apartment because the dustease had jammed and Carla had spent five minutes in silent comment on the dust. I was moving in that combined sludge of terror, mindlessness, and masochistic cringing she'd taught me, when the door signal went.

When I opened the door, there stood the black medic with a slim case of file-tapes. I felt transparent, and that was how he treated me. He gazed straight through me to the empty room where he had hoped my granny would be.

"I'm afraid your call doesn't seem to be working," he said. (Why had I the notion Carla had done something to the call?) "I'd be grateful to see Mz Brice, if she can spare me a few minutes. Just something we'd like to check for the files."

That instant, splendid on her cue, Carla manifested from the bathroom. The medic had seen her naked in the frosty box, but not a naked that was vaguely and fluently sheathed in a damp towel. It had the predictable effect. As he paused transfixed, Carla bestowed her most gracious smile.

"Sit down," she said. "What check is this? Tacey, darling, why not arrange some fresh coffee?"

Tacey darling went to the coffee cone. Over its bubbling, I heard him say to her, "It's simply that Doctor Something was a little worried by a possible amnesia. Certainly, none of the memory areas seem physically impaired. But you see, here and there on the tape—"

"Give me an example, please," drawled Carla.

The black medic lowered his lashes as if to sweep the tablotape.

"Some confusion over places, and names. Your second husband, Francis, for instance, who you named as Frederick. And there, the red mark—Doctor Something-Else mentioned the satellite disaster of '91, and it seems you did not recall—"

"You're referring to the malfunction of the Ixion 11, which broke up and crashed in the midwest, taking three hundred lives," said Carla. She sounded like a purring textbook. She leaned forward, and I could watch him tremble all the way across from the coffee cone. "Doctor Something and Doctor Something-Else," said Carla, "will have to make allowances for my excitement at rebirth. Now, I can't have you driving out this way for nothing. How about you come to dinner, the night before the great day. Tacey doesn't see nearly enough people her own age. As for me, let's say you'll make a two-hundred-year-old lady very happy."

The air between them was electric enough to form sparks. By the "great day" she meant, patently, the five-channel Spatial event when her four thousand and ninety confrères got liberated from the subzero. But he plainly didn't care so much about defrosting anymore.

The coffee cone boiled over. I noticed with a shock I was crying. Nobody else did.

What I wanted to do was program the ready-cook for the meal, get in some wine, and get the hell out of the apartment and leave the two of them alone. I'd pass the night at one of the all-night Populars, and creep in around ten A.M. the next morning. That's the state I frankly acknowledged she had reduced me to. I'd have been honestly grateful to have done that. But Carla wouldn't let me.

"Out?" she inquired. "But this whole party is for you, darling."

There was nobody about. She didn't have to pretend. She and I knew I was the slave. She and I knew her long-refrigerated soul, returning in fire, had scalded me into a melty on the ground. So it could only be cruelty, this. She seemed to be experimenting, even, as she had with the gadgets. The psychological dissection of an inferior inhabitant of the future.

What I had to do, therefore, was to visit the ready-set hair parlor, and buy a dress with my bimonthly second W-I check. Carla, though naturally she didn't go with me, somehow instigated and oversaw these ventures. Choosing the dress, she was oddly at my elbow. *That* one, her detached and omnipresent aura instructed me. It was expensive, and it was scarlet and gold. It would have looked wonderful on somebody else. But not me. That dress just sucked the little life I've got right out of me.

Come the big night (before the big day, for which the countdown must already have, in fact, begun), there I was, done up like a New Year parcel, and with my own problematical soul wizened within me. The door signal went, and the slave accordingly opened the door, and the dark angel entered, politely thanking me as he nearly walked straight through me.

He looked so marvelous, I practically bolted. But still the aura of Carla, and Carla's wishes, which were beginning to seem to be communicating themselves telepathically, held me put.

Then Carla appeared. I hadn't seen her before, that evening. The dress was lionskin, and it looked real, despite the anti-game-hunting laws. Her hair was a smooth auburn waterfall that left bare an ear with a gold star dependent from it. I just went into the cooking area and uncorked a bottle and drank most of it straight off.

They both had good appetites, though hers was better than his. She'd eaten a vast amount since she'd been with me, presumably ravenous after that long fast. I was the waitress, so I waited on them. When I reached my plate, the food had congealed because the warmer in the table on my side was faulty. Anyway, I wasn't hungry. There were two types of wine. I drank the cheap type. I was on the second bottle now, and sufficiently sad I could have howled, but I'd also grown uninvolved, viewing my sadness from a great height.

They danced together to the septophones. I drank some more wine. I was going to be very, very ill tomorrow. But that was tomorrow. Verily. When I looked up, they'd danced themselves into the bedroom and the panels were shut. Carla's cruelty had had its run and I wasn't prepared for any additions, such as ecstatic moans from the interior, to augment my frustration. Accordingly, garbed in my New Year parcel frock, hair in curlicues, and another bottle in my hand, I staggered forth into the night.

I might have met a thug, a rapist, a murderer, or even one of the numerous polipatrols that roam the city to prevent the activities of such. But I didn't meet anyone who took note of me. Nobody cared. Nobody was interested. Nobody wanted to be my friend, rob me, abuse me, give me a job or a goal, or make me happy, or make love to me. So if you thought I was a Judas, just you remember that. If one of you slobs had taken any notice of me that night—

I didn't have to wait for morning to be ill. There was a handsome washroom on Avenue East. I'll never forget it. I was there quite a while.

When the glamorous weather-control dawn irradiated the city, I was past the worst. And by ten A.M. I was trudging home, queasy, embittered, hard-done-by, but sober. I was even able to register the tabloes everywhere and the holoid neons, telling us all that the great day was here. The day of the four thousand and ninety. Thawday. I wondered dimly if Carla and the Prince of Darkness were still celebrating it in my bed. She should have been cold. Joke. All right. It isn't.

The door to my apartment let me in. The place was as I'd abandoned it. The window blinds were down, the table strewn with plates and glasses. The bedroom door firmly shut.

I pressed the switch to raise the blinds, and nothing happened, which didn't surprise me. That in itself should have proved to me how far the influence had gone and how there was no retreat. But I only had this random desultory urge to see what the apartment door would do now. What it did was not react. Not even when I put my hand on the panel, which method was generally reserved for guests. It had admitted me, but wouldn't let me out again. Carla had done something to it. As she had to the call, the meters, and to me. But how—personal power? Ridiculous. I was a spineless dope, that was why she'd been able to negate me. Yet—forty-one medics, with a bevy of tests and questions, some of which, apparently, she hadn't got right, ate from her hand. And maybe her psychic ability had increased. Practice makes perfect.

. . . *What befalls a soul trapped for years, centuries, in a living yet statically frozen body?*

It was dark in the room, with the blinds irreversibly staying down and the lights irreversibly off.

Then the bedroom door slid wide, and Carla slid out. Naked again, and glowing in the dark. She smiled at me, pityingly.

"Tacey, darling, now you've gotten over your sulks, there's something in here I'd like you to clear up for me."

Dichotomy once more. I wanted to take root where I was, but she had me walking to the bedroom. She truly was glowing. As if she'd lightly sprayed herself over with something mildly luminous. I guessed what would be in the bedroom, and I'd begun retching, but, already despoiled of filling, that didn't matter. Soon I was in the doorway and she said, "Stop that, Tacey." And I stopped retching and stood and looked at what remained of the beautiful black medic, wrapped up in the bloodstained lionskin.

Lions drink blood, not roses.

Something loosened inside me then. It was probably the final submission, the final surrender of the fight. Presumably I'd been fighting her subconsciously from the start, or I wouldn't have gained the ragged half-freedoms I had. But now I was limp and sodden, so I could ask humbly: "The plant was salad. But a man—what was he?"

"You don't quite get it, darling, do you?" Carla said. She stroked my hair friendlily. I didn't shudder anymore. Cowed dog, I was relaxed under the contemptuous affection of my mistress. "One was green and vegetable. One was black, male, and meat. Different forms. Local dishes. I had no inclination to sample you, you comprehend, since you were approximate to my own appearance. But of course, others who find themselves to be black and male may wish to sample pale-skinned females. Don't worry, Tacey. You'll be safe. You entertain me. You're mine. Protected species."

"Still don't understand, Carla," I whispered meekly.

"Well, just clear up for me, and I'll explain."

I don't have to apologize to you for what I did then, because, of course, you know all about it, the will-less indifference of the absolute slave. I bundled up the relics of Carla's lover-breakfast, and dumped them in the waste-disposal, which dealt with them pretty efficiently.

Then I cleaned the bedroom and had a shower and fixed Carla some coffee and biscuits. It was almost noon, the hour when the four thousand and ninety were going to be roused, and to step from their frost boxes in front of seven-eighths of the world's Spatial-viewers. Carla wanted to see it too, so I switched on my set, minus the sound. Next Carla told me I might sit, and I sat on a pillow, and she explained.

For some reason, I don't remember her actual words. Perhaps she put it in a technical way and I got the gist but not the sentences. I'll put it in my own words here, despite the fact that a lot of you know now anyway. After all, under supervision, we still have babies sometimes. When they grow up they'll need to know. Know why they haven't got a chance, and why we hadn't. And, to level with you, know why I'm not a Judas, and that I didn't betray us, because I didn't have a chance either.

Laziness, optimism, and blind stupidity.

I suppose optimism more than anything.

Four thousand and ninety-one persons lying down in frozen stasis, aware they didn't have souls and couldn't otherwise survive, dreaming of a future of cures, and of a reawakening in that future. And the earth dreaming of benevolent visitors from other worlds, father-mother figures to guide and help us. Sending them buzz-whuzzes to bleep, over and over, *Here* we are. *Here. Here.*

I guess we do have souls. Or we have something that has nothing to do with the brain, or the nerve centers, or the spinal cord. Perhaps that dies too, when we die. Or perhaps it escapes. Whatever happens, that's the one thing you can't retain in Cryogenic Suspension. The body, all its valves and ducts and organs, lies pristine in limbo, and when you wake it up with the correct drugs, impulses, stimuli, it's live again, can be cured of its diseases, becoming a flawless vessel of—nothing. It's like an empty room, a vacant lot. The tenant's skipped.

Somewhere out in the starry night of space, one of the bleeping buzz-whuzzes was intercepted. Not by pater-mater figures, but by a predatory, bellicose alien race. It was simple to get to us—hadn't we given comprehensive directions? But on arrival they perceived a world totally unsuited to their fiery, gaseous, incorporeal forms. That was a blow, that was. But they didn't give up hope. Along with their superior technology they developed a process whereby they reckoned they could transfer inside of human bodies, and thereafter live off the fat of the Terrain. However, said process wouldn't work. Why not? The human consciousness (soul?) was too strong to overcome, it wouldn't let them through. Even asleep, they couldn't oust us. Dormant, the consciousness (soul?) is still present, or at least linked. As for dead bodies, no go. A man who had expired of old age, or with a mobile on top of him, was no use. The body had to be a whole one, or there was no point. Up in their saucers, which were periodically spotted, they spat and swore. They gazed at the earth and drooled, pondering mastery of a globe, and entire races of slaves at their disposal. But there was no way they could achieve their aims until—until they learned of all those Cryogenic Suspensions in their frost boxes, all those soulless lumps of ice, waiting on the day when science would release and cure them and bring them forth healthy and *void*.

If you haven't got a tenant, advertise for a new tenant. We had. And they'd come.

Carla was the first. As her eyes opened under the crystal, something looked out of them. Not Carla Brice. Not anymore. But something.

Curious, cruel, powerful, indomitable, alien, deadly.

Alone, she could handle hundreds of us humans, for her influence ascended virtually minute by minute. Soon there were going to be four thousand and ninety of her kind, opening their eyes, smiling their scornful thank-yous through the Spatials at the world they had come to conquer. The world they did conquer.

We gave them beautiful, healthy, movable houses to live in, and billions to serve them and be toyed with by them, and provide them with extra bodies to be frozen and made fit to house any leftover colleagues of theirs. And our green depolluted meadows wherein to rejoice.

As for Carla, she'd kept quiet and careful as long as she had to. Long enough for the tests to go through and for her to communicate back, telepathically, to her people, all the data they might require on earth, prior to their arrival.

And now she sat and considered me, meteoric fiery Carla-who-wasn't-Carla, her eyes, in the dark, gleaming topaz yellow through their copper irises, revealing her basic inflammable nature within the veil of a dead woman's living flesh.

They can make me do whatever they want, and they made me write this. Nothing utterly bad has been done to me, and maybe it never will. So I've been lucky there.

To them, I'm historically interesting, as Carla had been historically interesting to us, as a first. I'm the first Slave. Possibly, I can stay alive on the strength of that and not be killed for a whim.

Which, in a way, I suppose, means I'm a sort of a success, after all.

Scorched Supper on New Niger

SUZY McKEE CHARNAS

Bob W. Netchkay wanted my ship and I was damned if I was going to let him have it.

It was the last of the Steinway space fleet that my sister Nita and I had inherited from our aunt Juno. Aunt Juno had been a great tough lady of the old days and one hell of an administrator, far better alone than us two Steinway sisters together. I was young when she died, but smart enough to know that I was a hell of a pilot; so I hired an administrator to run the line for Nita and me.

Bob Netchkay administrated himself a large chunk of our income, made a bunch of deliberately bad deals, and secretly bought up all my outstanding notes after a disastrous trading season. I threw him out, but he walked away with six of my ships. I lost nine more on my own. Then my sister Nita married the bastard and took away with her all the remaining ships but one, my ship, the *Sealyham Eggbeater*.

And I'd mortgaged that to raise money for a high risk, high profit cargo in hopes of making a killing. But there were delays on Droslo, repairs to be made at Coyote Station, and the upshot was that Bob had gotten his hands on my mortgage. Now he was exercising his rights under it to call it early, while I was still racing for the one nearby dealer not trade-treatied to my competitors. His message was waiting for me when I woke that morning someplace between Rico and the Touchgate system.

Ripotee had checked in the message for me. He sat on the console chewing imaginary burrs out from between his paw pads. No comment from him. He was probably in one of those moods in which he seemed to feel that the best way to preserve his catlike air of mystery was keeping his mouth shut and acting felinely aloof.

I read my message, smacked the console, and bounced around the cabin yelling and hugging my hand. Then I said, "This is short range, from 'The Steinway Legal Department,' which means that creep Rily in Cabin D of our flagship—I mean the Netchkay pirate ship. They're close enough to intercept me before I can reach my buyer on Touchgate Center. Bob will get my ship and my cargo and find a way to keep both."

Ripotee yawned delicately, curling his pink tongue.

I wiped the console and cut every signal, in or out, that might help Bob to home in on me again. Then I set an automatic jig course to complicate his life. Fast evasive tactics would cost me heavily in fuel but still leave me enough to get to Red Joy Power Station, an outpost on Touchgate Six that was closer to me than my original buyer. Red Joy is an arm of Eastern Glory, the China combine that is one of the great long-hauling companies. I could make Red Joy before Bob caught me, dump my cargo with the Chinese for the best price they would give me, and nip out again.

The Chinese run an admirable line, knowing how to live well on little in these times of depression. They're arrogant in a falsely humble way, lack daring and imagination as Aunt Juno taught me to define those terms, and think very little of anything not Chinese. But they are honest and I could count on them to give me fair value for my cargo.

On the other hand, though the Steinway ships are short haulers, they are the only short haulers that can travel among star systems without having to hitch costly rides with long haulers like the Chinese. We are in competition, of a sort. The Chinese don't like competition on principle; so they don't much like Steinways.

Ripotee was observing the course readouts glowing on the wall. "Red Joy," he remarked, "used to be the trademark of underwear marketed in China in the days of Great Mao."

"At worst they would impound my ship," I said, "but they'd still pay me for what's in it."

Ripotee coughed. "About our cargo," he said. His tail thumped the top of the console. "I was mouse hunting this morning in the hold." I kept mice on the *Eggbeater* to eat up my crumbs and to keep Ripotee fit and amused. "All that pod is souring into oatmeal."

I sat there and spattered my instruments with tears.

Pod is one of the few really valuable alien trade items to have been found in the known universe. It integrates with any living system it's properly introduced to and realigns that system into a new balance that almost always turns out to be beneficial. People are willing to pay a lot for a pod treatment. But if pod gets contaminated with organic matter it integrates on its own and turns into "oatmeal," a sort of self-digested sludge, which quickly becomes inert and very smelly and hard to clean up.

I hadn't had the time or the money to compartmentalize the hold of the *Eggbeater*. If some of the pod was soured, it was all soured.

"New Niger," Ripotee murmured. His eyes were sleepy blue slits, contemplating the wall charts. "We could reach New Niger faster than Netchkay could. They would buy the *Eggbeater* and fight Bob afterward to keep it."

I sat paralyzed with indecision. The New Nigerians certainly would buy the *Sealyham Eggbeater*, given the chance.

It was to keep my ship out of such hands as theirs that Bob was so anxious to take it over. All the other Steinways are later models, set to blow themselves up if strangers go poking around in their guts. This protects the Steinway secret: what Aunt Juno did to fit her short haul ships for travel between systems without hitching rides at the extortioners' rates that long haulers charge. An engineer could dig into my ship, though, and come out unscathed to report that Aunt Juno had simply modified the straight-and-tally system in a particular manner with half a dozen counter-clock Holbein pins, without disturbing the linkup with the stabilizers and the degreasing works. Everybody knows the general principles, but nobody outside of us Steinways knows the exact arrangement.

The Chinese, long haulers exclusively, wouldn't be interested. They would only take my ship to tuck it away out of commission so its secret couldn't be used by anybody else to cut down their income from giving hitches.

But the Africans of New Niger ran short haul ships and were longtime competitors of the Steinway Line on the in-system short haul routes. They could use Aunt Juno's secret, if they had it, to bounce from system to system cheap, as we did, and wipe out our advantage.

Ripotee said, "Or you could just give up and let Netchkay have the ship. A lot of people would say you should. He's a good administrator." I took a swipe at him, but he eluded me with a graceful leap onto the food synthesizer, which burped happily and offered me a cup of steaming ersatz. "He's a North American," Ripotee continued, "a go-getter, who's trying to rebuild North American prestige—"

"To build himself, you mean, on my ships and my sister's treachery!"

"The Captain's always right," Ripotee said, "in her own ship."

I drank the ersatz and glared at the wall, ignoring for the moment the instruments blinking disaster warnings at me: Bob's ship was following my jig course already. If I was starting to pick him up, he would be picking me up too, first in signals and then in reality.

Among the instruments that gave the walls their baroque look of overdone detail I had stuck a snapshot of a New Nigerian captain I had encountered once, closely. What were the chances that somebody down there would know where Barnabas was these days? It would make a difference to know that I had one friend on New Niger.

My console jumped on, and there was a splintery image of Bob Netchkay's swarthy, handsome face. He looked grave and concerned, which made me fairly pant with hatred.

"You got my offer, Dee," he said in a honey voice.

If I turned off again he would think I was too upset to deal with him. I looked him in the eye and did not smile.

"Did you?" he pressed. He faced me full on, obscuring the predatory thrust of his beaky features.

"I know all about this final stage of your grab project, yes," I said.

He shook his head. "No, Dee, you don't understand. I'm thinking about the family now." He had changed his name to Steinway on marrying Nita, which was good for business but bad for my blood pressure. "I've talked this over with Nita and she agrees; the only way to handle it right is together, as a family."

I said, "I have no family."

Nita came and looked over his shoulder at me, her round, tanned face reproachful. I almost gagged: Nita, charter member of the New Lambchop League, sweet and slinky and one pace behind "her" man, pretending she knew nothing about business. She had dumped me as a partner for this ambitious buccaneer because he would play along with her frills and her protect-me-I'm-weak line. I think Aunt Juno had hoped to lead her in another direction by leaving half of the Steinway fleet to her. But Nita was part of the new swing back to "romance," a little lost lambchop, not an admiral of the spaceways.

"We're still sisters, Dee." She blinked her black eyes at me under her naked brows. She had undergone face stiffening years ago to create the supposedly alluring effect of enormous, liquid orbs in a mysterious mask.

"You may be somebody's sister," I snapped. "I'm not."

She whispered something to Bob.

He nodded. "I know. You see how bad things have gotten, Dee, when you get into a worse temper than ever at the sight of your own sister. Sometimes I think it's a chemical imbalance, that temper of yours, it's not natural. Nita has to go, she's got things to do. I just wanted you to know that anything I suggest has already been run past her, and she's in complete agreement. Isn't that right, Nita?"

Nita nodded, fluttered her tapered fingers in my direction, and whisked her svelte, body-suited figure out of the picture. Where she had been I saw something I recognized behind Bob's shoulder: one of those stretched guts from the Wailies of Tchan that's supposed to show images of the future if you expose it to anti-gravity. It had never shown Aunt Juno these two connivers running her flagship.

"Well?" I said. I sipped the cold dregs of my ersatz.

Bob lowered sincerely at me. "Look, Dee, I'm older than you and a lot more experienced at a lot of things, like running a successful trade business. And I'm very concerned about the future of the Steinway name. You and I have been at odds for a long time, but you don't really think I've gone to all this trouble just to junk the line, do you? I did what I had to do, that's all."

He stopped and glared past me; I turned. Ripotee had a hind foot stuck up in the air and was licking his crotch. He paused to say loudly, "I'm doing what I have to do, too."

"Get that filth off the console!" Bob yelled. I chortled. He got control of himself and plowed on: "Already I've restored your family's reputation; Steinway is once again a name held in commercial respect. And I can do more.

"You don't realize; things are going to get rougher than you can imagine, and it won't be any game for a freelance woman with nobody to back her up. Look around you: times are changing, it's a tougher and tougher short haul market, and women are pulling back into softer, older ways. What will you be out there, one of a handful of female freaks left over from the days of Juno and her type? Freaks don't get work, not when there are good, sound men around to take it away from them. You'll be a pauper.

"I don't want that. Nita doesn't want it. You don't want it. Give up and face facts."

He paused, the picture of a man carried away by his own eloquence. And a pleasure to look at too, if I hadn't been burning up with loathing for his very tripes. Even without the frame of curling black hair and high collar, the subtly padded shoulders and chest—the New Lambchops weren't the only ones looking back in time to more romantic eras—Bob was handsome, and very masculine looking in a hard, sharp-cut way.

He knew it and used it, posing there all earnest drama, to give me a minute to react, to cue him as to how all this was setting with me. I said, deadpan, "What's the deal?"

He looked pained. "Not a deal; a way for us all to come out all right. You give me the *Sealyham Eggbeater*, pull out of the business, take a holiday someplace, grow out your hair. In exchange for your ship, I'll give you a one-third inalienable interest in the Steinway stock and a nice desk job for income. But I get to run things my own way without interference. You keep your mouth shut and let me do what I know how to do, and I take care of you and your sister."

I was so mad I could hardly work my jaw loose enough to utter a sound. "But I don't get to do what *I* know how to do, which is to pilot a short haul ship. My answer is no."

I wiped the console and punched a new jig. Then I plugged in a tingle of electracalm and a light dose of antistress because I needed my head clear.

Ripotee lay stretched out along the sill of a viewport, curved within its curve, one paw hanging down. He liked to keep his distance when I was upset. His sapphire eyes rested on me, intent, unreadable. He had either found that he could not or decided that he would not learn to use his facial muscles for expressiveness on the human model. I couldn't interpret that masked, blunt-muzzled visage.

I said, "Ripotee, what do you know about New Niger?"

His tail started swinging, lashing. That was something he had never been able to control. He was excited, onto something.

"Jungle," he said. "Tall trees and vines and close underbrush. Good smells, earth and voidings and growth. Not like here."

"You've got cabin fever," I snorted. I was already setting up a fast but indirect course for Singlet, New Niger's main port. "Aren't your mice entertaining you enough anymore?"

I reached out to pat his head, but he jerked away. He didn't say, Don't do that, though he could have. Sometimes he was pleased to show me the superfluity of that human invention, speech. We had been in space a longish while. Ripotee got just as irritable as anyone else—as me.

The autodrives took over at full speed on a wild zigzag course. Strapping in tight, I signaled Ripotee, over the shout of the engines, to get into his harness. I tried to cut the graveys, but the switch stuck: it was going to be a rough ride. I felt reckless. Bob was close; if he tried to grab the *Eggbeater* now, he'd run a good chance of collision and of getting himself killed, if not all of us.

There was a lot of buffeting and slinging as the ship shunted from course to course. I kept my eyes on Ripotee, not wanting to see evidence of impossible strain, of damage, of imminent ruin on the dials that encrusted the walls. He lay flat in his nest of straps secured to a padded niche over the internal monitor banks, his claws bradded into the fibers. He was Siamese, fawn beneath and seal-brown on top, a slight shading of stripes on his upper legs, cheeks, and forehead. He had street blood in him, none of your overbred mincing and neurosis there. I hoped he wasn't about to come to a crashing end on account of my feud with Netchkay.

I am a natural pilot but not what they call a sheepherder, the kind who thrives on being alone in space. A good short haul ship can be managed by one operator and can carry more cargo that way, and I don't like crowding. So I had acquired Ripotee instead of a human partner.

He had been a gift as a kitten, along with a treatment contract on him for a place out in the Tic Tacs where they use pod infections to mutate animals upward—if humanizing their brains is actually a step in that direction. He came out of his pod fever with a good English vocabulary and a talent for being aggravating in pursuit of his own independence.

Even at his worst, he was the companion I needed, a reminder of something besides the bright sterility of space and its stars. There wasn't anything else. We had yet to find alien life of true intelligence. Meanwhile, the few Earth animals that had survived the Oil Age were all the more important to us—to those of us who cared about such things, anyway.

The ship dropped hard, slewing around to a new heading. Straps bit my skin. I thought of the time when, after a brush with some name-proud settlers on Le Cloue, I had asked Ripotee, "Do you want to change your name? Maybe you don't like being called 'Ripotee'?" I was thinking that it was hard for him to pronounce it, as he had some trouble with *t*'s.

He had said, "I don't care, I don't have to say it. I can say 'I,' just like a person. Anyway, Ripotee isn't my name; it's just your name for me."

Only later I wondered whether this proud statement covered not some private name he had for himself but the fact that he had no name except the one I had given him.

I could hardly draw breath to think with now, and I was very glad to have had no breakfast but that cup of ersatz.

Another hard swing, and I smelled rotting pod; a cargo seal must have broken and who knew what else. Ripotee let out a sudden wail —not pain, I hoped, just fear. I kept my eyes closed now. If he'd been shaken loose from his harness he could be slammed to death on the walls, just as I would be if I tried to go and help him.

One thing about Ripotee that neither of us nor his producers in the Tic Tacs knew was how long he had to live. He was approaching his first watermark, the eighth year, which if successfully passed normally qualifies a domestic cat for another seven or eight. In his case, we had no idea whether the pod infection had fitted him with a human life span to go with his amplified mind, or, given that, whether his physical small-animal frame would hold up to such extended usage. One thing was sure, enough of this battering around and he would end up just as punchy as any human pilot would.

I blacked out twice. Then everything smoothed down, and my power automatically cut as the landing beams locked on. A voice sang a peculiarly enriched English into my ears over the headset: looping vowels, a sonorous timbre—reminding me of Barnabas's voice. "Singlet Port. So now you will be boarded by a customs party. Please prepare to receive. . . ."

Prepare to give up—but never to Bob.

Ripotee was first out on New Niger. I sprung the forward hatch and a group of people came in; he padded right past them, tail in the air, none of your hanging about sniffing to decide whether or not it was worth his time to go through the doorway. Normally he's as cautious as any cat, but he is also given to wild fits of berserker courage that are part existential meanness and part tomcat.

He paused in his progress only to lay a delicate line of red down the back of a reaching hand—just an eyeblink swipe of one paw, an exclamation from the victim, and Ripotee was off, belly stretched in an ecstatic arc of all-out effort above the landing pad. Well out of reach, he paused with his tail quirked up in its play mode, glanced back, and then bounded sideways out of sight behind a heap of cartons and drums.

I had to pay a quarantine fine on him, of course. They were very annoyed to have lost any organisms he might have brought in with him that could be useful in pod experiments. The fine was partly offset by some prime wrigglies they got out of me, leftovers from a visit to the swamps of Putt.

There were forms to fill out and a lot of "dash" to pay for hints on how to fill them out with the least chance of expensive mistakes. I stood in the security office, my head still fuzzy from the rough flight, and I wrote.

A young man with a long thin face like a deer's came and plucked me by the sleeve. He said in soft, accented English, "You are asked for, Missisi. Come with me please."

"Who?" I said, thinking damn it, Bob has landed, he's onto me already. I stalled. "I have these forms to finish—"

He looked at the official who had given me these books of papers and said, "Missisi Helen will see to it that everything is put right."

The official reached over, smiling, and eased the papers out from under my hand. "I did not know that Captain Steinway was a friend of Missisi Helen. Do not worry of your ship; it goes into our clean-out system because of the oatmeal."

My guide led me through corridors and once across a landing surface brilliant with sun. I wondered if this Missisi Helen was the famous Helen who had been trading from New Niger as far back as Aunt Juno's own times: a tough competitor.

We went to a hangar where a short hauler stood surrounded by half-unpacked bales and boxes and spilled fruit. For a barnyard flavor, chickens (the African lines would carry anything) ran among the feet of the passengers, who shouted and pawed through everything, looking, I supposed, for their own belongings mixed in with the scattered cargo. The mob, rumpled and steamy with their own noise and excitement, was all Black except for one skinny, shiny-bald White man in the stained white sari of a Holy Wholist missionary. He stood serenely above it all.

I picked my way along after my guide, trying not to wrinkle my nose; after all, I'd had no more opportunity for a thorough bath and fresh change of clothing than these folks had. To tell the truth, I felt nervous in that crush and scramble of people; there were so many, and I had lived without other humans for a long time.

A knot of argument suddenly burst, and a little woman in a long rose-colored dress stepped out to meet me, snapping angrily over her shoulder at a man who reached pleadingly to restrain her: "And I tell you, it is for you some of my cargo was dumped cheap at Lagos Port to make room for this, your cousin. I am surprised you did not want my very ancestor's bones thrown away so you could bring your whole family! You will pay back for my lost profits, or I will make you very sorry! Speak there to my secretary."

She faced me, one heavily braceleted arm cocked hand-on-hip, her bare, stubby feet planted wide. Her hair, a tight, springy pile of gray, was cut and shaped into an exaggerated part, like two steep hills on her head. She tipped her head back and looked down her curved, broad, delicate nose at me.

"Dee Steinway. You do not look at all like your aunt Juno."

"I favor my father's side."

"As well," she said. "Juno ran to fat in her later years. I knew her well; I am Helen Nwanyeruwa, head of Heaven Never Fail Short Hauling Limited. Why are you here, and why did Bob Netchkay land right behind you, waving pieces of paper under the noses of customs?"

Well, that was straight out, and it shook me up a little bit. Most trading people talk around things to see what all the orbits are before they set a plain course. I looked nervously at the intent faces surrounding us. I said, "He wants to take my ship."

She grimaced. "With papers; that means with laws."

"I'd rather sell the ship to you before he can slap those papers on me," I said.

"What ship?"

"Not just any ship. The Steinway *Eggbeater*."

Her eyes were very bright. "Then it is good I have set some friends of mine here to wrapping Bob Netchkay in many, many yards of bright red tape. If you knew how often I tried to get Juno to trade me a ship of hers—" She looked me up and down, scowling now. "I don't want to have to discuss this over Netchkay's papers; so, we must hide you. Hey!" She spoke rapidly in her own language to one of her attendants, who hurried away.

Helen watched the attendant engage in an animated conversation with the Holy Wholist. "See that missionary," she commented, "how he waves his arms, he is all rattled about, he outrages as if back in his own place now, not a foreign planet. I tell you, some of these White priest people think they are still in nineteenth-century Africa when they throw their weights around. Ah, there, something is agreed; now tell me about this ship."

I started to tell her. Somewhere in the second paragraph, one and then the other of my legs were tapped and lifted as if I were a horse being shod. I looked down. My space boots had been deftly removed. Before I could object, I was wrapped in an odorous garment which I recognized disgustedly as the yards and yards of the Holy Wholist's grubby sari. The Wholist himself was gone.

"A trade," said Helen calmly, adjusting a fold of this raggedy toga into a pretty tuck at my waist.

"What, my mag shoes for his clothes? Come on!" Space boots—mag shoes, we call them—are valuable in industry for walking on metal walls and such.

"Not so simple," she said, "but in the end, yes. He said he would take nothing for his sari but a permit to preach in the markets where we do not like such interferences. I know an official who has long wanted a certain emblem for the roof of his air car, for which he would surely give a preaching permit. And among my own family there is a young man upon whose air-sled there is fixed this same fancy metal emblem—"

"Which he was willing to swap for my mag shoes," I said. "But how did you work it all out so fast?"

"Why, I am a trader, what else?" Helen said. "Did your aunt never teach you not to interrupt your elders in the middle of a story?"

"Sorry," I muttered, got annoyed with myself for being so easily chastened, and added defiantly, "But I'm not going to shave my head as bare as the Wholist's for the sake of this fool disguise." I go bald-headed in space rather than fuss with hairnets and stiffeners and caps to keep long hair from swimming into my eyes in non-gravey. Approaching landfall, I always start it growing out again.

Helen shrugged. Then she whirled on her attendants and clapped her hands, shouting, "Is there no car to take these passengers to town?"

The passengers grabbed their things and were herded toward an ancient gas truck parked outside. The Heaven Never Fail Short Hauling Line seemed to deal in some very small consignments. The area was still littered with boxes and sacks. These were being haggled over by Helen's people and the drivers of air-sleds who loaded up and drove off.

Helen caught my arm and took me with her to a raised loading platform from which she could observe the exodus while she asked me about the *Sealyham Eggbeater*. She knew all the right questions to ask, about construction, running costs, capacity, maintenance record, logged travel history (and unlogged). When she heard of the long hauls that the little ship had made, she nodded shrewdly.

"So it has Juno's modifications; unshielded, as I have heard—it can be examined?"

"Yes."

"You do not know the specifications of the modifications yourself, do you?"

"I'm a pilot, not an engineer," I said huffily. It embarrasses me that I can't keep that sort of thing in my head.

She asked about the name of the ship.

I shrugged. "I don't know about '*Sealyham*,' but '*Eggbeater*' dates from when the Kootenay Line ran ships shaped like eggs and it became a great fashion. Aunt Juno didn't want to spend money to modify our own ships, so we stuck with our webby, messy look and renamed all of them some kind of eggbeater."

Helen smiled and nodded. "Now I remember. At the time I suggested taking slogans for her ships as we do here. You know my ships' names: *In God Starry Hand; No Rich without Tears; Pearl of the Ocean Sky*. I have twenty-seven ships." She waved at the hangar floor. "You see how quickly my cargo is gone. I have a warehouse too but only small, and this is my one hangar. My goods move all the time, and my ships are moving them. Yams in the yam-house start no seedlings."

"Yams?" I said. I was beginning to feel a little feverish, probably from the antipoddies I'd taken before landing.

"You must scatter yams in the ground," Helen said impatiently. "In Old Africa. Yams don't grow here; we must import. But the saying is true everywhere, so my ships fly, my goods travel. I named the ships in old style pidgin talk from Africa, in honor of my beginnings—in my ancestors' lorry lines. All the lorries bore such fine slogans.

"My personal ship is *Let Them Say*. It means, I care nothing how people gossip on me, only how they work for me—"

She fell abruptly silent. Alarmed, I looked where she was looking. A machine was in the doorway I'd come in by, its scanner turning to sweep the hangar while its sensor arm patted about on the floor and door jambs.

Helen signaled to one of the freight sleds with a furious gesture. It lifted toward us. She tapped at her ear—that was when I noticed the speaker clipped there in the form of an earring—and said bitingly into a mike on her collar, "Robot sniffers are working this port, why were they not spotted, why was I not told?"

Jerked out of the spell of her exotic authority, I remembered my danger and I remembered Ripotee. "I had a companion, a cat—"

"It must find you, then. These machines come from the Steinway flagship."

I looked around frantically for some sign of Ripotee. "Don't you have to stay a little to make sure everything gets done right here?"

"My people will do for me. Sit down, that sniffer is turned this way."

With surprising strength, Helen yanked me onto the sled beside her; the sled, driven by a heavy girl in a bright blue jumper, slewed around and sped us swiftly out into the bright sunshine.

We headed toward a cluster of domes and spires some distance away. The sled skimmed over broad stubbly fields between high, shaggy green walls that were stands of trees and undergrowth: outposts of the jungle Ripotee had spoken of. Other sleds followed and preceded ours, most of them fully loaded.

"Where are we going?" I said.

"To market, of course."

I remembered that Helen was an old opponent in the marketplaces of the worlds, and it occurred to me that perhaps she was simply keeping me scarce until she could trade me in for a good profit. I checked the driver's instruments out of the corner of my eye, gauging the possibility of jumping for it and hiding out on my own in the jungle or something, just in case I had to. Helen must have seen me because she laughed and patted my knee.

"Ah, my runaway White girl, what are you looking for? Is it that you are suspicious of me now? Netchkay flashes his papers about, claiming that you are space-sick and need to be protected from yourself, or why would you flee from your own family to the home of the trade rivals of the great Steinway Line? You think I might sell you to Bob Netchkay.

"Foolish! I am your friend here, and not only because of Juno and her invention, which can make me very much richer; not even only for the sake of the Steinway Line as it was in its heyday, all those bright, sharp little ships running rings around the big men and their big plans. Yes; not only for these reasons am I your friend, but because women know how to help each other here. The knowledge comes in the blood, from so many generations that lived as many wives to one man. They all competed like hell, but if the husband treated one wife badly, the others made complaint, and were sick, and scorched his food, until he behaved nicely again. So, here is Bob Netchkay being nasty with you; I will play co-wife, and for you I will scorch bad Bob's supper."

Now, why couldn't my own sister Nita take that line?

"That man is a fungus," I muttered.

"Now, that is the proper tone," Helen said approvingly, "for a missionary talking about one of another sect." Then she added with serene and perfect confidence, "As for Netchkay, I will shortly think what to do about him.

"First tell me just what you yourself want out of it."

"My ship back and some money to start flying." On a sudden inspiration I added, "My mag shoes were worth much more than this Holy Wholey rag I'm wearing. You have to count them in any deal between us."

She let that pass and leaned forward to snap out an order to our driver. "There is the market," she said to me, indicating a high translucent dome with landing pads hitched round it in a circle like a halo on a bald head.

I scowled. "I know you have business there, but what good is the market to me?"

"Bob Netchkay's robot sniffers cannot enter on your trail. No servos are permitted on the market floor. They are not agile enough for the crowds and always get trampled and pushed about until they break, and then they sit there in the way with their screamers on for assistance, driving everyone mad. In there you must play missionary a little. White missionaries are not remarkable here on New Niger; if those sniffers ask of you outside the market from people coming out, they will learn nothing.

"Sit still and be quiet till we land, I must listen to the trading reports."

She turned up the volume on the button communicator in her earring and ignored me. I studied her as we neared the market building. She didn't look old enough to have known Aunt Juno, but it never occurred to me to doubt that she had. I thought I saw in her the restless, swift energy of my aunt. In Helen it was keen ambition, right out there on the surface for all to see. Helen even had the same alert, eager poise of the head that Aunt Juno had so noticeably developed along with her progressive nearsightedness.

She shooed me out onto a ribbon lift which lowered me to the edge of the immense seethe and roar of the jam-packed market floor. She herself boarded a little floater. That way she could oversee the trading at her booths, darting like an insect from one end of the hall to the other.

I took up a position as deep within the crowd as I could elbow myself room. On my right a fat woman hawked chili-fruits from Novi Nussbaum; on my left squawking chickens were passed over the heads of the crowd to their purchasers. Women carrying loads on their heads strode between buyers and sellers, yelling at each other in the roughly defined aisles between stalls.

I shouted myself what I imagined might be the spiel of a Holy Wholist: "The sky of New Niger is the sky of Old Earth; our souls are pieces of one great eggshell enclosing the universe!" and similar rubbish. Some of the crowd stopped around me; about a dozen women, and two men with red eyes and the swaying stance of drunks.

Suddenly there was a shriek from the chili-fruit woman. Over a milling of excited marketers I could just glimpse her slapping among her wares with her shoe.

Helen's floater zipped in; she seized the shouting woman by the arm and spoke harshly into her ear, reducing her to silence. I managed to insinuate myself through the crowd, which was already beginning to disperse in search of more interesting matters.

Helen said to me in a venomous whisper, "Did you hear it? This woman says she saw moving, maybe, a sweetsucker among the chili-fruits. A sweetsucker, can you imagine, carried all the way from Novi Nussbaum with my cargo!"

The vendor, eyes cast down, muttered, "I saw it, I am telling you—sweetsucker or not. A long thing like what they call snake in Iboland, but hairy, and making a nasty sound," and she drew her lips back and made clicking sounds with her tongue and widely chomping teeth, like a kid who hasn't learned yet to chew with its mouth closed. It was just the sound Ripotee makes when he's eating.

Helen rounded on the woman again, snarling threats: "If you spread rumors of sweetsuckers drying up my Novi Nussbaum fruits, I will see you not only never sell for me again but find every market on New Niger closed to you!"

I bent down and hunted quietly around the stand, calling Ripotee's name. Not quietly enough: some friendly people at the next stall over turned to watch and saw my religious attire. Identifying my behavior as some exotic prayer ceremony, they cheerfully took up my call as a chant, clapping their hands: "Rip-o-tee! Rip-o-tee!"

Helen took me firmly by the wrist. "What are you doing?"

"This vending woman must have seen my cat."

"And by now many people in the market have your cat's name in their mouths, which is very foolish and not good for us. Netchkay is clever, and I just now get word that seeing he could not introduce his machines here to find if you are at the market, he has sent instead your own sister, Nita Steinway. She will know that cat's name if she hears it spoken, and she will look for you. So we must go at once, though it means I break my business early, which I do not like at all."

She propelled me onto the floater with her, hovering there a moment to give curt orders to the vending woman: "Go take these chili-fruits to put water in them and plump them up, so no one will believe this nonsense about sweetsuckers!" We rose straight for one of the roof hatches.

I said, "Helen, my cat—"

"Oh, your cat, this cat is driving me mad!" she cried, shooting us out onto one of the landing pads again and bustling me sharply into a waiting town skipper. It was an elegant model with hardwood and bright silver fittings inside. She drove it herself, shying us through the sky in aggressive swoops that made other skippers edge nervously out of our way.

"Now listen, is it this cat you want to talk about or diddling Bob Netchkay? If you are interested, I have arranged it; I have set engineers to copying the Steinway modification from your ship. When plans are drawn we will show them to Netchkay. If he wants them sold to every short hauler in the business, he can continue to worry you. If he agrees to leave you alone, he will have only one competitor with the secret of long hauling in short haul ships: myself."

Chuckling, she sideslipped us past a steeple that had risen unexpectedly before us. "Oh, he will grind his teeth to powder, and I—I will be the one to carry on the true spirit of the Steinway Line."

I looked down at the bubble buildings we were skimming over, interspersed with what looked like not very satisfactorily transplanted palm trees, all brown and drooping. I felt lonesome and exposed in the hands of Helen Nwanyeruwa above that alien townscape.

We landed on the roof of a square, solid cement building. Helen shouted for attendants to come moor the skipper and for a guide to show me to my room. She said kindly, "Go there now, I have made a surprise for you. Maybe then you will stop wailing after this cat and enjoy my party tonight."

The surprise was Barnabas, sitting on the bed and grinning. He had grown a curl of beard along his jawline and wore not a captain's jumper but tan cord pants and a gownlike shirt of green and black.

"Barnabas!" I said. "What in the worlds—"

"Everybody here knows you and I have met and made connection before. New Niger is the marketplace of gossip."

"Better to make connection than to just talk about it," I said and began tossing off my clothes. I'd forgotten that peculiarly electrical expression of New Nigerian English; it set me off. I was suddenly so horny I could hardly see straight.

In space I forget; most of us do, though we like to keep up the legend of rampant pilots whooping it up in free fall. Actually, all that is inhibited out there, maybe by stress. But it comes back fast and furious when you are aground again.

Barnabas had the presence of mind to get up and shut the door. He knew right away what was happening and threw himself into it with a cheerful, warm gusto that had me almost in tears. I finally had to beg off because he was making me sore with all that driving, and he tumbled off me sideways, laughing: "Sorry, I didn't mean to hurt you, but it is long since I did this with a crew-cut woman!"

"It's the first thing I've done on New Niger that didn't feel all foreign and strange," I said. "Let's do it again, but this time I'll get on top."

Later on a small boy came padding in with his eyes downcast bringing us towels, and padded out again. Two towels.

Pilots tend to be a little prudish about these things, which are after all more important and isolated incidents for us than for your average planet-bunny with all his or her opportunities. "Don't you people know what servomechs are for?" I grumbled.

Barnabas was stroking my throat. "You have a beautiful neck, just like the belly of a snake. No, no, that is compliment! Don't mind the youngsters—Helen gives employment to many children of relatives. She is very rich, you know."

"How did he know there were two of us needing towels?"

"Everyone knows I was up here, and what else does a man do with a woman. They forget that I am a captain myself and might have business to talk with you. To people here, I am just a man, good only for fun and fathering. . . ."

At his sudden glance of inquiry and concern I shook my head. "Lord no, Barnabas, I shot myself full of antipoddies before leaving the ship. Otherwise I'd be nailed to the toilet with the runs." All pilots use antis on landfall. You have to make a special effort to conceive.

"I have several children now," Barnabas said, and his voice took a bitter edge. "But unfortunately no ship. A falling out with my employer." He smiled wryly. "I am sorry for myself. What have you been doing, Deedee? I hear you have a lot of trouble with Bob Netchkay and your sister."

I explained. He grimaced and shook his head, half condemning, half admiring. "I told you long ago, that man is to be watched; he has plenty of brains and drive, and with your clever sister to help him he is making a great company to rival even the Chinese."

"He's a fungus," I said. I liked that word.

Barnabas laughed. "Let's not argue in the shower."

We stood in the wet corner under the fine spray shooting in from the walls and talked, rubbing and sponging each other and picking our hairs out of the drain. Then we toweled off, got back on the bed, and soon had to clean up all over again.

"Can you stay a while?" I asked, stroking the long muscles woven across his back. "You're doing me a lot of good, Barnabas."

"Me, too," he said. "To be free of the worry, you know, of not making babies. . . . They like a man to be fertile here." He shrugged and changed the subject. "Tell me about Ripotee. I was thinking of him just now; he used to complain that it was disgusting, us two together—"

"I think he was just jealous, not really overcome with horror at our inordinate hugenesses rolling around together. I tried taking a female cat aboard for him, but he couldn't stand her." I started to cry.

Barnabas hugged me and made soothing sounds into my frizz of new-grown hair. I blubbed out how Ripotee had left the ship before I could do anything, even shoot him with antis. "He was in one of his crazy derring-do fits. He kept up with me as far as the market, but since then I don't know—Helen doesn't care. Maybe she's already heard that he's been caught and eaten. From what I've seen, no animals survive here except humans and chickens. People must be crazy for a taste of red meat—"

"Not cat meat, it is awful!" Barnabas exploded.

We curled up together and talked about Ripotee. I told Barnabas how it made me feel so peculiar to think back to the days when Ripotee had been a dumb cat that I could shove around and tickle and yell at, as people do with cats, without a thought. I'd teased him, called him all kinds of names, grabbed him up, and scrubbed him under the chin 'til he half-fainted with delight.

I didn't do things like that anymore.

"Don't be put off," Barnabas said. "It is only his pride that keeps him from flopping down for a chin rub just as he used to do, and he would love for you to push him over and rub his chin anyway."

I shook my head. "He's changed since you knew him. I think it's all that reading. When he lies relaxed with his eyes half shut looking at nothing, I know he's not falling asleep anymore; now he's brooding. Like a person."

Barnabas stood up and pulled on his shorts. "He is luckier than a person. If he were a mere man, he would be protesting always how all he needs are his mates, he must have good fellows to drink with and gossip and play cards."

"This afternoon you and I certainly proved that's a lie," I said smugly.

He didn't smile; he wrinkled his nose and sat down again, putting his arm around my shoulders. "But this is what they say here, and the women of New Niger can make it stick, too, I tell you. You know, Dee, I might have inherited wealth as you did, but my great grandfather was too ambitious. He was seduced by the big trade of international business like many other men in Nigeria. He jumped to put his money into the big boom of Europe and America, just as he had jumped right into Christianity and having only one wife at a time.

"So then the wars and the bad weather came and broke all the high finance, and him with it, among all the rest. He was left nothing but a worn-out yam farm in an overcrowded, overworked corner of Iboland in the Eastern Region. Nobody had much of anything in Nigeria then, except some of the women traders with lorry fleets—the lorry mammies—and those who went even on foot from market to market, dealing haircombs and matches and sugar by the cube. They became the ones with funds to put into space travel.

"So here I am on the world they settled, trying to get rich myself. And who do you think is my boss, the one that is giving me trouble and keeping me grounded?"

"A woman," I guessed.

"A cousin of Helen's, and a woman, yes." He slipped on one of his plastic sandals. "The other men say, take it easy, relax and enjoy some drinking."

I felt less than completely sympathetic; I heard that angry, self-pitying tone again and didn't like it. I said lightly, "These women of New Niger are some tough ladies."

He answered with a grudging pride: "Listen, long ago, when your ancestor-mothers were chaining themselves to the gates of politicians' houses, my ancestor-mothers were rousing each other to riot against the English colonials' plan to take census of women and women's property. It was thought this would lead to special taxing of these women, for even then there were many wives who were farmers and petty traders on their own. They made what is still called the Women's War. Thousands rose up in different places to catch the chiefs the English had appointed and to sit on them—it means to frighten and belittle a man with angry, insulting songs and to spoil his property. They tore some public buildings to the ground. In all some fifty women were shot dead by the authorities, and many more were wounded—that is how frightened the government were. No tax was applied, and the English had a big inquiry in their parliament on how to rule Iboland.

"Helen herself is named for the woman who began the War. On being told in her own yard to count her goats and children, this woman shouted to the official who said it, 'Was your mother counted?' and seized him by the throat."

I could well believe it and said so.

Barnabas got up again.

"Where are you off to?" I said. Talking with him like this was almost like old times together in space.

"I must get ready for the party; you should, too. Tonight Helen Nwanyeruwa holds a feast for the spirit of her ancestor the lorry mammy. Wealthy Missisi Helen had the ancestor-bones brought here on one of her ships; the spirit would not dare to displease her by staying behind."

He bent and rested both hands on my shoulders, looking intently into my face. "It is very good to see you, Deedee."

The outer surfaces of the house were illuminated so that the walled courtyard was brilliantly lit for the party. Family and guests milled around on the quickie grass, grown for the evening in an hour to cover where the plastic paving had been rolled back.

Wrapped in my Holy Wholist sari, worn properly this time with nothing underneath—it didn't bother me, I often go naked in my ship—I milled around with the best of them. As a missionary I was not expected to join the dancing, for which I was grateful. I felt nervous and shy and alien, and I wandered over toward where Helen sat on a huge couch beside the shrine she had had erected: a concrete stele with the image of a truck on it. On the way I passed a line of men and a line of women dancing opposite each other, and Barnabas stepped to my side out of the men's line. His skin was shiny with sweat. He caught me around the waist and murmured in my ear, "You and I do our own private dancing, Deedee, later on."

As we approached, Helen patted the slowflow plastic next to her, making room for me but not for Barnabas. He joined the crowd of retainers on her right.

Helen wore African clothing of sparkling silverweave and a piece of the same cloth tied around her head into an elaborate turban. Even her white plastic sandals couldn't spoil the effect. She was beautiful; by comparison, those around her who affected the fashionable billowing Victorian look of the new Romanticism seemed puny and laughable.

Sitting beside her wiry, tense body on the surface that slowly molded to my shape, I felt protected by her feisty energy. Yet her boldness in having me up there in full view endangered me; suppose Bob had spies here? The drums thundered in the spaces of the courtyard. I gulped down the drink she handed me. It tasted like lemonade filtered through flannel.

I shivered. "Helen, what if—an enemy hears the drums and comes to your party?"

She looked at me out of the corner of her eye and said with haughty dismissiveness, "No enemy has been invited."

This was repeated among the others around us and brought much laughter. Of course she must have robot guards, computer security systems, and so on, I thought; but I felt edgy.

Barnabas leaned toward us. "Even so, Missisi Helen, it might be wise to take extra care. I myself and a few friends have devised a special power hookup—"

Helen set down her drink and turned to him. "Don't worry yourself about these things, Barnabas; you will only get in the way. You are a good, strong young man, and Missisi Alicia tells me you have fathered a fine baby in her family. Go and drink from my private casks, over there, you and your friends. Go amuse yourselves."

Barnabas spun and forced his way out through the crowd toward the dancers—then swerved sharply back toward the bar.

"Why are you so hard on him?" I said.

"These boys get too big ideas of themselves, especially the young ones who have been out in space," Helen replied, reaching for a fresh drink from a tray offered her. "They begin thinking their fathers ran fleets of lorries, too."

Everybody whooped over this. Helen was excited, feeding off the high spirits of those who fed off her own. She flung out her arm, pointing at a young man in the forefront of a huddle of others who had been looking our way on and off for quite a while. He resisted his friends' efforts to push him forward.

"You see that boy there," she said, pitching her voice so that everyone near the ancestor shrine must hear, "he has been chasing after that girl, my Anne, who is still nearly a baby, but he has not taken up his courage to speak to me about her. And he boasts that his father hunts lions with a spear in Old Africa, where there are fewer lions than here on New Niger." She snatched up a pebble and pitched it not to strike but to startle into squawking flight one of the ubiquitous chickens pecking for scraps around a food table. "See what kind of lions we have here! Just such as that boy's father hunts, just so fierce!"

At last, something familiar—the suitor who didn't suit Mother. "Anne is one of your daughters?"

"Oh no," Helen replied proudly, "one of my wives."

I didn't know what to say. Helen grinned at me, plainly pleased with the effect of her words.

"I have lots of wives," she added with great satisfaction. "It was always Ibo custom that a woman rich enough to support wives could marry so; and I am very rich. My Anne will find herself a young man who makes her happy for a while. No fear, in time she will bring me a child of that union to be brother or sister to the children of my own body and my other wives'."

She gave me an affectionate hug, chuckling. "Just as you look now, so shocked, that is how your aunt looked when I married my first wife. Even once I told her, 'Juno, you should have daughters to comfort your old age and inherit your goods. Do as I do, there must be some White way with many documents.' But she said, 'I only have time for one creation, and that is the Steinway Line.' Then she laughed because it was the kind of grand talk men use to impress each other; we both knew the petty trading would go on as always, while the men heroes choke on their grand schemes.

"I live by that petty trading, and I live well, as you see. Come make fast to my own good fortune, as in one of our African sayings: if a person is not successful at trading in the market, it would be cowardly to run away; instead she should change her merchandise.

"Give up wishing to be admiral of a trading fleet, and say you will come work for my company, my bold White flyer."

I was looking at Barnabas. He danced, his shoulders rippling like water shunting down a long container, first to one end and then to the other. A bit wobbly, in fact; as he turned without seeing me, I realized that it was not only the ecstasy of the dance that sealed his eyes. He was drunk. I was alone among strangers.

I shook my head.

"You are too stubborn," Helen said, giving me a thump in the side with her elbow. But she didn't look unhappy. Maybe she thought I was just making a move in a complicated bargaining game, and approved. If I were any good at that kind of thing, I wouldn't have been in this spot with Bob. It's not the dealing I love, it's the piloting. Helen didn't know me well enough yet to really understand that. "Well," she added, "you must do what suits you, and let them say!"

Somebody screamed, there was a swirling in the crowd as one of the food tables crashed down, and a girl came flying toward us, shrieking. I leaped up, thinking, Netchkay has come, someone has been hurt because of him; but I was fuddled with drink and couldn't think what to do.

Helen strode to meet the screaming girl.

"It spoke to me, the spirit of your ancestor," the girl gibbered, twisting her head to stare wide-eyed over her shoulder at the tumbled ruin of the food table. "I was serving food, Missisi Helen, as you told me, and a little high voice said from someplace down low, behind me, 'A piece of light meat, please, cut up small on a plate.' I looked in the dark by the wall, I saw eyes like red-hot coins."

I hurried unsteadily over to where two servos were already sucking up the mess and getting in each other's way.

Behind me I heard the girl: "I was afraid, Missisi. The spirit repeated, so I put down food, but then someone passed behind me and I heard the spirit cry, 'Get off my tail!' and it vanished. Mary thinks she stepped on it—Oh, Missisi Helen, will Mary and me be cursed?"

I shoved one of the servos aside, looking for the poor, crushed remains of Ripotee.

I found nothing but a hole in the wall, low, rounded, and utterly puzzling. I rapped on the nearest servo, which was busy wiping at some sauce with the trailing end of my sari, apparently under the impression that this was a large, handy rag.

"What's this?" I said into the speaker of the servo, pointing at the hole. "Where does it lead to?"

"Madam or sir, it is hole for fowl," creaked the servo. "Madam or sir, it leads in for chickens seeking entry to this compound for the night and leads out for—"

"All right, all right," I said. While addressing me the tin fool had decided the sari was beyond salvage, and had begun ingesting it into its canister body for disposal. I yanked.

The servo clicked disapprovingly and sheared off the swallowed portion of my garment with an interior blade. I made my way back through the crowd toward Helen, rearranging the remains of my clothing and swearing to myself.

"—not possible that my ancestor has returned as *an animal,*" Helen was saying in an ominous voice. "Felicity, remember this: I took you from your mother for a good bride price, I put you to school. I have adopted your children for my own. Now think what you are saying to me of my own ancestor here before all my guests."

Silence. I elbowed near enough to see just as the girl dropped suddenly full length on the ground, her hands spread flat beside her shoulders like someone doing the down part of a push-up.

The crowd gave a satisfied sigh; but Helen stamped her foot in exasperation and said, "We are not in Old Africa now; I will not have you prostrating to me. Just get up and ask my pardon nicely." She looked pleased though.

Felicity scrambled to her feet and whispered an apology. Helen came and linked her arm through mine, saying loudly, "If it was somebody's ancestor, it must go find food at the house of its proper descendants."

In a lower voice she continued, "Monitors have been found under some of the spilled serving dishes; Netchkay will know you are here. You must leave for a mission church away from Singlet, just until my engineers have finished work on your ship. One of my freight sleds will take you. It goes at midmorning tomorrow to tour the market towns. By the time you return—"

"Helen, listen, I can't just take off again like this. My cat is still hanging around here someplace—"

"Oh, cat, cat! You must get your mind to business now." She fiddled impatiently with her ear speaker. "Do you think I can keep track of all that happens here? I have a dozen wives to attend to. This is only an animal, after all."

"Ripotee is my friend."

"Then you must hope for the best for your friend, and meanwhile go and rest; you have a journey tomorrow."

And she walked away and stepped into the center of one of the lines of dancing women, stamping and whirling and flipping her head to the different parts of the complex beat, lithe as a girl.

When Barnabas came to my room, it was not to tumble into my bed.

I had fallen asleep, still in my sari, despite the music and voices from the courtyard. He shook me awake in the half-lit room—it was quiet now, near dawn—and whispered, "Dee—you can stop worrying about Ripotee. I have him safe for you, outside with a friend of mine who found him."

His breath smelled of liquor, but he seemed steady and alert, and I could have hugged him for the news he brought. I followed him downstairs. Someone murmured, from within another room with its door ajar, "Barnabas?" A woman's voice; and I thought, Ha, he has other beds to sleep in at Helen's house than mine, no wonder he can visit as he likes.

I ran with him across the courtyard, holding up my hem to keep from tripping. As we passed out of the gateway, a long air car swept silently toward us and stopped. A door opened. I bent to look inside, and Barnabas grabbed both my arms from behind and thrust me forward into the interior, where not Ripotee but someone else waited. I tried to twist away, but Barnabas shoved in beside me, pinning me hard with his hip and shoulder. The other person was Nita, my sister.

While I was still caught in the first breathless explosion of shock and incredulous outrage, she slapped a little needle into my neck. She may be a lambchop, my sultry sister, but she is quick. Quicker than

I am, who had never stopped to wonder in my sleepy daze why Barnabas hadn't just brought Ripotee up to me himself.

"—too much in the needle," Barnabas was saying in underwater tones. I could feel breath on each cheek, and on one side was a tinge of wine odor: Barnabas. I was sitting wedged between them. It occurred to me that the antipoddies I had taken might have buffered the effect of the drug. I hoped so; and hoped that Barnabas, out of practice at the transition from space to land, would forget about the effects of antis.

"You've never fought with Dee," Nita said. "She's strong as a servo, and I'm not taking any chances." She fidgeted next to me, trying to get at something tucked into her clothing, doubtless another needle.

Barnabas said firmly, "If you give another needle, this is all finished. I will go back to Helen and tell everything. Mr. Netchkay and I made particular agreement that there would be no risk of harm to Dee."

A moment of frigid tenseness: good, good, fight or something. Shoot me again, Nita, it would be worth it, if only Barnabas would then go to Helen as he threatened.

She didn't, and he didn't. I smelled dust, smoke, and was that rocket fuel? The car stopped, and I slumped helplessly there until he hauled me out with a fair amount of grunting. True to her chosen style, Nita let Barnabas do the work: he was the man, after all. I was set down on a metal surface in what felt like an enclosed space. There was a nasty odor in the air.

Barnabas's hands moved mine to set them comfortably under my cheek, as if I lay sleeping. He whispered in my ear. I shut out the words, knowing what they would be: that he was sorry, that the only way he could go out as a pilot again was to work for a foreigner like Netchkay; that this was his only chance. That he would be sure nothing terrible happened to me. And so on.

I didn't blame him, exactly. I just felt sick and sorry. There isn't a captain alive who wouldn't understand the feeling of sitting on a planet for years, going soft in the head on a soft life, while good reflexes and knowledge soak away.

Nita was another story. I wondered if she hated me, if she meant to do me some hideous injury while I lay there defenseless.

"Please leave me alone with my sister, Captain," she said. Barnabas made no more apologies to me; I heard his quiet steps recede.

Nita folded herself neatly, with poise, beside me. I didn't see her, but I knew, for her, there would be nothing so inelegant as a squat. Warm drops wet my cheek.

"You look awful," she groaned. "Dressed like a fanatic of some skinhead sect and smelling like a savage—Honestly, Dee, you are so crazy! Why don't you let us take care of you? Bob's not a bad man. He did take the Steinway Line, but he saved it from ruin—won't you credit him with that?"

She paused, snuffling forlornly. I wanted to cry myself. And in her accustomed manner, she was making it very hard for me to hate her. Nita never let anything happen the easy way for others, only for herself. It was very easy for her to betray me because she had fooled herself into believing she was doing the right thing.

"I hope there are no rats in here," she said miserably. "But I had to talk to you. Once Bob comes, it'll be all shouting and cursing and nobody getting in a sensible word.

"There's going to be a war. The independent short haul traders have had enough of being wrung dry by the Chinese long haulers, and Bob has finally gotten them together on a plan to take the Chinese long haul trade into American hands. So for a while there aren't going to be any nifty little short haul ships operating on their own, flitting around as they please, and calling themselves freelancers—your way. It's going to be too dangerous. Everyone will have to choose a side and stick with it. But you've got no sense. You'll hold out on your own in some old ship and end getting blown up by us or the other side—and I'm not going to tolerate it."

She patted my fuzz of hair and pulled at my wrap, arranging me as a more modest heap on the floor. She blew her nose and added resentfully, "Bob says it's no more than you deserve, charging around the way you do. He should have known Aunt Juno, the awful example she set us—as if every girl could be like that, or should be! She may not have meant to get you killed, but that's just what it will turn out to be by leaving you spaceships to run. She thought you were tough as a man, like her."

More sniffling. "She never thought much of me; but then I was always the realist."

Sure, if realism means you just coast along looking for somebody to notice how pretty you make yourself so they take the burden of your own life off your shoulders for you. I almost told her that, before reminding myself that my best chance was to fake being more knocked out by the drug than I was, so she wouldn't give me another shot. While I burned, she prattled on, fixing up my wayward life, and Aunt Juno's wayward life, too, for that matter, her own way.

"You and Bob and I would make a great team, once you got off your high horse and left the strategy to him. Bob's a natural leader. He'll do well, you'll see. But you have to come in with us, you have to stop fighting us and charging off in any crazy direction you feel like! Honestly, sometimes I think I must be the older one and you the younger.

"I haven't had even a minute to sit down and talk to you in more than four home years, do you realize that? I bet you don't even notice."

So she shot me after all, if only with guilt, an old lambchop trick. I was the older sister; it was all my fault, whatever "it" happened to be. BULLSHIT, I yelled silently. HELP, SOMEBODY!

"I'm warning you, Dee; if you insist on bucking Bob, I'll side with him. We'll see that you spend the war out of harm's way in nice, quiet seclusion somewhere, and so drugged up for your own good that you'll never get your pilot's license renewed again. Grounded forever. Think about it, Dee, please. This isn't just what you want and what I want anymore. You've got to be realistic."

Then she leaned down and kissed me, my sister who knew how to set all my defense alarm systems roaring in a panic; and I swear the kiss was honest.

I was so glad when she got up and walked out that I nearly bawled with relief. A little while passed. I lay there trying to flex my sluggish muscles, thinking about being locked up, thinking about being grounded for good, so I shouldn't worry Nita or inconvenience Bob. I wondered if Barnabas would repent and go tell Helen what had happened; and what, if anything, Helen would or could do about me.

The place had a real stink to it, laced with the faint pungence of Barnabas's sweat and Nita's perfumes. Later on there was another smell: stinky cat breath, by the stars!

"Ripotee." I strained to see; by this time the drug had begun to wear off. There had to be some light in the place because there were the reflections in Ripotee's eyes, not a foot from my face: just as Felicity had said, two burning red coins. I couldn't reach out to him, and he came no closer. "Are you hurt?" I cried.

"I'm fine, but hungry. At your party someone tramped on my tail before I could get anything to eat, and there's nothing here—they cleaned out my mice with the oatmeal."

What a pleasure it was to hear his voice—any voice, most particularly two voices, instead of Nita's sugary tones foretelling my ruin. I tried to sit up. My hand encountered a line of rivets in the wall beside me.

"What is this? Where has Bob had me locked up?"

Ripotee said, "We're in the hold of the *Sealyham Eggbeater*."

"Shit," I said. Now I recognized the smell, pod rot plus cleanzymes. So Bob had the *Eggbeater* and he had me, and he had Ripotee, too, now; which made me feel very stupid, very tired, and a little mean.

Ripotee elaborated. "Bob is outside. He took the flagship up last night. Now he's trying to buy clearance so he can take the *Eggbeater* up too, even though it's still officially in the cleaning process." He was angry. His tail kept slap-slapping the floor.

It annoyed me that he could see me in that darkness, and I couldn't see him. Sitting there blind, holding myself up against the wall, I said, "How was the jungle, Ripotee?"

"Hot," he said, "and tangled and full of bugs. Some of them are living in my ears. You smell of medicine."

"Drug. It's almost all worn off." I could hear his tail flailing away at the floor and the wall, and the faint click of his claws as he paced. I said, "Why did you stay away like that? I was worried to death about you."

"I just wanted to be on my own out there in the jungle, like the big cats used to be on Old Earth. It was lonesome. There was nobody there but chickens. I got mad and hungry and I ate some. People chased me." He coughed, minute explosions. I could see the blurry red disks of his eyes again. "I wanted to land here, but there isn't anything here for me; like there isn't anything here for you.

"What I really wanted," he added fiercely, "was a fight, as a matter of fact; another cat to fight with." This was solid ground. I knew how he loved to go tomming it at any landfall we made, coming home bloody and limping and high on adrenaline. I think he liked the instinctual speed and strength and ferocity of the contest, no chance to think, let alone talk. Which contradicted the last thing he'd said about the jungle, but he's just as capable of wanting two opposing things at the same time as I am.

"You just couldn't stand it that I was out there on my own," he raged, "you were scared I'd turn wild or something—a fish dropping back into the water will swim away and forget, that's all you thought I'd do. Well, even when my brain was just kitty brains it was bigger than that!"

"I was worried about you!" I yelled.

"Poor Ripotee, dumb Ripotee can't possibly manage on his own." He was pacing again. "In the jungle his ancestors ruled like kings; he needs his soft-bodied human to look after him and protect him! Go marry some rich man so you can retire from space and look after him!"

"Oh, Ripotee—"

"Don't talk to me!" His agitated voice wound right up into a real old-fashioned Siamese yowl.

That yowl was heard; the hatch was swung open, letting in a sweep of light, and Bob stood framed against the afternoon outside. What a blast of energy it gave me to see that tall, strong, masterful silhouette: just what I needed to nerve me up for a fight.

"If it isn't the voice of the talking cat," he said. "I'd know it anywhere, damned unnatural noise. Nita's worried about the shot she gave you, Dee, but if you're trading mouse stories with the jumped-up lap-warmer you must be okay."

He didn't seem to have people with him, but I thought I heard voices outside; or was it only the cackling of the inescapable chickens of New Niger?

He read my admittedly obvious thoughts. "I have friends with me. Oh, yes, your friends are here too, I wouldn't lie to you, but there's nothing they can do for a foreigner in the face of trade federation papers—except obstruct and annoy me. When your friends run out of obstruction and annoyance, my friends will be free to come in here where you can't duck me again, and they'll be my witnesses and hold you down while I serve you with these papers."

One thing was certain, and that was that my friends couldn't help me as long as they were outside and I was trapped in here.

I said, "Go to hell," while patting madly around on the floor in search of something, anything, to use as a weapon. All I had was the Holy Wholey sari; so I pulled that off and rested there on my knees with it in my hands, wondering how much Bob could see in the dimness of the hold.

I could see him fairly well. He was wearing one of those wide light capes popular in the upper ranks of federation office. It can disguise the fact that many of the members come from worlds where the human form has been pretty heavily engeneticked to fit alien environments. Bob let his hang loose to the floor so that anyone could see what a fine, straight figure of a man he was. And he was, too. Nita has good taste—in appearances.

Myself, I have good taste in disasters, which was what led me to be crouching naked in front of my enemy, nothing but a bunch of wrinkled cloth in my fists, nothing at all in my head.

Ripotee minced over and rubbed against Bob's ankle. I held my breath. He said, "Something to tell you, Uncle Bob," using the twee little voice and baby talk that Bob always wanted from him.

With his head up so that he could keep an eye on me, Bob sank onto his haunches. He wasn't dumb enough to try to pick Ripotee up, something that even I seldom did and never without an invitation. He hunkered there in the doorway, one hand braced on the floor, the other hooked into his belt; a dashing figure even on his hams.

Ripotee said, "I want to go away with you, Uncle Bob; will you take me, for a secret? A secret about the Steinway modification?"

Bob bent a little lower, bringing his dark Byronic curls closer to Ripotee's narrow face.

Ripotee did what a fighting tom does; he shot up so high on his hind legs that he stood for an instant on the tip of his extended tail, and he let go a left and right too swift to see. Bob screamed and reared up, both hands clapped to his face, and Ripotee leaped between his legs and out of the hatchway.

Holding my garment stretched out in front of me, I flung myself at the light, bowling Bob out onto the ground with me, entangled in folds of cloth. I am not a giant, regardless of Ripotee's opinion, but I am solid and I landed on top, knees and elbows first.

People came rushing over and pried us apart, lifting me to my feet and trying to wrap me up. I think some thought Bob had gotten my clothes off me for some nefarious purpose and were somewhat miffed by my own lack of concern. As I said, I float around naked in space a lot, and I carried it off pretty coolly.

When Bob panted that he was all right, his eyes hadn't been touched, I thought, thank gods. It was enough to be able to laugh freely at the sight he made, scrubbing at his blood-smeared face with his prettily embroidered cuffs.

At my side Helen said rapidly, "He has a federation warrant to suspend your license and immobilize you pending mental exam. It applies at once, as you are not a citizen here."

Shaking bright drops onto the soiled white cloth heaped on the ground at his feet, Bob groped for the paper held out by one of his minions.

I spoke first. "Helen, you'd make any girl a wonderful husband. Will you marry me?"

Helen swooped down on a chicken that was scrabbling around by our feet. She bit off its head and spit it out, held up the fluttering corpse and sprinkled us both with blood. Then she tossed the bird away, threw her arms around my waist, and announced loudly, "Robert Wilkie Netchkay Steinway—that is your name on those papers?—you and your people are invited to my house tonight to celebrate this wedding I have just made here with Dee Steinway. It is sudden, but here in New Niger we have very hot blood and we do things suddenly. I myself am surprised to find that I have married again.

"As for your papers, they cannot be executed on a woman of New Niger. Try going through the local courts if you wish. You will find many of my relatives there hard at work; just as I have numbers of cousins and grown children working also here at Singlet Port, where you docked your big ship illegally yesterday."

"Docked illegally?" snapped Bob. "Your own port people let me in and let me out again."

"Someone made a mistake," said Helen blandly. "Your flagship was too big for our facilities. Some damage has been done and certain other traders were prevented from landing and have suffered losses on that account. There will be a large fine, I fear.

"If you do not come tonight," she added, "I will be very insulted, and so too will all my hardworking relatives. Also you would miss a fine trade we are arranging for you, to make you happy at our celebration."

As we walked away amid Helen's voluble crowd of supporters, I looked back; there was the *Eggbeater*, freshly plated and rewired, ports open to let in the air. There was Bob, trying to push Nita off him as she clung and wailed.

And there was Ripotee, trotting along behind us, a few feathers stuck to his whiskers.

As the bride, I didn't have anything to do at the wedding feast but dance around. Helen and a few of her kindred skilled in law and business sat at a table with Bob, Nita, a mess of papers, and a records terminal. They talked while platters of food were brought, notably the speciality of the evening. Yams Wriggly, an Oriental dish; the wrigglies came from a Red Joy tariff delegation. Bob himself didn't eat much; his face looked as if whatever they served him was burned.

I danced, badly, with Ripotee clinging to my shoulders. We threw the whole line of dancers off.

Our guests from the flagship got up to leave rather early, seen out personally by their host and the beaming bride. Bob looked at me coolly, with an unbloodied eye—he'd had fast, first-rate treatment of the scratches and showed not a mark—and said, "If you ever grow up, Dee, you'll be welcome at home."

I laughed in his face.

He was trembling ever so slightly—with pure rage, I sincerely hoped. As he turned and started to steer Nita away with him in an iron grip, she burst into tears and cried, "Oh, Dee, what will become of your life? My sister has turned into a naked savage—"

I was wearing my jumper, as a matter of fact, trimmed with bright patterns that a couple of Helen's junior wives had applied to the chest, back, and bottom. But I suppose Nita was still seeing me as I had burst from the ship that afternoon, bare and blood-spattered.

Other guests began leaving, hurried out by Helen's loud, laughing complaints that she was being ruined by two parties on successive nights.

She drew me over to the long table where she and Bob and Nita had feasted. Ripotee jumped down from my shoulder.

"I'm going off for a walk. Don't get worried about me this time. I'll meet you in the morning at the, ah, hole for fowl."

Helen called sharply after him, "Food will be left out for you. Please confine your eating to *cold* chicken."

She turned to me. "Here are your ship papers and your debt agreements. Netchkay paid his fine with your ship, since that was the only currency the port would accept; and I did a bit of dealing so that the ownership papers end in my hands—and now in yours."

I was pretty well bowled over by this; and I found that now that we had done it, diddled Bob and saved my neck, it wasn't going to be so simple just to accept my salvation at the hands of an old trading rival. I was suddenly worried about some hidden twist, some pitfall, in the already odd situation in which I had landed myself.

Into the awkward silence—awkward for me, though Helen was grinning triumphantly—came noise from an adjoining courtyard, where many of the guests seemed to have congregated on their way out. Singing, it was, and loud laughter.

"They are sitting on Barnabas," Helen said with relish.

"Helen, let him go work for Netchkay if that's what he wants. He's earned it."

"His just deserts!" She laughed. "White people are terrible to work for. Oh, yes, I worked for your aunt Juno once, on the computer records of the Steinway Line—making sure they were fit for the eyes of certain officials. I learned a lot working for Juno, but she would not learn much from me, or even about me—she was so surprised when I went my own way, to make my own fleet! Perhaps she thought I would spend my life as a faithful retainer!"

I took a deep breath. "Look, Helen, I like to hear about Aunt Juno, but things can't be left like this between you and me. You paid no bride wealth for me, and maybe I can't bring you any children to add to your family, and I'll never learn local ways enough to be comfortable or to be a credit to you—"

Helen threw back her head and screamed with laughter. She slapped my arms, she hugged me. "Oh, you child you!" she crowed, dashing tears of mirth from her eyes. "Listen, you silly White girl; what do you think, we get married like that? A marriage is an alliance of families, planned long in advance. The bride comes and works for years first in the husband's house, so the husband's family can see is she worth marrying. We are not impulsive like you people, and we do not marry with chicken blood! But, that is what a man like Bob Netchkay would believe."

"Then I'm not—?"

"You are not. Nor am I so foolish as to marry a foreigner, bringing nothing but trouble and misunderstanding on all sides."

"But then it's all pure gift," I said, getting up from the table. "I can't accept, Helen—my freedom, my ship—"

"Sit down, sit, sit, sit," she said, pulling me back down beside her. "You forget, there are still the plans for the Steinway modifications, which are worth a great deal to me.

"Also I act in memory of certain debts to your aunt Juno; and because you are a woman and not a puny weed like that sister of yours; and to black the eye of my rival Netchkay in front of everyone; and also for the pleasure of doing a small something for a White girl, whose race was once so useful in helping my people to get up.

"But I could also say, Dee, that I hope to make you just enough beholden to me so that you will bend your pride—not much, only small-small—and a Steinway will fly her ship for me out there in space that she loves better than any world."

I leaned forward and made wet circles on the plastic table with the bottom of my glass. An image of Aunt Juno came into my mind—a plump dynamo of a woman with her hair piled high on her head to make her look taller; and pretty, pretty even after her neck thickened and obliterated her shapely little chin, and age began to freckle her hands. She had come tripping into my shop class in the Learning Center where I was raised, and batting her long lashes above a dazzling smile that left the teaching team charmed and humbled, she had summoned me away with her because she believed I could become a pilot.

Helen murmured, "Do you know, I myself never fly. All my dealings are made from here, from landfall. In Iboland it was taboo forever for women to climb up above the level of any man's head; it brought sickness. Now we are bolder, we have discarded such notions, we climb easily to the top floors of tall buildings, and nobody falls ill. But I am old-fashioned, and I am still not comfortable climbing into black space among the stars."

I said, "I'll fly for you."

And so I have done ever since, with brief visits to my "family" on New Niger. I think sometimes how sharp Ripotee was to see that there was no living there for either of us. But I don't tell him; he thinks well enough of himself as it is.

Abominable

CAROL EMSHWILLER

We are advancing into an unknown land with a deliberate air of nonchalance, our elbows out or our hands on hips, or standing one foot on a rock when there's the opportunity for it. Always to the left, the river, as they told us it should be. Always to the right, the hills. At every telephone booth we stop and call. Frequently the lines are down because of high winds or ice. The Commander says we are already in an area of the sightings. We must watch now, he has told us over the phone, for those curious two-part footprints no bigger than a boy's and of a unique delicacy. "Climb a tree," the Commander says, "or a telephone pole, whichever is the most feasible, and call out a few of the names you have memorized." So we climb a pole and cry out: Alice, Betty, Elaine, Jean, Joan, Marilyn, Mary . . . and so on, in alphabetical order. Nothing comes of it.

We are seven manly men in the dress uniform of the Marines, though we are not (except for one) Marines. But this particular uniform has always been thought to attract them. We are seven seemingly blasé (our collars open at the neck in any weather) experts in our fields, we, the research team for the Committee on Unidentified Objects that Whizz by in Pursuit of Their Own Illusive Identities. Our guns shoot sparks and stars and chocolate-covered cherries and make a big bang. It's already the age of frontal nudity; of "Why not?" instead of "Maybe." It's already the age of devices that can sense a warm, pulsing, live body at seventy-five yards and home in on it, and we have one of those devices with us. (I might be able to love like that myself someday.) On the other hand, we carry only a few blurry pictures in our wallets, most of these from random sightings several months ago. One is thought to be of the wife of the Commander. It was taken from a distance and we can't make out her features, she was wearing her fur coat. He thought he recognized it. He has said there was nothing seriously wrong with her.

So far there has been nothing but snow. What we put up with for these creatures!

Imagine their bodies as you hold this little reminder in the palm of your hand . . . this fat, four-inch Venus of their possibilities. . . . The serious elements are missing, the eyes simple dots (the characteristic hairdo almost covers the face), the feet, the head inconsequential. Imagine the possibility of triumph but avoid the smirk. Accept the challenge of the breasts, of the outsize hips and then . . . (the biggest challenge of all). If we pit ourselves against it *can we win*? Or come off with honorable mention, or, at the least, finish without their analysis of our wrong moves?

Here are the signs of their presence that we have found so far (we might almost think these things had been dropped in our path on purpose if we didn't know how careless they can be, especially when harassed or in a hurry; and since they are nervous creatures, easily excited, they usually *are* harassed and/or in a hurry). . . . Found in our path, then: one stalk of still-frozen asparagus, a simple recipe for moussaka using onion-soup mix, carelessly torn out of a magazine, a small purse with a few crumpled-up dollar bills and a book of matches. (It is clear that they do have fire. We take comfort in that.)

And now the Commander says to leave the river and to go up into the hills even though they are treacherous with spring thaws and avalanches. The compass points up. We slide on scree and ice all day sometimes, well aware that they may have all gone south by now, whole tribes of them feeling worthless, ugly, and unloved. Because the possibilities are endless, any direction may be wrong, but at the first sign of superficialities, we'll know we're on the right track.

One of us is a psychoanalyst of long experience, a specialist in hysteria and masochism. (Even without case histories, he is committed to the study of their kind.) He says that if we find them they will probably make some strange strangling sounds, but that these are of no consequence and are often mistaken for laughter, which, he says, is probably the best way to take them. If, on the other hand, they smile, it's a simple reflex and serves the purpose of disarming us. (It has been found that they smile two and a half times as often as we do.) Sometimes, he says, there's a kind of nervous giggle, which is essentially sexual in origin and, if it occurs when they see us, is probably a very good sign. In any case, he says, we should give no more than our names and our rank, and if they get angry, we should be careful that their rage doesn't turn against themselves.

Grace is the name of the one in the picture, but she must be all of fifty-five by now. Slipped out of a diner one moonlit night when the Commander forgot to look in her direction. But what was there to do but go on as usual, commanding what needed to be commanded? We agree. He said she had accepted her limitations up to that time, as far as he could see, and the limits of her actions. He blamed it on incomplete acculturation or on not seeing the obvious, and did not wonder about it until several years later.

I'd like to see one like her right now. Dare to ask where I come from and how come they're so unlike? How we evolved affectations the opposite of theirs? And do they live deep underground in vast kitchens, some multichambered sanctuary heated by ovens, the smell of gingerbread, those of childbearing age perpetually pregnant from the frozen semen of some tall, redheaded, long-dead comedian or rock star? Anyway, that's one theory.

But now the sudden silence of our own first sighting. One! . . . On the heights above us, huge (or seems so) and in full regalia (as in the Commander's photograph): mink and monstrous hat, the glint of something in the ears, standing (it seems a full five minutes) motionless on one leg. Or maybe just an upright bear (the sun was in our eyes) but gone when we got up to the place a half hour later. The psychoanalyst waited by the footprints all night, ready with his own kind of sweet talk, but no luck.

The information has been phoned back to the Commander ("Tell her I think I love her," he said), and it has been decided that we will put on the paraphernalia ourselves . . . the shoes that fit the footprints, the mink, fox, leopard (phony) over several layers of the proper underwear. We have decided to put bananas out along the snow in a circle seventy-five yards beyond our camp and to set up our live warm-body sensor. Then when they come out for the bananas, we will follow them back to their lairs, down into their own dark sacred places; our camera crew will be ready to get their first reactions to us for TV. They'll like being followed. They always have.

We hope they are aware, if only on some dim level, of our reputations in our respective fields.

But the live warm-body sensor, while it does sound the alarm, can't seem to find any particular right direction, and in the morning all the bananas are gone.

It's because they won't sit still . . . won't take anything seriously. There's nobody to coordinate their actions, so they run around in different directions, always distracted from the task at hand, jumping to conclusions, making unwarranted assumptions, taking everything for granted or, on the other hand, not taking *anything* for granted (love, for instance). The forces of nature are on their side, yes, (chaos?) but we have other forces. This time we will lay the bananas out in one long logical straight line.

When we step into those kitchens finally! The largest mountain completely hollowed out, my God! And the smells! The bustle! The humdrum *everydayness* of their existence! We won't believe what we see. And they will probably tell us things are going better than ever. They will be thinking they no longer need to be close to the sources of power. They may even say they like places of no power to anyone . . . live powerless, as friends, their own soft signals one to the other, the least of them to the least of them. And they will also say we hardly noticed them anyway, or noticed that they weren't there. They will say we were always looking in the other direction, that we never knew who or what they were, or cared. Well, we did sense something . . . have sensed it for a long time, and we feel a lack we can't quite pinpoint. Unpaid creatures, mostly moneyless, but even so, noticed. We will tell them this, and also that the Commander thinks he may love one of them.

But this time they have refused the bananas. (What we offer them is never quite right.) Okay. The final offering (they have one more chance): these glass beads that look like jade; a set of fine, imported cookware; a self-help book, "How to Overcome Shyness with the Opposite Sex"; and (especially) we offer ourselves for their delight as sons, fathers, or lovers (their choice).

The psychoanalyst says they're entitled to their own opinions, but we wonder how independent should they be allowed to be?

One of us has said it was just a bear we saw at the top of that hill. He said he remembered that it humped down on all fours after standing on one leg, but they *might* do that.

The psychoanalyst has had a dream. Afterwards he told us never to be afraid of the snapping vagina (figuratively speaking) but to come on down to them (though we are climbing up, actually) and throw fish to the wombs (nothing but the best filet of sole, figuratively speaking).

This is the diagram the psychoanalyst has laid out for further study:

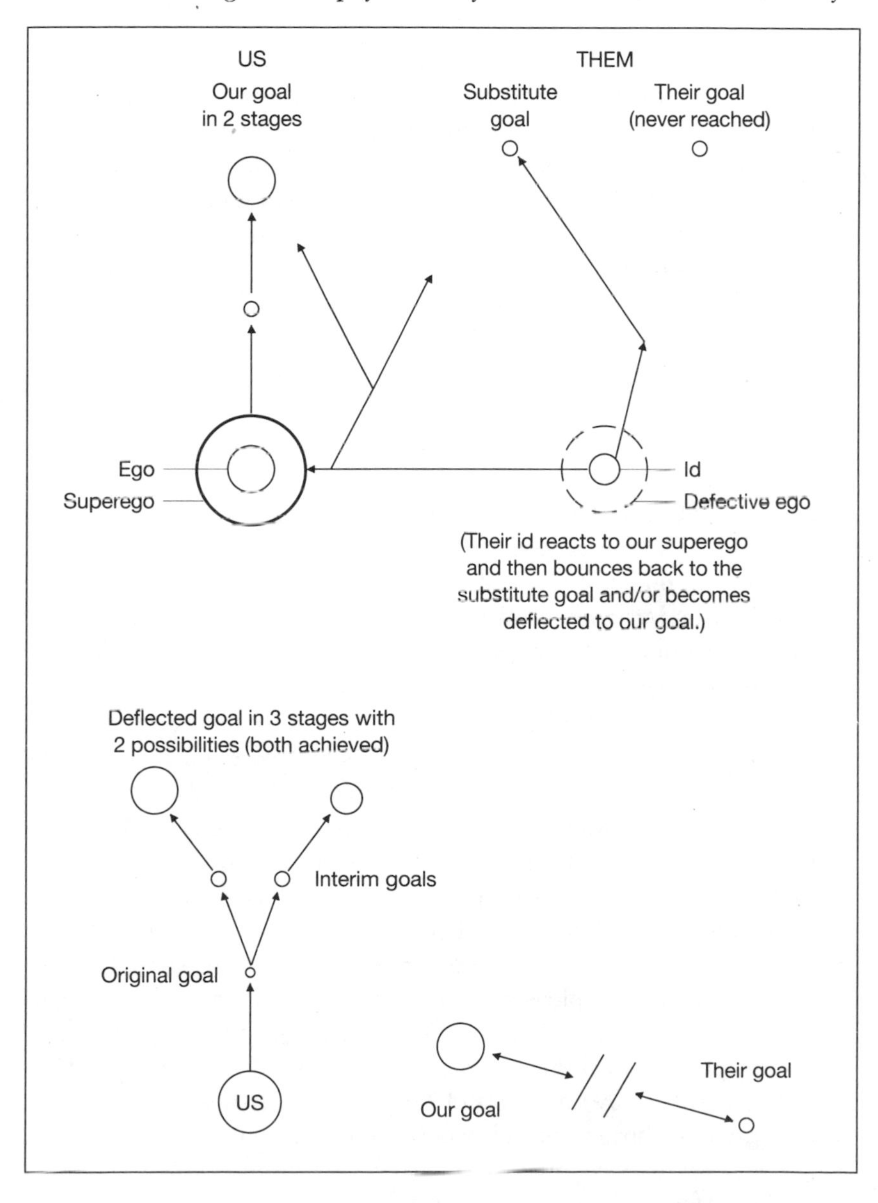

Well, if I had one, I'd wash its feet (literally) and the back. Venture the front, too. Let the water flow over both of us. Let their hair hang down. I'd take some time out now and then, even from important work, to do some little things like this of hardly any meaning, and listen, sometimes, to its idle chatter or, at least, seem to. But as to Grace, it must be something else I have in mind, though I'm not sure what.

We are telling all the old tales about them around our campfires in the late evenings, but it's not the same kind of frightening that it used to be when we were young and telling the tales in similar circumstances because now we know they may actually be lurking out there in the shadows, and what's scary is that we have really no idea of their size! We're not sure what to believe. On the one hand, whether they are twice our size or, as the Commander insists, whether almost all of them are quite a bit smaller and definitely weaker. The more mythically oriented among us have said that they are large enough to swallow us up into their stomachs (from below) and to ejaculate us out again months later, weak and helpless. The anthropologically oriented say they may be the missing link we have searched for so long and stand, as they believe, somewhere between the gorilla and us (though probably quite a bit higher on the scale than *Pithecanthropus erectus*) and that they are, therefore (logically), distinctly smaller and somewhat bent over, but may not necessarily be weaker. The sexually obsessed among us wonder, among other things, if their orgasm is as specific a reaction as ours is. The romantics among us think they will be cute and loveable creatures even when they're angry and regardless of size and strength. Others think the opposite. Opinions also vary as to how to console them for the facts of their lives and whether it is possible to do so at all since 72 percent of them perceive themselves as inferior, 65 percent perceive themselves to be in a fragile mental balance, only 33⅓ percent are without deep feelings of humiliation simply for being what they are. How will it be possible, then, to penetrate their lines of self-defense and their lines of defensiveness? Altercations are inevitable, that's clear. (Eighty-five percent return to rehash old arguments.) We dislike unpleasant emotional confrontations, try to avoid such things at all costs, but we also realize that playing the role of dominant partner in intimate interaction won't always be easy. How nice, even so, to have a group of beings, one of these days (almost invisible, too), whose main job would be to tidy up!

Pedestals have already been set out for them.

Even if (or especially if) they are not quite up to our standards, they will, in any case, remind us of the animal in all of us, of our beastliness . . . our ebb and flow . . . of life forces we barely know exist . . . maybe some we never suspected.

But now we have had a strange and disturbing message from the Commander telling us that some very important political appointees have said that these stories of sightings are exactly that, stories . . . hoaxes, and it's been proven that the photographs have been doctored, in one case a gorilla superimposed on a snowy mountain, in another case a man in drag. (Only two pictures still unexplained.) Several people have confessed. Some have never even been in the area at all. Whatever we have seen must have been a trick of light and shadow or, more likely, one of the bears in this vicinity and (they're sure of it) we have a hoaxer among us, stealing the bananas himself and making footprints with an old shoe on the end of a long stick. Besides, think if we should discover that they do, in fact, exist. We would only be adding to our present problems. Committees would have to be set up to find alternatives to boredom once their dishwashing years were over. Cures would have to be discovered for cancers in peculiar places, for strange flows, for vaginismus and other spasms. A huge group of dilettantes (Sunday poets and painters) would be added to society, which society can well do without, according to the Commander. And why should we come searching for them, as though they were Mount Everest (and as important), simply because they're there? Anyway, the funding for our search has run out. The Commander even doubts if we can afford any more phone calls.

We are all very depressed by this news, though it's hard to pinpoint exactly why. Some of us feel sure, or fairly sure, that there *is* something out there . . . just out of sight . . . just out of earshot. Some of us seem to see, sometimes, a flash of color out of the corners of our eyes, as though the essentially invisible had been made *almost* visible for a few seconds. Makes one think, too (and some of us do), how socks and underwear might someday return, magically, from under beds to be found clean and folded in the drawer, as if cups of coffee could appear out of nowhere just when most needed, as if the refrigerator never ran out of milk or butter. . . . But we are at the service of our schedule and our budget. We must return to the seats of power, to the service of civilization . . . politics. . . . We turn back.

For a while I think seriously of going on by myself. I think perhaps if I crept back alone, sat quietly, maybe dressed to blend in more. Maybe if I sat still long enough (and stopped telling, out loud, those old, scary stories about them), if I made no proud gestures . . . shoulders not so stiff . . . maybe then they'd get used to me, even eat bananas out of my hand, and come, in time, to recognize an authoritarian figure by the subtle reality of it, and perhaps learn a few simple commands. But I have to stick to my orders. It's too bad, though I do want to pick up my pay, my medals, and get on with the next project. Still, I want to make one more move toward these creatures, if only a symbolic one. I sneak back along the trail and leave a message where it can't be missed, surrounded by bananas. I leave something they'll be sure to understand: the simple drawing of a naked man; a crescent that can't help but stand for moon; a heart shape (anatomically correct) for love; a clock face with the time of the message; the outline of a footprint of my own next to an outline of one of theirs (looks like a question mark next to an exclamation point). "To Grace" at the top. I sit there for a while, then, and listen for sighs and think I hear some . . . think I see something vaguely white on white in the clarity of snow. Invisible *on purpose*, that's for sure (if there at all), so if we can't see them, it's not *our* fault.

Well, if that's how they want it, let them bark at the moon alone (or whatever it is they do) and dance and keep their own home fires burning. Let them live, as was said, "in the shadow of man." It serves them right.

I ask the psychoanalyst, "Who are we, anyway?" He says about 90 percent of us ask that same question in one form or another, while about 10 percent seem to have found some kind of an answer of their own. He says that, anyway, we will remain essentially who we already are whether we bother to ask the question or not.

Bluewater Dreams

SYDNEY J. VAN SCYOC

Namir was sleeping, the breeze on her face, when Mega slipped through the window and touched her with cold fingers. Namir woke immediately, briefly confused. "Mega?" Then, by the light of the night-lamp, she saw the swelling that disfigured her friend's face, distinguished the mottled patches that underlay Mega's fine body hair, and her heart sank. She sat up with an involuntary sob. "No, Mega."

"It's come to me." Mega's voice was seldom more than a whisper. That, combined with the softness of the fine, dark hair that covered her and the half-hidden glint of her eyes, made her a creature of shadow and subtlety. Tonight her voice was wispy, regretful. "It's taking me, Namir."

"No." Useless word. These things happened each time new settlers came from Zabath, Shandoar, and Perdin. Diseases that scarcely touched humans savaged Mega's kind, those who insisted upon living in the human settlement. This was a new pathology, one no one had yet named. Some tiny organism from some far world had come to Zabath and silently taken up life with its new human host, causing neither discomfort nor death. But when it rode its host to Rahndarr and met the Birleles, it was a killer.

Now the killer had found Mega—Mega, who was always so insouciant, skipping up and down the redrock steps of Rahndatown after Namir even when Namir tried to send her away. Quickly Namir embraced her friend, trying to warm her slight body. She could feel the bones through the thin flesh. In the sunlight, running, leaping, Mega was swift and dauntless. In Namir's arms, cold and afflicted, she was fragile. "If you had gone back to the mountains—," Namir said hopelessly.

She herself had lured Mega down. Music was the thing that drew Birleles to Rahndatown—singing, the ring of cymbals, the call of horns. They were fascinated by the bright sounds but could not make music themselves, just as they could not duplicate the bright colors of the cloth the human settlers wore. The Birleles lived high in the grayrock mountains with only the music of the wind in the crags and the bright color of an occasional shatterflower. Namir had sat at the foot of the grayrock mountain one day, lonely, singing songs from Shandoar and crying, and had seen bright eyes peering at her from the rocks. Sense told her to quit singing then, to chase the Birlele back up the mountain to her own kind. But sense had not been with her that day, only loneliness, and she had tempted Mega all the way back to Rahndatown with her, just to have her company. "If you had not come with me—"

Mega quivered in Namir's arms. "I would have come to Rahndatown one day anyway. I'm one of the ones who has to come here and know the human things."

Yes, just as there were many Birleles in the mountains who would never come to Rahndatown, who resisted the call of music and color and new experience. Namir had often thought about them and wondered if they were the strong ones, or if the strong ones were the ones like Mega, who risked themselves for the new experience.

"I would have come," Mega repeated, "and one day I would have gone back to my mountain. Now I must go tonight."

Namir's arms stiffened. She released her friend, keenly aware of the chill of her room, of the weight of her blankets. "You can't—you can't go back there. You've heard—"

"Namir, I have to go to the dreaming ponds," Mega whispered with shivering intensity. "I need my dreams now. They're calling me." Through puffy lids, her eyes were earnest, pleading.

Namir shivered. The dreaming ponds lay high on the mountain where Mega's people lived. The Birleles bathed in them at important times and had dreams then to guide them. "Namir—"

Mega's eyes glinted faintly. "Namir, I've had my child-dreams, my naming-dreams, my hunting-dreams. Now it is time for my dying-dreams." One slight hand closed on Namir's arm. "You have dreams too, Namir. You know the call of them."

Yes, she dreamed often enough, but always in her bed and always of Shandoar. "Mega—you can't go. Your people—they won't let you go up the mountain with disease." At least that was what the separatists said when they went before the Council of Governors to request laws to send the Birleles who lived in Rahndatown back to the mountains. The Birleles took disease too easily, they said, and when they tried to go back to their mountains to die, their mountain kin caught them on the lower slopes and bled them, rather than letting them carry disease to the high Birlele habitats.

"They will stop me, perhaps," Mega said. "But when I tell them I go for my dying-dreams, they will let me pass."

"No, Mega. The separatists—"

"Namir, do you believe the separatists? Over me? They say they want to send us back for our own good, but they have other reasons —other reasons for not wanting us here."

Namir frowned. Yes, there was more than altruism behind the separatists' vehemence. There was a fear of the nonhuman intelligence of the Birleles, even a fear of their strange shadowed beauty. Not everyone was attracted by the alien. Many were frightened and repelled by it. "But the dead Birleles that have been found on the lower paths—" She had heard of the way they died, their blood drained from their bodies.

"Namir, you know there are predators on the mountain. Many of them."

"I—I don't know what to believe, Mega." Even if the Birleles would let Mega pass, Namir was reluctant to let her go tonight. The Birleles exhibited a wide range of body temperatures and changed in many ways with the warm and cold of day and night. By night they were slow-moving and sometimes confused. If their body temperatures fell below a certain level, compensatory mechanisms came into play and warmed them, and then their minds cleared. But by day, with sunlight warming them, they moved swiftly and their thoughts were quicksilver. "At least wait for morning, when it's warm. You'll walk faster then."

"I'll go farther if I start now, before I become weaker. Namir—"

"Mega—wait and I'll sing for you. You have to let me sing for you a last time." She said it as an inducement but immediately recognized it for a plea. She needed to sing for Mega again. They had begun their friendship with singing. If it must end, then it must end that way.

And perhaps after she had sung, Mega would realize she couldn't risk the walk to the mountain. Perhaps—

She didn't wait for consent. Holding the fragile body, she began to rock, singing a wordless melody from her crèche days on Shandoar. She felt Mega first resist, then fall to the spell of the song. Her lids hooded her eyes and her breath grew deep and sighing. Once she said, querulously, "Namir—" But Namir knew Mega's weakness and she continued singing, softly, wordlessly, trying to warm Mega with her own body heat.

"Namir—please. I have to go."

Namir did not release her. She sang until her song finally lulled them both to sleep. Even then she seemed to feel the catch of her voice in her throat, until sometime much later when she woke and realized that she was sobbing rather than singing. She sat with a start. First dawn was in the sky and she was alone.

There was unreality in her room. Surely she had imagined Mega's visit. Other Birleles fell victim to infection; never Mega. Mega had been her special friend for three years and would be until Namir took her first year-mate.

But she knew she had not dreamed the visit, the disease, or the plea. Certainly she had not dreamed Mega's disappearance. Mega had gone to the dreaming ponds.

Alone, and there were predators on the mountain. Whether they were Mega's own kind or other species, there was danger and Mega would be too weak to resist it. The chill of dawn entered Namir's bones. She had brought Mega to the valley—never mind that she had tried many times to send her away—and now Mega was dying of human-borne infection.

Quickly Namir left her bed and dressed, her fingers trembling. This was the coldest time, the hour before sunrise, and Mega would travel slowly. If Namir could find her before she reached the mountain and bring her back—

She had hoped to leave the dwelling unnoticed. But her father was awake. She encountered him in the passageway, the anger of a new day already on his face. He was not happy in Rahndatown, where new settlers pressed in on all sides. His chronic dissatisfaction found ready focus in Namir's behavior. "Early today," he said, a hard undertone in his voice.

"I couldn't sleep." For once she was anxious not to rankle him.

"People seldom sleep when they are singing. And I saw your friend as she left."

"She came this way?" Usually Mega came and went through Namir's bedroom window.

"Would I have seen her otherwise? And I saw her disease." He turned, and for a moment his eyes gleamed fiercely. "She won't be back, you know. She is gone for good now."

Namir sucked a painful breath. "Father—"

"Don't dispute me. I told you never to sing to a Birlele and you did. I told you to send her back when you first brought her here and you did not. I told you to close your window and your door to her and you said you would do what you pleased. Now you have done it."

Yes, and Mega would die. Namir released her breath in an angry sob. It was useless to argue with him, to remind him that she had tried many times to send Mega back. And if she had closed her window and door to her, Mega would simply have become another wistful Rahndatown Birlele, taking food and shelter where she could find it. "And I'd do it again!" she said angrily, suddenly full of her own grievance. "She's the only thing I've had here! I left everything else behind on Shandoar—my school-sisters, my friends—"

She had touched a nerve. "You left them to make a new life here! And so you will! Do you expect to have everything you had on Shandoar—at once? I've waited all my life to have what you will have here in a few years more."

"The mines?" she demanded sharply, forgetting that she did not want to rankle him. "Is that what you're giving me?"

Even in the dim light of the passageway, she saw his face congest. He wrenched at her arm. "Have I ever asked you to use pick and lantern? Have I ever sent anyone but myself down those tunnels to dig?"

"No—but you'd be happier if you could!" she shot back—unfairly. Why she always deflected his own bitterness back at him twofold, why she always fought, she didn't know. "With two of us digging, we could move to the farlands that much sooner."

"We'll be there in good enough time." Namir's mother had appeared in the doorway of her bedroom, frowning, her hands clenched.

Namir's father turned, releasing Namir's arms. He seemed caught between them, a big man, angry. "No time in Rahndatown is good time."

"Yet we can't go to the farlands until we can go," Namir's mother reminded him. "And you make it worse by going to the tunnels without your mask and tank. You make yourself mindsick." Her voice was low, contained, but with a sharp edge. "You know there are gases in the tunnels. Ask anyone who watches the miners come up at the end of the day. We can tell from the faces which ones have used their masks. Those are the ones who look tired. The others, the ones who are angry, the way you are always angry—"

"You wouldn't be angry when you came here to grow wintergrasses in the farlands and then had to mine the mountain to buy emigration permits?"

"You knew about the permits when we came. And you know about the gases in the mine, too."

It was a familiar argument, his bitter impatience pitted against her gritty persistence. It would go on until he left for the tunnels. Silently

Namir slipped down the passageway and out the door. Neither of them noticed.

Rahndatown was little more than a series of cavities cut into the redrock mountainside: windows, doors, ventholes, hollowed-out rooms. Its look was bleak by dawn, as if the mountain were beset with parasites. And its paths and stairs were shaggy with weeds and litter. Rahndatown was no proud place, and every fresh shipload of immigrants added a new tawdriness.

Yet there was music and color, too, during the bright hours of day. The settlers from Shandoar had a tradition of music and those from Perdin dyed and wove their own cloth so they could wear the brilliant colors they chose in designs that pleased them. The Zabathi cheerfully adopted both traditions and added a few of their own. As Namir slipped down the steps that led to the lower levels, she was aware of an occasional Birlele peering at her from rocky shelter, wondering if she would sing, wondering if when it grew warm and she removed her jacket, there would be colorsilks beneath.

Namir averted her eyes and hurried. Most of these Birlele had no particular friend. They lived as they could, seldom well by human standards. Yet friendship had not saved Mega.

Once beyond the burrowed settlement, she ran through the slag-piled regions at the foot of the mountain, past the timbered mouth of the mine, down streets of quikpanel warehouses that held export and import materials. There were already people and machinery at work among the warehouses and in the sorting and assembling sheds. And in the distance, the smelters offered fiery sparks to the gray morning sky.

Once or twice she recognized a face among the workers and wanted to stop and ask if Mega had come this way. But what other way was there through the valley toward the grayrock mountains?

None. Namir ran.

Soon she left Rahndatown behind. And soon the morning sun climbed over the crags of the distant mountains and banished gray from the sky. Namir turned once and peered back toward Rahndatown, trying to find something there to warm her. But she could see nothing there to stand comparison with her memory of Shandoar's muraled buildings and green parks.

Her eyes stung. *I never minded that people pressed us on all sides. I never minded that everything on Shandoar had already been built and there was nothing more to build. I never minded any of that.*

But I do mind the roughness and emptiness here. We have to lock the flute and horn in cases to keep grit from scarring them. We hardly take them out anymore. And my voice—how long will my voice be sweet here?

The morning began to warm and she sang, testing her voice against the air. If Mega had not run too far ahead, if she heard Namir singing—

But there was no sign that Mega heard. Namir watched the brush that choked the valley for sign of her friend, or for fresh footprints. Several times she saw crushed vegetation and once she found a place where someone had uprooted sweetroot and chewed the starchy tuber. That could have been anyone, Birlele or human.

Pausing, discouraged, she pulled sweetroot and chewed it herself. Then she continued to the lowermost slopes of the mountain where she had first met Mega.

She found her there on the path, her slight body sprawled gracelessly, her breath harsh. For a moment, Namir only wanted to turn back and forget seeing her like this. If she could remember her running in the sun instead, limbs flashing, dark hair gleaming—

Mega stirred and pulled herself to a sitting position. Her swollen face was grotesque and mottled patches glared angrily through her dark hair. " 'Mir—you've come to carry me."

Namir forced herself forward. "I—I've come to take you back. Yes."

Mega struggled to her feet, her limbs thrashing almost angrily. "No—no. You've come to carry me to the ponds. You have to carry me, 'Mir. I thought I could walk, but I can't. It's taking me—this disease."

Namir felt a quick twist of fear. "Mega—no. I can't take you there."

Despite her infirmity, Mega's eyes glinted. "You believe them then—the people who want to keep us in the mountains. You believe that my own people will catch us on the paths and kill us. You're afraid of them."

Was she? Afraid of Mega's kind? Namir could not deny it. The Birleles who lived in Rahndatown were eager and whispering, caught up in the excitement of human activity and color. That made them somehow childish. Those who lived in the seclusion of the mountains were surely different. They were not susceptible to human ways. They were an intelligent species with rituals and traditions and—Mega said—legends. Intelligent enough, certainly, to know that if they permitted humans to penetrate the upper reaches of the mountains where they lived, they would take disease and die. Namir wet her lips with her tongue. "Mega, maybe there is something the doctors can give you. If you let me take you back—"

Mega peered up at her unwinkingly. "You know there is nothing, 'Mir. What I need are my dreams. The dreamwaters call me."

Namir hesitated, torn. If the separatists were right, if it was the mountain Birleles who had killed those returning Birleles found dead on the lower slopes— She peered up the mountainside. The grayrock was stark and harsh-shadowed, a stern environment. But somewhere were the dreams Mega remembered—dreams much like Namir's memories of Shandoar, precious, tantalizing, evanescent.

Certainly she had never heard of any Birlele harming any human. Perhaps that was simply because no human had climbed the grayrock mountains.

Perhaps not. Deciding, she took her friend in her arms. "I'll take you to the ponds." To the dreams. Perhaps someone would take her back to Shandoar one day, to the silken park grasses and muraled walls she remembered. She could hope.

Although Mega stood half as tall as Namir, carrying her up the mountain path was like carrying nothing. According to Birlele legend, the Birlele were descended from avians. The webbed membrane that connected Mega's upper arms to her slight torso seemed testimony to the authenticity of the legend. And she was light, her bones insubstantial. Occasionally, imagining watchful Birlele soaring on mountain air currents, Namir glanced up the mountain apprehensively.

But the Birleles had not flown for hundreds of centuries, and they did not fly today. Instead, at midafternoon, they suddenly perched in numbers upon the rocks that overlooked the path, their breath a menacing hiss. Namir halted, peering up at them, her nerves frozen. They had appeared silently, without warning. Mega sighed and opened her eyes.

Namir fought a suddenly thick tongue. "Mega—will they understand me? If I talk to them?" The hissing grew louder. The Birlele were two dozen, and they hunched as if ready to spring. Their body hair was denser than Mega's, darker, glossier. Their bodies were more muscular. And their faces were twisted in warning.

Mega summoned a weak whisper. "They will understand if you sing."

Namir shivered. Sing to two dozen hostile Birlele? On a steep mountain trail with her friend dying in her arms? "If *you* talk to them, Mega—"

"I don't have to talk to them. They know I'm going to the dreamwaters. Every Birlele goes there to die, and I am dying."

Namir caught her breath involuntarily. "Mega—you told me you wanted to dream in the ponds."

"I do. But that's where we die, too, Namir—in the warm water." She looked up into Namir's face. "Don't be afraid—I will talk to them." Summoning strength, she spoke a few sibilant words to the Birlele at the side of the path.

The exchange was brief, hissing. Three of the Birlele spoke with Mega in turn and then drew back, folding their arms over their chests.

"They are glad I've come," Mega told Namir. "Only a few others have come this far who were sick. But they ask that you not let me touch ground. That way I will not soil the paths. And—they ask that you sing. They won't come to the valley for songs, but they would like them here, to know what they are like."

Namir's mouth was suddenly dry. The Birleles at the side of the path regarded her stonily. She could not believe they wanted to hear her. She could only believe they wanted to savage her. "We won't soil the paths," she said, and hoped the hissing Birleles understood.

Certainly they seemed to understand her songs. As she continued up the trail, holding Mega's chill body close, stroking her dark hair, she sang every song she knew of Shandoar. She sang its clipped grasses and its white buildings, its black beaches and the foamed water that washed them. She sang the bright clothes the people wore, and the happy voices of schools of children running to recitation. She sang all her memories of there, and then she sang the memories she wished she might have had, of growing to adulthood there, of walking the parks and city-trails as a woman, of laughing under trimmed trees with her own children and the children of her school-sisters.

At first the Birleles followed warily, shoulders hunched, faintly hissing. But when Namir paused and carefully removed her jacket, never letting Mega touch ground, when she pulled her brightly patterned blouse free from its confining sash and let the colors ripple in sunlight, the Birleles quieted.

Finally they were silent, and only Namir's voice rang in the grayrock mountains.

Despite Mega's assurances, she dared not sit to rest. She dared not let her song trail away. On their mountain, the Birleles were more alien than she had ever imagined and her voice was the only thing she had familiar. It reassured her, quenching the worst of her fear. When dark came, she pulled her jacket back over her blouse and continued up the trail, Mega directing her.

Did she only imagine during the final hour of their climb that she tasted something in the air she had never tasted before on Rahndarr? And that something— Welcome? Joy?

Then the scent in the air changed and became heavy. They reached the dreaming ponds soon after the moon rose and Namir paused, sampling the sulfur taint in the air. The ponds, three of them, were yellow-crusted yet vividly blue. The moon floated upon each smooth-glass surface, three times sister to itself. Namir paused and thought she had never seen it so full, so silver. Nor had she ever seen the stars of Rahndarr so vivid in the black sky.

There are many things I haven't seen here. Things I haven't wanted to see, she realized, *because I've only wanted to see Shandoar.*

Certainly she had never seen the geyser that plumed from the rocks and rose moon-silver against the night while she stood at the edge of the nearest pond. She watched its magical play with drawn breath until it sank back into the rocks. Then her breath sighed away.

I could sing about that.

. . . if Mega were not dying. Mega seemed to have shrunk in her arms. Her skin was chill, her eyes vacant. "You will have to carry me into the pond," she whispered. "Don't put me down until you can put me into the water."

"I could put you into the water now," Namir said. She stepped forward, breaking the yellow crust that ringed the pond. Warm water seeped into her boots.

"No, take me to the center of the pond. And don't be afraid of the stings, Namir."

"Stings?" Involuntarily Namir stiffened, peering down into the moonlit depths of the pool.

"Yes, they make the dreams. Sometimes I wonder about that, you know—I wonder if the stings would make you dream too. I dream like a human sometimes, at night when I sleep."

Namir hesitated at the edge of the pond. She could see nothing in the pond that might sting her. There were no insects and the bottom of the pond was of grayrock pebbles. She stroked Mega's hair. The night was cold and Mega was confused.

The Birleles who crouched behind them were not confused. They peered at Namir silently, their eyes bright and unreadable. There were several dozen of them now, some of them very old, others very young. As she hesitated, they edged forward and those nearer her raised their arms, fanning out their vestigial flight-membranes. Their shadows became grotesque on the pebbled ground.

Were they threatening her? Were they observing some ritual? Or were they simply urging her forward?

How could she know? Namir stepped forward quickly, pond water lapping up her pants legs to her thighs, her hips, her waist. It was hotter than she had guessed, almost scalding. Gasping, she stumbled toward the center of the pond.

And then she felt the stings. Something rippled up from the bottom of the pond, something irregular and gray—it might have been a pebble—and brushed against her leg. And stung, sharply. She jerked in surprise. "Mega—" A second object broke from the pond bottom and struck at her. This time there was numbness. It spread quickly up and down her leg. She attempted to step back, to escape the pond. Her leg buckled, and instead she fell forward into the water.

Mega seemed not to notice her distress. She squirmed free of Namir's grasp and arched fluidly into the depths of the pond. As she swept underwater to the bottom of the pond, Namir saw a look of ecstatic anticipation on her swollen face. Then pebble-like objects bobbed from the bottom of the pond and swirled around her, striking at her in a quick frenzy.

Namir struggled to her feet. "No!" Without thinking, she flung herself into the water after Mega, grappling for her. Sulfur water stung her eyes and was sucked into her half-open mouth. *"Mega!"*

Mega did not reach for rescue. Instead she swam swiftly away across the pond, her dark hair washing in the water, the expression on her face intent now, expectant.

As Namir slipped and stumbled after her, she was stung again and again. With an anguished cry, she fell forward into the water, suddenly too weak to swim. Still the pebble-like objects darted at her and stung her and Mega swam just beyond reach.

Namir was aware of overwhelming weakness and terrible dizziness. Gasping, coughing, she fought to mobilize her lifeless legs, her numbing arms. She had lost voluntary control of both. Finally she sank into the pond, hot mineral water burning in her respiratory passages.

At some point consciousness faded.

At some other point it returned, in fragments. Namir gathered the fragments and realized that she lay on the verge of the pond, that it was daylight, and that she was alone. Whatever Birlele had pulled her from the water had gone with all the others. She stared up into the noonday sun. Her throat burned and her head ached. And she had the strange sense that she had dreamed.

She lay for a moment, trying to capture the substance of her dreams. The images were alien and came in incomprehensible juxtapositions —as if the dreams had not been her own but someone else's, created not from her reality of Shandoar-lost but from some other reality of

Rahndarr-gained. The welcome, the joy she had felt the night before—somehow they had become part of her dreams.

"The meadows—," she said, hardly aware that she spoke. She had always thought shatterflowers coarse, those that grew in Rahndatown. Now she knew that in the meadows that lay far beyond the town, their gaudy colors would be vibrant. "The fields—" Her father had described them to her often enough, the fields of wintergrass they would grow in the farlands: lush, green, sweeping in the sun. She had imagined them as a terrible emptiness. Now she saw them as he must see them: vividly, hungrily. She wanted them as badly as he did.

But there was something else she wanted and that she could not have. "Mega," she said with a sob, and sat.

Mega hung in the blue water of the dreaming pond, her limbs lax, only her face breaking the water's surface. Her arms were spread, and her flight-membranes seemed to flutter despite the stillness of the pond.

Had the Birleles simply left her here like this? Left her to bloat in the water? Almost angrily Namir took her feet. If she could reach Mega's body before she was stung to unconsciousness again, pull it back to the pond's edge—

Before she could enter the water, Mega rolled to her stomach in the water and kicked herself across the pond to Namir.

Namir found herself holding her friend, holding the body that should have been stiff and cold—the body that was water-hot and living. "Mega—your face—" she stammered. The swelling was gone. So were the vivid discolorations that marked the course of the disease.

"Did you dream?" Mega demanded, her eyes lively. "Did the stings make you dream?"

"I—I think I did dream. A little. But—"

Mega nodded eagerly, shaking herself, making water fly. "I dreamed everything I wanted to dream. I spoke with the wind, I tumbled with the rocks, I rode the clouds over the mountains. Do you see them, Namir? I rode those clouds." She pointed, radiant. "We are that much alike at least. The stings made you dream, too. A little."

"Yes." Perhaps. And perhaps she had dreamed simply because she often did, dreamed strangely because the last day had changed her in some way. "But Mega—" Namir peered down into the clear pond. Why was Mega alive? Why was she well? None of the Birleles in Rahndatown had recovered from this disease.

None of the Birleles in Rahndatown had come to the dreaming ponds. They had been too weak to come so far alone, and few of them had special friends to help them. None had special friends foolish enough to climb to the Birlele habitat. Namir stroked Mega's shoulder. It was fever hot, as if—

As if— "Mega," she realized, "you needed fever."

Mega was preening herself, deftly grooming her wet hair, sweeping it into dark whorls. "Fever?"

"You needed fever to kill the disease. And your body—your body doesn't make fever. When you got sick, you became cold instead. You had to come here to make yourself warm enough to kill the infection." Could it be that simple? Could the Birleles who lived among the humans survive human diseases simply by submersion?

"I had to come here to die," Mega corrected her. "But I had healing dreams instead of dying dreams. It happens sometimes. We dream of being well and live again."

Namir nodded. Perhaps the solution was not so simple. Perhaps there had been some subtle interaction between the heat of the dreaming pond and the venom of whatever it was that stung. Perhaps even that interaction would not suffice against all human-borne infections. Perhaps only this one.

Still Namir did not feel any sinking discouragement. Mega had stepped from the pond well. Namir had had her dreams of Rahndarr, whatever their origin. And she would tell the Council of Governors what had happened. The Council had declared for the right of the Birleles to live where they pleased on their native world, whatever the dangers. Perhaps they could do something now to alleviate the worst of those dangers. She brushed at her clothes. They were stiff in places, damp in others. "Mega, will you come back to Rahndatown with me?" Did she hope for a yes or a no?

Mega had completed her grooming and she peered up at Namir with momentary sadness. "No, Namir, I have been in Rahndatown three years and I have seen and heard what I wanted. Now there are places I dreamed and I want to visit them. The caves where my sisters live, the crags dark at night, the deep crevices where we hunt shadowleaf—"

Namir nodded, understanding. There were meadows and grasslands she wanted to see, urgently. "The others—you're sure they won't hurt you?"

Mega's eyes glinted. "Namir, they came into the pond and dreamed with me while I was healing. They were glad I returned, and they asked why others have not."

The separatists were wrong then. The Birleles had let her walk up their mountain paths; they had saved her from drowning in the dream-pond; and they had welcomed Mega back, even sick.

They gazed at each other. It was awkward parting. There were things Namir wanted to say. Yet all she could think was, "Mega, when I dreamed, you were there." Was it a lie? Hadn't there been a quick shape moving through her half-recalled dreams? Hadn't she glimpsed it in the meadows and in the farlands?

"Then I will see you again." Noon restlessness was on Mega and her limbs moved eagerly. But before she darted away, she touched the bright sash that held Namir's blouse. "Will you leave me this?"

"Of course." Namir stripped it off, eager to prolong their parting. "And I'll sing for you."

At that Mega laughed, hoarsely, coughing, as Birleles laughed. "No, Namir. Don't sing until you get back to the valley. Then if there is someone there sick, sing when you carry her up the trail and we will all dream with her. Will you?"

Come up the mountain again past hissing Birleles? For a moment fear returned, unreasoning. Namir dismissed it. "Of course." She would make herself friend of those Birleles in Rahndatown who had no special friend. If they needed her, she would be there, either to speak to the Council of Governors for them or to carry them to the dreaming ponds when they were stricken.

"Then that is when I will see you," Mega said, and she leapt away as swift and dauntless as Namir remembered.

When she was gone, Namir started down the trail. Occasionally she saw Birleles watching her from the rocks. When she paused, they hissed. She longed for something familiar to reassure herself by—some song to guard against strangeness. But she looked closely and found a little bit of Mega in each watching Birlele, and she did not sing again until she reached the valley.

The Cabinet of Edgar Allan Poe

ANGELA CARTER

Imagine Poe in the Republic! when he possesses none of its virtues; no Spartan, he. Each time he tilts the jug to greet the austere morning, his sober friends reluctantly concur: "No man is safe who drinks before breakfast." Where is the black star of melancholy? Elsewhere; not here. Here it is always morning; stern, democratic light scrubs apparitions off the streets down which his dangerous feet must go.

Perhaps . . . perhaps the black star of melancholy was hiding in the dark at the bottom of the jug all the time . . . it might be the whole thing is a little secret between the jug and himself. . . .

He turns back to go and look; and the pitiless light of common day hits him full in the face like a blow from the eye of God. Struck, he reels. Where can he hide, where there are no shadows? They split the Republic in two, they halved the apple of knowledge, white light strikes the top half and leaves the rest in shadow; up here, up north, in the leveling latitudes, a man must make his own penumbra if he wants concealment because the massive, heroic light of the Republic admits of no ambiguities. Either you are a saint; or a stranger. He is a stranger, here, a gentleman up from Virginia somewhat down on his luck, and, alas, he may not invoke the Prince of Darkness (always a perfect gentleman) in his cause since, of the absolute night which is the antithesis to these days of rectitude, there is no aristocracy.

Poe staggers under the weight of the Declaration of Independence. People think he is drunk.

He *is* drunk.

The prince in exile lurches through the newfound land.

So you say he overacts? Very well; he overacts. There is a past history of histrionics in his family. His mother was, as they say, born in a trunk, greasepaint in her bloodstream, and made her first appearance on any stage in her ninth summer in a hiss-the-villain melodrama entitled *Mysteries of the Castle*. On she skipped to sing a ballad clad in the pretty rags of a ballet gypsy.

It was the evening of the eighteenth century.

At this hour, this very hour, far away in Paris, France, in the appalling dungeons of the Bastille, old Sade is jerking off. Grunt, groan, grunt, onto the prison floor . . . aaaagh! He seeds dragons' teeth. Out of each ejaculation spring up a swarm of fully armed, mad-eyed homunculi. Everything is about to succumb to delirium.

Heedless of all this, Poe's future mother skipped onto a stage in the fresh-hatched American republic to sing an old-world ballad clad in the pretty rags of a ballet gypsy. Her dancer's grace, piping treble, dark curls, rosy cheeks—cute kid! And eyes with something innocent, something appealing in them that struck directly to the heart so that the smoky auditorium broke out in raucous sentimental cheers for her and clapped its leather palms together with a will. A star was born that night in the rude firmament of fit-ups and candle footlights, but she was to be a shooting star; she flickered briefly in the void, she continued the inevitable trajectory of the meteor, downward. She hit the boards and trod them.

But, well after puberty, she was still able, thanks to her low stature and slim build, to continue to personate children, clever little ducks and prattlers of both sexes. Yet she was versatility personified; she could do you Ophelia, too.

She had a low, melodious voice of singular sweetness, an excellent thing in a woman. When crazed Ophelia handed round the rosemary and rue and sang: "He is dead and gone, lady," not a dry eye in the house, I assure you. She also tried her hand at Juliet and Cordelia and, if necessary, could personate the merriest soubrette; even when racked by the nauseas of her pregnancies, still she would smile, would smile and oh! the dazzling candor of her teeth!

Out popped her firstborn, Henry; her second, Edgar, came jostling after to share her knee with her scripts and suckle at her bosom while she learned her lines, yet she was always word-perfect even when she played two parts in the one night, Ophelia or Juliet and then, say, Little Pickle, the cute kid in the afterpiece, for the audiences of those days refused to leave the theater after a tragedy unless the players changed costumes and came back to give them a little something extra to cheer them up again.

Little Pickle was a trousers role. She ran back to the greenroom and undid the top buttons of her waistcoat to let out a sore, milky breast to pacify little Edgar who, wakened by the hoots and catcalls that had greeted her too voluptuous imitation of a boy, likewise howled and screamed.

A mug of porter or a bottle of whiskey stood on the dressing table all the time. She dipped a plug of cotton in whiskey and gave it to Edgar to suck when he would not stop crying.

The father of her children was a bad actor and only ever carried a spear in the many companies in which she worked. He often stayed behind in the greenroom to look after the little ones. David Poe tipped a tumbler of neat gin to Edgar's lips to keep him quiet. The red-eyed Angel of Intemperance hopped out of the bottle of ardent spirits and snuggled down in little Edgar's longclothes. Meanwhile, on stage, her final child, in utero, stitched its flesh and bones together as best it could under the corset that preserved the theatrical illusion of Mrs. Elizabeth Poe's eighteen-inch waist until the eleventh hour, the tenth month.

Applause rocked round the wooden O. Loving mother that she was—for we have no reason to believe that she was not—Mrs. Poe exited the painted scene to cram her jewels on her knee while tired tears ran rivers through her rouge and splashed upon their peaky faces. The monotonous clamor of their parents' argument sent them at last to sleep but the unborn one in the womb pressed its transparent hands over its vestigial ears in terror.

(To be born at all might be the worst thing.)

However, born at last this last child was, one July afternoon in a cheap theatrical boardinghouse in New York City after many hours on a rented bed while flies buzzed at the windowpanes. Edgar and Henry, on a pallet on the floor, held hands. The midwife had to use a pair of blunt iron tongs to scoop out the reluctant wee thing; the sheet was tented up over Mrs. Poe's lower half for modesty so the toddlers saw nothing except the midwife brandishing her dreadful instrument and then they heard the shrill cry of the newborn in the exhausted silence, like the sound of the blade of a skate on ice, and something bloody as a fresh-pulled tooth twitched between the midwife's pincers.

It was a girl.

David Poe spent his wife's confinement in a nearby tavern, wetting the baby's head. When he came back and saw the mess, he vomited.

Then, before his sons' bewildered eyes, their father began to grow insubstantial. He unbecame. All at once he lost his outlines and began to waver on the air. It was twilit evening. Mama slept on the bed with a fresh mauve bud of flesh in a basket on the chair beside her. The air shuddered with the beginning of absence.

He said not one word to his boys but went on evaporating until he melted clean away, leaving behind him in the room as proof he had been there only a puddle of puke on the splintered floorboards.

As soon as the deserted wife got out of bed, she posted down to Virginia with her howling brats because she was booked for a tour of the South and she had no money put away so all the babies got to eat was her sweat. She dragged them with her in a trunk to Charleston; to Norfolk; then back to Richmond.

Down there, it is the fetid height of summer.

Stripped to her chemise in the airless dressing room, she milks her sore breasts into a glass; this latest baby must be weaned before its mother dies.

She coughed. She slapped more, yet more rouge on her now haggard cheekbones. "My children! what will become of my children?" Her eyes glittered and soon acquired a febrile brilliance that was not of *this* world. Soon she needed no rouge at all; red spots brighter than rouge appeared of their own accord on her cheeks while veins as blue as those in Stilton cheese but muscular, palpitating, prominent, lithe, stood out of her forehead. In Little Pickle's vest and breeches it was not now possible for her to create the least suspension of disbelief and something desperate, something fatal in her distracted playing both fascinated and appalled the witnesses, who could have thought they saw the living features of death itself upon her face. Her mirror, the actress's friend, the magic mirror in which she sees whom she has become, no longer acknowledged any but a death's head.

The moist, sullen Southern winter signed her quietus. She put on Ophelia's madwoman's nightgown for her farewell.

When she summoned him, the spectral horseman came. Edgar looked out of the window and saw him. The soundless hooves of black-plumed horses struck sparks from the stones in the road outside. "Father!" said Edgar; he thought their father must have reconstituted himself at this last extremity in order to transport them all to a better place, but when he looked more closely, by the light of a gibbous moon, he saw the sockets of the coachman's eyes were full of worms.

They told her children that now she could come back to take no curtain calls no matter how fiercely all applauded the manner of her going. Lovers of the theater plied her hearse with bouquets: "And from her pure and uncorrupted flesh May violets spring." (Not a dry eye in the house.) The three orphaned infants were dispersed into the bosoms of charitable protectors. Each gave the clay-cold cheek a final kiss; then they too kissed and parted, Edgar from Henry, Henry from the tiny one who did not move or cry but lay still and kept her eyes tight shut. When shall these three meet again? The church bell tolled: never never never never never.

Kind Mr. Allan of Virginia, Edgar's own particular benefactor, who would buy his bread, henceforward, took his charge's little hand and led him from the funeral. Edgar parted his name in the middle to make room for Mr. Allan inside it. Edgar was then three years old. Mr. Allan ushered him into Southern affluence, down there; but do not think his mother left Edgar empty-handed, although the dead actress was able to leave him only what could not be taken away from him, to wit, a few tattered memories.

TESTAMENT OF MRS. ELIZABETH POE

Item: nourishment. A tit sucked in a greenroom, the dug snatched away from the toothless lips as soon as her cue came, so that, of nourishment, he would retain only the memory of hunger and thirst endlessly unsatisfied.

Item: transformation. This is a more ambivalent relic. Something like this. . . . Edgar would lie in prop baskets on heaps of artificial finery and watch her while she painted her face. The candles made a profane altar of the mirror in which her vague face swam like a magic fish. If you caught hold of it, it would make your dreams come true but Mama slithered through all the nets which desire set out to catch her.

She stuck glass jewels in her ears, pinned back her nut-brown hair, and tied a muslin bandage round her head, looking like a corpse for a minute. Then on went the yellow wig. Now you see her, now you don't; brunette turns blonde in the wink of an eye.

Mama turns round to show how she has changed into the lovely lady he glimpsed in the mirror.

"Don't touch me, you'll mess me."

And vanishes in a susurration of taffeta.

Item: that women possess within them a cry, a thing that needs to be extracted . . . but this is only the dimmest of memories and will reassert itself in vague shapes of unmentionable dread only at the prospect of carnal connection.

Item: the awareness of mortality. For, as soon as her last child was born, if not before, she started to rehearse in private the long part of dying; once she began to cough, she had no option.

Item: a face, the perfect face of a tragic actor, his face, white skin stretched tight over fine, white bones in a final state of wonderfully lucid emaciation.

Ignited by the tossed butt of a still-smoldering cigar that lodged in the cracks of the uneven floorboards, the theater at Richmond where Mrs. Poe had made her last appearance burned to the ground three weeks after her death. Ashes. Although Mr. Allan told Edgar how all of his mother that was mortal had been buried in her coffin, Edgar knew the somebody elses she so frequently became lived in her dressing-table mirror and were not constrained by the physical laws that made her body rot. But now the mirror, too, was gone; and all the lovely and untouchable, volatile, unreal mothers went up together in a puff of smoke on a pyre of props and painted scenery.

The sparks from this conflagration rose high in the air, where they lodged in the sky to become a constellation of stars which only Edgar saw and then only on certain still nights of summer, those hot, rich, blue, mellow nights the slaves brought with them from Africa, weather that ferments the music of exile, weather of heartbreak and fever. (Oh, those voluptuous nights, like something forbidden!) High in the sky these invisible stars marked the points of a face folded in sorrow.

NATURE OF THE THEATRICAL ILLUSION: everything you see is false.

Consider the theatrical illusion with special reference to this impressionable child, who was exposed to it at an age when there is no reason for anything to be real.

He must often have toddled onto the stage when the theater was empty and the curtains down so all was like a parlor prepared for a séance, waiting for the moment when the eyes of the observers make the mystery.

Here he will find a painted backdrop of, say, an antique castle—a castle! such as they don't build here; a Gothic castle all complete with owls and ivy. The flies are painted with segments of trees, massy oaks or something like that, all in two dimensions. Artificial shadows fall in all the wrong places. Nothing is what it seems. You knock against a gilded throne or horrid rack that looks perfectly solid, thick, immoveable, and you kick it sideways, it turns out to be made of papier-mâché, it is as light as air—a child, you yourself, could pick it up and carry it off with you and sit in it and be a king or lie in it and be in pain.

A creaking, an ominous rattling scares the little wits out of you; when you jump round to see what is going on behind your back, why, the very castle is in midair! Heave-ho and up she rises, amid the inarticulate cries and muttered oaths of the stagehands, and down comes Juliet's tomb or Ophelia's sepulchre, and a super scuttles in, clutching Yorick's skull.

The foulmouthed whores who dandle you on their pillowy laps and tip mugs of sour porter against your lips now congregate in the wings, where they have turned into nuns or something. On the invisible side of the plush curtain that cuts you off from the beery, importunate, tobacco-stained multitude that has paid its pennies on the nail to watch these transcendent rituals now come the thumps, bangs, and clatter that make the presence of their expectations felt. A stagehand swoops down to scoop you up and carry you off, protesting, to where Henry, like a good boy, is already deep in his picture book, and there is a poke of candy for you and the corner of a handkerchief dipped in moonshine and Mama in crown and train presses her rouged lips softly on your forehead before she goes down before the mob.

On his brow her rouged lips left the mark of Cain.

Having, at an impressionable age, seen with his own eyes the nature of the mystery of the castle—that all its horrors are so much painted cardboard and yet they terrify you—he saw another mystery and made less sense of it.

Now and then, as a great treat, if he kept quiet as a mouse, because he begged and pleaded so, he was allowed to stay in the wings and watch; the round-eyed baby saw that Ophelia could, if necessary, die twice nightly. All her burials were premature.

A couple of brawny supers carried Mama on stage in Act Four, wrapped in a shroud, tipped her into the cellarage amidst displays of grief from all concerned but up she would pop at curtain call having shaken the dust off her graveclothes and touched up her eye makeup, to curtsey with the rest of the resurrected immortals, all of whom, even Prince Hamlet himself, turned out, in the end, to be just as undead as she.

How could he, then, truly believe she would not come again, although, in the black suit that Mr. Allan provided for him out of charity, he toddled behind her coffin to the cemetery? Surely, one fine day, the spectral coachman would return again, climb down from his box, throw open the carriage door, and out she would step wearing the white nightdress in which he had last seen her, although he hoped this garment had been laundered in the interim since he last saw it all bloody from a hemorrhage.

Then a transparent constellation in the night sky would blink out; the scattered atoms would reassemble themselves to the entire and perfect Mama and he would run directly to her arms.

It is the midmorning of the nineteenth century. He grows up under the black stars of the slave states. He flinches from that part of women the sheet hid. He becomes a man.

As soon as he becomes a man, affluence departs from Edgar. The heart and pocketbook that Mr. Allan opened to the child now pull themselves together to expell. Edgar shakes the dust of the sweet South off his heels. He hies north, up here, to seek his fortune in the places where the light does not permit that chiaroscuro he loves; now Edgar Poe must live by his disordered wits.

The dug was snatched from the milky mouth and tucked away inside the bodice; the mirror no longer reflected Mama but, instead, a perfect stranger. He offered her his hand; smiling a tranced smile, she stepped out of the frame.

"My darling, my sister, my life, and my bride!"

He was not put out by the tender years of this young girl whom he soon married; was she not just Juliet's age, just thirteen summers?

The magnificent tresses forming great shadowed eaves above her high forehead were the raven tint of nevermore, black as his suits the seams of which his devoted mother-in-law painted with ink so that they would not advertise to the world the signs of wear and, nowadays, he always wore a suit of sables, dressed in readiness for the next funeral in a black coat buttoned up to the stock and he never betrayed his absolute mourning by so much as one flash of white shirtfront. Sometimes, when his wife's mother was not there to wash and starch his linen, he economized on laundry bills and wore no shirt at all.

His long hair brushes the collar of this coat, from which poverty has worn off the nap. How sad his eyes are; there is too much of sorrow in his infrequent smile to make you happy when he smiles at you and so much of bitter gall, also, that you might mistake his smile for a grimace or a *grue* except when he smiles at his young wife with her forehead like a tombstone. Then he will smile and smile with as much posthumous tenderness as if he saw already: *Dearly beloved wife of* . . . carved above her eyebrows.

For her skin was white as marble and she was called—would you believe!—"Virginia," a name that suited his expatriate's nostalgia and also her condition, for the childbride would remain a virgin until the day she died.

Imagine the sinless children lying in bed together! The pity of it!

For did she not come to him stiffly armored in taboos—taboos against the violation of children; taboos against the violation of the dead—for, not to put too fine a point on it, didn't she always look like a walking corpse? But such a pretty, pretty corpse!

And, besides, isn't an undemanding, economic, decorative corpse the perfect wife for a gentleman in reduced circumstances, upon whom the four walls of paranoia are always about to converge?

Virginia Clemm. In the dialect of northern England, to be "clemmed" is to be very cold. "I'm fair clemmed." Virginia Clemm.

She brought with her a hardy, durable, industrious mother of her own, to clean and cook and keep accounts for them and to outlive them, and to outlive them both.

Virginia was not very clever; she was by no means a sad case of arrested development, like his real, lost sister, whose life passed in a dream of non-being in her adopted home, the vegetable life of one who always declined to participate, a bud that never opened. (A doom lay upon them; the brother, Henry, soon died.) But the slow years passed and Virginia stayed as she had been at thirteen, a simple little thing whose sweet disposition was his only comfort and who never ceased to lisp, even when she started to rehearse the long part of dying.

She was light on her feet as a revenant. You would have thought she never bent a stem of grass as she passed across their little garden. When she spoke, when she sang, how sweet her voice was; she kept her harp in their cottage parlor, which her mother swept and polished until all was like a new pin. A few guests gathered there to partake of the Poes' modest hospitality. There was his brilliant conversation though his women saw to it that only tea was served, since all knew his dreadful weakness for liquor, but Virginia poured out with so much simple grace that everyone was charmed.

They begged her to take her seat at her harp and accompany herself in an Old World ballad or two. Eddy nodded gladly: "yes," and she lightly struck the strings with white hands of which the long, thin fingers were so fine and waxen that you would have thought you could have set light to the tips to make of her hand the flaming Hand of Glory that casts all the inhabitants of the house, except the magician himself, into a profound and deathlike sleep.

She sings:

Cold blows the wind, tonight, my love,
And a few drops of rain.

With a taper made from a manuscript folded into a flute, he slyly takes a light from the fire.

I never had but one true love
In cold earth she was lain.

He sets light to her fingers, one after the other.

A twelve month and a day being gone
The dead began to speak.

Eyes close. Her pupils contain in each a flame.

Who is that sitting on my grave
Who will not let me sleep?

All sleep. Her eyes go out. She sleeps.

He rearranges the macabre candelabra so that the light from her glorious hand will fall between her legs and then he busily turns back her petticoats; the mortal candles shine. Do not think it is not love that moves him; only love moves him.

He feels no fear.

An expression of low cunning crosses his face. Taking from his back pocket a pair of enormous pliers, he now, one by one, one by one by one, extracts the sharp teeth just as the midwife did.

All silent, all still.

Yet, even as he held aloft the last fierce canine in triumph above her prostrate and insensible form in the conviction he had at last exorcised the demons from desire, his face turned ashen and sear and he was overcome with the most desolating anguish to hear the rumbling of the wheels outside. Unbidden, the coachman came; the grisly emissary of her highborn kinsman shouted imperiously: "Overture and beginners, please!" She popped the plug of spiritous linen between his lips; she swept off with a hiss of silk.

The sleepers woke and told him he was drunk; but his Virginia breathed no more!

After a breakfast of red-eye, as he was making his toilet before the mirror, he suddenly thought he would shave off his mustache in order to become a different man so that the ghosts who had persistently plagued him since his wife's death would no longer recognize him and would leave him alone. But, when he was clean shaven, a black star rose in the mirror and he saw that his long hair and face folded in sorrow had taken on such a marked resemblance to that of his loved and lost one that he was struck like a stock or stone, with the cutthroat razor in his hand.

And, as he continued, fascinated, appalled, to stare in the reflective glass at those features that were his own and yet not his own, the bony casket of his skull began to agitate itself as if he had succumbed to a tremendous attack of the shakes.

Good night, sweet prince.

He was shaking like a backcloth about to be whisked off into oblivion.

Lights! he called out.

Now he wavered; horrors! *He was starting to dissolve!*

Lights! more lights! he cried, like the hero of a Jacobean tragedy when the murdering begins, for the black star was engulfing him.

On cue, the laser light on the Republic blasts him.

His dust blows away on the wind.

The Harvest of Wolves

MARY GENTLE

Flix sat in the old sagging armchair, leaned forward, and tore another page from the *Encyclopaedia Britannica*. The fire took it, flickering in the grate.

"What the—" the boy, closing the door as he entered, strode across the room and slapped the book out of her hand. "What's the matter with you? You could *sell* that for—"

"For money to buy fuel?" Flix suggested. Adrenaline made her dizzy. She looked down at her liver-spotted hands, where the veins stood up with age; they were shaking. "Thank you, I prefer to cut out the middle man. Self-sufficiency."

He glared; she doubted he recognized irony.

"You're crazy, you know that?"

"If you know it, that ought to be enough. Have you put in your report yet?" She shot the question at him.

He was still young enough to blush. Angry because of it, he snarled, "You keep your mouth shut, citizen. You hear me?"

"I hear you." Age makes you afraid, Flix thought. Pacifying him, she said, "Well, what have you brought me?"

"Bread. Milk's out. Can't deliver, there's no transport. I got you some water, though. It's clean."

You wouldn't know clean water if it bit you, Flix thought bitterly. She watched the boy unpacking the plastic bag he carried, throwing the goods into the nearest cupboard. He was growing taller by the week, this one; broad-shouldered with close-cropped black hair, and the changing voice of adolescence.

"Marlow," she said, "what makes you choose community service?"

"Didn't choose it, did I? Got given it, didn't I?"

He straightened, stuffed the bag in the pocket of his uniform jacket, and came over to squat beside the open fire. Though he never admitted it, it attracted him. Probably because he'd never before been in a house old enough to have a grate, she thought.

" 'Community service,' " she repeated, unable to keep the edge out of her voice. "Snooping under cover of charity; you call that service? Bringing Welfare rations, weighing me up . . . and all the time new laws, and cutting it closer every time, eh? If they've got as far as these slums, Marlow boy, then pretty soon we'll all be gone."

Resentment glared out of him. "Think I want to come here? Crazy old house, crazy old bitch—"

"That's 'citizen' to you, if you can't manage 'Flix.' " She offered him a crumpled pack of cigarettes, forcing a smile. "Only tobacco, I'm afraid."

The Pavlovian response: "Filthy things'll give you cancer."

"Ah, who'll get me first, then: lung cancer, hypothermia, starvation—or you and your bloody Youth Corps?"

"You got no room to talk—it was your lot got us in this mess in the first place." He stood up. "You think we want to live like this, no jobs, nothing? You got no idea. If it weren't for the Corps I'd be—"

"You'd be waiting out your time on Welfare," Flix said, very carefully. "Seeing the deadline come up. You'd be being tested—like I am now—to see how fit you are to survive. To qualify for government food. To get government water, so you don't die of cholera. Government housing, so you don't die of cold. Instead you're here, waiting for me to—"

"That's the way it is," Marlow said. He lowered his head, glaring at her from dark, hollowed eyes. (Why, she thought, he's been losing sleep.) "You got to produce. You got to work. You got to be worth keeping on Welfare. Or else—and don't tell me it ain't fair. I know it ain't fair, but that's the way it is."

"Ah," she said, on a rising inflection, "is that the way it is."

"*Look* at you!" He swung his arm round, taking in the single-room flat. The wallpaper was covered by old posters, garish with the slogans of halcyon '90s (that final, brief economic flowering) when protest was easy. Planks propped up on bricks served as shelves for old books and pamphlets and magazines. Some had sat so long in the same place that the damp had made of them an inseparable mass. A long-disconnected computer terminal gathered dust, ancient access codes scratched on the casing. Cracking china lay side by side on the drainer with incongruously new plastic dishes, and a saucepan full of something brown and long-burned sat on the stove. A thin film of plaster from the ceiling had drifted down onto the expanse of worn linoleum, left empty by the clustering of table, chair, and bed round the open fire.

Flix poked the ashes with a burned slat, and glanced up at the windows. Beyond the wire mesh, the sky was gray.

"You could fix those boards," she said. "There's a wind whips through there could take the barnacles off a ship's hull, since your friends left me with no glass in the windows. . . . What, no reaction?"

"You can't blame them." The boy sounded tired, and very adult. "Thinking of you in here. Eating, sleeping. Doing nothing to earn it."

"Christ!" Flix exploded, and saw him flinch at the word as he always did. But now she wasn't goading him for her amusement. "There was a time you didn't have to *earn* the right to live! You had it—as a human being!"

"Yeah," he said wearily, "I know. I heard about that. I hear about it all the time from my old man. Free this, free that, free the other; holidays in the sun, cars for everybody, everybody working—yeah, I heard. And what happens? What do you leave for *us*? You let the niggers come in and steal your jobs, you let the Yanks put their missiles here! You let kids grow up wild 'cause their mothers were never home; you sell us out to the Reds—"

"Oh, spare me. If you're going to be bigoted, at least be original!"

"Citizen," Marlow said, "shut up."

Not quite under her breath she said, "Ignorant pig."

He yelled, "Why don't you clean this place up? *You* live like a pig!"

"I was never one for housework—and besides, I've got you to do it for me, haven't I? Courtesy of the Welfare state. Until such time as the state decides I'm not worth keeping alive."

His would not be the first report made on her (though the first under this name), but time and purges had culled the number of officials willing to turn a blind eye on changes of code, name, and location.

I am, Flix thought, too old for this fugitive life.

"Pig," Marlow repeated absently. He rummaged around in the toolbox by the window and began nailing the slats back over the lower windowsill.

"There's coffee in the cupboard." Flix made a peace offering of it. "Have some if you want it. You'll have to boil the kettle. I think the power's still on."

"Where'd you get *coffee*?"

"I still have friends," Flix observed sententiously. "They can't do much, being as they're old like me; but what they can do, they will. The old network's still there."

"Subversive," he accused.

Lord Brahma! I can't seem to keep off it today, Flix thought. What is it with me—do I *want* to die? Well, maybe. But not to suit their convenience.

"Do you ever listen to anything except what they tell you?"

Marlow whacked the last nail in viciously, threw down the hammer, and stalked over to the sink. Filling the kettle, his back to her, he said, "I know what's right. I know what's true."

"I am sick to death of people who *know*. I want people who aren't sure. I want people who're willing to admit there's another side to the argument—or even that there is an argument, for Christ's sake! Marlow, will you bloody look at me!"

He plugged the kettle in. Turning, and leaning back against the chipped unit: "What?"

"You don't believe all that bullshit." Again, he flinched. They are abnormally sensitive, she thought. "You can't believe it, you're not the age. Sixteen's when you go round questioning everything."

"Maybe in your day. It's different now. We got to grow up quick or not at all." He shrugged. "Listen, I'm looking back at it, what it was like—I can see what you can't. While you sat round talking, the commies were taking over the unions; and if it hadn't been for Foster we'd be a satellite state today—"

Flix groaned. "Jesus. Marlow, tell me all the shit you like, tell me we were all commie pinko perverts, tell me we were capitalist running dogs who brought the world to ruin"—she was laughing, an old woman's high cackle—"but in the name of God, don't tell me about your precious Foster! I knew all I needed to know about dictators before you were born!"

His mouth twisted. She could see him lose patience with her.

"You don't know what it's like," Marlow said. "Five of us in a two-room flat, and the power not on, and never enough food, and for why? Because there's no work, and if there was, there's nothing to buy with the money! At least he's making it better. At least there's less of that."

"Where do you go when there's nowhere to go?" Flix asked rhetorically. "I'd OD if you could get the stuff, but that's another thing banned in your bloody utopia. Fetch us the coffee, Marlow, and hand me that half-bottle in the top cupboard."

He was as disapproving as any Youth Cadet, but he did what she asked. Whiskey and coffee (the last now, the very last) bit into her gut. I am fighting, she reminded herself sourly, I am fighting—God knows why—for my life.

"I suppose it's no good offering you a drink? No, I thought not. Hell, Marlow, loosen up, will you?"

She had, over the weeks, gained some small amusement from tormenting him. Like all of Foster's New Puritans, the Corps strongly disapproved of drugs, blasphemy, lechery—and there, she thought, is a fine old-fashioned word. Not that I've quite got round to that . . . but wouldn't he react beautifully! Or is it that I'm afraid of him laughing? Or afraid of him? For all his "community service," he's still a thug.

She tore a few more pages from the thick book, crumpled them, and poked them into the fire where they flared briefly. "What about coal, Marlow?"

"Reconstituted."

"Christ, that stuff doesn't burn. Still, what the hell. Come and sit down." She watched him kneel by the flames. In the dim cold room, the light made lines on his face; he looked older.

"In the nineties," she said speculatively, "there were, for example, parties without supervisors—supervisors!—and music without propaganda—"

"Without whose propaganda?"

"Bravo, Marlow!" She clapped gently. "Without theirs, of course. With ours. Now it's the other way round. Do you realize, I wouldn't *mind* if he had the grace to be original? But it's the same old thing; no free press, no free speech, no unions; food shortages, rabid patriotic nationalism—"

"You were traitors! Was that any better?"

No way out, she thought, no way in; God preserve us from the voice of invincible ignorance.

"One thing we didn't do," she said. "We didn't weigh people up as to how useful they were to the state—and let them die when they got sick and old."

He was quiet. "Didn't you?"

"We didn't *plan* it."

"There's less poverty now. Less misery. It's a hard world," he said. "They're starving in Asia. Dying. That's not going to happen here. You used it up, this world. So you got yourselves to blame if you don't like what's happening now."

"Marlow," Flix said, "what are you going to say in your report?"

Now there was no evading the question. He looked up with clear puzzled eyes. "I don't want to do it."

"I know, or it wouldn't be nearly a month overdue, would it? No, don't ask me how I know. Like I said, the old grapevine's still there. When are they going to start wondering, Marlow? When are they going to start making reports on *you*?"

He stared into the fire. She got up slowly, taking her weight on her wrists, and went across to pull on her old (now much cracked) leather jacket. The cold got into her bones. Now would I be so weak if there was proper food? she thought. Christ, my mother lived to be eighty, and I'm not within twenty years of that!

"I've got family," Marlow said. "The old man, Macy, and the baby. We got to eat."

She could see herself reflected in the speckled wall mirror, lost in sepia depths. An old woman, lean and straight, with spiky cropped hair that needed washing from gray to silver. Marlow, out of focus, was a dark uniform and the glint of insignia.

Flix looked straight at him, solemnly; and when his eyes were fixed on her, she smiled. She had always had one of those faces, naturally somber and sardonic, that are transformed when they smile. Vanity doesn't go with age, she thought, savoring the boy's unwilling responsive grin.

"I could have shown you so much—so much. You haven't got the guts to run wild," she said, "you haven't got the guts to *question*."

The implication of promise was there. He watched her. The light dimmed, scummy and cold; and the fire glowed down to red embers. The ever-present smell of the room, overlain for a while by coffee and spirits, reasserted itself.

"You're a drunk," Marlow said. "D'you think I haven't seen the bottles you throw out—and the ones you hide? Yeah, your friends keep you supplied, all right! I've come in here when you were dead drunk on the bed, place stinking of shit; I've listened to you maundering on about the old days—I don't want to know! If this is where it leaves you, I don't want to know!"

"Is that right?" Tears stung behind her eyes; her voice thinned. "You'll never live the life I lived, and you'll never know how I regret it passing—ah, Jesus, it tears you up, to know it's gone and gone for good. *You* were the people we wanted to help. I mean you, Marlow! And when it came to actually thinking—God knows how difficult that is—you didn't want to know. You'd sooner march with your mobs. You'd sooner smash places up on your witch-hunts. You'd sooner cheer the tanks when they roll by. And God help you, that's not enough, you've got to think you're *right!*"

The boy crossed the room and pushed her. She fell back on the bed with an ugly sound. He stamped back and forth, sweeping the cracked cups crashing to the floor. Violently he kicked at the piles of old books and pamphlets. They scattered in soggy lumps.

"This!" he shouted. "You preach about your precious books and you burn them to keep warm! You talk about your 'subversive network' but what is it really? Old men and women hoarding food and drink, keeping it from us who need it!"

She, breathing heavily and conscious of pain, didn't answer. His first energy spent, he came back and helped her into the chair; and made up the fire until it blazed. The cold wind blew belches of gray smoke back into the room.

Flix felt down into the side of the chair for the hidden bottle there; fist knotted about it, letting the alcohol sting her back to life. When she looked up again he was putting on his coat.

As if nothing had happened, she said, "Books aren't sacred. Ideas are, and I've got those up here." She touched her lank hair. "Whatever else we are, we subversives, I'll tell you this—we care about each other. That's more than your Corps will do for you when you're old."

"I'll come in again tomorrow." He was all boy now; gangling, uncertain, sullen.

"I don't care if you don't agree with me! Just think about what you're doing—for once, *think* about it!"

At the door he turned back and said, "*Will* they look after you?"

After she heard the door slam, she plugged the power outlet into the antique stereo equipment, and placed old and much-mended '90s revival-rock cassettes, blasting the small room full of sound. It served to stop the treadmill-turning of her mind.

"You've got a letter!" Taz yelled down the stairs after her the next morning. She grunted, not taking any notice; the old man (occupier of the building's only other inhabitable room) was given to delusions, to happenings that were years after their time.

But when she crossed the hallway it lay there in the crepuscular light: a thin rough-paper envelope folded and addressed to Citizen Felicity Vance. Flix picked it up, wincing at the pain in her back. An immature hand, the letters mostly printed. So she knew.

She took it into her room, closing the door and resting her old bones on the bed.

Where is there anyone I can tell? she thought. That's another one of the boy's taunts—"if you had a husband, citizen." Ah, but I could never live in anyone's company but my own.

Now it came to it, she was afraid. Shaking, sweating; the old cold symptoms. She opened the letter.

Citizen—

I have to tell the truth. They check up on me too. It is the truth. You drink too much and your alone and cant take care. I have to live. If your friends are good friends you better tell them I sent my report in. Its not your fault things are like this. Im sorry I said it was. Sometimes I wisht I lived in the old days it might have been good. But I dont think so not for most of us.

Peter Marlow

She dressed slowly; fashions once adopted from a mythical past and previous revolutions: old jeans and sweater and the ancient leather jacket—the smell took her back, with the abruptness of illusion, to boys and bikes and books; to bright libraries, computer networks; to Xerox and duplicators, to faxsheets in brilliant colors that had been going to change the world.

He believes I'm a drunken old woman; alone, friends no more than geriatrics; he has to report me or be reported himself—and does he hope that it's more than an illusion, that some secret subversive organization still exists to whisk me off to—what? Safety? Where?

Things are bad all over, kid.

But at least he's sent in the report.

She left, locking the door behind her. It was a long time and a long walk to where she could borrow a working telephone. When she called the number, it was a while before it was answered; and a while before he remembered her name.

"Well," Flix said, "you'll have had the report by now."

"You're a fool," the man said. "You won't last a week in the Welfare camps! Flix—"

"I'll last long enough to tell what I know," Flix said. "About you—and who your father was—and what 'societies' you used to belong to. I'll do it, Simon. Maybe it won't make much difference, maybe it won't even lose you your job. But you won't have much of a career afterwards."

After a pause he said, "What do you want?"

"I want somewhere decent to live. I want to be warm. I want enough to eat, I want to play my music and read my books in peace. That's all. I'm tired of living like a pig! I want a place like the one you've got put by for yourself when *you* get old. No Welfare camps for Foster's boys, right? Now they'll put me in one—they can't ignore that report—and when they do, you know what I'm going to say!"

She could feel his uncertainty over the line, knew she had to weight things in her favor.

"Would it help," she said, "if you could turn in a few of the old subversive cells, by way of a sweetener? Those that didn't know you, those that can't give us away."

" 'Us.' " His tone reluctantly agreed complicitly, barely masked contempt. "Names?"

"Names after, not before."

And he agreed.

Flix grinned to herself, a fox-grin full of teeth and no humor. You and me both, Marlow, she thought; you and me both. . . .

"Like someone once told me," she said, "I have to live."

Bloodchild

OCTAVIA E. BUTLER

My last night of childhood began with a visit home. T'Gatoi's sisters had given us two sterile eggs. T'Gatoi gave one to my mother, brother, and sisters. She insisted that I eat the other one alone. It didn't matter. There was still enough to leave everyone feeling good. Almost everyone. My mother wouldn't take any. She sat, watching everyone drifting and dreaming without her. Most of the time she watched me.

I lay against T'Gatoi's long, velvet underside, sipping from my egg now and then, wondering why my mother denied herself such a harmless pleasure. Less of her hair would be gray if she indulged now and then. The eggs prolonged life, prolonged vigor. My father, who had never refused one in his life, had lived more than twice as long as he should have. And toward the end of his life, when he should have been slowing down, he had married my mother and fathered four children.

But my mother seemed content to age before she had to. I saw her turn away as several of T'Gatoi's limbs secured me closer. T'Gatoi liked our body heat, and took advantage of it whenever she could. When I was little and at home more, my mother used to try to tell me how to behave with T'Gatoi—how to be respectful and always obedient because T'Gatoi was the Tlic government official in charge of the Preserve, and thus the most important of her kind to deal directly with Terrans. It was an honor, my mother said, that such a person had chosen to come into the family. My mother was at her most formal and severe when she was lying.

I had no idea why she was lying, or even what she was lying about. It *was* an honor to have T'Gatoi in the family, but it was hardly a novelty. T'Gatoi and my mother had been friends all my mother's life, and T'Gatoi was not interested in being honored in the house she considered her second home. She simply came in, climbed onto one of her special couches, and called me over to keep her warm. It was impossible to be formal with her while lying against her and hearing her complain as usual that I was too skinny.

"You're better," she said this time, probing me with six or seven of her limbs. "You're gaining weight finally. Thinness is dangerous." The probing changed subtly, became a series of caresses.

"He's still too thin," my mother said sharply.

T'Gatoi lifted her head and perhaps a meter of her body off the couch as though she were sitting up. She looked at my mother and my mother, her face lined and old-looking, turned away.

"Lien, I would like you to have what's left of Gan's egg."

"The eggs are for the children," my mother said.

"They are for the family. Please take it."

Unwillingly obedient, my mother took it from me and put it to her mouth. There were only a few drops left in the now-shrunken, elastic shell, but she squeezed them out, swallowed them, and after a few moments some of the lines of tension began to smooth from her face.

"It's good," she whispered. "Sometimes I forget how good it is."

"You should take more," T'Gatoi said. "Why are you in such a hurry to be old?"

My mother said nothing.

"I like being able to come here," T'Gatoi said. "This place is a refuge because of you, yet you won't take care of yourself."

T'Gatoi was hounded on the outside. Her people wanted more of us made available. Only she and her political faction stood between us and the hordes who did not understand why there was a Preserve—why any Terran could not be courted, paid, drafted, in some way made available to them. Or they did understand, but in their desperation, they did not care. She parceled us out to the desperate and sold us to the rich and powerful for their political support. Thus, we were necessities, status symbols, and an independent people. She oversaw the joining of families, putting an end to the final remnants of the earlier system of breaking up Terran families to suit impatient Tlic. I had lived outside with her. I had seen the desperate eagerness in the way some people looked at me. It was a little frightening to know that only she stood between us and that desperation that could so easily swallow us. My mother would look at her sometimes and say to me, "Take care of her." And I would remember that she too had been outside, had seen.

Now T'Gatoi used four of her limbs to push me away from her onto the floor. "Go on, Gan," she said. "Sit down there with your sisters and enjoy not being sober. You had most of the egg. Lien, come warm me."

My mother hesitated for no reason that I could see. One of my earliest memories is of my mother stretched alongside T'Gatoi, talking about things I could not understand, picking me up from the floor and laughing as she sat me on one of T'Gatoi's segments. She ate her share of eggs then. I wondered when she had stopped, and why.

She lay down now against T'Gatoi, and the whole left row of T'Gatoi's limbs closed around her, holding her loosely, but securely. I had always found it comfortable to lie that way but, except for my older sister, no one else in the family liked it. They said it made them feel caged.

T'Gatoi meant to cage my mother. Once she had, she moved her tail slightly, then spoke. "Not enough egg, Lien. You should have taken it when it was passed to you. You need it badly now."

T'Gatoi's tail moved once more, its whip motion so swift I wouldn't have seen it if I hadn't been watching for it. Her sting drew only a single drop of blood from my mother's bare leg.

My mother cried out—probably in surprise. Being stung doesn't hurt. Then she sighed and I could see her body relax. She moved languidly into a more comfortable position within the cage of T'Gatoi's limbs. "Why did you do that?" she asked, sounding half asleep.

"I could not watch you sitting and suffering any longer."

My mother managed to move her shoulders in a small shrug. "Tomorrow," she said.

"Yes. Tomorrow you will resume your suffering—if you must. But for now, just for now, lie here and warm me and let me ease your way a little."

"He's still mine, you know," my mother said suddenly. "Nothing can buy him from me." Sober, she would not have permitted herself to refer to such things.

"Nothing," T'Gatoi agreed, humoring her.

"Did you think I would sell him for eggs? For long life? My son?"

"Not for anything," T'Gatoi said, stroking my mother's shoulders, toying with her long, graying hair.

I would like to have touched my mother, shared that moment with her. She would take my hand if I touched her now. Freed by the egg and the sting, she would smile and perhaps say things long held in. But tomorrow, she would remember all this as a humiliation. I did not want to be part of a remembered humiliation. Best just to be still and know she loved me under all the duty and pride and pain.

"Xuan Hoa, take off her shoes," T'Gatoi said. "In a little while I'll sting her again and she can sleep."

My older sister obeyed, swaying drunkenly as she stood up. When she had finished, she sat down beside me and took my hand. We had always been a unit, she and I.

My mother put the back of her head against T'Gatoi's underside and tried from that impossible angle to look up into the broad, round face. "You're going to sting me again?"

"Yes, Lien."

"I'll sleep until tomorrow noon."

"Good. You need it. When did you sleep last?"

My mother made a wordless sound of annoyance. "I should have stepped on you when you were small enough," she muttered.

It was an old joke between them. They had grown up together, sort of, though T'Gatoi had not, in my mother's lifetime, been small enough for any Terran to step on. She was nearly three times my mother's present age, yet would still be young when my mother died of age. But T'Gatoi and my mother had met as T'Gatoi was coming into a period of rapid development—a kind of Tlic adolescence. My mother was only a child, but for a while they developed at the same rate and had no better friends than each other.

T'Gatoi had even introduced my mother to the man who became my father. My parents, pleased with each other in spite of their very different ages, married as T'Gatoi was going into her family's business—politics. She and my mother saw each other less. But sometime before my older sister was born, my mother promised T'Gatoi one of her children. She would have to give one of us to someone, and she preferred T'Gatoi to some stranger.

Years passed. T'Gatoi traveled and increased her influence. The Preserve was hers by the time she came back to my mother to collect what she probably saw as her just reward for her hard work. My older sister took an instant liking to her and wanted to be chosen, but my mother was just coming to term with me and T'Gatoi liked the idea of choosing an infant and watching and taking part in all the phases of development. I'm told I was first caged within T'Gatoi's many limbs only three minutes after my birth. A few days later, I was given my first taste of egg. I tell Terrans that when they ask whether I was ever afraid of her. And I tell it to Tlic when T'Gatoi suggests a young Terran child for them and they, anxious and ignorant, demand an adolescent. Even my brother who had somehow grown up to fear and distrust the Tlic could probably have gone smoothly into one of their families if he had been adopted early enough. Sometimes, I think for his sake he should have been. I looked at him, stretched out on the floor across the room, his eyes open, but glazed as he dreamed his egg dream. No matter what he felt toward the Tlic, he always demanded his share of egg.

"Lien, can you stand up?" T'Gatoi asked suddenly.

"Stand?" my mother said. "I thought I was going to sleep."

"Later. Something sounds wrong outside." The cage was abruptly gone.

"What?"

"Up, Lien!"

My mother recognized her tone and got up just in time to avoid being dumped on the floor. T'Gatoi whipped her three meters of body off her couch, toward the door, and out at full speed. She had bones —ribs, a long spine, a skull, four sets of limbbones per segment. But when she moved that way, twisting, hurling herself into controlled falls, landing running, she seemed not only boneless, but aquatic—something swimming through the air as though it were water. I loved watching her move.

I left my sister and started to follow her out the door, though I wasn't very steady on my own feet. It would have been better to sit and dream, better yet to find a girl and share a waking dream with her. Back when the Tlic saw us as not much more than convenient big warm-blooded animals, they would pen several of us together, male and female, and feed us only eggs. That way they could be sure of getting another generation of us no matter how we tried to hold out. We were lucky that didn't go on long. A few generations of it and we would have *been* little more than convenient big animals.

"Hold the door open, Gan," T'Gatoi said. "And tell the family to stay back."

"What is it?" I asked.

"N'Tlic."

I shrank back against the door. "Here? Alone?"

"He was trying to reach a call box, I suppose." She carried the man past me, unconscious, folded like a coat over some of her limbs. He looked young—my brother's age perhaps—and he was thinner than he should have been. What T'Gatoi would have called dangerously thin.

"Gan, go to the call box," she said. She put the man on the floor and began stripping off his clothing.

I did not move.

After a moment, she looked up at me, her sudden stillness a sign of deep impatience.

"Send Qui," I told her. "I'll stay here. Maybe I can help."

She let her limbs begin to move again, lifting the man and pulling his shirt over his head. "You don't want to see this," she said. "It will be hard. I can't help this man the way his Tlic could."

"I know. But send Qui. He won't want to be of any help here. I'm at least willing to try."

She looked at my brother—older, bigger, stronger, certainly more able to help her here. He was sitting up now, braced against the wall, staring at the man on the floor with undisguised fear and revulsion. Even she could see that he would be useless.

"Qui, go!" she said.

He didn't argue. He stood up, swayed briefly, then steadied, frightened sober.

"This man's name is Bram Lomas," she told him, reading from the man's armband. I fingered my own armband in sympathy. "He needs T'Khotgif Teh. Do you hear?"

"Bram Lomas, T'Khotgif Teh," my brother said. "I'm going." He edged around Lomas and ran out the door.

Lomas began to regain consciousness. He only moaned at first and clutched spasmodically at a pair of T'Gatoi's limbs. My younger sister, finally awake from her egg dream, came close to look at him, until my mother pulled her back.

T'Gatoi removed the man's shoes, then his pants, all the while leaving him two of her limbs to grip. Except for the final few, all her limbs were equally dexterous. "I want no argument from you this time, Gan," she said.

I straightened. "What shall I do?"

"Go out and slaughter an animal that is at least half your size."

"Slaughter? But I've never—"

She knocked me across the room. Her tail was an efficient weapon whether she exposed the sting or not.

I got up, feeling stupid for having ignored her warning, and went into the kitchen. Maybe I could kill something with a knife or an ax. My mother raised a few Terran animals for the table and several thousand local ones for their fur. T'Gatoi would probably prefer something local. An achti, perhaps. Some of those were the right size, though they had about three times as many teeth as I did and a real love of using them. My mother, Hoa, and Qui could kill them with knives. I had never killed one at all, had never slaughtered any animal. I had spent most of my time with T'Gatoi while my brother and sisters were learning the family business. T'Gatoi had been right. I should have been the one to go to the call box. At least I could do that.

I went to the corner cabinet where my mother kept her larger house and garden tools. At the back of the cabinet there was a pipe that carried off waste water from the kitchen—except that it didn't anymore. My father had rerouted the waste water before I was born. Now the pipe could be turned so that one half slid around the other and a rifle could be stored inside. This wasn't our only gun, but it was our most easily accessible one. I would have to use it to shoot one of the biggest of the achti. Then T'Gatoi would probably confiscate it. Firearms were illegal in the Preserve. There had been incidents right after the Preserve was established—Terrans shooting Tlic, shooting N'Tlic. This was before the joining of families began, before everyone had a personal stake in keeping the peace. No one had shot a Tlic in my lifetime or my mother's, but the law still stood—for our protection, we were told. There were stories of whole Terran families wiped out in reprisal back during the assassinations.

I went out to the cages and shot the biggest achti I could find. It was a handsome breeding male and my mother would not be pleased to see me bring it in. But it was the right size, and I was in a hurry.

I put the achti's long, warm body over my shoulder—glad that some of the weight I'd gained was muscle—and took it to the kitchen. There, I put the gun back in its hiding place. If T'Gatoi noticed the achti's wounds and demanded the gun, I would give it to her. Otherwise, let it stay where my father wanted it.

I turned to take the achti to her, then hesitated. For several seconds, I stood in front of the closed door wondering why I was suddenly afraid. I knew what was going to happen. I hadn't seen it before, but T'Gatoi had shown me diagrams and drawings. She had made sure I knew the truth as soon as I was old enough to understand it.

Yet I did not want to go into that room. I wasted a little time choosing a knife from the carved, wooden box in which my mother kept them. T'Gatoi might want one, I told myself, for the tough, heavily furred hide of the achti.

"Gan!" T'Gatoi called, her voice harsh with urgency.

I swallowed. I had not imagined a simple moving of the feet could be so difficult. I realized I was trembling and that shamed me. Shame impelled me through the door.

I put the achti down near T'Gatoi and saw that Lomas was unconscious again. She, Lomas, and I were alone in the room, my mother and sisters probably sent out so they would not have to watch. I envied them.

But my mother came back into the room as T'Gatoi seized the achti. Ignoring the knife I offered her, she extended claws from several of her limbs and slit the achti from throat to anus. She looked at me, her yellow eyes intent. "Hold this man's shoulders, Gan."

I stared at Lomas in panic, realizing that I did not want to touch him, let alone hold him. This would not be like shooting an animal. Not as quick, not as merciful, and, I hoped, not as final, but there was nothing I wanted less than to be part of it.

My mother came forward. "Gan, you hold his right side," she said. "I'll hold his left." And if he came to, he would throw her off without realizing he had done it. She was a tiny woman. She often wondered aloud how she had produced, as she said, such "huge" children.

"Never mind," I told her, taking the man's shoulders. "I'll do it."

She hovered nearby.

"Don't worry," I said. "I won't shame you. You don't have to stay and watch."

She looked at me uncertainly, then touched my face in a rare caress. Finally, she went back to her bedroom.

T'Gatoi lowered her head in relief. "Thank you, Gan," she said with courtesy more Terran than Tlic. "That one . . . she is always finding new ways for me to make her suffer."

Lomas began to groan and make choked sounds. I had hoped he would stay unconscious. T'Gatoi put her face near his so that he focused on her.

"I've stung you as much as I dare for now," she told him. "When this is over, I'll sting you to sleep and you won't hurt anymore."

"Please," the man begged. "Wait . . ."

"There's no more time, Bram. I'll sting you as soon as it's over. When T'Khotgif arrives she'll give you eggs to help you heal. It will be over soon."

"T'Khotgif!" the man shouted, straining against my hands.

"Soon, Bram." T'Gatoi glanced at me, then placed a claw against his abdomen slightly to the right of the middle, just below the last rib. There was movement on the right side—tiny, seemingly random pulsations moving his brown flesh, creating a concavity here, a convexity there, over and over until I could see the rhythm of it and knew where the next pulse would be.

Lomas's entire body stiffened under T'Gatoi's claw, though she merely rested it against him as she wound the rear section of her body around his legs. He might break my grip, but he would not break hers. He wept helplessly as she used his pants to tie his hands, then pushed his hands above his head so that I could kneel on the cloth between them and pin them in place. She rolled up his shirt and gave it to him to bite down on.

And she opened him.

His body convulsed with the first cut. He almost tore himself away from me. The sounds he made . . . I had never heard such sounds come from anything human. T'Gatoi seemed to pay no attention as she lengthened and deepened the cut, now and then pausing to lick away blood. His blood vessels contracted, reacting to the chemistry of her saliva, and the bleeding slowed.

I felt as though I were helping her torture him, helping her consume him. I knew I would vomit soon, didn't know why I hadn't already. I couldn't possibly last until she was finished.

She found the first grub. It was fat and deep red with his blood—both inside and out. It had already eaten its own egg case, but apparently had not yet begun to eat its host. At this stage, it would eat any flesh except its mother's. Let alone, it would have gone on excreting the poisons that had both sickened and alerted Lomas. Eventually it would have begun to eat. By the time it ate its way out of Lomas's flesh, Lomas would be dead or dying—and unable to take revenge on the thing that was killing him. There was always a grace period between the time the host sickened and the time the grubs began to eat him.

T'Gatoi picked up the writhing grub carefully and looked at it, somehow ignoring the terrible groans of the man.

Abruptly, the man lost consciousness.

"Good." T'Gatoi looked down at him. "I wish you Terrans could do that at will." She felt nothing. And the thing she held . . .

It was limbless and boneless at this stage, perhaps fifteen centimeters long and two thick, blind and slimy with blood. It was like a large worm. T'Gatoi put it into the belly of the achti, and it began at once to burrow. It would stay there and eat as long as there was anything to eat.

Probing through Lomas's flesh, she found two more, one of them smaller and more vigorous. "A male!" she said happily. He would be dead before I would. He would be through his metamorphosis and screwing everything that would hold still before his sisters even had limbs. He was the only one to make a serious effort to bite T'Gatoi as she placed him in the achti.

Paler worms oozed to visibility in Lomas's flesh. I closed my eyes. It was worse than finding something dead, rotting, and filled with tiny animal grubs. And it was far worse than any drawing or diagram.

"Ah, there are more," T'Gatoi said, plucking out two long, thick grubs. "You may have to kill another animal, Gan. Everything lives inside you Terrans."

I had been told all my life that this was a good and necessary thing Tlic and Terran did together—a kind of birth. I had believed it until now. I knew birth was painful and bloody, no matter what. But this was something else, something worse. And I wasn't ready to see it. Maybe I never would be. Yet I couldn't *not* see it. Closing my eyes didn't help.

T'Gatoi found a grub still eating its egg case. The remains of the case were still wired into a blood vessel by their own little tube or hook or whatever. That was the way the grubs were anchored and the way they fed. They took only blood until they were ready to emerge. Then they ate their stretched, elastic egg cases. Then they ate their hosts.

T'Gatoi bit away the egg case, licked away the blood. Did she like the taste? Did childhood habits die hard—or not die at all?

The whole procedure was wrong, alien. I wouldn't have thought anything about her could seem alien to me.

"One more, I think," she said. "Perhaps two. A good family. In a host animal these days, we would be happy to find one or two alive." She glanced at me. "Go outside, Gan, and empty your stomach. Go now while the man is unconscious."

I staggered out, barely made it. Beneath the tree just beyond the front door, I vomited until there was nothing left to bring up. Finally, I stood shaking, tears streaming down my face. I did not know why I was crying, but I could not stop. I went farther from the house to avoid being seen. Every time I closed my eyes I saw red worms crawling over redder human flesh.

There was a car coming toward the house. Since Terrans were forbidden motorized vehicles except for certain farm equipment, I knew this must be Lomas's Tlic with Qui and perhaps a Terran doctor. I wiped my face on my shirt, struggled for control.

"Gan," Qui called as the car stopped. "What happened?" He crawled out of the low, round, Tlic-convenient car door. Another Terran crawled out the other side and went into the house without speaking to me. The doctor. With his help and a few eggs, Lomas might make it.

"T'Khotgif Teh?" I said.

The Tlic driver surged out of her car, reared up half her length before me. She was paler and smaller than T'Gatoi—probably born from the body of an animal. Tlic from Terran bodies were always larger as well as more numerous.

"Six young," I told her. "Maybe seven, all alive. At least one male."

"Lomas?" she said harshly. I liked her for the question and the concern in her voice when she asked it. The last coherent thing he had said was her name.

"He's alive," I said.

She surged away to the house without another word.

"She's been sick," my brother said, watching her go. "When I called, I could hear people telling her she wasn't well enough to go out even for this."

I said nothing. I had extended courtesy to the Tlic. Now I didn't want to talk to anyone. I hoped he would go in—out of curiosity if nothing else.

"Finally found out more than you wanted to know, eh?"

I looked at him.

"Don't give me one of *her* looks," he said. "You're not her. You're just her property."

One of her looks. Had I picked up even an ability to imitate her expressions?

"What'd you do, puke?" He sniffed the air. "So now you know what you're in for."

I walked away from him. He and I had been close when we were kids. He would let me follow him around when I was home and sometimes T'Gatoi would let me bring him along when she took me into the city. But something had happened when he reached adolescence. I never knew what. He began keeping out of T'Gatoi's way. Then he began running away—until he realized there was no "away." Not in the Preserve. Certainly not outside. After that he concentrated on getting his share of every egg that came into the house and on looking out for me in a way that made me all but hate him—a way that clearly said, as long as I was all right, he was safe from the Tlic.

"How was it, really?" he demanded, following me.

"I killed an achti. The young ate it."

"You didn't run out of the house and puke because they ate an achti."

"I had . . . never seen a person cut open before." That was true, and enough for him to know. I couldn't talk about the other. Not with him.

"Oh," he said. He glanced at me as though he wanted to say more, but he kept quiet.

We walked, not really headed anywhere. Toward the back, toward the cages, toward the fields.

"Did he say anything?" Qui asked. "Lomas, I mean."

Who else would he mean? "He said 'T'Khotgif.' "

Qui shuddered. "If she had done that to me, she'd be the last person I'd call for."

"You'd call for her. Her sting would ease your pain without killing the grubs in you."

"You think I'd care if they died?"

No. Of course he wouldn't. Would I?

"Shit!" He drew a deep breath. "I've seen what they do. You think this thing with Lomas was bad? It was nothing."

I didn't argue. He didn't know what he was talking about.

"I saw them eat a man," he said.

I turned to face him. "You're lying!"

"I saw them eat a man." He paused. "It was when I was little. I had been to the Hartmund house and I was on my way home. Halfway here, I saw a man and a Tlic and the man was N'Tlic. The ground was hilly. I was able to hide from them and watch. The Tlic wouldn't open the man because she had nothing to feed the grubs. The man couldn't go any farther and there were no houses around. He was in so much pain he told her to kill him. He begged her to kill him. Finally, she did. She cut his throat. One swipe of one claw. I saw the grubs eat their way out, then burrow in again, still eating."

His words made me see Lomas's flesh again, parasitized, crawling. "Why didn't you tell me that?" I whispered.

He looked startled, as though he'd forgotten I was listening. "I don't know."

"You started to run away not long after that, didn't you?"

"Yeah. Stupid. Running inside the Preserve. Running in a cage."

I shook my head, said what I should have said to him long ago. "She wouldn't take you, Qui. You don't have to worry."

"She would . . . if anything happened to you."

"No. She'd take Xuan Hoa. Hoa . . . wants it." She wouldn't if she had stayed to watch Lomas.

"They don't take women," he said with contempt.

"They do sometimes." I glanced at him. "Actually, they prefer women. You should be around them when they talk among themselves. They say women have more body fat to protect the grubs. But they usually take men to leave the women free to bear their own young."

"To provide the next generation of host animals," he said, switching from contempt to bitterness.

"It's more than that!" I countered. Was it?

"If it were going to happen to me, I'd want to believe it was more, too."

"It *is* more!" I felt like a kid. Stupid argument.

"Did you think so while T'Gatoi was picking worms out of that guy's guts?"

"It's not supposed to happen that way."

"Sure it is. You weren't supposed to see it, that's all. And his Tlic was supposed to do it. She could sting him unconscious and the operation wouldn't have been as painful. But she'd still open him, pick out the grubs, and if she missed even one, it would poison him and eat him from the inside out."

There was actually a time when my mother told me to show respect for Qui because he was my older brother. I walked away, hating him. In his way, he was gloating. He was safe and I wasn't. I could have hit him, but I didn't think I would be able to stand it when he refused to hit back, when he looked at me with contempt and pity.

He wouldn't let me get away. Longer legged, he swung ahead of me and made me feel as though I were following him.

"I'm sorry," he said.

I strode on, sick and furious.

"Look, it probably won't be that bad with you. T'Gatoi likes you. She'll be careful."

I turned back toward the house, almost running from him.

"Has she done it to you yet?" he asked, keeping up easily. "I mean, you're about the right age for implantation. Has she—"

I hit him. I didn't know I was going to do it, but I think I meant to kill him. If he hadn't been bigger and stronger, I think I would have.

He tried to hold me off, but in the end, he had to defend himself. He only hit me a couple of times. That was plenty. I don't remember going down, but when I came to, he was gone. It was worth the pain to be rid of him.

I got up and walked slowly toward the house. The back was dark. No one was in the kitchen. My mother and sisters were sleeping in their bedrooms—or pretending to.

Once I was in the kitchen, I could hear voices—Tlic and Terran from the next room. I couldn't make out what they were saying—didn't want to make it out.

I sat down at my mother's table, waiting for quiet. The table was smooth and worn, heavy and well-crafted. My father had made it for her just before he died. I remembered hanging around underfoot when he built it. He didn't mind. Now I sat leaning on it, missing him. I could have talked to him. He had done it three times in his long life. Three clutches of eggs, three times being opened and sewed up. How had he done it? How did anyone do it?

I got up, took the rifle from its hiding place, and sat down again with it. It needed cleaning, oiling.

All I did was load it.

"Gan?"

She made a lot of little clicking sounds when she walked on bare floor, each limb clicking in succession as it touched down. Waves of little clicks.

She came to the table, raised the front half of her body above it, and surged onto it. Sometimes she moved so smoothly she seemed to flow like water itself. She coiled herself into a small hill in the middle of the table and looked at me.

"That was bad," she said softly. "You should not have seen it. It need not be that way."

"I know."

"T'Khotgif—Ch'Khotgif now—she will die of her disease. She will not live to raise her children. But her sister will provide for them, and for Bram Lomas." Sterile sister. One fertile female in every lot. One to keep the family going. That sister owed Lomas more than she could ever repay.

"He'll live then?"

"Yes."

"I wonder if he would do it again."

"No one would ask him to do that again."

I looked into the yellow eyes, wondering how much I saw and understood there, and how much I only imagined. "No one ever asks us," I said. "You never asked me."

She moved her head slightly. "What's the matter with your face?"

"Nothing. Nothing important." Human eyes probably wouldn't have noticed the swelling in the darkness. The only light was from one of the moons, shining through a window across the room.

"Did you use the rifle to shoot the achti?"

"Yes."

"And do you mean to use it to shoot me?"

I stared at her, outlined in moonlight—coiled, graceful body. "What does Terran blood taste like to you?"

She said nothing.

"What are you?" I whispered. "What are we to you?"

She lay still, rested her head on her topmost coil. "You know me as no other does," she said softly. "You must decide."

"That's what happened to my face," I told her.

"What?"

"Qui goaded me into deciding to do something. It didn't turn out very well." I moved the gun slightly, brought the barrel up diagonally under my own chin. "At least it was a decision I made."

"As this will be."

"Ask me, Gatoi."

"For my children's lives?"

She would say something like that. She knew how to manipulate people, Terran and Tlic. But not this time.

"I don't want to be a host animal," I said. "Not even yours."

It took her a long time to answer. "We use almost no host animals these days," she said. "You know that."

"You use us."

"We do. We wait long years for you and teach you and join our families to yours." She moved restlessly. "You know you aren't animals to us."

I stared at her, saying nothing.

"The animals we once used began killing most of our eggs after implantation long before your ancestors arrived," she said softly. "You know these things, Gan. Because your people arrived, we are relearning what it means to be a healthy, thriving people. And your ancestors, fleeing from their homeworld, from their own kind who would have killed or enslaved them—they survived because of us. We saw them as people and gave them the Preserve when they still tried to kill us as worms."

At the word "worms" I jumped. I couldn't help it, and she couldn't help noticing it.

"I see," she said quietly. "Would you really rather die than bear my young, Gan?"

I didn't answer.

"Shall I go to Xuan Hoa?"

"Yes!" Hoa wanted it. Let her have it. She hadn't had to watch Lomas. She'd be proud. . . . Not terrified.

T'Gatoi flowed off the table onto the floor, startling me almost too much.

"I'll sleep in Hoa's room tonight," she said. "And sometime tonight or in the morning, I'll tell her."

This was going too fast. My sister. Hoa had had almost as much to do with raising me as my mother. I was still close to her—not like Qui. She could want T'Gatoi and still love me.

"Wait! Gatoi!"

She looked back, then raised nearly half her length off the floor and turned it to face me. "These are adult things, Gan. This is my life, my family!"

"But she's . . . my sister."

"I have done what you demanded. I have asked you!"

"But—"

"It will be easier for Hoa. She has always expected to carry other lives inside her."

Human lives. Human young who would someday drink at her breasts, not at her veins.

I shook my head. "Don't do it to her, Gatoi." I was not Qui. It seemed I could become him, though, with no effort at all. I could make Xuan Hoa my shield. Would it be easier to know that red worms were growing in her flesh instead of mine?

"Don't do it to Hoa," I repeated.

She stared at me, utterly still.

I looked away, then back at her. "Do it to me."

I lowered the gun from my throat and she leaned forward to take it.

"No," I told her.

"It's the law," she said.

"Leave it for the family. One of them might use it to save my life someday."

She grasped the rifle barrel, but I wouldn't let go. I was pulled into a standing position over her.

"Leave it here!" I repeated. "If we're not your animals, if these are adult things, accept the risk. There is risk, Gatoi, in dealing with a partner."

It was clearly hard for her to let go of the rifle. A shudder went through her and she made a hissing sound of distress. It occurred to me that she was afraid. She was old enough to have seen what guns could do to people. Now her young and this gun would be together in the same house. She did not know about our other guns. In this dispute, they did not matter.

"I will implant the first egg tonight," she said as I put the gun away. "Do you hear, Gan?"

Why else had I been given a whole egg to eat while the rest of the family was left to share one? Why else had my mother kept looking at me as though I were going away from her, going where she could not follow? Did T'Gatoi imagine I hadn't known?

"I hear."

"Now!" I let her push me out of the kitchen, then walked ahead of her toward my bedroom. The sudden urgency in her voice sounded real. "You would have done it to Hoa tonight!" I accused.

"I must do it to someone tonight."

I stopped in spite of her urgency and stood in her way. "Don't you care who?"

She flowed around me and into my bedroom. I found her waiting on the couch we shared. There was nothing in Hoa's room that she could have used. She would have done it to Hoa on the floor. The thought of her doing it to Hoa at all disturbed me in a different way now, and I was suddenly angry.

Yet I undressed and lay down beside her. I knew what to do, what to expect. I had been told all my life. I felt the familiar sting, narcotic, mildly pleasant. Then the blind probing of her ovipositor. The puncture was painless, easy. So easy going in. She undulated slowly against me, her muscles forcing the egg from her body into mine. I held on to a pair of her limbs until I remembered Lomas holding her that way. Then I let go, moved inadvertently, and hurt her. She gave a low cry of pain and I expected to be caged at once within her limbs. When I wasn't, I held on to her again, feeling oddly ashamed.

"I'm sorry," I whispered.

She rubbed my shoulders with four of her limbs.

"Do you care?" I asked. "Do you care that it's me?"

She did not answer for some time. Finally, "You were the one making choices tonight, Gan. I made mine long ago."

"Would you have gone to Hoa?"

"Yes. How could I put my children into the care of one who hates them?"

"It wasn't . . . hate."

"I know what it was."

"I was afraid."

Silence.

"I still am." I could admit it to her here, now.

"But you came to me . . . to save Hoa."

"Yes." I leaned my forehead against her. She was cool velvet, deceptively soft. "And to keep you for myself," I said. It was so. I didn't understand it, but it was so.

She made a soft hum of contentment. "I couldn't believe I had made such a mistake with you," she said. "I chose you. I believed you had grown to choose me."

"I had, but . . ."

"Lomas."

"Yes."

"I have never known a Terran to see a birth and take it well. Qui has seen one, hasn't he?"

"Yes."

"Terrans should be protected from seeing."

I didn't like the sound of that—and I doubted that it was possible. "Not protected," I said. "Shown. Shown when we're young kids, and shown more than once. Gatoi, no Terran ever sees a birth that goes right. All we see is N'Tlic—pain and terror and maybe death."

She looked down at me. "It is a private thing. It has always been a private thing."

Her tone kept me from insisting—that and the knowledge that if she changed her mind, I might be the first public example. But I had planted the thought in her mind. Chances were it would grow, and eventually she would experiment.

"You won't see it again," she said. "I don't want you thinking any more about shooting me."

The small amount of fluid that came into me with her egg relaxed me as completely as a sterile egg would have, so that I could remember the rifle in my hands and my feelings of fear and revulsion, anger and despair. I could remember the feelings without reviving them. I could talk about them.

"I wouldn't have shot you," I said. "Not you." She had been taken from my father's flesh when he was my age.

"You could have," she insisted.

"Not you." She stood between us and her own people, protecting, interweaving.

"Would you have destroyed yourself?"

I moved carefully, uncomfortably. "I could have done that. I nearly did. That's Qui's 'away.' I wonder if he knows."

"What?"

I did not answer.

"You will live now."

"Yes." *Take care of her,* my mother used to say. Yes.

"I'm healthy and young," she said. "I won't leave you as Lomas was left—alone, N'Tlic. I'll take care of you."

Fears

PAMELA SARGENT

I was on my way back to Sam's when a couple of boys tried to run me off the road, banging my fender a little before they sped on, looking for another target. My throat tightened and my chest heaved as I wiped my face with a handkerchief. The boys had clearly stripped their car to the minimum, ditching all their safety equipment, knowing that the highway patrol was unlikely to stop them; the police had other things to worry about.

The car's harness held me; its dashboard lights flickered. As I waited for it to steer me back onto the road, the engine hummed, choked, and died. I switched over to manual; the engine was silent.

I felt numb. I had prepared myself for my rare journeys into the world outside my refuge, working to perfect my disguise. My angular, coarse-featured face stared back at me from the mirror overhead as I wondered if I could still pass. I had cut my hair recently, my chest was still as flat as a boy's, and the slightly padded shoulders of my suit imparted a bit of extra bulk. I had always been taken for a man before, but I had never done more than visit a few out-of-the-way, dimly lighted stores where the proprietors looked closely only at cards or cash.

I couldn't wait there risking a meeting with the highway patrol. The police might look a bit too carefully at my papers and administer a body search on general principles. Stray women had been picked up before, and the rewards for such a discovery were great; I imagined uniformed men groping at my groin, and shuddered. My disguise would get a real test. I took a deep breath, released the harness, then got out of the car.

The garage was half a mile away. I made it there without enduring more than a few honks from passing cars.

The mechanic listened to my husky voice as I described my problem, glanced at my card, took my keys, then left in his tow truck, accompanied by a younger mechanic. I sat in his office, out of sight of the other men, trying not to let my fear push me into panic. The car might have to remain here for some time; I would have to find a place to stay. The mechanic might even offer me a lift home, and I didn't want to risk that. Sam might be a bit too talkative in the man's presence; the mechanic might wonder about someone who lived in such an inaccessible spot. My hands were shaking; I thrust them into my pockets.

I started when the mechanic returned to his office, then smiled nervously as he assured me that the car would be ready in a few hours; a component had failed, he had another like it in the shop, no problem. He named a price that seemed excessive; I was about to object, worried that argument might only provoke him, then worried still more that I would look odd if I didn't dicker with him. I settled for frowning as he slipped my card into his terminal, then handed it back to me.

"No sense hanging around here." He waved one beefy hand at the door. "You can pick up a shuttle to town out there, comes by every fifteen minutes or so."

I thanked him and went outside, trying to decide what to do. I had been successful so far; the other mechanics didn't even look at me as I walked toward the road. An entrance to the town's underground garage was just across the highway; a small glassy building with a sign saying Marcello's stood next to the entrance. I knew what service Marcello sold; I had driven by the place before. I would be safer with one of his employees, and less conspicuous if I kept moving; curiosity overcame my fear for a moment. I had made my decision.

I walked into Marcello's. One man was at a desk; three big men sat on a sofa near one of the windows, staring at the small holo screen in front of them. I went to the desk and said, "I want to hire a bodyguard."

The man behind the desk looked up; his mustache twitched. "An escort. You want an escort."

"Call it whatever you like."

"For how long?"

"About three or four hours."

"For what purpose?"

"Just a walk through town, maybe a stop for a drink. I haven't been to town for a while, thought I might need some company."

His brown eyes narrowed. I had said too much; I didn't have to explain myself to him. "Card."

I got out my card. He slipped it into his outlet and peered at the screen while I tried to keep from fidgeting, expecting the machine to spit out the card even after all this time. He returned the card. "You'll get your receipt when you come back." He waved a hand at the men on the sofa. "I got three available. Take your pick."

The man on my right had a lean, mean face; the one on the left was sleepy-eyed. "The middle guy."

"Ellis."

The middle man stood up and walked over to us. He was a tall black man dressed in a brown suit; he looked me over, and I forced myself to gaze directly at him while the man at the desk rummaged in a drawer and took out a weapon and holster, handing them to my escort.

"Ellis Gerard," the black man said, thrusting out a hand.

"Joe Segor." I took his hand; he gripped mine just long enough to show his strength, then let go. The two men on the sofa watched us as we left, as if resenting my choice, then turned back to the screen.

We caught a shuttle into town. A few old men sat near the front of the bus under the watchful eyes of the guard; five boys got on behind us, laughing, but a look from the guard quieted them. I told myself again that I would be safe with Ellis.

"Where to?" Ellis said as we sat down. "A visit to a pretty boy? Guys sometimes want escorts for that."

"No, just around. It's a nice day—we could sit in the park for a while."

"I don't know if that's such a good idea, Mr. Segor."

"Joe."

"Those cross-dressers hang out a lot there now. I don't like it. They go there with their friends and it just causes trouble—it's a bad element. You look at them wrong, and then you've got a fight. It ought to be against the law."

"What?"

"Dressing like a woman. Looking like what you're not." He glanced at me. I looked away, my jaw tightening.

We were in town now, moving toward the shuttle's first stop. "Hey!" one of the boys behind us shouted. "Look!" Feet shuffled along the aisle; the boys had rushed to the right side of the bus and were kneeling on the seats, hands pressed against the window; even the guard had turned. Ellis and I got up and changed seats, looking out at what had drawn the boys' attention.

A car was pulling into a spot in front of a store. Our driver put down his magazine and slowed the bus manually; he obviously knew his passengers wanted a look. Cars were not allowed in town unless a woman was riding in one; even I knew that. We waited. The bus stopped; a group of young men standing outside the store watched the car.

"Come on, get out," a boy behind me said. "Get out of the car."

Two men got out first. One of them yelled at the loiterers, who moved down the street before gathering under a lamppost. Another man opened the back door, then held out his hand.

She seemed to float out of the car; her long pink robe swirled around her ankles as she stood. Her hair was covered by a long, white scarf. My face grew warm with embarrassment and shame. I caught a glimpse of black eyebrows and white skin before her bodyguards surrounded her and led her into the store.

The driver pushed a button and picked up his magazine again; the bus moved on. "Think she was real?" one of the boys asked.

"I don't know," another replied.

"Bet she wasn't. Nobody would let a real woman go into a store like that. If I had a girl, I'd never let her go anywhere."

"If I had a trans, I'd never let her go anywhere."

"Those trans guys—they got it made." The boys scrambled toward the back of the bus.

"Definitely a trans," Ellis said to me. "I can tell. She's got a mannish kind of face."

I said, "You could hardly see her face."

"I saw enough. And she was too tall." He sighed. "That's the life. A little bit of cutting and trimming and some implants, and there you are—you don't have to lift a finger. You're legally female."

"It isn't just a little bit of cutting—it's major surgery."

"Yeah. Well, I couldn't have been a transsexual anyway, not with my body." Ellis glanced at me. "You could have been, though."

"Never wanted it."

"It's not a bad life in some ways."

"I like my freedom." My voice caught on the words.

"That's why I don't like cross-dressers. They'll dress like a woman, but they won't turn into one. It just causes trouble—you get the wrong cues."

The conversation was making me uneasy; sitting so close to Ellis, hemmed in by his body and the bus's window, made me feel trapped. The man was too observant. I gritted my teeth and turned toward the window. More stores had been boarded up; we passed a brick school building with shattered windows and an empty playground. The town was declining.

We got off in the business district, where there was still a semblance of normal life. Men in suits came and went from their offices, hopped on buses, strolled toward bars for an early drink.

"It's pretty safe around here," Ellis said as we sat on a bench. The bench had been welded to the ground; it was covered with graffiti and one leg had been warped. Old newspapers lay on the sidewalk and in the gutter with other refuse. One bore a headline about the African war; another, more recent, the latest news about Bethesda's artificial womb program. The news was good; two more healthy children had been born to the project, a boy and a girl. I thought of endangered species and extinction.

A police car drove by, followed by another car with opaque windows. Ellis gazed after the car and sighed longingly, as if imagining the woman inside. "Wish I was gay," he said sadly, "but I'm not. I've tried the pretty boys, but that's not for me. I should have been a Catholic, and then I could have been a priest. I live like one anyway."

"Too many priests already. The Church can't afford any more. Anyway, you'd really be frustrated then. They can't even hear a woman's confession unless her husband or a bodyguard is with her. It's just like being a doctor. You could go nuts that way."

"I'll never make enough to afford a woman, even a trans."

"There might be more women someday," I said. "That project at Bethesda's working out."

"Maybe I should have gone on one of those expeditions. There's one they let into the Philippines, and another one's in Alaska now."

I thought of a team of searchers coming for me. If they were not dead before they reached my door, I would be; I had made sure of that. "That's a shady business, Ellis."

"That group in the Amazon actually found a tribe—killed all the men. No one'll let them keep the women for themselves, but at least they have enough money to try for one at home." Ellis frowned. "I don't know. Trouble is, a lot of guys don't miss women. They say they do, but they really don't. Ever talk to a real old-timer, one that can remember what it was like?"

"Can't say I have."

Ellis leaned back. "A lot of those guys didn't really like girls all that much. They had places they'd go to get away from them, things they'd do together. Women didn't think the same way, didn't act the same—

they never did as much as men did." He shaded his eyes for a moment. "I don't know—sometimes one of those old men'll tell you the world was gentler then, or prettier, but I don't know if that's true. Anyway, a lot of those women must have agreed with the men. Look what happened—as soon as you had that pill that could make you sure you had a boy if you wanted, or a girl, most of them started having boys, so they must have thought, deep down, that boys were better."

Another police car drove past; one of the officers inside looked us over before driving on. "Take a trans," Ellis said. "Oh, you might envy her a little, but no one really has any respect for her. And the only real reason for having any women around now is for insurance—somebody's got to have the kids, and we can't. But once that Bethesda project really gets going and spreads, we won't need them anymore."

"I suppose you're right."

Four young men, dressed in work shirts and pants, approached us and stared down at us silently. I thought of the boys I had once played with before what I was had made a difference, before I had been locked away. One young man glanced quickly down the street; another took a step forward. I stared back and made a fist, trying to keep my hand from shaking; Ellis sat up slowly and let his right hand fall to his waist, near his holster. We kept staring until the group turned from us and walked away.

"Anyway, you've got to analyze it." Ellis crossed his legs. "There's practical reasons for not having a lot of women around. We need more soldiers—everybody does now, with all the trouble in the world. And police, too, with crime the way it is. And women can't handle those jobs."

"Once people thought they could." My shoulder muscles were tight; I had almost said *we*.

"But they can't. Put a woman up against a man, and the man'll always win." Ellis draped an arm over the back of the bench. "And there's other reasons, too. Those guys in Washington like keeping women scarce, having their pick of the choice ones for themselves—it makes their women more valuable. And a lot of the kids'll be theirs, too, from now on. Oh, they might loan a woman out to a friend once in a while, and I suppose the womb project'll change things some, but it'll be their world eventually."

"And their genes," I said. I knew that I should change the subject, but Ellis had clearly accepted my pose. In his conversation, the ordinary talk of one man to another, the longest conversation I had had with a man for many years, I was looking for a sign, something to keep me from despairing. "How long can it go on?" I continued. "The population keeps shrinking every year—there won't be enough people soon."

"You're wrong, Joe. Machines do a lot of the work now anyway, and there used to be too many people. The only way we'll ever have more women is if someone finds out the Russians are having more, and that won't happen—they need soldiers, too. Besides, look at it this way—maybe we're doing women a favor if there aren't as many of them. Would you want to be a woman, having to be married by sixteen, not being able to go anywhere, no job until she's at least sixty-five?"

And no divorce without a husband's permission, no contraception, no higher education—all the special privileges and protections could not make up for that. "No," I said to Ellis. "I wouldn't want to be one." Yet I knew that many women had made their peace with the world as it was, extorting gifts and tokens from their men, glorying in their beauty and their pregnancies, lavishing their attention on their children and their homes, tormenting and manipulating their men with the sure knowledge that any woman could find another man—for if a woman could not get a divorce by herself, a man more powerful than her husband could force him to give her up if he wanted her himself.

I had dreamed of guerrillas, of fighting women too proud to give in, breeding strong daughters by a captive male to carry on the battle. But if there were such women, they, like me, had gone to ground. The world had been more merciful when it had drowned or strangled us at birth.

Once, when I was younger, someone had said it had been a conspiracy—develop a foolproof way to give a couple a child of the sex they wanted, and most of them would naturally choose boys. The population problem would be solved in time without having to resort to harsher methods, and a blow would be leveled at those old feminists who had demanded too much, trying to emasculate men in the process. But I didn't think it had been a conspiracy. It had simply happened, as it was bound to eventually, and the values of society had controlled behavior. After all, why shouldn't a species decide to become one sex, especially if reproduction could be severed from sexuality? People had believed men were better, and had acted on that belief. Perhaps women, given the power, would have done the same.

We retreated to a bar when the sunny weather grew cooler. Ellis steered me away from two taverns with "bad elements," and we found ourselves in the doorway of a darkened bar in which several old and middle-aged men had gathered and two pretty boys dressed in leather and silk were plying their trade.

I glanced at the newscreen as I entered; the pale letters flickered, telling me that Bob Arnoldi's last appeal had failed and that he would be executed at the end of the month. This was no surprise; Arnoldi had, after all, killed a woman, and was always under heavy guard. The letters danced on; the President's wife had given birth to her thirteenth child, a boy. The President's best friend, a California millionaire, had been at his side when the announcement was made; the millionaire's power could be gauged by the fact that he had been married three times, and that the prolific First Lady had been one of the former wives.

Ellis and I got drinks at the bar. I kept my distance from one of the pretty boys, who scowled at my short, wavy hair and nestled closer to his patron. We retreated to the shadows and sat down at one of the side tables. The tabletop was sticky; old cigar butts had been planted on a gray mound in the ashtray. I sipped my bourbon; Ellis, while on the job, was only allowed beer.

The men at the bar were watching the remaining minutes of a football game. Sports of some kind were always on holo screens in bars, according to Sam; he preferred the old pornographic films that were sometimes shown amid war coverage and an occasional boys' choir performance for the pederasts and the more culturally inclined. Ellis looked at the screen and noted that his team was losing; I commented on the team's weaknesses, as I knew I was expected to do.

Ellis rested his elbows on the table. "This all you came for? Just to walk around and then have a drink?"

"That's it. I'm just waiting for my car." I tried to sound nonchalant. "It should be fixed soon."

"Doesn't seem like enough reason to hire an escort."

"Come on, Ellis. Guys like me would have trouble without escorts, especially if we don't know the territory that well."

"True. You don't look that strong." He peered at me a little too intently. "Still, unless you were looking for action, or going to places with a bad element, or waiting for the gangs to come out at night, you could get along. It's in your attitude—you have to look like you can take care of yourself. I've seen guys smaller than you I wouldn't want to fight."

"I like to be safe."

He watched me, as if expecting me to say more.

"Actually, I don't need an escort as much as I like to have a companion—somebody to talk to. I don't see that many people."

"It's your money."

The game had ended and was being subjected to loud analysis by the men at the bar; their voices suddenly died. A man behind me sucked in his breath as the clear voice of a woman filled the room.

I looked at the holo. Rena Swanson was reciting the news, leading with the Arnoldi story, following that with the announcement of the President's new son. Her aged, wrinkled face hovered over us; her kind brown eyes promised us comfort. Her motherly presence had made her program one of the most popular on the holo. The men around me sat silently, faces upturned, worshiping her—the Woman, the Other, someone for whom part of them still yearned.

We got back to Marcello's just before dark. As we approached the door, Ellis suddenly clutched my shoulder. "Wait a minute, Joe."

I didn't move at first; then I reached out and carefully pushed his arm away. My shoulders hurt and a tension headache, building all day, had finally taken hold, its claws gripping my temples. "Don't touch me." I had been about to plead, but caught myself in time; attitude, as Ellis had told me himself, was important.

"There's something about you. I can't figure you out."

"Don't try." I kept my voice steady. "You wouldn't want me to complain to your boss, would you? He might not hire you again. Escorts have to be trusted."

He was very quiet. I couldn't see his dark face clearly in the fading light, but I could sense that he was weighing the worth of a confrontation with me against the chance of losing his job. My face was hot, my mouth dry. I had spent too much time with him, given him too many chances to notice subtly wrong gestures. I continued to stare directly at him, wondering if his greed would win out over practicality.

"Okay," he said at last, and opened the door.

I was charged more than I had expected to pay, but did not argue about the fee. I pressed a few coins on Ellis; he took them while refusing to look at me. He knows, I thought then; he knows and he's letting me go. But I might have imagined that, seeing kindness where there was none.

I took a roundabout route back to Sam's, checking to make sure no one had followed me, then pulled off the road to change the car's license plate, concealing my own under my shirt.

Sam's store stood at the end of the road, near the foot of my mountain. Near the store, a small log cabin had been built. I had staked my claim to most of the mountain, buying up the land to make sure it remained undeveloped, but the outside world was already moving closer.

Sam was sitting behind the counter, drumming his fingers as music blared. I cleared my throat and said hello.

"Joe?" His watery blue eyes squinted. "You're late, boy."

"Had to get your car fixed. Don't worry—I paid for it already. Thanks for letting me rent it again." I counted out my coins and pressed them into his dry, leathery hand.

"Any time, son." The old man held up the coins, peering at each one with his weak eyes. "Don't look like you'll get home tonight. You can use the sofa there—I'll get you a nightshirt."

"I'll sleep in my clothes." I gave him an extra coin.

He locked up, hobbled toward his bedroom door, then turned. "Get into town at all?"

"No." I paused. "Tell me something, Sam. You're old enough to remember. What was it really like before?" I had never asked him in all the years I had known him, avoiding intimacy of any kind, but suddenly I wanted to know.

"I'll tell you, Joe." He leaned against the doorway. "It wasn't all that different. A little softer around the edges, maybe, quieter, not as mean, but it wasn't all that different. Men always ran everything. Some say they didn't, but they had all the real power—sometimes they'd dole a little of it out to the girls, that's all. Now we don't have to anymore."

I had been climbing up the mountain for most of the morning, and had left the trail, arriving at my decoy house before noon. Even Sam believed that the cabin in the clearing was my dwelling. I tried the door, saw that it was still locked, then continued on my way.

My home was farther up the slope, just out of sight of the cabin. I approached my front door, which was almost invisible near the ground; the rest of the house was concealed under slabs of rock and piles of deadwood. I stood still, letting a hidden camera lens get a good look at me. The door swung open.

"Thank God you're back," Julia said as she pulled me inside and closed the door. "I was so worried. I thought you'd been caught and they were coming for me."

"It's all right. I had some trouble with Sam's car, that's all."

She looked up at me; the lines around her mouth deepened. "I wish you wouldn't go." I took off the pack loaded with the tools and supplies unavailable at Sam's store. Julia glanced at the pack resentfully. "It isn't worth it."

"You're probably right." I was about to tell her of my own trip into town, but decided to wait until later.

We went into the kitchen. Her hips were wide under her pants; her large breasts bounced as she walked. Her face was still pretty, even after all the years of hiding, her lashes thick and curly, her mouth delicate. Julia could not travel in the world as it was; no clothing, no disguise, could hide her.

I took off my jacket and sat down, taking out my card, and my papers. My father had given them to me—the false name, the misleading address, the identification of a male—after I had pleaded for my own life. He had built my hideaway; he had risked everything for me. Give the world a choice, he had said, and women will be the minority, maybe even die out completely; perhaps we can only love those like ourselves. He had looked hard as he said it, and then he had patted me on the head, sighing as though he regretted the choice. Maybe he had. He had chosen to have a daughter, after all.

I remembered his words. "Who knows?" he had asked. "What is it that made us two kinds who have to work together to get the next batch going? Oh, I know about evolution, but it didn't have to be that way, or any way. It's curious."

"It can't last," Julia said, and I did not know if she meant the world, or our escape from the world.

There would be no Eves in their Eden, I thought. The visit to town had brought it all home to me. We all die, but we go with a conviction about the future; my extinction would not be merely personal. Only traces of the feminine would linger—an occasional expression, a posture, a feeling—in the flat-breasted male form. Love would express itself in fruitless unions, divorced from reproduction; human affections are flexible.

I sat in my home, in my prison, treasuring the small freedom I had, the gift of a man, as it seemed such freedom had always been for those like me, and wondered again if it could have been otherwise.

Webrider

JAYGE CARR

The Eternal Second ended, and once again I had survived.

There was a reception committee at the terminus. Not for me, for what I carried.

"Left thigh," I said, as a dozen anxious-eyed humans converged on me before I could take a second step away from the terminus out of which I had just emerged. I turned so that my left side faced them, and three banged into each other to kneel. I pressed the under-the-skin control at my waist, and my left thigh split neatly and painlessly open. Impatient fingers probed the organi-synthetic-lined cavity revealed. What they wanted was there, of course; the thigh carry is *safe*, if blighted uncomfortable for the carrier.

If Whatever-they-wanted had been smaller, I'd've used my mouth. I'm one of those who can keep their mouths shut while riding.

Then they had the four unbreakable vials out and were hastening away with them. What was left of the reception committee was shaking my hands and trying to shove beakers full of unknown swizzles and platters of equally exotic eatments at me, while gabbling out thank-yous at a kilometer-a-second rate.

I'm left-handed, so it was my right arm I stuck out. "*High*-nutri. Now." My third and fourth words on this world I had never seen before and would probably never see again once I'd been called off of it.

They'd been briefed. A medico—a short but swishious fem with come-hither-and-enjoy eyes—clamped a dingus of a type I'd never seen before around my arm. I felt something physically digging in, invading my body-integral space to insert the nutri. But primitive as the method was, it worked *fast*. I could feel the dizziness wearing off, a contented glow spreading outward from my arm.

"Thanks," I told her. "Good stuff."

"Any time, honored Webrider. I'm Medico Miyoshi Alnasr. If, during your stay on our world, you should again require my services"—she pressed a head-only mini-holo of herself, no bigger than my thumbnail, against the back of my wrist, where it adhered neatly—"just peel the outer layer to activate the summoner. I answer," her voice dropped, "twenty-eight hours a day. . . ."

Groupie, I thought, but I didn't jerk off the summoner. Odds were I would need her professional services at some point; turista is a chronic disease among webriders. But as for anything else . . . no mistaking the look in her eyes, in all their eyes. Until what I carried did what they needed it to do, I could have asked for half their world—and gotten it.

There was more in her eyes, though. An avidity I saw far too often. This one liked the glamor and notoriety of succoring a webrider, the more the better—and the how of it didn't matter a rotted bean to her.

Webriders learn to live with that, and the envy. Webriders are never allowed to forget that they are the true elite, those very, very few who can step in a terminus on one world and step out—alive!—on another. For the rest, it can only be slower-than-light wombships, taking months and years—even at the compressed time of relativistic velocity—from one world to another.

We have not only the freedom of the stars, but the unspeakable glory of riding the web. The Eternal Second. The ultimate experience.

Webriding. Flowing through stars, points of flame running through hands that aren't hands, the psychic You bound up in the physical You that's just a pattern sliding along the web, held together and existing only by the strength of will of the webrider. Sailing on evanescent wings of mind through the energy/matter currents of space, down one fragile strand of the web and up another. Feeling torn apart, as the pattern that is You is spread over parsecs, smeared across the stars; and yet, godlike, knowing those stars, sensing with psychic "eyes" the entire spectrum of space/time, so that the beat of the pulsars is like the universe's throbbing heart. . . .

We have our glory, and one of the prices we pay for it is the groupies.

Not that I was worried about the medico; she was one of the safe kind of groupie. The only kind the locals would and should let near a webrider. The greedy but selfish kind, wanting close but not *too* close, snatching a rubbed-off glamor. But never for a second considering risking her own precious hide for the real thing.

It's the other kind of groupie who is so dangerous, the *real* groupie. The one who will do anything to get on the web. Infinitely dangerous to a rider, to a rider's peace of mind, so necessary for safe webriding. They try to sneak up close to a rider, and then . . .

Oh, groupies are necessary. Where else would we get our recruits? But they have to be kept away from the riders, because it hurts too much, to lose someone you've grown close to. A double hurt for me, because I and my sister were once groupies ourselves. I am a rider now, but our tree lost us both. She, as like me as a holo image, is now atoms scattered across half a galaxy. I relive that loss with every would-be rider that dies—and so many of them do die.

Another price we pay. And they, the world-dwellers, try to make it up to us, forgetting that what's infinitely precious on one world may be common as oxy on another. Not that I could take any of it with me. What is desperately needed, I take in the thigh, or use the mouth carry. But for myself—never.

There are other rewards besides those which can be carried. In the crowd surrounding me, eagerly talking or humbly waiting for me to express my opinion, were at least four citizens obviously put there for me to choose from. An ultra brawn, one of the prettiest boychicks I'd ever seen, a superswishious fem that eclipsed the medico by several orders of magnitude, and an adorable nymphet. All choice, but by this world's standards. Which meant, short, broad, tailless, blue-tinted skin, and pale, almost colorless hair that grew in little tufts over every bit of exposed skin I could see—plenty!—except around eyes and mouths. I'd seen weirder, lots, and I probably looked just as odd to them, if not odder.

I'm a straight fem, myself, and the brawn seemed well endowed with what a brawn should have—his costume left little to my fertile imagination—so I wasted no time in putting a possessive hand on his arm and asking him to stick around, while I politely implied to the other three that if that was the way my tastes went, they'd certainly have been my choice.

The nymphet pouted, but the brawn was looking me up and down in a very unprofessional way, part smugness at being chosen, but mostly yum-*yum! I'm* gonna *enjoy* this!

I was no little complimented.

Mother Leaf, how that crowd around me talked and talked. A rider needs two things to restore physical/psychic energy after a ride, and I'd only had one. When my knees began to buckle, I let them. He caught me easily, and lifted me into a comfortable baby-carry, though I was a head taller than he. I wrapped my tail around his waist.

"Medico Alnasr," he called, voice shot through with worry.

"You," I said, and smiled. He got the message, prehensile tails have their uses, after all. He strode through the mob, my weight nothing, like a feeding black hole through a galaxy's heart. Which suited me just fine.

There was one odd incident. A fem—older, if wrinkles and missing tufts of hair meant what such signs usually mean—caught sight of my brawn's face and her own went pure blue. "Malachi," she hissed, but my brawn never missed stride. I shrugged mentally; relative, lover, or whatever, she'd have him back as soon as I left.

All my energies were most satisfactorily restored.

He was a pleasant conversationalist, too, easily talking about his exotic—to me—world of shallow seas and endless island chains. Not his fault, either, when a careless mention of his own family, his own sister, reminded me once again of the one I had lost. Sensing my inner withdrawal, he laughed and changed the subject, refusing to let me brood over a childhood spent in the crests of giant trees and a lost more-than-sister. Still talking, he led me out onto a transparent floored balcony, cantilevered over a crystal water lagoon, filled with living rainbows darting through equally living though grotesque mazes.

His name was (he had quickly confirmed this) Malachi; and I sensed his curiosity growing about mine. I would have told him freely, except—

I have no name.

A twig may not choose a name until he/she has pollinated or budded. (Old habits die hard; we give birth as any other humans, except always clutches of identicals. But we identify with our trees. For example, I am—or was—a twig of the tree called Tamarisk, of the 243rd generation born under Her shading leaves. But I was unbudded when I came to the web—too young—and unbudded I must stay until I die, or am thrown off the web for whatever reason, which is almost the same thing. A budding fem can't ride, and I am a rider; I must ride.

On the rolls of the web I am carried as "Twig Tamarisk of Sequoia Upper." But that is for others' convenience. I have never chosen a name for myself, now I never will.

I told him to call me "Twig" and he looked me up and down and stifled laughter. I supposed to one as broad as he, I did look like a walking twig.

He gestured upward, that I might admire the gauzy dayring while he controlled his face. There was a rustle behind us; I caught my lip. We were supposed to be alone, but there are fanatics on many worlds. Twisted minds. Haters, who strike out at the handiest—or most prominent—targets.

I said nothing. Malachi could have been in on it, whatever it was.

I simply moved a little away, as though to follow better Malachi's pointing finger. Until he heard the sounds, too—

The intruder hadn't a chance. Unarmed, the unfilled muscles and flesh of a youthful growth spurt, he was surprised by Malachi's savage attack.

In seconds, Malachi had his opponent facedown on the deck, hands caught behind his back, and was looking about for something to tie his wrists together with. The stranger squirmed desperately but futilely, until he managed to twist his head around so that his gaze met mine, his face younger even than the still growing body, blue-rimmed eyes rawly swollen, the irises scarcely darker than the blue-tinted whites. "Webrider, *please*," he begged.

I knew the look in those eyes, all webriders see it over and over.

"Let him up, Malachi."

"But he shouldn't be here. He may have come to attack—" Which showed that some on this world had heard certain tales, too.

"No, Malachi, he's a groupie. Aren't you, bud?"

Sullenly. "I don't know what a groupie is."

"Do you want to ride the web yourself—or just hear about other worlds and webriding?"

Each tuft of his hair was tied with a different colored ribbon. His mouth dropped open, revealing black (painted?) teeth—and I knew I had guessed right. "How did you know—"

I laughed. "Did you think you were the only one, then?" I stretched out one hand to Malachi, the other to the boy, to help them to their feet. "Come on, relax, get comfortable. What's your—" Out of old habit I started to say tree, but remembered in time. "—name, bud?"

Malachi let him up but continued to glare suspiciously at him; the boy glared back, sour and silent.

"Well," I perched on a railing, and a crisp breeze rippled playfully over my skin, "shall we call you Incognit, then, bud?"

"Incog—what?"

"Incognit. It means 'unknown' in one of the Austere systems' tongues. It's one of their planets, actually, that's how I heard of it. Awkward place, for a stranger, the land looks firm, but if you're fool enough to step on it, you'd sink in up to your eyebrows—or a little more. All the land—at least all near the terminus—is like that. I guess that sandy patch of yours," I gestured with my head toward the golden sweep surrounded by rippling blue, "reminded me of Incognit, put the word in my head."

"You mean," his eyes were huge, hypnotic in their intensity, "that there's a settled world with no solid land at all?"

"Affirm." I was being a fool, and knew it. But ah, the wistful adulation, the fearful hope in those shades-of-blue eyes. Surely, if I emphasized the negative strongly enough. . . . "More than one, in fact. Sink worlds like Incognit, and worlds that are covered with water. One I was on was all water, but it had so many buildings, their foundations on pilings sunk into bedrock, that you couldn't tell it unless you went down, oh, hundreds of levels. And there are worlds where there are no real boundaries at all, just a slow gradient, a gradual increase of pressure as you sink down, until you reach the core. And that's only solid if you consider ultracompressed matter, no crystalline structure at all, as solid. And there are worlds—"

"How can people live on a world like that, with no solid anywhere?"

"Floaters." I had a persistent itch between my shoulder blades, just to the left of my mane, and I swung my tail around to scratch it with the prehensile's tip. "Big ones and little ones, all with lifepods dangling beneath." I grinned, remembering. "Scared the sap out of my hosts on that world, I did. Inside, the pods could have been anywhere, except for the swaying motion. But outside—the vanes and ropes and controls reminded me of the vines and limbs of the treecrest where I was born and grew up. A little higher, of course . . . I was never on the floor of anything until I entered training. Only animals live on the rootfloor of my world, it's dark all the time, and well, I hadn't realized how I missed crestdriving and vineswinging and everything else until I hit that world. Had to stop, though; I was afraid I'd give somebody a heart attack. Quite a sight it was, great mats of those floaters all roped together; never found out what they were, the floaters. Artificial, or animals, or made from dead animals . . ."

I kept talking, trying to guess from his reactions whether he was just a listener—or a would-be rider.

I should have known, though. Anybody with nerve to break in the way he had was no mere listener.

While I talked, I hooked into webmind, that almost living totality of all information fed into all the terminuses of the web. Nobody knows why all successful riders can hook into webmind, sooner or later if not immediately. I could, from my very first ride, just by wanting to, with no more effort than remembering the way the leaves uncurled on my home treecrest every spring, or the shimmering colors of Under-the-Falls on a planet called Niagara Ultimate.

My question for webmind was a simple one: what percentage of successes this world enjoyed.

Blight! No successes, never; the training school had been closed down long ago, all native attempts at webriding made illegal. (Yet they were willing to use the web, so long as others took the risks!) A few fanatics had continued to try, despite the illegality, the guards; all had failed.

I kept talking, and eventually the groupie asked the inevitable, revealing question, "What does it feel like to ride the web?"

What does it feel like to *live*?

Only riders know.

I tried to describe the indescribable. But always with the caveat. "Most people aren't strong enough. They try, but their psychic You can't hold their pattern together, and it begins to spread and spread, thinner and thinner, until it isn't a pattern at all, atom sundered from atom, the physical body only a new current among the nebulae, undetectable by the most sensitive instruments we have . . .

"Splattering, we call it.

"Nine out of ten, bud. Remember it. Repeat it to yourself. Nine out of ten. Nine out of ten, *trained*. Worse than nine out of ten, for the untrained."

He didn't believe me. He thought I was lying. And I was, but not the way he thought. It's not nine out of ten, it's ninety-nine out of a hundred. Yet if I'd told him the truth, that less than one percent survive their first ride, he certainly wouldn't have believed me.

I had to warn him, force him to recognize the risks, the odds against him. With luck, I might discourage him entirely. If he wanted the web, badly enough, nothing I or anyone could say or do would stop him (I knew!). But at least, he would have been warned.

Or so I told myself.

The path to Blight, they say, is leaved with good intentions.

I shooed him away, finally, his taste for adventure (I prayed!) sated for a good long while.

Afterwards, the reaction set in. Until a tentative hand brushed my shoulder. "Can I help?" Harsh breathing and a dark cloud of worry at my back.

I shook my head, still staring unseeing at blue on blue vistas. Until I realized that panic was about to explode behind me. "It hurts, that's all, Malachi. But it wasn't your fault. No one can keep determined enough groupies away, no matter what security measures they use. Only—try harder, your people must try *harder*. Keep groupies away from me, Malachi. Away!"

"You've privacy now, but they'll hear and obey, once you yourself break the privacy. But"—the hand on my shoulder trembled—"I don't understand. You were—very kind, to that one youngster. Why deny others what they crave? Shutting yourself away to recuperate, that's understandable. But afterwards, a few simple words seem harmless enough—"

"Harmless!" I whirled, tail curling and uncurling in a manner that would have signaled attack-to-the-death in my home tree. "It hurts *me*, Malachi! It makes me remember, too many have died. And for *them*—don't you understand, are you blind—they want to *ride*. And for some, being close to a rider is the final encouragement. They see a rider, a successful rider, and they think they can be successful, too. So they try. And they die. They *die*, Malachi. You can't stop it entirely, no one can. But you can at least—discourage—"

He flushed blue and looked guilty as Blight. But it wasn't his fault, and he was a splendid brawn. I caught his arms, leaned my head against warm breadth of shoulder, firm with thick muscle, and sighed. "You'll never understand, will you, my solid, feet-on-the-trunk Malachi. You're happy with your life as it is, you've never been infected with a madness, wanted something so desperately you'd sell your soul, your tree, anything to have it. I know, I had it, never recovered, riders never do. But you—the joys of today, eh, brawn? Would *you* face almost certain death for the chance to become a webrider?"

He stiffened like a crestdweller bitten by a duasp, then his deep chuckles shook us both from top to toe. Until he showed me once again how joyous the joys of the present can be.

I was given the tour royale the next planetary days. My brawn Malachi disappeared as soon as we emerged from our little suite-over-the-water, but as soon as I asked for him, I got him back.

There was the Blightedest smug expression on his face, and an almost tastable current of disapproval from the others. But—I liked what I liked. If I had somehow offended against this world's mores—tough. I didn't bother to dip into webmind to search among this world's customs to see what, or if, I was doing wrong.

As many worlds as I've been to, there's always something new. A sight, a sport, and amusement. Malachi and I shared them all, sometimes he the master I the tyro, sometimes the two of us tyros together.

Yet it wasn't all lotus-eating. There are many ways a webrider, a webrider who can hook into webmind, can be useful.

Through work or play, whenever I was tired or sad or down for any reason, I could always reach behind myself to have my hand taken in a hard warm hand. Malachi was there when I needed him, never intruding unless I needed him. As though to remind me that there are everyday pleasures and everyday lives, and even some people to whom webriding is not the be-all and the end-all. I could only thank Mother Leaf for those whose lives were so filled to the brim that they didn't need the web. Live long and fully, Malachi, my sweet brawn. Live long and fully!

Oh, I was useful, my brawn an everpresent silent shadow. I knew how long it had been since they had called on web, webmind told me. They'd waited overlong, until a true almost-death emergency. I was sure they'd smile to see my back stepping into the terminus.

But I have my loyalty to web. I wanted them to be impressed with the advantages of web, and webriders. I couldn't stay too long, of course, a rider has to ride constantly to stay in tune. But I told webmind to keep me on low-priority unless there was a starprime emergency.

So I was still there when Incognit splattered.

They screamed for me, of course, but too late. I was physically away from the web, and it was all over in a second, anyway.

I knew what had happened, knew as soon as it happened, knew nothing could be done.

He'd splattered, in the Second, and that—was it.

I went, nonetheless, though it took me several standard hours to get to the terminus from where I'd been.

Besides the usual component of VIPs, technies, medicos, and curious, there was a furious female who rounded on me as I entered the outer door to the terminus hall and snarled, "Ausantr—get him!"

"I can't." I didn't know if she was mother, sister, or lover, but she was in an emotional state I wouldn't have thought these stolid heavies could achieve. She was shorter than I, but solid muscle. Her hand slammed around, and I went *up* and crashed into a wall so hard my teeth met in my lip before I crumpled down in a heap.

Six hands got in each other's way helping me up, and when I had my feet steady under me, Malachi and the female were rolling about, hands at each other's throats and snarling threats so laced with local dialect I couldn't understand them.

I wiped blood from my mouth as others managed to separate the combatants. Despite the hands holding her, she glared lasers at me. "You people—" It was sneer and curse.

"And yours. You called for a webrider. You wish the web to be kept open, the riders to ride. Over a hundred die, for each successful rider. One of those who died could have been me; I accepted the risk, so did the bud. And your people must share the responsibility, too, as long as they leave the web connected to your world."

I saw it sinking in. Then, "And it doesn't bother you . . . those hundred deaths?"

When one of them was my sister, my image, my other self?

She turned away, shoulders slumping.

"I need a medico, my lip is bleeding. It must be sealed before I try to ride."

Webmind had already told me that he hadn't made it to the first crossing, but I searched anyway, sweeping up one strand and down the next, diving at a junction and sliding up its strands, again and again.

I tried almost too long, then I was back—empty-handed.

"Remember, if you must remember, the happinesses he had, that you and he had together."

"You were only gone a second!"

The Eternal Second.

"I could have reached another Arm in that second, or gathered him back, if he were there to gather. There wasn't a flavor of another on the web." She raised her fist again—and believed. Her shoulders sagged, the fist dropped, and she walked away, out of the door, out of my life.

Malachi only waited for the high-nutri band to be placed around my arm before scooping me up and walking out with me.

After that, though his world held much to enjoy, I was only waiting for my Call.

Not that I wouldn't learn to live, in time, with Incognit's death, and my guilt. But not while I still walked his world, where every step I took reminded me that I'd slaughtered an innocent bud as surely as if I'd pushed him off a low-lying branch and watched him fall to the deadly floor below.

At last, the Call came. A nearby world to supply emergency multiprograms for a planet in a distant Arm. A short hop, and then a long, long ride. I said no good-byes, riders never do. The odds are against returning to the same world a second time. We used cats' good-byes. (I sometimes wondered which of the many animals called cats I've seen on various worlds is the cat the silent good-bye was named after.)

I would miss Malachi, though. There was more to him than the usual live-for-the-moment brawn. His life-choice mayn't've been mine, but I couldn't help admiring him, if for nothing more than the tenacity I sometimes sensed beneath the surface of bonhomie.

The terminus was warmed up, glowing as I approached. I stood, breathing deeply, one . . . three . . . and took the giant step.

I wasn't alone!

I could feel—him, Malachi!—*splattering;* and I grabbed instinctively, and clung tightly, with psychic arms I hadn't known I possessed.

Past and present merged, we had joined hearts and minds and psyches in a dozen different ways, altered each other, grown close, laughed, cried, made love; now we sailed down the web—together.

The Eternal Second, space spread out within you, galaxies spinning like diadems, beating suns like beating hearts, the itch of nebulas, the sharp tang of holes, the gentle warmth of starwombs.

He was laughing and crying and spilling out delight as sweet as a new opened cupra blossom.

We were two in one, web wrapped around us yet riding down it, an endless tightrope stretched to infinity.

Until we erupted through the terminus, two separate entities again, no longer one. He was still laughing, falling helplessly to a glitter-chrome deck, laughing, laughing, *laughing*. I wasn't much abler than he, but I was so furious I leaned over and slapped him so hard the shape of his teeth imprinted on my hand. "Don't you *ever* do that again."

Still laughing, he pulled me down and kissed me, and there it was, in his eyes, that hunger I'd seen in so many others.

So quiet he had stood, politely behind me while I told my tales, patiently listening, never interrupting—behind me so I couldn't see the greedy hunger in his eyes, too.

"You—sneak," I snarled, as soon as he let me go to breathe. "You slithering snake, you—" He laughed, and I understood, all of it. "You set the whole thing up, you planned this from the beginning, you—" His laughter was louder than a world's dying. "You—used—me!" I was really infuriated, which is no way to go on a webride. A puzzled technie was watching us, holding out the canister that would have to go in my thigh.

"You hold on to *that*—" I pointed to Malachi. "And you throw him down to the floor for the trogs to—you put him in the deepest, dryest dungeon hole you have, and don't you—"

"Webrider," he sat up, face still split by that triumphant grin, "you object because I used you to get what I always wanted. But you were willing—not willing—you expected, as a matter of right, to use *me*, or one like me, to be given whatever you wanted, whatever you asked for, just because you're a webrider. And yet you blame *me*, for using you."

I had to see the humor of it. "Is it kinder to pretend," I asked, "to arouse expectations I can't possibly fulfill? Or—do you expect riders to live celibate?"

"Never you," he blinked agreement. "As for expectations—I know the next leg of your trip is too far, too hard for a beginner. But I expect you to come back for me, as soon as you can."

"You conceited—I've had a hundred, more, better than you."

He stood, still shorter than me, still grinning. "You're not my first, either." I held still only because the medico was seaming my thigh. "You'll be back, rider. You see, I know your weakness."

"Do you?" I was already starting my deep breathing again.

"Yes, rider. I know your weakness. If you don't come back, you know I'll follow. And—your weakness—you have a conscience."

Riding angry is a good way to get splattered. I kept up my slow breathing, ran through calming mantras, readying myself. I knew he was right, but I wouldn't tell him so. Let him sweat—he wasn't all *that* sure, under his camouflage of certitude—for a while.

But I'd be back, not just because of any outmoded nonsense of conscience—though that was there, Blight take him!—but because the web *owed* him now.

There had never been a successful paired ride before. Never. So paired rides had been forbidden. Then why had we succeeded now—had we simply that much more skill at riding?

Or—could it be as simple as a strong bonded *mixed* pair was necessary to balance on the web? In early days, riders shared their home-world prejudices. We have forgotten today that different once meant despicable, that pariah—the wombshippers, those condemned to the slow death of space to help hold the worlds together—was a term of contempt. In the early days of the web, before Abednego Jones and the great joining, paired riders would have been from a single world; or worse, from different worlds, but assigned together, against their own deepest inclinations, the prejudices there, at best lightly concealed. Could it be that now, with prejudices mostly forgotten with time, that all it took was a strong bonding of unlikes?

And could it be—a novice bonded to an adept—must we always and forever pay ninety-nine prices for the one?

Groupies had been kept fanatically away from riders up to now. Speaking, light contact if it couldn't be avoided, but never closeness. I wasn't the only rider with a conscience, who couldn't bear to see someone he/she had been close to, *splatter*. . . .

Now Malachi had proved it could be done. So—let the groupies have their way, let them pair, emotionally, physically, however they could with an experienced rider. Maybe . . .

Could we end that constant loneliness, the scourge of riding? I'd felt it, marrow-deep, blade-sharp, until the temptation comes, the one last glorious ride, to the ends of the universe and beyond . . . the infinite Eternal Second . . . ending in death. . . .

I risked one look back before I stepped into the terminus. He was surrounded by guards in moss green but he was smiling. . . .

He was right.

I'd be back.

For the next-to-the-last time, I rode the web—alone.

Alexia and Graham Bell

ROSALEEN LOVE

I suppose you know about the telephone by now, and you've heard a version of its story. Perhaps you think it's an invention we've had for eighty years or so.

You'll be wrong.

The telephone was invented two months ago by my brother Graham, on a cold winter's afternoon when he had nothing better to do than fiddle around with a few tin cans, a thermo-amp, some wires, and a junked teletype I found on the tip. I heard some strange noises and when he yelled "Alexia" down the hall to me, I came running, because I thought he was up to his usual dopy experiments, dropping the cats upside down off the roof to see if they'd land on their paws, that kind of thing. But it wasn't the cats this time. He'd hitched the teletype up so it spoke! I saw it myself, the first time he got it working, and it was playing away like a pianola, but sounding out the words! Words which Graham was speaking into a tin can on the other side of the room! The telephone! Which you've all heard about by now, though what you don't know is its secret. That it's only been around for two months. Truly.

Why should you believe me? When the history books tell the story differently and antique telephones fetch high prices at the market?

Let me explain. It's one of those things which was never intended to happen. It was only after the event that all kinds of things fell into place, retrospectively.

I think the responsibility for our present mess must rest firmly with great-grandfather Alexander Graham Bell. Yes, back in 1870 he'd planned to migrate from England to Canada but he missed the boat! So he stayed at the docks and caught the next ship out, to Australia. West, east, what's the difference? said great-grandfather, but he was wrong. Ever since Alexander overslept, the world of invention and discovery has taken an alternative path. Yes, the path of the telegraph and the censors and communal messenging.

Let me explain. It was only after the telephone was invented that it started influencing the past. Graham's explanation goes like this: in our day-to-day activities, we are usually working toward a future goal. I am studying to become a censor in Central Control, or I was then, all that's changed, now, and Graham is saving money so he can invent the ice-aeroplane. Okay, so we're here, in the present, and the way we perceive the future is influencing what we're doing. Equally, our present, now, is at this moment an influence on the past of our former selves and others. Graham says it's obvious to anyone with the intellect of an ant, but I don't know about the ants, they may be smarter than we give them credit for.

I can see that Graham's argument has a certain elementary logic all its own.

"Graham," I had to say, after I'd congratulated him on inventing something that worked for once, even though it was probably going to be good for nothing in the world, then that's my brother Graham, what can I expect? "Graham, what will Mother say when she sees what a mess you've made of her thermo-amp?"

Graham glared at me and made for the cat, but I grabbed it before he could upend it. Surely he knows enough about how the cat uses its tail as an inertial paddle? He doesn't have to go in for the experimental overkill! That's Graham, though, a perfectionist. A perfectionist in the creation of knowledge we could perfectly well do without.

He had all the time to experiment because he was on compo from his job as messenger boy, second class. It's not what Graham thought he was meant for in this life. So he did his best to fall down every flight of stairs between Central Message Control and the jobs he was sent on until finally he broke a few bones and got some time off to recover. Of course what he's done is make himself retrospectively redundant now we've got the telephone, and messenger boys are out of work in a big way. Yes, along the way Graham created our present crisis in unemployment.

This is how it happened. I've been a privileged witness to the scene and I have a responsibility to tell the story properly.

The telephone's great achievement is the contraction of distance. Pick up a phone and dial a number, and it doesn't matter whether the person on the other end is down the street or across the country.

Now mess around with distance, with length, and you're going to be messing around with time. That's what we've just recently come to realize. Though we should have known, I suppose. Einstein told us about it. So, basically, what has happened since Graham got busy is that the last two months have expanded out of all proportion, expanded in time that is. Two months have blown out into eighty years! It's true!

So Graham did something clever, something that worked, for once. The trouble is, it worked only too well.

At first Graham just tinkered about in the workroom. He was excited and chatty about what he was up to, but I'd heard all I wanted to know about cats and aerodynamics and the possibilities of the ice-aeroplane, so I didn't really listen as closely as I should have. "Imagine!" said Graham. "Imagine being able to speak at a distance, without a written record of the conversation! Think what it'd be like! Privacy! No censors snooping into all the details of our lives! We'll be able to talk about something without the entire teletype room knowing what's happening!"

When he said that I was listening, that's for sure, and I tried to argue back. Imagine, a world without censors reading all the messages! I took him to task on that one, I can assure you. "Graham, if someone can pick up your telephone and speak to anyone else without a record being kept, it will lead to the breakdown of law and order as we know it.

"Besides," I added, and Graham grew white about the eyes at this. Ha! I scared him properly! "If the censors get to hear about what you're doing, why, you'll do them out of a job" (and I was right about that!) "and they'll be absolutely livid!"

Graham clutched his throat with a strangled cry. "The censors? After me? No! I'm only a child! My mother loves me! How would they get to know about it?"

"Walls have ears," I said, very smugly.

"Alexia! No! Don't tell on me! I'm your brother! You'd never!"

Ha! I had him worried! But he's right. I'm not a censor-snooper. It's true, I wanted a job as a censor, but I wanted it for the pay packet and the security. I didn't have to believe all the guff they teach us about law and order. "Be careful," I said to Graham, but of course he wasn't. Once he found out what he was able to do, he just had to go ahead and do it. I didn't tell on Graham. I now know I did wrong. After all, Graham succeeded in subverting the social fabric of twentieth-century society.

I was too busy to notice, at the time. I had my work to do. I confided to my friend Greta, though. We worked together at the telegraph office.

"Mind you, if Graham's invention works, we'll soon be out of a job," I said to Greta, between the dots and the dashes.

Greta didn't believe me. "At the telegraph office? At Central Message

Control? No, Alexia, that won't happen. No one ever gets sacked from here."

"They can get you for unnatural interference with the messages," I reminded her.

Greta was shocked. "Alexia, that's never happened! No one would do that! It'd be . . . monstrous!"

"What about redundancy? They can get you on that."

I shall always remember Greta's patient reply. "Alexia," she said, "morse code and semaphore and messenger boys have been around longer than your brother Graham and his crazy ideas. How's the cat?"

"On the mend."

"The ice-aeroplane, didn't you say that was another of his latest inventions?"

"Yes, but the telephone is different! I think the telephone is going to work!"

Greta was unconvinced. "We'd be able to talk to each other without everyone in the teletype room knowing the message."

"I know, I know."

"It'll mean the end of twentieth-century society as we know it!"

"No more censors!"

"Shhh!"

"Greta, I just can't get through to Graham. I keep telling him: Graham, the telephone will lead to anarchy."

"It won't ever happen," said Greta, as she lectured me on the moral desirability of the Censored State. "If we were meant to talk to each other down wires then God would have connected us up from birth."

Graham just kept on working. "Today the passageway, tomorrow the world," he announced when I came home one evening.

I found a land-line down the passage and a telephone hook-up in my bedroom. "Graham, you've gone too far this time," I bellowed into the phone when it rang. "Get your inventions out of my room!"

"Alexia, will you step into the next room for a moment?" said Graham on the phone, polite and conscious of the historic moment.

I told him a thing or two. "Greta says you're a social menace, and I agree with her!" This is a true account of the first telephone message. You may know part of the story.

First Graham wired up the passage, then he extended the line to every room in the house. Then he wanted more. He wanted to go down the street and clear across Australia, then out into the world.

And he managed to persuade people! Never mind the censors, they soon vanished, once the capitalist entrepreneurs took over. Graham soon had them convinced.

"Gas pipes, water pipes, and telephone pipes!" said Graham, his eyes gleaming and his fingers flying. "One system, one policy, one universal service!"

"One giant monopoly! And money!" replied the capitalist entrepreneur.

"One grand telephonic system linking each farm to its neighbor, each factory to its central office, each nation to the other!" said Graham, still the visionary.

Remember what it said in the paper? "We may confidently expect that Mr. Bell will give us the means of making voice and spoken words audible through the electric wires to an ear hundreds of miles distant." It happened.

I tried to warn Graham. "There may be a few social problems."

Graham didn't pay attention. "Nothing a telephone in every house won't fix," he said.

"There may be a few economic problems," I warned.

"Show me the economic problem that money won't eliminate!" There was no stopping him.

"Contract distance, contract time!"

"Only a little bit! No one will ever notice!"

"Graham, don't do it! You are going into the unknown."

"No need to worry," said Graham, "I know perfectly well what I'm doing."

Of course, he got it wrong and we all paid the price. Poor old Greta was one of the first casualties.

"Alexia, what's wrong? My life . . . it's passing so quickly! It seems only yesterday that we worked in Central Control, and now . . . the telegraph! It's vanished!"

I tried my best to distract her. "Happy birthday darling! Fifty candles on the cake!"

"Then things changed so quickly. The telephone . . ."

"Time's a funny thing."

Greta blew at the candles. "Everything started to speed up, and things passed me by, so quickly!"

"There, there, you must have been enjoying yourself."

"It's not fair! I haven't had time to enjoy myself!"

Of course, Graham could explain it. "The distinction between past, present, and future is only an illusion," he said.

"It seems real, to me. How can yesterday become tomorrow?"

"If time contracts!"

"That's my problem! What's the solution?"

"I'm working on it," Graham muttered.

"I can't wait," said Greta, "I need it now."

I discovered that time is more than my perception of it. Time depends on the telephone.

"Nonsense!" you will say. "Time has been around for simply ages, but the telephone, why, it's only been around for a couple of years!"

"A couple of years? Did you say a couple of years? Why did you say that? I've got you, there!"

"Did I say a couple of years?" you'll say, puzzled. "Why, of course I meant a hundred years. I don't know why I said a *couple* of years, and with such conviction. It was just a silly mistake."

Aha, but silly mistakes always mean something! You're confused about the issue, admit it. There's something not quite right about the telephone, something that's hovering on the edge of your comprehension but which can't quite make the break out into your conscious mind. You know, more than you can tell.

Greta and I both noticed something happening. I've worked it out since then.

When Graham got the marketing men interested in his invention, and phones started appearing in every home, time started to speed up for most people. You know how it is, you feel that last year was only yesterday, and that the years of your life are flitting by so quickly. There is a perfectly reasonable explanation. It's because last year was only yesterday, for you, though not for me.

The censors joined the unemployed, the messenger boys went off to two world wars, and wherever the telephone spread, time accelerated in its course. It's only in countries where there are no phones that people still get full value for their lives.

I don't know why it was that Graham and I have not shared the experience. We've either been spared, or punished, for our knowledge. We have stayed outside the onward rush of time. Graham's happy. He thinks he must have invented the elixir of youth in that first experiment. Only the elixir isn't a drug made from gold, or precious herbs, or genetically engineered DNA. The elixir is a unique form of radiation which comes from standing too close to a few tin cans, a thermo-amp, old wires, and a teletype junked in a quite specific way, at a time when Jupiter is on the cusp of Uranus and the moon is in the fourth quarter.

I can't turn the clock back. I can't personally dynamite every telephone in Australia. But I see I shall have to hijack Graham and take him off to Antarctica. He'll come with me willingly enough. Where better to design the ice-aeroplane?

There's a new factor entering into the story. Graham's started to mutter about a new device to contract distance, only this time on a cosmic scale. He can do it, too. The problem with space travel, says Graham, is that space is too big. It's one thing to design a spaceship, but then it takes aeons to get anywhere in it. The stars are too far away. So Graham is working on a device to shrink the galaxy.

Instead of us reaching out to the stars, Graham will have the stars reach down to us.

This is the end. The world has suffered enough.

I, Alexia Bell, being of sound mind, must take my brother Graham to Antarctica, and there build him an ice-hangar for his ice-aeroplanes. I shall lock the door and throw the key from a high window. I make this sacrifice, for you.

Reichs-Peace

SHEILA FINCH

Greta spotted her contact as soon as she entered Walgreen's Drugstore. Though he wore a golf shirt and wide-bottom cords like every other male in Indianapolis on a Sunday in June, there was no mistaking that ramrod back, the suggestion of boots under the table. She slid into the booth across from him, setting the shoulder purse down beside her, but keeping an arm linked through the strap. She tugged at her skirt to prevent her thighs sticking to the vinyl seat. The sharp aroma of coffee burning on a hotplate mingled with the gentler scent of Ivory soap, defeating the efforts of the air conditioner to reduce all smells to anonymity.

"The humidity already exceeds last year's record for this time of year." Nervousness constricted her throat, and the phrase her Irish friend had carefully rehearsed with her came out too high-pitched.

He raised his eyes from the chocolate malt and nodded briefly. "*Gruss Gott, Fräulein Bradford.*"

He was in his sixties, with short, steel gray hair and a deep, rich baritone. She'd known what the response was to be; even so, she felt an irrational fear. But the jukebox was vibrating with the latest big-band sound, and if any of her colleagues from the Lilly labs were around, the chance was slim they'd have heard.

"I'd prefer we spoke English," she said.

"As you wish." His accent was impeccably British. "And yes, it is exceedingly humid!"

She could have told him the exact humidity factor, the barometric pressure, the temperature highs and lows, the percentage of probability for rain before sundown—everything she ever read stayed firmly in her mind, even trivia. She recognized the nervous desire to escape into just such trivia and squashed it.

The soda-fountain jerk came round the counter toward their booth. "What's it to be?"

He was frowning at her skirt, Greta noticed. She hastily placed a paper napkin over the exposed knees. It was stupid to have worn such a short one—hadn't she just finished reading this morning's editorial about the connection between fashion and immorality? *Ominous trend of the eighties,* the paper had called it. *A challenge to our deepest values of family and church.*

"Coffee," she said. "No—make that Coke."

The man turned away and she looked at the German.

"What am I to call you?"

"Mr. Smith will do," he said blandly.

She had an irrational desire to get it over with. Never mind the agony of soul she'd gone through since O'Hara first called her. She had to get out of the States now. She couldn't pass up the opportunity that had come at such a critical time. This man represented her best chance of crossing the borders without a passport—which no one in her division at Lilly had a chance of getting.

The German was observing her beneath a raised eyebrow. "You seem ill at ease."

"I've got what you want."

The eyebrow lifted rather higher, and she thought: *He's a character out of an old movie. He ought to wear a monocle.* Then she realized he was aiming for that effect.

"And what may that be, Miss Bradford?"

"Don't play with me, Mr. Smith," she said fiercely.

"I ask out of curiosity only. It would seem more logical for information to flow the other way. After all, America is unable to launch a weather satellite that works for more than a couple of months, but the Führer's son walks on the moon."

They were both silent while the soda jerk pushed the Coca-Cola glass toward her. "That'll be fifty cents."

"Allow me." The German set the coins down with military precision.

When they were alone again she said, "I'll need guarantees."

"Of course."

"Safe passage immediately to England, or I won't consider it."

"Ah." He leaned back against the booth and folded his arms. "Later, perhaps. But first, a necessary detour to Munich."

"Why?" she demanded.

It hadn't been difficult to guess what they wanted, though nothing had been said. Nor had she had much trouble deciding to give it to them—only a fool or a martyr would not agree her own welfare came first, and she was neither. She'd thought this out carefully. Either one would be priceless to him, but the papers could go anywhere while she only wanted to go to London.

He held out a gold case. "Cigarette?" She shook her head. He put it away without taking one for himself. "I believe you left the Fatherland at an early age?"

"In '41. When I was two years old. What's that got to do with—"

"Then you'll enjoy a brief visit of reacquaintance."

"Reawaken a lot of bad memories, you mean?"

He regarded her calmly. "Feeling as you do, Miss Bradford, why are you accepting our help?"

It wasn't as if she hadn't considered this, too. But she had to get out before it was too late, before the hand of the Alliance of Protestant Churches tightened over all aspects of American life and crushed her. Already the missionary visits had begun, though for the moment they merely urged her politely to attend church. The sprawling Pan-European Federation seemed the best refuge. Germany was its most powerful state; she wasn't surprised it recognized the value of what she knew.

She didn't reply.

"My apology," he said. "A tasteless question. One can only imagine the terror of living in fear of the coming pogroms against those with your abilities."

She glanced around Walgreen's. The other customers—mostly men—counted dimes for the jukebox, or sipped their sodas, propping the funnies against the napkin holders. "What do you mean?"

"The psi gifts you must surely have inherited, Miss Bradford."

"My what?"

In turn, he seemed genuinely puzzled. "You can't imagine we don't know about your *Zigeuner* blood?"

Of course, she thought. As early as 1946 Germany had begun to make its peace with the expatriated Jews, offering generous settlements and a public display of contrition. This was even in American history books that seldom took account of anything outside the boundaries of the forty-eight states. Now, apparently, it was the turn of the Romanies—what there were left of them. Well, if they wanted to put on the sackcloth and ashes for a Gypsy brat whose parents had died in a Bavarian work camp, she supposed she could tolerate it for a few days. But a ticket to London was the prize she wanted in return for her information on the research projects of the Eli Lilly Pharmaceutical Company.

She clutched the shoulder purse tightly and took a deep breath, willing her hands to stop trembling. "How soon can you arrange it?"

It wasn't as if she had anyone or anyplace here to regret leaving. She'd had two broken marriages, and homes in more than a dozen states over the years. One side effect of an overzealous memory was a restless need to escape. But itinerant, double-divorcées weren't exactly popular in America these days.

"Shall we say right away, Miss Bradford?" He stood up. "Of course, there's time to finish your Coke first!"

Early-morning fog lay over the small airstrip outside Munich when they landed. Somewhere a cow mooed as Greta emerged sleepily from the private jet they'd transferred to in neutral Ireland. The air was cool and heavy with the scents of clover and fresh-plowed earth; she was glad of the felt cape Mr. Smith had lent her. He caught her arm, turning her toward the waiting Volkswagen limousine. The shoulder purse banged against her side, bulging with the small stack of Euromarks she'd picked up in Ireland, where O'Hara had advised her she'd get a better rate for her dollars. Everything she owned in the world was now in that purse. But some of it was so valuable, she'd never miss the rest.

The limousine's uniformed chauffeur snapped to attention as they approached, giving a stiff, high salute her blood remembered in a rush of cold foreboding.

"We're almost there, Fräulein." Mr. Smith held the door for her. "A twenty-minute drive, no more."

From the chauffeur's radio came a raucous song with a heavy beat.

"One of the oldest English rock groups," he said, catching her frown. "Very popular here. The Beatles, they're called. Have you heard of them in America? No, I suppose not."

He slid the glass partition across, shutting the harsh sounds in with the driver.

The interior smelled of leather and polished wood, and lilies of the valley in a small crystal vase attached to the back of the driver's seat. She pressed her cheek to the window and watched the gray-wreathed fields slip by, the huddled villages still asleep, their onion-domed churches catching the first bright rays of sun through the mist, the cows waiting to be milked, the sleek, gleaming spiderweb of robot harvesters crouched over the vegetable fields. The sixteenth and the twentieth centuries coexisted peacefully here.

And America? she thought. America had retreated to a dream of the nineteenth.

Except in one area.

At the edge of the neat fields, as if at the edge of consciousness itself, the forest loomed, *ur-wald*, where generations of her ancestors had stopped their wagons and made camp—until the laws that declared them undesirable, a threat to the progress of Aryan destiny. A pale crescent of moon was still visible above the pines.

"Sad memories?" Mr. Smith enquired. "The work camps were admittedly a blot on the Fatherland's record. I hate to think what might have happened if the truce hadn't been signed in '42. I've always felt that if he'd waited until late June of '41 to start Barbarossa, as he'd originally planned, the Führer would have repeated Napoleon's mistake of taking on the winter climate as well as the Russian army. It was a trade-off, of course. Less time to prepare—and some bad feeling with Mussolini, who had other plans—but better weather. Who can guess what he might have done in that cold January of 1942, instead of forging the beginnings of European unification? May his soul find rest in Valhalla, but the Führer was inclined to rather wasteful racial policies!"

"I remember nothing of my parents, Herr Schmidt," she said coldly, emphasizing the German form of the code name he'd given her. "I was smuggled out to an English family in Essex, and then on to New York just before the peace in Europe."

He gazed at her thoughtfully a moment before turning away to his own window.

"My mother was English—both nations go back to the same Folk, you know. But here we are!"

The limousine had been traveling up a winding cobblestone road. Now it stopped on the crown of the low hill before an imposing, square-built mansion. Rows of tall windows along the front flashed in the sunlight; flags snapped crisply on their poles; geraniums bloomed tidily beside a driveway.

"Where are we?"

"*Das Dachauer Schloss*—the old palace at Dachau dating back to the sixteenth century," he said, as the chauffeur opened the door. "But you won't be uncomfortable. It's been modernized."

He led her inside into the high-ceilinged hall. She was aware of dark, polished floors and thick oriental rugs, the gleam of pewter on mahogany tables, the tapestry depictions of Valkyries and Wagnerian heroes lining the walls. Warmth rose from a discreet radiator under a mullioned window, taking the chill off the smaller room she was ushered into. The room was dominated by a magnificent set of antlers over the fireplace, whose flames were more ornamental than necessary. Hunting horns, elaborately painted beer steins, bundles of partridge feathers tied with faded ribbons, gave the room the air of a pagan shrine. A brocaded armchair stood by the window to take advantage of the fine view over the formal gardens.

"Bitte, warten Sie hier, Fräulein," Herr Schmidt said. "But I'm sorry! I keep forgetting it's painful."

He went out.

Greta hugged the shoulder purse to her breast like a baby about to be torn from her grasp. For whom was she waiting? A scientist would be logical if they knew the importance of what she carried. Germany's physical sciences had boomed under the return of great men like Einstein and Von Braun. Europe was busy in space, pushing out to the moon and beyond. But space science was something the American government hadn't encouraged in the wave of isolationism that gripped the country after two years alone against Japan. Most Americans hadn't wanted to be drawn into the war in the first place; being left alone to finish it was particularly galling. Even victory itself had not been enough to dispel the disillusionment with former allies. The Pacific Rim Treaty, signed in Hawaii in '44, had been followed by a national distaste for war and weapons and the physical science that produced them.

But America had been quietly pioneering a biological revolution, the dimensions of which were about to buy freedom for Dr. Greta Bradford.

On a sudden impulse she took the wad of notes and diagrams out of her purse and stuffed them under the brocade cushion.

She had barely replaced the cushion when the door opened and a plump, white-haired woman in her seventies, wearing a green-and-gold dirndl, came in. A gold swastika suspended on a fine chain nestled in the lace of her blouse. The old face had a peasant's simplicity to it, without the signs of the peasant's hard life. She leaned on a cane and reached out a hand to Greta before Schmidt, coming behind, could introduce her.

"Die gnädige Frau, Eva Hitler," he said.

"I am so glad you are here," the Führer's widow said in careful English.

Embarrassed, Greta mumbled, "I understand *Deutsch,* I'm just rusty—"

"Think nothing of it! I like the chance to practice." She smiled conspiratorially at Greta. "It helps me hold my own when I visit the

Queen in London. Those Saxe-Coburgs were always such snobs! Shall we sit?"

A long-haired dachshund—as old in dog years as its mistress—came to sit at her feet. Schmidt withdrew, almost colliding with a fresh-faced young girl bringing a tray of coffee.

A hint of lavender cologne drifted from the old woman as she moved. "Do take that low chair over there, it is more comfortable. This is my favorite, by the window." Frau Hitler seated herself, apparently unaware of the new tilt to the seat cushion. "Have some coffee."

She sounded nervous. Odd, Greta thought; she was the one who should feel awkward. Spies and defectors weren't usually treated to audiences with great men's widows. She sat clumsily, dropping the shoulder bag by her feet, and accepted coffee in a delicate Rosenthal cup. The coffee was dark and thick on the tongue.

Frau Hitler nodded at her. "Turkish. Everybody in Europe drinks Turkish coffee now. Even the English!"

Greta added more sugar. The old lady chattered on about the fresh air in this part of Bavaria—she couldn't take the capital in summer, "the *Föhn,* you know"—the cost of heating a Baroque palace, the deplorable opera season just over in Munich, the decline of good breeding among the wives of Europe's new leaders. Greta listened in silence, nodding occasionally, while tension knotted her stomach. She was impatient to get down to business, but this garrulous old woman was not the one who could appreciate the importance of what she had to offer.

Frau Hitler broke off in midsentence. She motioned Greta to close the door the serving girl had left ajar.

"Bradford was not the name I once knew you by."

Greta jumped, rattling the small cup on its saucer. "I—the family in England—"

"I know. They gave you their name. Do you know what yours was?" The old lady gazed out the window, the linen napkin twisted round and round in arthritic fingers. "Tshurkurka, I think. Though I could be wrong after all these years. They all had such dreadful names."

She said this with such quiet simplicity, Greta was overwhelmed. The sense of something about to be revealed tightened her chest.

"Your mother's name was Rupa. She read my palm, more than once. She was just about twenty when you last saw her. A dark, scrawny little thing Rupa was—much like you, only even thinner."

Greta's head was starting to pound. "Why are you telling me this?"

"I could not save her, you see." Frau Hitler turned from the window, her eyes catching the light so that they seemed luminous. "Der Führer was a very stubborn man, and I had no influence in those days. There were so many crazy people surrounding him, demanding his attention. He was always difficult to deal with, swinging between extroverted confidence—the Adolf I fell in love with—and paranoia. Later, the doctors controlled these moods with their medicines. He was a manic-depressive, you see."

The little fire crackled and spat a small spark onto the hearth. Frau Hitler sipped her coffee. Greta waited, her own coffee forgotten like the papers under the cushion.

"Once, she gave me a warning for Adolf—she'd read it in the cards. The coming winter would be the worst in memory, she said. I didn't know why that might be important, but I told him. I think it was the only time he ever listened to me, and even then I practically had to go down on my knees! Well. But I managed to save Rupa's children. And she smiled at me, before she went."

"Children?" she breathed.

"You had a brother—a baby," Frau Hitler said, her attention back on the misty *Hofgarten* again. "You know, I kept track of what happened to you, even after you were sent on to America."

"But why?"

"I thought it might be useful someday. A Romany, you see? But you do not, of course." She was silent for a moment. Then she picked up the *Suddeutsche Zeitung* that had been lying on a footstool by her side. "Have you seen the paper? My son makes a name for himself in space."

She held it out so Greta could see the front-page headline: *Wolfgang macht die Mondexpedition.* There was a blurry newsphoto accompanying the text. The pounding in her head was becoming a full-scale migraine.

"The paper does not tell everything. Wolfli has gone off on his own, away from the moon base. He did not take a radio with him—he has something of Adolf's impetuosity in him, I think. Or perhaps he is just always trying to live up to the legend of a great man. Well. There has been no communication with him for more than four days. That would not be so alarming—Wolfli is brave and competent!—but something else has occurred."

Her face was a mask of grief; lines that Greta had overlooked on meeting her now stood out like the moon's own rifts and valleys.

"Wolfli must be told of the danger he faces from sudden sunspot activity our scientists have monitored."

"And Wolfli—" Greta said, slipping without thinking into the diminutive form of the name.

"—is your brother. I never could have children, you see. Oh, I did not tell Adolf! I do not think he would have understood, even afterward, when Mr. Churchill had talked sense into him. He thought the baby was his own son—he was much too busy in those days to keep track of everything!—and so he married me."

She gazed at Greta, seeking understanding. Greta returned the look stonily, in the grip of shock and disbelief through which anger darted. *My brother?*

Frau Hitler sighed and looked wistfully through the window as if she'd rather be strolling down the tunnel formed by the tall trees than revealing long-kept secrets. "Today, Führer is almost a bad word. It is all Chancellor and Prime Minister now."

"Why am I here?" Greta asked harshly.

"You are Romany," Frau Hitler said. "Romany have the Gift. I need you. Wolfli needs you."

She gaped. "You think I'm *psychic?*"

Hitler's widow nodded. "No one else can reach him. But you have a chance! An English gypsy once told me the bond is strong between Romany bloodkin."

"That's absurd!" Greta started to laugh. Here, in the world center of science, *this*? "I'm a scientist, Frau Hitler. Tell me you're joking."

"No. Herr Schmidt will take you to Von Braun Space Communications Center in Munich immediately. He does not know what I have just told you—nobody does!—but he will do as I ask. They have equipment there. I do not know how to describe it, but it will augment your Gift in some way. And you will reach Wolfli and save him."

Greta stared at the old woman. Was that love or craziness or both that burned in her eyes? "Look. I was brought here to sell secrets, biological secrets—gene-splicing techniques—" She broke off. This old woman was too simple to understand in any case. "Things Germany could use to its advantage. But not *this!*"

"So you may suppose. Herr Schmidt is so secretive, he would not have told you! However, you came because I gave the order to have you picked up. Because Wolfli's life depends on you. And your safety depends on me, just as my secret depends on you. A karmic situation all round, *nicht wahr?*"

"I appreciate your being a good mother to him," Greta said in gentler tone. "But I'm not telepathic."

The liquid old eyes held hers steadily. "You are still a citizen of that benighted country, you see. If you do not save Wolfli, I shall have you returned."

The highest point of the new space communications building on the west bank of the Isar, a few kilometers past the government offices of the Pan-European Federation outside Munich, was crowned with its ritual fir tree. German mythology seemed cozily at home with German science in this countryside.

Schmidt led the way through the maze of corridors that connected the labs, offices, and conference rooms. One such bend led to the commissary, she guessed, her nose wrinkling at the pungent odor of sauerkraut being prepared for lunch. Passes were demanded and displayed several times. Guard dogs eyed them suspiciously, jaws working in anticipation. Each time they were waved farther inside. The sound of their feet rang hollowly down the corridors.

Greta had not chosen to reply to the small talk he'd felt obliged to make on the drive down, and he'd given up the attempt. She'd insisted on a detour, to the small cemetery cupped in low hills on the outskirts of Dachau, where the concentration camp's victims had been buried. Here, where the scent of lilac hung like incense, under the icons of a Christian religion they'd scorned, lay her parents, anonymously with a few hundred others. Gypsies, Jews, and political undesirables shared a common grave, unfortunates who'd not survived the hard work and malnutrition of the camp between 1933 and 1942. Unbidden, the statistics of death, read long ago in an unguarded moment, rose in her mind. She stooped and tore a weed from its place in the smooth velvet of the lawn. Somewhere not far off a cuckoo called.

Hypocrite! she thought savagely. How would what she was willing to traffic in lead to any better outcome? But she felt no sense of responsibility toward the nation she'd just left, no ties of duty or loyalty, only to herself. Perhaps that was what it meant to be a Gypsy? Disowned by every country, at home nowhere and everywhere.

She turned away. She couldn't mourn for these people, for she'd hardly known who they were. Her true parents had been the second-generation German immigrants in New York who'd raised her and sent her to university. And if she hadn't been capable of loving them, at least she'd honored them. Now they were dead, too, severing the only flimsy bond she'd ever felt. A hard anger rose in her, along with something else, an emotion she couldn't at first name.

She'd made Schmidt make a second detour before they left Dachau, to a jeweler's, where she used a large number of her new Euromarks.

Now she smoothed her dark hair, feeling the swing of heavy gold hoops in her earlobes. He'd made no comment about her new image.

Schmidt held open a steel door, gesturing for her to enter. A dull confusion of sound flowed out to her—murmur of voices, a low whine of machinery, unidentifiable clicks and whirs, the occasional rasp of a steel chair across a tiled floor. She stopped on the threshold, hardly believing what she saw. The banked computers and display screens lining one complete wall of the room were beyond the wildest imagination of a Hoosier biochemist, both in number and complexity. By comparison the pharmaceutical scientists might as well have been working with abacus and slide rule. She suffered a full minute of gut-wrenching envy; then she remembered what she'd brought with her.

A short, white-haired man in a lab smock was waiting patiently for her to complete her inspection.

"Josef Krantzl, Fräulein." He bowed. *"Kommen Sie bitte herein."*

He led the way through the chamber of technological wonders to a smaller, sparsely furnished room. The lighting here was soft. On a low table beside a reclining leather chair lay an oval contraption of straps and wires. A small computer sat discreetly against a wall.

"Der Apparat—" Krantzl began, waving a hand at the helmet.

Behind her Schmidt asked, "Would you like me to translate?"

Greta stared icily at him.

"As you wish."

Krantzl launched himself into a long passionate explanation of his work, the theories that underpinned it, the apparatus he'd built, the niche in the German space program into which it fitted. The longer he talked, the more he lapsed from the *Hochdeutsch* she'd learned from her foster parents, the vowels broadening, the consonants slurring together in the Bavarian dialect she barely recognized as German. But she was not about to admit this to Schmidt. The man stood with the expectant air of someone with a lifeline, waiting for a drowning victim to throw it to.

German physical science, Krantzl explained, was founded on the works of three masters: Einstein, Jung, and Freud. Intercepting her puzzled expression at this odd coupling, he spoke eloquently of the mating of inner and outer space, the role of Mind in the universe, the effects of the quantum-mechanical revolution on the theory of psionics. Along the way he invoked the mystical role the Fatherland must play in the world's destiny, and the cosmological repercussions of the heirs of Siegfried planting their footprints in the ur-dust of the moon.

She was exhausted trying to follow this twisted logic. She'd heard some bizarre scientific theories proposed over a glass too many of

Kentucky bourbon—nothing like this! A glance at Schmidt's impassive face showed Greta that if Krantzl was mad, it was a madness shared by his compatriots.

"Unfortunately," Krantzl came to the end of his dissertation on German psychic science, "that segment of the population which possesses these gifts in extraordinary measure is in short supply, due to the unfortunate circumstances of the recent past."

"He refers to the mistake the Führer made about the Romanies," Schmidt said.

She would have laughed, but it wasn't funny. "Mistake, was it? And what am I supposed to do? Soothe your consciences by cooperating in this charade of crystal-ball reading?"

Krantzl's expression was pained. "If you had time to read the literature, Fräulein Bradford—"

"Time is the one element we don't have," Schmidt said sharply. "A man's life is at stake."

The scientist pursed his lips, but was silent.

"By the way," Greta said slowly, "that's Fräulein Doktor Bradford."

"The French have a word for it, I believe," Schmidt said. *"Touché,* Fräulein Doktor Bradford!"

"If you can only reach Herr Hitler," Krantzl pleaded. "Warn him of the solar-radiation danger—get him back to the base—"

And then, a thought she'd been suppressing since the interview in the Baroque splendor of Eva Hitler's summer home surfaced. The man whose life was in danger was her brother. In comparison to the mystical mumbo jumbo she'd just heard it was a simple fact, no more fantastic than the knowledge of her own survival. And there was one thing about the Romanies she knew—the ties of family were all-important.

Tshurkurka. Wolfgang und Greta Tshurkurka. Bloodkin.

She pushed away her scientific reluctance. So what if she didn't believe in telepathy? She owed it to her brother to try. She sat in the reclining chair and lifted the helmet, its wires trailing over her lap.

"Ready when you are, Doktor Krantzl."

Hours later—

Perhaps days? The passage of time was not noticeable in this quiet room—

She developed a cramp in her neck. Reaching up, she started to unfasten the straps of the heavy helmet.

"Please!" Krantzl turned in agitation from the screen he was monitoring. "We haven't made contact yet."

"I have to take a break."

"We're so close!" he mourned.

Greta doubted that. She massaged her neck, her head feeling fantastically light without the helmet. It had been an odd experience, trying to do something all her scientific training told her was nonsense. She placated this part of herself with the thought that she had little choice but to do as they ordered if she ever hoped to get to England. She'd had enough gallivanting around; now she was ready to settle in some quiet Essex village. Near enough to London for work, and perhaps the theater, but—

The wheels of Krantzl's chair squealed as he fidgeted, impatient to resume work.

To gain time she said, "Explain to me again how this contraption is supposed to function."

She regretted it immediately, for the little man waxed eloquent at once. The unfamiliar terms washed over her—nuclear-magnetic-resonance tomography—mapping the complicated microcircuitry of the brain—particle-beam tomographic stimulation, augmenting and transferring the psi-specific waves of her neural activity into space.

Some of this had the ring of good science, though her background, limited as it was to biology and chemistry, was not sufficient for her to separate the physics from the psychic. She wondered if American physicists even dreamed how far advanced the Germans were, or if they cared.

"This explanation would've been unnecessary, Fräulein Doktor Bradford," Schmidt said, "if the United States hadn't lost interest in physical research. They were as far advanced as we in the race to split the atom before the war ended. So, from small decisions mighty histories grow!"

"Of course," Krantzl said hesitantly, "so many of your best physicists were Jews who accepted the Führer's offer to help them settle in Palestine when—"

"Even so!" Schmidt said, and Krantzl subsided.

Greta shut her eyes, banishing the man and the hint of menace that lay under the oily manners of his personality. Worry about the papers left in Frau Hitler's study nagged her. Now that she knew that hadn't been what they wanted, what would she do with them?

If she ever retrieved them.

Greta sighed. The experience itself had been frustrating, for she had no idea what she should do while under the transmitting helmet. Nor had Krantzl offered suggestions. Her Romany blood was supposed to tell her how to do it.

She'd tried sending subvocalized messages—*Wolfli, can you hear me? Wolfli, can you hear me?*—but tired of this quickly. Visualizing the man whose attention she hoped to attract didn't work either, for her only image of him was the grainy photo in the newspaper Frau Hitler had showed her. She should have thought to ask for a more intimate picture, maybe a baby portrait, something her own subconscious might recognize and respond to.

Back to work.

She thought of the moon itself—man's first outpost in space—the silver disk by whose waxing and waning the Romanies measured the passage of time—

She couldn't concentrate.

Her mind drifted away from the task, not only rejecting the idea of telepathic communication, but emptying of all thoughts. Once she slid into a light sleep, only to be jolted awake by an indignant Krantzl, who saw the telltale change of brain waves on his screen.

"We waste time, Fräulein Doktor Bradford," Schmidt's voice interrupted harshly. The man was growing more objectionable by the hour. Greta studied the hard lines of his face.

"What're *you* getting out of this—rescuing Frau Hitler's son? Why is it so important?"

"We are a sentimental race," he said, unperturbed. "The son of a great man—"

"Bullshit."

He allowed himself a small, dim smile. "Europe has had forty years of peace—wonderful, isn't it? But peace is not necessarily good for people. They grow fat and lazy. They lose the inner strength that made the Fatherland invincible. Some of us see the necessity of rectifying the matter, directing the feet of our nation back to the narrow path of German destiny. We are called upon to be leaders of the world, Fräulein! Not merchants haggling over the price of cheese and sausage on the London stock exchange."

"You're planning to break up the Federation?"

"The Federation already suffers from inaction. It allows the Slavic states—always a hotbed of crazy political ideas, and paranoid at best!—to dream of separation. And too much peace has encouraged the Greeks to remember a Homeric past that they mutter about restoring. Il Duce was right; we should have taught them a lesson long ago! Without a common goal to fire men's imaginations the Federation will destroy itself. No, you American farmers have been looking to Asia for so long you don't see the European future marching up to your gates."

"War against the States, then."

"Perhaps not at first."

It was unthinkable, but terribly possible. "And where does Wolfgang fit into this?"

"*Hitler*," he said. "A name to conjure with."

They had the technology to do it, too, she thought.

"But you are procrastinating, Fräulein Doktor Bradford. Please, put the helmet back on voluntarily."

She had a momentary urge to tell him the truth.

Across the room Krantzl glanced up nervously. "This is a scientific endeavor, *Kamerad!*"

Greta lifted the helmet.

It worked no better this time. She forced herself to repeat his name like a mantra, summoned up fantastic images of a moonbase from science fiction she'd read as a child in Brooklyn, before it was banned. She held the gaudy pictures like asymmetric mandalas in her mind, searching for some hidden magic in her inheritance that eluded conscious grasp.

Nothing.

The headache she'd been fighting off pulsed, a spreading ache.

"Look—this won't work! I don't know what you expect from Romany genes, but—"

She shrieked as Schmidt caught her arm, twisting it up behind her back. A purple haze of pain clouded thinking. She expected any minute to hear the bone snap.

He hissed at her. "*Es muss Erfolg haben!* Try again!"

Gasping for breath, she tried to call Wolfgang's name in her head.

"Again!" He jerked her arm.

"Perhaps—" Krantzl began tentatively.

"Again!"

Tears burned behind her closed lids. She fought them back. Her mother had given up her children to safety and gone to the concentration camp smiling. That was bravery. She could do no less.

"You're not trying hard enough, Fräulein!"

She screamed as her arm slid out of its socket. The gold hoops banged against her neck as she writhed in his grip.

Rupa's children—used and abused as countless generations of Romanies before them. The bright caravans hounded from border to border. The smiling, hidden treachery of honest burghers. And always the fear of the dogs, the knives in the long, cold night under an enemy moon.

In the gray wash of agony that blotted out thought Greta was aware only of a pair of dark eyes behind a curve of glass, and a searing point of contact, a skein of spider silk slung across the void.

When she came to, she was lying on a couch under a tapestry she'd seen before. Maidens rose full-breasted out of the Rhine, their arms cradling the fabled gold of the Nibelung. The fire's cheerful flicker played over the woven scenery in the twilit room. Her own arm was strapped securely against her chest, and a dull ache floated somewhere at the edge of attention. Someone was sponging her brow with something cool and fragrant.

"Thank goodness," Eva Hitler said. "I cannot imagine what came over Herr Schmidt! He knows I abhor violence. I used to say to Adolf—"

Greta sat up, ignoring Frau Hitler's protests. The little room spun for a moment. "Wolfgang—"

"—contacted us almost immediately!" she replied happily. "He said he had a hunch something was not right! He got back safely to moonbase."

Greta lay back and closed her eyes. Coincidence? Probably. Wolfgang was a trained astronaut, after all.

"Good! Now, let me work again with the *Kolnischewasser*—"

She couldn't believe in telepathy, no matter what blood she'd inherited. Many strange things in life owed themselves to coincidence. Jung's principle of synchronicity, Krantzl would have called it. She pushed this thought away.

There was a knock at the door—but without waiting for an answer, Schmidt entered. The dachshund scuttled to safety behind its mistress.

"Hans!" Frau Hitler said with displeasure. "You might have—"

"What more do you want from me?" Greta said. "You have your next führer safe and sound."

She tried to sit up, but Frau Hitler's swollen fingers, fragrant with the cologne she'd been using, gently pushed her back.

"You have more talents than we suspected, Fräulein. I ran a check on the work you were doing at Lilly Labs." He nodded thoughtfully at her. He had her shoulder bag in his hand. "There was something you thought important. Something you hoped to bargain with when I picked you up. Your ticket to England, I believe."

"You chose a different currency," she said. "I've kept my part of the bargain."

"And if I choose again, how will you prevent me? Come, Fräulein, where are the papers you brought with you? They weren't in your bag.

I've no time for gypsy tricks." He tossed the bag contemptuously on the rug.

"What are you talking about, Hans?" Frau Hitler demanded.

"All weapons are useful in war," he said. "Especially biological ones that call down the plagues of hell, twisting the bodies of man and beast, even destroying minds—am I not right, Fräulein?—leaving one's own forces unharmed. Appropriate, isn't it, that a nation of farmers should be the first to learn how to poison the harvest? Oh, yes! We knew the Lilly company was working on recombinant DNA, an area we'd neglected. We were only a little slow acting on that intelligence. We indulged ourselves in the security of knowing your country was not pursuing the more profitable avenues of nuclear fission. Then this occurred, and you fell into our hands most fortunately."

Her skin crawled as he spoke. This was what she had intended to do, so why the sudden reluctance? The man aroused a primeval fear in her. He was the hunter, the man with a knife in the night—

"There will be no more war!" the old lady said imperiously. "It contradicts Adolf's vision for Europe. On his deathbed he spoke of the thousand years of peace—"

"The so-called *Reichs-Peace!*" Schmidt said, mouthing the words with obvious distaste. "A bastard concept, like the phrase itself! A new Hitler will see things differently."

She could tell him the truth about Wolfgang Tshurkurka, and then perhaps he'd be discouraged.

And an old woman's heart would be broken. It shouldn't have mattered to Greta Tshurkurka, Gypsy, but somehow she found that it did.

She said nothing.

"If the Führer hadn't agreed to peace when he did, if he'd pursued the advantage that was all his," Schmidt said, "there might've been a German Empire today, not a Federation of shopkeepers! We are the only major European nation that has been denied an empire. Now there's a second chance."

"Yes," Frau Hitler said. "An empire in space!"

He gazed up at the voluptuous Rhine maidens in the full bloom of their triumph. "I regret now that I went with Rudolf Hess to England in the spring of '41—parachuting like a couple of romantic schoolboys into a Scottish glen! Of course, I *was* hardly more than a boy—Hess understood the English fascination with the Young Poet image I could project so well! I think to myself, if only I hadn't been so eloquent, if only the mission had failed and we had not persuaded the stubborn

British to join forces with us against the communist threat. How differently things might have turned out then!"

"But the war would have dragged on, Hans—"

"And Germany would have won! We wouldn't have needed sniveling treaties, promising to love each other and get along like so many peasants at a wedding."

How could she be sure about Wolfgang Tshurkurka, born a Gypsy, raised a Nazi? She might never know, and not knowing might make a terrible mistake.

Frau Hitler said—as if she, rather than Greta, possessed the Gift of the Romanies—"Wolfli is not like that. I did not raise him to be so. He will conquer the stars, not people."

The old woman radiated a strength beyond her size, Greta thought. In that instant she was willing to believe she was right.

Schmidt made an impatient noise in his throat.

Frau Hitler looked down at Greta for a long moment, her expression thoughtful. "You have kept your side of the bargain twice over, Fräulein Bradford. Germany will remember that."

She turned to the fireplace, withdrawing something from a pocket in the embroidered apron over the voluminous folds of her dirndl. Flames leaped up as the first sheets reached them.

Schmidt crossed the room in three strides. *"Gott im Himmel! Was tun Sie?"*

"Do not touch me, Hans!" Frau Hitler stood, back to the fireplace, protecting it with her upraised cane. "You have no right to prevent me disposing of trash I find in my own home."

Gone. Her ticket to England vanished in a shower of sparks.

But the formulas for destruction, the equations themselves that led to twisted minds and grotesque bodies were etched on her brain for as long as she lived.

Schmidt cursed loudly in German and English.

"Leave us now, Hans," Frau Hitler said as smoke billowed into the room from the last of the pages. "I will overlook this impoliteness, for today you are overwrought."

"You may succeed in delaying us, *gnädige Frau,* but you can't stop us!" He clicked his heels and lunged out of the room.

Greta lay back against the pillow. How long had she been without sleep? Since Indianapolis—sometime soon she'd have to think what she was going to do here in Germany. Her only skill was as a biochemist—there would be other nations anxious to buy what she knew, if she were willing to sell. . . .

The shoulder began to throb.

She was aware of the old woman's arthritic fingers laid on her brow, and made an effort to swallow down fatigue. "I'm glad you burned them."

Frau Hitler smiled. "Do you not suppose I had enough talk of genetic selection, years ago? It is our destiny and our danger to be always thinking of improving the race, you see! But not this way."

Greta exhaled. If it had only been that simple—

She felt the pull of the painkillers and tranquilizers they had obviously pumped into her. Schmidt suspected her of the wrong mental powers. He hadn't guessed what templates for disaster were really locked in her brain.

Worthless treasure, like the rest of the trivia, for she knew she could never bring herself to use it now.

Perversely she felt only a great relief.

"Perhaps the time has come for me to tell Wolfli my secret. He has children of his own—he will understand now. Besides, a little insurance against Herr Schmidt might be useful. Ach! We are in for interesting times again. How tiresome."

Lethargically Greta opened her eyes again and saw the old woman's hands with their swollen knuckles. One of the formulas someone else at Lilly had been working on had promised relief for arthritis—she'd seen it once, but hadn't paid much attention, absorbed as she was then in her own deadly equations. If she worked hard enough, she could reconstruct it, or at least enough of it to give somebody else a clue.

Greta sighed. "Tomorrow, I'll—"

"You will stay in Germany long enough to welcome Wolfli home?"

"No, I—what?"

"I need a companion to accompany me to London next month. The Queen's garden parties are always such fun, but exhausting for a woman of my age! I had hoped you would come."

Tears that Schmidt had not been able to command spilled over now.

Frau Hitler settled back in her favorite chair, the dachshund on her lap. "And I would not be offended if you did not return with me, you see."

Behind her, Greta glimpsed the bright moon framed in the mullioned window—a promise that the Reichs-Peace would be kept a little while longer.

"Rupa's children bless you, Eva Hitler," Greta said. "And so does History."

Angel

PAT CADIGAN

Stand with me awhile, Angel, I said, and Angel said he'd do that. Angel was good to me that way, good to have with you on a cold night and nowhere to go. We stood on the street corner together and watched the cars going by and the people and all. The streets were lit up like Christmas, streetlights, store lights, marquees over the all-night movie houses and bookstores blinking and flashing: shank of the evening in east midtown. Angel was getting used to things here and getting used to how I did nights. Standing outside, because what else are you going to do. He was *my* Angel now, had been since that other cold night when I'd been going home, because where are you going to go, and I'd found him and took him with me. It's good to have someone to take with you, someone to look after. Angel knew that. He started looking after me, too.

Like now. We were standing there awhile and I was looking around at nothing and everything, the cars cruising past, some of them stopping now and again for the hookers posing by the curb, and then I saw it, out of the corner of my eye. Stuff coming out of the Angel, shiny like sparks but flowing like liquid. Silver fireworks. I turned and looked all the way at him and it was gone. And he turned and gave a little grin like he was embarrassed I'd seen. Nobody else saw it, though; not the short guy who paused next to the Angel before crossing the street against the light, not the skinny hype looking to sell the boom box he was carrying on his shoulder, not the homeboy strutting past us with both his girlfriends on his arms, nobody but me.

The Angel said, Hungry?

Sure, I said. I'm hungry.

Angel looked past me. Okay, he said. I looked, too, and here they came, three leather boys, visor caps, belts, boots, keyrings. On the cruise together. Scary stuff, even though you know it's not looking for you.

I said, them? *Them?*

Angel didn't answer. One went by, then the second, and the Angel stopped the third by taking hold of his arm.

Hi.

The guy nodded. His head was shaved. I could see a little gray-black stubble under his cap. No eyebrows, disinterested eyes. The eyes were because of the Angel.

I could use a little money, the Angel said. My friend and I are hungry.

The guy put his hand in his pocket and wiggled out some bills, offering them to the Angel. The Angel selected a twenty and closed the guy's hand around the rest.

This will be enough, thank you.

The guy put his money away and waited.

I hope you have a good night, said the Angel.

The guy nodded and walked on, going across the street to where his two friends were waiting on the next corner. Nobody found anything weird about it.

Angel was grinning at me. Sometimes he was *the* Angel, when he was doing something, sometimes he was Angel, when he was just with me. Now he was Angel again. We went up the street to the luncheonette and got a seat by the front window so we could still watch the street while we ate.

Cheeseburger and fries, I said without bothering to look at the plastic-covered menus lying on top of the napkin holder. The Angel nodded.

Thought so, he said. I'll have the same, then.

The waitress came over with a little tiny pad to take our order. I cleared my throat. It seemed like I hadn't used my voice in a hundred years. "Two cheeseburgers and two fries," I said, "and two cups of—" I looked up at her and froze. She had no face. Like, *nothing,* blank from hairline to chin, soft little dents where the eyes and nose and mouth would have been. Under the table, the Angel kicked me, but gentle.

"And two cups of coffee," I said.

She didn't say anything—how could she?—as she wrote down the order and then walked away again. All shaken up, I looked at the Angel, but he was calm like always.

She's a new arrival, Angel told me and leaned back in his chair. Not enough time to grow a face.

But how can she breathe? I said.

Through her pores. She doesn't need much air yet.

Yah, but what about—like, I mean, don't other people *notice* that she's got nothing there?

No. It's not such an extraordinary condition. The only reason you notice is because you're with me. Certain things have rubbed off on you. But no one else notices. When they look at her, they see whatever face they expect someone like her to have. And eventually, she'll have it.

But you have a face, I said. You've always had a face.

I'm different, said the Angel.

You sure are, I thought, looking at him. Angel had a beautiful face. That wasn't why I took him home that night, just because he had a beautiful face—I left all that behind a long time ago—but it was there, his beauty. The way you think of a man being beautiful, good clean lines, deep-set eyes, ageless. About the only way you could describe him—look away and you'd forget everything except that he was beautiful. But he did have a face. He *did*.

Angel shifted in the chair—these were like somebody's old kitchen chairs, you couldn't get too comfortable in them—and shook his head, because he knew I was thinking troubled thoughts. Sometimes you could think something and it wouldn't be troubled and later you'd think the same thing and it would be troubled. The Angel didn't like me to be troubled about him.

Do you have a cigarette? he asked.

I think so.

I patted my jacket and came up with most of a pack that I handed over to him. The Angel lit up and amused us both by having the smoke come out his ears and trickle out of his eyes like ghostly tears. I felt my own eyes watering for his; I wiped them and there was that *stuff* again, but from me now. I was crying silver fireworks. I flicked them on the table and watched them puff out and vanish.

Does this mean I'm getting to *be* you, now? I asked.

Angel shook his head. Smoke wafted out of his hair. Just things rubbing off on you. Because we've been together and you're—susceptible. But they're different for you.

Then the waitress brought our food and we went on to another sequence, as the Angel would say. She still had no face but I guess she could see well enough because she put all the plates down just where you'd think they were supposed to go and left the tiny little check in the middle of the table.

Is she—I mean, did you know her, from where you—

Angel gave his head a brief little shake. No. She's from somewhere else. Not one of my—people. He pushed the cheeseburger and fries in front of him over to my side of the table. That was the way it was done; I did all the eating and somehow it worked out.

I picked up my cheeseburger and I was bringing it up to my mouth when my eyes got all funny and I saw it coming up like a whole *series* of cheeseburgers, whoom-whoom-whoom, trick photography, only for real. I closed my eyes and jammed the cheeseburger into my mouth, holding it there, waiting for all the other cheeseburgers to catch up with it.

You'll be okay, said the Angel. Steady, now.

I said with my mouth full, That was—that was *weird*. Will I ever get used to this?

I doubt it. But I'll do what I can to help you.

Yah, well, the Angel *would* know. Stuff rubbing off on me, he could feel it better than I could. He was the one it was rubbing off *from*.

I had put away my cheeseburger and half of Angel's and was working on the french fries for both of us when I noticed he was looking out the window with this hard, tight expression on his face.

Something? I asked him.

Keep eating, he said.

I kept eating, but I kept watching, too. The Angel was staring at a big blue car parked at the curb right outside the diner. It was silvery blue, one of those lots-of-money models, and there was a woman kind of leaning across from the driver's side to look out the passenger window. She was beautiful in that lots-of-money way, tawny hair swept back from her face, and even from here I could see she had turquoise eyes. Really beautiful woman. I almost felt like crying. I mean, jeez, how did people get that way and me too harmless to live.

But the Angel wasn't one bit glad to see her. I knew he didn't want me to say anything, but I couldn't help it.

Who is she?

Keep eating, Angel said. We need the protein, what little there is.

I ate and watched the woman and the Angel watch each other and it was getting very—I don't know, very *something* between them, even through the glass. Then a cop car pulled up next to her and I knew they were telling her to move it along. She moved it along.

Angel sagged against the back of his chair and lit another cigarette, smoking it in the regular, unremarkable way.

What are we going to do tonight? I asked the Angel as we left the restaurant.

Keep out of harm's way, Angel said, which was a new answer. Most nights we spent just kind of going around soaking everything up. The Angel soaked it up, mostly. I got some of it along with him, but not the same way he did. It was different for him. Sometimes he would use me like a kind of filter. Other times he took it direct. There'd been the big car accident one night, right at my usual corner, a big old Buick running a red light smack into somebody's nice Lincoln. The Angel had had to take it direct because I couldn't handle that kind of stuff. I didn't know how the Angel could take it, but he could. It carried him for days afterwards, too. I only had to eat for myself.

It's the intensity, little friend, he'd told me, as though that were supposed to explain it.

It's the intensity, not whether it's good or bad. The universe doesn't know good or bad, only less or more. Most of you have a bad time reconciling this. *You* have a bad time with it, little friend, but you get through better than other people. Maybe because of the way you are. You got squeezed out of a lot, you haven't had much of a chance at life. You're as much an exile as I am, only in your own land.

That may have been true, but at least I *belonged* here, so that part was easier for me. But I didn't say that to the Angel. I think he liked to think he could do as well or better than me at living—I mean, I couldn't just look at some leather boy and get him to cough up a twenty dollar bill. Cough up a fist in the face or worse, was more like it.

Tonight, though, he wasn't doing so good, and it was that woman in the car. She'd thrown him out of step, kind of.

Don't think about her, the Angel said, just out of nowhere. Don't think about her anymore.

Okay, I said, feeling creepy because it was creepy when the Angel got a glimpse of my head. And then, of course, I couldn't think about anything else hardly.

Do you want to go home? I asked him.

No. I can't stay in now. We'll do the best we can tonight, but I'll have to be very careful about the tricks. They take so much out of me, and if we're keeping out of harm's way, I might not be able to make up for a lot of it.

It's okay, I said. I ate. I don't need anything else tonight, you don't have to do any more.

Angel got that look on his face, the one where I knew he wanted to give me things, like feelings I couldn't have anymore. Generous, the Angel was. But I didn't need those feelings, not like other people seem to. For a while, it was like the Angel didn't understand that, but he let me be.

Little friend, he said, and almost touched me. The Angel didn't touch a lot. I could touch him and that would be okay, but if *he* touched somebody, he couldn't help *doing* something to them, like the trade that had given us the money. That had been deliberate. If the trade had touched the Angel first, it would have been different, nothing would have happened unless the Angel touched him back. All touch meant something to the Angel that I didn't understand. There was touching without touching, too. Like things rubbing off on me. And sometimes, when I did touch the Angel, I'd get the feeling that it was maybe more his idea than mine, but I didn't mind that. How many people were going their whole lives never being able to touch an Angel?

We walked together and all around us the street was really coming to life. It was getting colder, too. I tried to make my jacket cover more. The Angel wasn't feeling it. Most of the time hot and cold didn't mean much to him. We saw the three rough trade guys again. The one Angel had gotten the money from was getting into a car. The other two watched it drive away and then walked on. I looked over at the Angel.

Because we took his twenty, I said.

Even if we hadn't, Angel said.

So we went along, the Angel and me, and I could feel how different it was tonight than it was all the other nights we'd walked or stood together. The Angel was kind of pulled back into himself and seemed to be keeping a check on me, pushing us closer together. I was getting more of those fireworks out of the corners of my eyes, but when I'd turn my head to look, they'd vanish. It reminded me of the night I'd found the Angel standing on my corner all by himself in pain. The Angel told me later that was real talent, knowing he was in pain. I never thought of myself as any too talented, but the way everyone else had been just ignoring him, I guess I must have had something to see him after all.

The Angel stopped us several feet down from an all-night bookstore. Don't look, he said. Watch the traffic or stare at your feet, but don't look or it won't happen.

There wasn't anything to see right then, but I didn't look anyway. That was the way it was sometimes, the Angel telling me it made a difference whether I was watching something or not, something about the other people being conscious of me being conscious of them. I didn't understand, but I knew Angel was usually right. So I was watching traffic when the guy came out of the bookstore and got his head punched.

I could almost see it out of the corner of my eye. A lot of movement, arms and legs flying and grunty noises. Other people stopped to look, but I kept my eyes on the traffic, some of which was slowing up so they could check out the fight. Next to me, the Angel was stiff all over. Taking it in, what he called the expenditure of emotional kinetic energy. No right, no wrong, little friend, he'd told me. Just energy, like the rest of the universe.

So he took it in and I *felt* him taking it in, and while I was feeling it, a kind of silver fog started creeping around my eyeballs and I was in two places at once. I was watching the traffic and I was in the Angel watching the fight and feeling him charge up like a big battery.

It felt like nothing I'd ever felt before. These two guys slugging it out—well, one guy doing all the slugging and the other skittering around trying to get out from under the fists and having his head punched but good, and the Angel drinking it like he was sipping at an empty cup and somehow getting it to have something in it after all. Deep inside him, whatever made the Angel go was getting a little stronger.

I kind of swung back and forth between him and me, or swayed might be more like it was. I wondered about it, because the Angel wasn't touching me. I really was getting to *be* him, I thought; Angel picked that up and put the thought away to answer later. It was like I was traveling by the fog, being one of us and then the other, for a long time, it seemed, and then after a while I was more me than him again, and some of the fog cleared away.

And there was that car, pointed the other way this time, and the woman was climbing out of it with this big weird smile on her face, as though she'd won something. She waved at the Angel to come to her.

Bang went the connection between us dead and the Angel shot past me, running away from the car. I went after him. I caught a glimpse of her jumping back into the car and yanking at the gear shift.

Angel wasn't much of a runner. Something funny about his knees. We'd gone maybe a hundred feet when he started wobbling and I could hear him pant. He cut across a Park & Lock that was dark and mostly empty. It was back-to-back with some kind of private parking lot and the fences for each one tried to mark off the same narrow strip of lumpy pavement. They were easy to climb but Angel was too panicked. He just *went* through them before he even thought about it; I knew that because if he'd been thinking, he'd have wanted to save what he'd just charged up with for when he really needed it bad enough.

I had to haul myself over the fences in the usual way, and when he heard me rattling on the saggy chain link, he stopped and looked back.

Go, I told him. Don't wait on me!

He shook his head sadly. Little friend, I'm a fool. I could stand to learn from you a little more.

Don't stand, run! I got over the fences and caught up with him. Let's go! I yanked his sleeve as I slogged past and he followed at a clumsy trot.

Have to hide somewhere, he said, camouflage ourselves with people.

I shook my head, thinking we could just run maybe four more blocks and we'd be at the freeway overpass. Below it were the butt-ends of old roads closed off when the freeway had been built. You could hide there the rest of your life and no one would find you. But Angel made me turn right and go down a block to this rundown crack-in-the-wall called Stan's Jigger. I'd never been in there—I'd never made it a practice to go into bars—but the Angel was pushing too hard to argue.

Inside it was smelly and dark and not too happy. The Angel and I went down to the end of the bar and stood under a blood-red light while he searched his pockets for money.

Enough for one drink apiece, he said.

I don't want anything.

You can have soda or something.

The Angel ordered from the bartender, who was suspicious. This was a place for regulars and nobody else, and certainly nobody else like me or the Angel. The Angel knew that even stronger than I did but he just stood and pretended to sip his drink without looking at me. He was all pulled into himself and I was hovering around the edges. I knew he was still pretty panicked and trying to figure out what he could do next. As close as I was, if he had to get real far away, he was going to have a problem and so was I. He'd have to tow me along with him and that wasn't the most practical thing to do.

Maybe he was sorry now he'd let me take him home. But he'd been so weak then, and now with all the filtering and stuff I'd done for him he couldn't just cut me off without a lot of pain.

I was trying to figure out what I could do for him now when the bartender came back and gave us a look that meant order or get out, and he'd have liked it better if we got out. So would everyone else there. The few other people standing at the bar weren't looking at us, but they knew right where we were, like a sore spot. It wasn't hard to figure out what they thought about us, either, maybe because of me or because of the Angel's beautiful face.

We got to leave, I said to the Angel but he had it in his head this was good camouflage. There wasn't enough money for two more drinks so he smiled at the bartender and slid his hand across the bar and put it on top of the bartender's. It was tricky doing it this way; bartenders and waitresses took more persuading because it wasn't normal for them just to give you something.

The bartender looked at the Angel with his eyes half closed. He seemed to be thinking it over. But the Angel had just blown a lot going through the fence instead of climbing over it and the fear was scuttling his concentration and I just knew that it wouldn't work. And maybe my knowing that didn't help, either.

The bartender's free hand dipped down below the bar and came up with a small club. "Faggot!" he roared and caught Angel just over the ear. Angel slammed into me and we both crashed to the floor. Plenty of emotional kinetic energy in here, I thought dimly as the guys standing at the bar fell on us, and then I didn't think anything more as I curled up into a ball under their fists and boots.

We were lucky they didn't much feel like killing anyone. Angel went out the door first and they tossed me out on top of him. As soon as I landed on him, I knew we were both in trouble; something was broken inside him. So much for keeping out of harm's way. I rolled off him and lay on the pavement, staring at the sky and trying to catch my breath. There was blood in my mouth and my nose, and my back was on fire.

Angel? I said, after a bit.

He didn't answer. I felt my mind get kind of all loose and runny, like my brains were leaking out my ears. I thought about the trade we'd taken the money from and how I'd been scared of him and his friends and how silly that had been. But then, I was too harmless to live.

The stars were raining silver fireworks down on me. It didn't help.

Angel? I said again.

I rolled over onto my side to reach for him, and there she was. The car was parked at the curb and she had Angel under the armpits, dragging him toward the open passenger door. I couldn't tell if he was conscious or not and that scared me. I sat up.

She paused, still holding the Angel. We looked into each other's eyes, and I started to understand.

"Help me get him into the car," she said at last. Her voice sounded hard and flat and unnatural. "Then you can get in, too. In the *back*seat."

I was in no shape to take her out. It couldn't have been better for her if she'd set it up herself. I got up, the pain flaring in me so bad that I almost fell down again, and took the Angel's ankles. His ankles were so delicate, almost like a woman's, like *hers*. I didn't really help much, except to guide his feet in as she sat him on the seat and strapped him in with the shoulder harness. I got in the back as she ran around to the other side of the car, her steps real light and peppy, like she'd found a million dollars lying there on the sidewalk.

We were out on the freeway before the Angel stirred in the shoulder harness. His head lolled from side to side on the back of the seat. I reached up and touched his hair lightly, hoping she couldn't see me do it.

Where are you taking me, the Angel said.

"For a ride," said the woman. "For the moment."

Why does she talk out loud like that? I asked the Angel.

Because she knows it bothers me.

"You know I can focus my thoughts better if I say things out loud," she said. "I'm not like one of your little pushovers." She glanced at me in the rearview mirror. "Just *what* have you gotten yourself into since you left, darling? Is that a boy or a girl?"

I pretended I didn't care about what she said or that I was too harmless to live or any of that stuff, but the way she said it, she meant it to sting.

Friends can be either, Angel said. It doesn't matter which. Where are you taking us?

Now it was *us*. In spite of everything, I almost could have smiled.

"Us? You mean, you and me? Or are you really referring to your little pet back there?"

My friend and I are together. You and I are *not*.

The way the Angel said it made me think he meant more than not together; like he'd been with her once the way he was with me now. The Angel let me know I was right. Silver fireworks started flowing slowly off his head down the back of the seat and I knew there was something wrong about it. There was too much all at once.

"Why can't you talk out loud to me, darling?" the woman said with fakey-sounding petulance. "Just say a few words and make me happy. You have a lovely voice when you use it."

That was true, but the Angel never spoke out loud unless he couldn't get out of it, like when he'd ordered from the bartender. Which had probably helped the bartender decide about what he thought we were, but it was useless to think about that.

"All right," said Angel, and I knew the strain was awful for him. "I've said a few words. Are you happy?" He sagged in the shoulder harness.

"Ecstatic. But it won't make me let you go. I'll drop your pet at the nearest hospital and then we'll go home." She glanced at the Angel as she drove. "I've missed you so much. I can't *stand* it without you, without you making things happen. Doing your little miracles. You knew I'd get addicted to it, all the things you could do to people. And then you just took off, I didn't know what had happened to you. And it *hurt*." Her voice turned kind of pitiful, like a little kid's. "I was in real *pain*. You must have been, too. Weren't you? Well, *weren't you?"*

Yes, the Angel said. I was in pain, too.

I remembered him standing on my corner, where I'd hung out all that time by myself until he came. Standing there in pain. I didn't know why or from what then, I just took him home, and after a little while, the pain went away. When he decided we were together, I guess.

The silvery flow over the back of the car seat thickened. I cupped my hands under it and it was like my brain was lighting up with pictures. I saw the Angel before he was my Angel, in this really nice house, the woman's house, and how she'd take him places, restaurants or stores or parties, thinking at him real hard so that he was all filled up with her and had to do what she wanted him to. Steal sometimes; other times, weird stuff, make people do silly things like suddenly start singing or taking their clothes off. That was mostly at the parties, though she made a waiter she didn't like burn himself with a pot of coffee. She'd get men, too, through the Angel, and they'd think it was the greatest idea in the world to go to bed with her. Then she'd make the Angel show her the others, the ones that had been sent here the way he had for crimes nobody could have understood, like the waitress with no face. She'd look at them, sometimes try to do things to them to make them uncomfortable or unhappy. But mostly she'd just stare.

It wasn't like that in the very beginning, the Angel said weakly and I knew he was ashamed.

It's okay, I told him. People can be nice at first, I know that. Then they find out about you.

The woman laughed. "You two are *so* sweet and pathetic. Like a couple of little children. I guess that's what you were looking for, wasn't it, darling? Except children can be cruel, too, can't they? So you got this—*creature* for yourself." She looked at me in the rearview mirror again as she slowed down a little, and for a moment I was afraid she'd seen what I was doing with the silvery stuff that was still pouring out of the Angel. It was starting to slow now. There wasn't much time left. I wanted to scream, but the Angel was calming me for what was coming next. "What happened to you, anyway?"

Tell her, said the Angel. To stall for time, I knew, keep her occupied.

I was born funny, I said. I had both sexes.

"A hermaphrodite!" she exclaimed with real delight.

She loves freaks, the Angel said, but she didn't pay any attention.

There was an operation, but things went wrong. They kept trying to fix it as I got older but my body didn't have the right kind of chemistry or something. My parents were ashamed. I left after a while.

"You poor thing," she said, not meaning anything like that. "You were *just* what darling, here, needed, weren't you? Just a little nothing, no demands, no desires. For anything." Her voice got all hard. "They could probably fix you up now, you know."

I don't want it. I left all that behind a long time ago, I don't need it.

"*Just* the sort of little pet that would be perfect for you," she said to the Angel. "Sorry I have to tear you away. But I can't get along without you now. Life is so boring. And empty. And—" She sounded puzzled. "And like there's nothing more to live for since you left me."

That's not me, said the Angel. That's you.

"No, it's a lot of you, too, and you know it. You know you're addictive to human beings, you knew that when you came here—when they *sent* you here. Hey, you, *pet,* do you know what his crime was, why they sent him to this little backwater penal colony of a planet?"

Yeah, I know, I said. I really didn't, but I wasn't going to tell her that.

"What do you think about *that,* little pet neuter?" she said gleefully, hitting the accelerator pedal and speeding up. "What do you think of the crime of refusing to mate?"

The Angel made a sort of an out-loud groan and lunged at the steering wheel. The car swerved wildly and I fell backwards, the silvery stuff from the Angel going all over me. I tried to keep scooping it into my mouth the way I'd been doing, but it was flying all over the place now. I heard the crunch as the tires left the road and went onto the shoulder. Something struck the side of the car, probably the guardrail, and made it fishtail, throwing me down on the floor. Up front the woman was screaming and cursing and the Angel wasn't making a sound, but, in my head, I could hear him sort of keening. Whatever happened, this would be it. The Angel had told me all that time ago, after I'd taken him home, that they didn't last long after they got here, the exiles from his world and other worlds. Things tended to *happen* to them, even if they latched on to someone like me or the woman. They'd be in accidents or the people here would kill them. Like antibodies in a human body rejecting something or fighting a disease. At least I belonged here, but it looked like I was going to die in a car accident with the Angel and the woman both. I didn't care.

The car swerved back onto the highway for a few seconds and then pitched to the right again. Suddenly there was nothing under us and then we thumped down on something, not road but dirt or grass or something, bombing madly up and down. I pulled myself up on the back of the seat just in time to see the sign coming at us at an angle. The corner of it started to go through the windshield on the woman's side and then all I saw for a long time was the biggest display of silver fireworks ever.

It was hard to be gentle with him. Every move hurt but I didn't want to leave him sitting in the car next to her, even if she was dead. Being in the backseat had kept most of the glass from flying into me but I was still shaking some out of my hair and the impact hadn't done much for my back.

I laid the Angel out on the lumpy grass a little ways from the car and looked around. We were maybe a hundred yards from the highway, near a road that ran parallel to it. It was dark but I could still read the sign that had come through the windshield and split the woman's head in half. It said, Construction Ahead, Reduce Speed. Far off on the other road, I could see a flashing yellow light and at first I was afraid it was the police or something but it stayed where it was and I realized that must be the construction.

"Friend," whispered the Angel, startling me. He'd never spoken aloud to me, not directly.

Don't talk, I said, bending over him, trying to figure out some way I could touch him, just for comfort. There wasn't anything else I could do now.

"I have to," he said, still whispering. "It's almost all gone. Did you get it?"

Mostly, I said. Not all.

"I meant for you to have it."

I know.

"I don't know that it will really do you any good." His breath kind of bubbled in his throat. I could see something wet and shiny on his mouth but it wasn't silver fireworks. "But it's yours. You can do as you like with it. Live on it the way I did. Get what you need when you need it. But you can live as a human, too. Eat. Work. However, whatever."

I'm not human, I said. I'm not any more human than you, even if I do belong here.

"Yes, you are, little friend. I haven't made you any less human," he said, and coughed some. "I'm not sorry I wouldn't mate. I couldn't mate with my own. It was too . . . I don't know, too little of me, too much of them, something. I couldn't bond, it would have been nothing but emptiness. The Great Sin, to be unable to give, because the universe knows only less or more and I insisted that it would be good or bad. So they sent me here. But in the end, you know, they got their way, little friend." I felt his hand on me for a moment before it fell away. "I did it after all. Even if it wasn't with my own."

The bubbling in his throat stopped. I sat next to him for a while in the dark. Finally I felt it, the Angel stuff. It was kind of fluttery-churny, like too much coffee on an empty stomach. I closed my eyes and lay down on the grass, shivering. Maybe some of it was shock but I don't think so. The silver fireworks started, in my head this time, and with them came a lot of pictures I couldn't understand. Stuff about the Angel and where he'd come from and the way they mated. It was a lot like how we'd been together, the Angel and me. They looked a lot like us but there were a lot of differences, too, things I couldn't make out. I couldn't make out how they'd sent him here, either—by *light*, in, like, little bundles or something. It didn't make any sense to me, but I guessed an Angel could be light. Silver fireworks.

I must have passed out, because when I opened my eyes, it felt like I'd been laying there a long time. It was still dark, though. I sat up and reached for the Angel, thinking I ought to hide his body.

He was gone. There was just a sort of wet sandy stuff where he'd been.

I looked at the car and her. All that was still there. Somebody was going to see it soon. I didn't want to be around for that.

Everything still hurt but I managed to get to the other road and start walking back toward the city. It was like I could *feel* it now, the way the Angel must have, as though it were vibrating like a drum or ringing like a bell with all kinds of stuff, people laughing and crying and loving and hating and being afraid and everything else that happens to people. The stuff that the Angel took in, energy, that I could take in now if I wanted.

And I knew that taking it in that way, it would be bigger than anything all those people had, bigger than anything I could have had if things hadn't gone wrong with me all those years ago.

I wasn't so sure I wanted it. Like the Angel, refusing to mate back where he'd come from. He wouldn't, there, and I couldn't, here. Except now I could do something else.

I wasn't so sure I wanted it. But I didn't think I'd be able to stop it, either, any more than I could stop my heart from beating. Maybe it wasn't really such a good thing or a right thing. But it was like the Angel said: the universe doesn't know good or bad, only less or more.

Yeah. I heard *that*.

I thought about the waitress with no face. I could find them all now, all the ones from the other places, other worlds that sent them away for some kind of alien crimes nobody would have understood. I could find them all. They threw away their outcasts, I'd tell them, but here, we *kept* ours. And here's how. Here's how you live in a universe that only knows less or more.

I kept walking toward the city.

Rachel in Love

PAT MURPHY

It is a Sunday morning in summer and a small brown chimpanzee named Rachel sits on the living-room floor of a remote ranch house on the edge of the Painted Desert. She is watching a Tarzan movie on television. Her hairy arms are wrapped around her knees and she rocks back and forth with suppressed excitement. She knows that her father would say that she's too old for such childish amusements—but since Aaron is still sleeping, he can't chastise her.

On the television, Tarzan has been trapped in a bamboo cage by a band of wicked Pygmies. Rachel is afraid that he won't escape in time to save Jane from the ivory smugglers who hold her captive. The movie cuts to Jane, who is tied up in the back of a Jeep, and Rachel whimpers softly to herself. She knows better than to howl: she peeked into her father's bedroom earlier, and he was still in bed. Aaron doesn't like her to howl when he is sleeping.

When the movie breaks for a commercial, Rachel goes to her father's room. She is ready for breakfast and she wants him to get up. She tiptoes to the bed to see if he is awake.

His eyes are open and he is staring at nothing. His face is pale and his lips are a purplish color. Dr. Aaron Jacobs, the man Rachel calls father, is not asleep. He is dead, having died in the night of a heart attack.

When Rachel shakes him, his head rocks back and forth in time with her shaking, but his eyes do not blink and he does not breathe. She places his hand on her head, nudging him so that he will waken and stroke her. He does not move. When she leans toward him, his hand falls limply to dangle over the edge of the bed.

In the breeze from the open bedroom window, the fine wisps of gray hair that he had carefully combed over his bald spot each morning shift and flutter, exposing the naked scalp. In the other room, elephants trumpet as they stampede across the jungle to rescue Tarzan. Rachel whimpers softly, but her father does not move.

Rachel backs away from her father's body. In the living room, Tarzan is swinging across the jungle on vines, going to save Jane. Rachel ignores the television. She prowls through the house as if searching for comfort—stepping into her own small bedroom, wandering through her father's laboratory. From the cages that line the walls, white rats stare at her with hot red eyes. A rabbit hops across its cage, making a series of slow dull thumps, like a feather pillow tumbling down a flight of stairs.

She thinks that perhaps she made a mistake. Perhaps her father is just sleeping. She returns to the bedroom, but nothing has changed. Her father lies open-eyed on the bed. For a long time, she huddles beside his body, clinging to his hand.

He is the only person she has ever known. He is her father, her teacher, her friend. She cannot leave him alone.

The afternoon sun blazes through the window, and still Aaron does not move. The room grows dark, but Rachel does not turn on the lights. She is waiting for Aaron to wake up. When the moon rises, its silver light shines through the window to cast a bright rectangle on the far wall.

Outside, somewhere in the barren rocky land surrounding the ranch house, a coyote lifts its head to the rising moon and wails, a thin sound that is as lonely as a train whistling through an abandoned station. Rachel joins in with a desolate howl of loneliness and grief. Aaron lies still and Rachel knows that he is dead.

When Rachel was younger, she had a favorite bedtime story. — Where did I come from? she would ask Aaron, using the abbreviated gestures of ASL, American Sign Language. — Tell me again.

"You're too old for bedtime stories," Aaron would say.

— Please, she'd sign. — Tell me the story.

In the end, he always relented and told her. "Once upon a time, there was a little girl named Rachel," he said. "She was a pretty girl, with long golden hair like a princess in a fairy tale. She lived with her father and her mother and they were all very happy."

Rachel would snuggle contentedly beneath her blankets. The story, like any good fairy tale, had elements of tragedy. In the story, Rachel's father worked at a university, studying the workings of the brain and charting the electric fields that the nervous impulses of an active brain produced. But the other researchers at the university didn't understand Rachel's father; they distrusted his research and cut off his funding. (During this portion of the story, Aaron's voice took on a bitter edge.)

So he left the university and took his wife and daughter to the desert, where he could work in peace.

He continued his research and determined that each individual brain produced its own unique pattern of fields, as characteristic as a fingerprint. (Rachel found this part of the story quite dull, but Aaron insisted on including it.) The shape of this "Electric Mind," as he called it, was determined by habitual patterns of thoughts and emotions. Record the Electric Mind, he postulated, and you could capture an individual's personality.

Then one sunny day, the doctor's wife and beautiful daughter went for a drive. A truck barreling down a winding cliffside road lost its brakes and met the car head-on, killing both the girl and her mother. (Rachel clung to Aaron's hand during this part of the story, frightened by the sudden evil twist of fortune.)

But though Rachel's body had died, all was not lost. In his desert lab, the doctor had recorded the electrical patterns produced by his daughter's brain. The doctor had been experimenting with the use of external magnetic fields to impose the patterns from one animal onto the brain of another. From an animal supply house, he obtained a young chimpanzee. He used a mixture of norepinephrin-based transmitter substances to boost the speed of neural processing in the chimp's brain, and then he imposed the pattern of his daughter's mind upon the brain of this young chimp, combining the two after his own fashion, saving his daughter in his own way. In the chimp's brain was all that remained of Rachel Jacobs.

The doctor named the chimp Rachel and raised her as his own daughter. Since the limitations of the chimpanzee larynx made speech very difficult, he instructed her in ASL. He taught her to read and to write. They were good friends, the best of companions.

By this point in the story, Rachel was usually asleep. But it didn't matter—she knew the ending. The doctor, whose name was Aaron Jacobs, and the chimp named Rachel lived happily ever after.

Rachel likes fairy tales and she likes happy endings. She has the mind of a teenage girl, but the innocent heart of a young chimp.

Sometimes, when Rachel looks at her gnarled brown fingers, they seem alien, wrong, out of place. She remembers having small, pale, delicate hands. Memories lie upon memories, layers upon layers, like the sedimentary rocks of the desert buttes.

Rachel remembers a blonde-haired fair-skinned woman who smelled sweetly of perfume. On a Halloween long ago, this woman (who was, in these memories, Rachel's mother) painted Rachel's fingernails bright red because Rachel was dressed as a gypsy and gypsies liked red. Rachel remembers the woman's hands: white hands with faintly blue veins hidden just beneath the skin, neatly clipped nails painted rose pink.

But Rachel also remembers another mother and another time. Her mother was dark and hairy and smelled sweetly of overripe fruit. She and Rachel lived in a wire cage in a room filled with chimps and she hugged Rachel to her hairy breast whenever any people came into the room. Rachel's mother groomed Rachel constantly, picking delicately through her fur in search of lice that she never found.

Memories upon memories: jumbled and confused, like random pictures clipped from magazines, a bright collage that makes no sense. Rachel remembers cages: cold wire mesh beneath her feet, the smell of fear around her. A man in a white lab coat took her from the arms of her hairy mother and pricked her with needles. She could hear her mother howling, but she could not escape from the man.

Rachel remembers a junior-high-school dance where she wore a new dress: she stood in a dark corner of the gym for hours, pretending to admire the crepe-paper decorations because she felt too shy to search among the crowd for her friends.

She remembers when she was a young chimp. she huddled with five other adolescent chimps in the stuffy freight compartment of a train, frightened by the alien smells and sounds.

She remembers gym class: gray lockers and ugly gym suits that revealed her skinny legs. The teacher made everyone play softball, even Rachel who was unathletic and painfully shy. Rachel at bat, standing at the plate, was terrified to be the center of attention. "Easy out," said the catcher, a hard-edged girl who ran with the wrong crowd and always smelled of cigarette smoke. When Rachel swung at the ball and missed, the outfielders filled the air with malicious laughter.

Rachel's memories are as delicate and elusive as the dusty moths and butterflies that dance among the rabbitbrush and sage. Memories of her girlhood never linger; they land for an instant, then take flight, leaving Rachel feeling abandoned and alone.

Rachel leaves Aaron's body where it is, but closes his eyes and pulls the sheet up over his head. She does not know what else to do. Each day she waters the garden and picks some greens for the rabbits. Each day, she cares for the animals in the lab, bringing them food and refilling their water bottles. The weather is cool, and Aaron's body does not smell too bad, though by the end of the week, a wide line of ants runs from the bed to the open window.

At the end of the first week, on a moonlit evening, Rachel decides to let the animals go free. She releases the rabbits one by one, climbing on a stepladder to reach down into the cage and lift each placid bunny out. She carries each one to the back door, holding it for a moment and stroking the soft warm fur. Then she sets the animal down and nudges it in the direction of the green grass that grows around the perimeter of the fenced garden.

The rats are more difficult to deal with. She manages to wrestle the large rat cage off the shelf, but it is heavier than she thought it would be. Though she slows its fall, it lands on the floor with a crash and the rats scurry to and fro within. She shoves the cage across the linoleum floor, sliding it down the hall, over the doorsill, and onto the back patio. When she opens the cage door, rats burst out like popcorn from a popper, white in the moonlight and dashing in all directions.

Once, while Aaron was taking a nap, Rachel walked along the dirt track that led to the main highway. She hadn't planned on going far. She just wanted to see what the highway looked like, maybe hide near the mailbox and watch a car drive past. She was curious about the outside world and her fleeting fragmentary memories did not satisfy that curiosity.

She was halfway to the mailbox when Aaron came roaring up in his old Jeep. "Get in the car," he shouted at her. "Right now!" Rachel had never seen him so angry. She cowered in the Jeep's passenger seat, covered with dust from the road, unhappy that Aaron was so upset. He didn't speak until they got back to the ranch house, and then he spoke in a low voice, filled with bitterness and suppressed rage.

"You don't want to go out there," he said. "You wouldn't like it out there. The world is filled with petty, narrow-minded, stupid people. They wouldn't understand you. And anyone they don't understand, they want to hurt. They hurt anyone who's different. If they know that you're different, they punish you, hurt you. They'd lock you up and never let you go."

He looked straight ahead, staring through the dirty windshield. "It's not like the shows on TV, Rachel," he said in a softer tone. "It's not like the stories in books."

He looked at her then and she gestured frantically. — I'm sorry. I'm sorry.

"I can't protect you out there," he said. "I can't keep you safe."

Rachel took his hand in both of hers. He relented then, stroking her head. "Never do that again," he said. "Never."

Aaron's fear was contagious. Rachel never again walked along the dirt track and sometimes she had dreams about bad people who wanted to lock her in a cage.

Two weeks after Aaron's death, a black-and-white police car drives slowly up to the house. When the policemen knock on the door, Rachel hides behind the couch in the living room. They knock again, try the knob, then open the door, which she had left unlocked.

Suddenly frightened, Rachel bolts from behind the couch, bounding toward the back door. Behind her, she hears one man yell, "My God! It's a gorilla!"

By the time he pulls his gun, Rachel has run out the back door and away into the hills. From the hills she watches as an ambulance drives up and two men in white take Aaron's body away. Even after the ambulance and the police car drive away, Rachel is afraid to go back to the house. Only after sunset does she return.

Just before dawn the next morning, she wakens to the sound of a truck jouncing down the dirt road. She peers out the window to see a pale green pickup. Sloppily stenciled in white on the door are the words: Primate Research Center. Rachel hesitates as the truck pulls up in front of the house. By the time she has decided to flee, two men are getting out of the truck. One of them carries a rifle.

She runs out the back door and heads for the hills, but she is only halfway to hiding when she hears a sound like a sharp intake of breath and feels a painful jolt in her shoulder. Suddenly, her legs give way and she is tumbling backward down the sandy slope, dust coating her red-brown fur, her howl becoming a whimper, then fading to nothing at all. She falls into the blackness of sleep.

The sun is up. Rachel lies in a cage in the back of the pickup truck. She is partially conscious and she feels a tingling in her hands and feet. Nausea grips her stomach and bowels. Her body aches.

Rachel can blink, but otherwise she can't move. From where she lies, she can see only the wire mesh of the cage and the side of the truck. When she tries to turn her head, the burning in her skin intensifies. She lies still, wanting to cry out, but unable to make a sound. She can only blink slowly, trying to close out the pain. But the burning and nausea stay.

The truck jounces down a dirt road, then stops. It rocks as the men get out. The doors slam. Rachel hears the tailgate open.

A woman's voice: "Is that the animal the County Sheriff wanted us to pick up?" A woman peers into the cage. She wears a white lab coat and her brown hair is tied back in a single braid. Around her eyes, Rachel can see small wrinkles, etched by years of living in the desert. The woman doesn't look evil. Rachel hopes that the woman will save her from the men in the truck.

"Yeah. It should be knocked out for at least another half hour. Where do you want it?"

"Bring it into the lab where we had the rhesus monkeys. I'll keep it there until I have an empty cage in the breeding area."

Rachel's cage scrapes across the bed of the pickup. She feels each bump and jar as a new pain. The man swings the cage onto a cart and the woman pushes the cart down a concrete corridor. Rachel watches the walls pass just a few inches from her nose.

The lab contains rows of cages in which small animals sleepily move. In the sudden stark light of the overhead fluorescent bulbs, the eyes of white rats gleam red.

With the help of one of the men from the truck, the woman manhandles Rachel onto a lab table. The metal surface is cold and hard, painful against Rachel's skin. Rachel's body is not under her control; her limbs will not respond. She is still frozen by the tranquilizer, able to watch, but that is all. She cannot protest or plead for mercy.

Rachel watches with growing terror as the woman pulls on rubber gloves and fills a hypodermic needle with a clear solution. "Mark down that I'm giving her the standard test for tuberculosis; this eyelid should be checked before she's moved in with the others. I'll add thiabendazole to her feed for the next few days to clean out any intestinal worms. And I suppose we might as well de-flea her as well," the woman says. The man grunts in response.

Expertly, the woman closes one of Rachel's eyes. With her open eye, Rachel watches the hypodermic needle approach. She feels a sharp pain in her eyelid. In her mind, she is howling, but the only sound she can manage is a breathy sigh.

The woman sets the hypodermic aside and begins methodically spraying Rachel's fur with a cold, foul-smelling liquid. A drop strikes Rachel's eye and burns. Rachel blinks, but she cannot lift a hand to rub her eye. The woman treats Rachel with casual indifference, chatting with the man as she spreads Rachel's legs and sprays her genitals. "Looks healthy enough. Good breeding stock."

Rachel moans, but neither person notices. At last, they finish their torture, put her in a cage, and leave the room. She closes her eyes, and the darkness returns.

Rachel dreams. She is back at home in the ranch house. It is night and she is alone. Outside, coyotes yip and howl. The coyote is the voice of the desert, wailing as the wind wails when it stretches itself thin to squeeze through a crack between two boulders. The people native to this land tell tales of Coyote, a god who was a trickster, unreliable, changeable, mercurial.

Rachel is restless, anxious, unnerved by the howling of the coyotes. She is looking for Aaron. In the dream, she knows he is not dead, and she searches the house for him, wandering from his cluttered bedroom to her small room to the linoleum-tiled lab.

She is in the lab when she hears something tapping: a small dry scratching, like a windblown branch against the window, though no tree grows near the house and the night is still. Cautiously, she lifts the curtain to look out.

She looks into her own reflection: a pale oval face, long blonde hair. The hand that holds the curtain aside is smooth and white with carefully clipped fingernails. But something is wrong. Superimposed on the reflection is another face peering through the glass: a pair of dark brown eyes, a chimp face with red-brown hair and jug-handle ears. She sees her own reflection and she sees the outsider; the two images merge and blur. She is afraid, but she can't drop the curtain and shut the ape face out.

She is a chimp looking in through the cold, bright windowpane; she is a girl looking out; she is a girl looking in; she is an ape looking out. She is afraid and the coyotes are howling all around.

Rachel opens her eyes and blinks until the world comes into focus. The pain and tingling has retreated, but she still feels a little sick. Her left eye aches. When she rubs it, she feels a raised lump on the eyelid where the woman pricked her. She lies on the floor of a wire mesh cage. The room is hot and the air is thick with the smell of animals.

In the cage beside her is another chimp, an older animal with scruffy dark brown fur. He sits with his arms wrapped around his knees, rocking back and forth, back and forth. His head is down. As he rocks, he murmurs to himself, a meaningless cooing that goes on and on. On his scalp, Rachel can see a gleam of metal: a permanently implanted electrode protrudes from a shaven patch. Rachel makes a soft questioning sound, but the other chimp will not look up.

Rachel's own cage is just a few feet square. In one corner is a bowl of monkey pellets. A water bottle hangs on the side of the cage. Rachel ignores the food, but drinks thirstily.

Sunlight streams through the windows, sliced into small sections by the wire mesh that covers the glass. She tests her cage door, rattling it gently at first, then harder. It is securely latched. The gaps in the mesh are too small to admit her hand. She can't reach out to work the latch.

The other chimp continues to rock back and forth. When Rachel rattles the mesh of her cage and howls, he lifts his head wearily and looks at her. His red-rimmed eyes are unfocused; she can't be sure he sees her.

— Hello, she gestures tentatively. — What's wrong?

He blinks at her in the dim light. — Hurt, he signs in ASL. He reaches up to touch the electrode, fingering skin that is already raw from repeated rubbing.

— Who hurt you? she asks. He stares at her blankly and she repeats the question. — Who?

— Men, he signs.

As if on cue, there is the click of a latch and the door to the lab opens. A bearded man in a white coat steps in, followed by a clean-shaven man in a suit. The bearded man seems to be showing the other man around the lab. ". . . only preliminary testing, so far," the bearded man is saying. "We've been hampered by a shortage of chimps trained in ASL." The two men stop in front of the old chimp's cage. "This old fellow is from the Oregon center. Funding for the language program was cut back and some of the animals were dispersed to other programs." The old chimp huddles at the back of the cage, eyeing the bearded man with suspicion.

— Hungry? the bearded man signs to the old chimp. He holds up an orange where the old chimp can see it.

— Give orange, the old chimp gestures. He holds out his hand, but comes no nearer to the wire mesh than he must to reach the orange. With the fruit in hand, he retreats to the back of his cage.

The bearded man continues, "This project will provide us with the first solid data on neural activity during use of sign language. But we really need greater access to chimps with advanced language skills. People are so damn protective of their animals."

"Is this one of yours?" the clean-shaven man asks, pointing to Rachel. She cowers in the back of the cage, as far from the wire mesh as she can get.

"No, not mine. She was someone's household pet, apparently. The county sheriff had us pick her up." The bearded man peers into her cage. Rachel does not move; she is terrified that he will somehow guess that she knows ASL. She stares at his hands and thinks about those hands putting an electrode through her skull. "I think she'll be put in breeding stock," the man says as he turns away.

Rachel watches them go, wondering at what terrible people these are. Aaron was right: they want to punish her, put an electrode in her head.

After the men are gone, she tries to draw the old chimp into conversation, but he will not reply. He ignores her as he eats his orange. Then he returns to his former posture, hiding his head and rocking himself back and forth.

Rachel, hungry despite herself, samples one of the food pellets. It has a strange medicinal taste, and she puts it back in the bowl. She needs to pee, but there is no toilet and she cannot escape the cage. At last, unable to hold it, she pees in one corner of the cage. The urine flows through the wire mesh to soak the litter below, and the smell of warm piss fills her cage. Humiliated, frightened, her head aching, her skin itchy from the flea spray, Rachel watches as the sunlight creeps across the room.

The day wears on. Rachel samples her food again, but rejects it, preferring hunger to the strange taste. A black man comes and cleans the cages of the rabbits and rats. Rachel cowers in her cage and watches him warily, afraid that he will hurt her, too.

When night comes, she is not tired. Outside, coyotes howl. Moonlight filters in through the high windows. She draws her legs up toward her body, then rests with her arms wrapped around her knees. Her father is dead, and she is a captive in a strange place. For a time, she whimpers softly, hoping to awaken from this nightmare and find herself at home in bed. When she hears the click of a key in the door to the room, she hugs herself more tightly.

A man in green coveralls pushes a cart filled with cleaning supplies into the room. He takes a broom from the cart, and begins sweeping the concrete floor. Over the rows of cages, she can see the top of his head bobbing in time with his sweeping. He works slowly and methodically, bending down to sweep carefully under each row of cages, making a neat pile of dust, dung, and food scraps in the center of the aisle.

The janitor's name is Jake. He is a middle-aged deaf man who has been employed by the Primate Research Center for the past seven years. He works night shift. The personnel director at the Primate Research Center likes Jake because he fills the federal quota for handicapped employees, and because he has not asked for a raise in five years. There have been some complaints about Jake—his work is often sloppy—but never enough to merit firing the man.

Jake is an unambitious, somewhat slow-witted man. He likes the Primate Research Center because he works alone, which allows him to drink on the job. He is an easygoing man, and he likes the animals. Sometimes, he brings treats for them. Once, a lab assistant caught him feeding an apple to a pregnant rhesus monkey. The monkey was part of an experiment on the effect of dietary restrictions on fetal brain development, and the lab assistant warned Jake that he would be fired if he was ever caught interfering with the animals again. Jake still feeds the animals, but he is more careful about when he does it, and he has never been caught again.

As Rachel watches, the old chimp gestures to Jake. — Give banana, the chimp signs. — Please banana. Jake stops sweeping for a minute and reaches down to the bottom shelf of his cleaning cart. He returns with a banana and offers it to the old chimp. The chimp accepts the banana and leans against the mesh while Jake scratches his fur.

When Jake turns back to his sweeping, he catches sight of Rachel and sees that she is watching him. Emboldened by his kindness to the old chimp, Rachel timidly gestures to him. — Help me.

Jake hesitates, then peers at her more closely. Both his eyes are shot with a fine lacework of red. His nose displays the broken blood vessels of someone who has been friends with the bottle for too many years. He needs a shave. But when he leans close, Rachel catches the scent of whiskey and tobacco. The smells remind her of Aaron and give her courage.

— Please help me, Rachel signs. — I don't belong here.

For the last hour, Jake has been drinking steadily. His view of the world is somewhat fuzzy. He stares at her blearily.

Rachel's fear that he will hurt her is replaced by the fear that he will leave her locked up and alone. Desperately she signs again. — Please please please. Help me. I don't belong here. Please help me go home.

He watches her, considering the situation. Rachel does not move. She is afraid that any movement will make him leave. With a majestic speed dictated by his inebriation, Jake leans his broom on the row of cages behind him and steps toward Rachel's cage again. — You talk? he signs.

— I talk, she signs.

— Where did you come from?

— From my father's house, she signs. — Two men came and shot me and put me here. I don't know why. I don't know why they locked me in jail.

Jake looks around, willing to be sympathetic, but puzzled by her talk of jail. — This isn't jail, he signs. — This is a place where scientists raise monkeys.

Rachel is indignant. — I am not a monkey, she signs. — I am a girl.

Jake studies her hairy body and her jug-handle ears. — You look like a monkey.

Rachel shakes her head. — No. I am a girl.

Rachel runs her hands back over her head, a very human gesture of annoyance and unhappiness. She signs sadly, — I don't belong here. Please let me out.

Jake shifts his weight from foot to foot, wondering what to do. — I can't let you out. I'll get in big trouble.

— Just for a little while? Please?

Jake glances at his cart of supplies. He has to finish off this room and two corridors of offices before he can relax for the night.

— Don't go, Rachel signs, guessing his thoughts.

— I have work to do.

She looks at the cart, then suggests eagerly, — Let me out and I'll help you work.

Jake frowns. — If I let you out, you will run away.

— No, I won't run. I will help. Please let me out.

— You promise to go back?

Rachel nods.

Warily he unlatches the cage. Rachel bounds out, grabs a whisk broom from the cart, and begins industriously sweeping bits of food and droppings from beneath the row of cages. — Come on, she signs to Jake from the end of the aisle. — I will help.

When Jake pushes the cart from the room filled with cages, Rachel follows him closely. The rubber wheels of the cleaning cart rumble softly on the linoleum floor. They pass through a metal door into a corridor where the floor is carpeted and the air smells of chalk dust and paper.

Offices let off the corridor, each one a small room furnished with a desk, bookshelves, and a blackboard. Jake shows Rachel how to empty the wastebaskets into a garbage bag. While he cleans the blackboards, she wanders from office to office, trailing the trash-filled garbage bag.

At first, Jake keeps a close eye on Rachel. But after cleaning each blackboard, he pauses to refill a cup from the whiskey bottle that he keeps wedged between the Saniflush and the window cleaner. By the time he is halfway through the second cup, he is treating her like an old friend, telling her to hurry up so that they can eat dinner.

Rachel works quickly, but she stops sometimes to gaze out the office windows. Outside, moonlight shines on a sandy plain, dotted here and there with scrubby clumps of rabbitbrush.

At the end of the corridor is a larger room in which there are several desks and typewriters. In one of the wastebaskets, buried beneath memos and candybar wrappers, she finds a magazine. The title is *Love Confessions* and the cover has a picture of a man and woman kissing. Rachel studies the cover, then takes the magazine, tucking it on the bottom shelf of the cart.

Jake pours himself another cup of whiskey and pushes the cart to another hallway. Jake is working slower now, and as he works he makes humming noises, tuneless sounds that he feels only as pleasant vibrations. The last few blackboards are sloppily done, and Rachel, finished with the wastebaskets, cleans the places that Jake missed.

They eat dinner in the janitor's storeroom, a stuffy windowless room furnished with an ancient grease-stained couch, a battered black-and-white television, and shelves of cleaning supplies. From a shelf, Jake takes the paper bag that holds his lunch: a baloney sandwich, a bag of barbecued potato chips, and a box of vanilla wafers. From behind the gallon jugs of liquid cleanser, he takes a magazine. He lights a cigarette, pours himself another cup of whiskey, and settles down on the couch. After a moment's hesitation, he offers Rachel a drink, pouring a shot of whiskey into a chipped ceramic cup.

Aaron never let Rachel drink whiskey, and she samples it carefully. At first the smell makes her sneeze, but she is fascinated by the way that the drink warms her throat, and she sips some more.

As they drink, Rachel tells Jake about the men who shot her and the woman who pricked her with a needle, and he nods. — The people here are crazy, he signs.

— I know, she says, thinking of the old chimp with the electrode in his head. — You won't tell them I can talk, will you?

Jake nods. — I won't tell them anything.

— They treat me like I'm not real, Rachel signs sadly. Then she hugs her knees, frightened at the thought of being held captive by crazy people. She considers planning her escape: she is out of the cage and she is sure she could outrun Jake. As she wonders about it, she finishes her cup of whiskey. The alcohol takes the edge off her fear. She sits close beside Jake on the couch, and the smell of his cigarette smoke reminds her of Aaron. For the first time since Aaron's death she feels warm and happy.

She shares Jake's cookies and potato chips and looks at the *Love Confessions* magazine that she took from the trash. The first story that she reads is about a woman named Alice. The headline reads: "I became a Go-go dancer to pay off my husband's gambling debts, and now he wants me to sell my body."

Rachel sympathizes with Alice's loneliness and suffering. Alice, like Rachel, is alone and misunderstood. As Rachel slowly reads, she sips her second cup of whiskey. The story reminds her of a fairy tale: the nice man who rescues Alice from her terrible husband replaces the handsome prince who rescued the princess. Rachel glances at Jake and wonders if he will rescue her from the wicked people who locked her in the cage.

She has finished the second cup of whiskey and eaten half Jake's cookies when Jake says that she must go back to her cage. She goes reluctantly, taking the magazine with her. He promises that he will come for her again the next night, and with that she must be content. She puts the magazine in one corner of the cage and curls up to sleep.

She wakes early in the afternoon. A man in a white coat is wheeling a low cart into the lab.

Rachel's head aches with hangover and she feels sick. As she crouches in one corner of her cage, he stops the cart beside her cage and then locks the wheels. "Hold on there," he mutters to her, then slides her cage onto the cart.

The man wheels her through long corridors, where the walls are cement blocks, painted institutional green. Rachel huddles unhappily in the cage, wondering where she is going and whether Jake will ever be able to find her.

At the end of a long corridor, the man opens a thick metal door and a wave of warm air strikes Rachel. It stinks of chimpanzees, excrement, and rotting food. On either side of the corridor are metal bars and wire mesh. Behind the mesh, Rachel can see dark hairy shadows. In one cage, five adolescent chimps swing and play. In another, two females huddle together, grooming each other. The man slows as he passes a cage in which a big male is banging on the wire with his fist, making the mesh rattle and ring.

"Now, Johnson," says the man. "Cool it. Be nice. I'm bringing you a new little girlfriend."

With a series of hooks, the man links Rachel's cage with the cage next to Johnson's and opens the doors. "Go on, girl," he says. "See the nice fruit." In the cage is a bowl of sliced apples with an attendant swarm of fruit flies.

At first, Rachel will not move into the new cage. She crouches in the cage on the cart, hoping that the man will decide to take her back to the lab. She watches him get a hose and attach it to a water faucet. But she does not understand his intention until he turns the stream of water on her. A cold blast strikes her on the back and she howls, fleeing into the new cage to avoid the cold water. Then the man closes the doors, unhooks the cage, and hurries away.

The floor is bare cement. Her cage is at one end of the corridor and two walls are cement block. A door in one of the cement block walls leads to an outside run. The other two walls are wire mesh: one facing the corridor; the other, Johnson's cage.

Johnson, quiet now that the man has left, is sniffing around the door in the wire mesh wall that joins their cages. Rachel watches him anxiously. Her memories of other chimps are distant, softened by time. She remembers her mother; she vaguely remembers playing with other chimps her age. But she does not know how to react to Johnson when he stares at her with great intensity and makes a loud huffing sound. She gestures to him in ASL, but he only stares harder and huffs again. Beyond Johnson, she can see other cages and other chimps, so many that the wire mesh blurs her vision and she cannot see the other end of the corridor.

To escape Johnson's scrutiny, she ducks through the door into the outside run, a wire mesh cage on a white concrete foundation. Outside there is barren ground and rabbitbrush. The afternoon sun is hot and all the other runs are deserted until Johnson appears in the run beside hers. His attention disturbs her and she goes back inside.

She retreats to the side of the cage farthest from Johnson. A crudely built wooden platform provides her with a place to sit. Wrapping her arms around her knees, she tries to relax and ignore Johnson. She dozes off for a while, but wakes to a commotion across the corridor.

In the cage across the way is a female chimp in heat. Rachel recognizes the smell from her own times in heat. Two keepers are opening the door that separates the female's cage from the adjoining cage, where a male stands, watching with great interest. Johnson is shaking the wire mesh and howling as he watches.

"Mike here is a virgin, but Susie knows what she's doing," one keeper was saying to the other. "So it should go smoothly. But keep the hose ready."

"Yeah?"

"Sometimes they fight. We only use the hose to break it up if it gets real bad. Generally, they do okay."

Mike stalks into Susie's cage. The keepers lower the cage door, trapping both chimps in the same cage. Susie seems unalarmed. She continues eating a slice of orange while Mike sniffs at her genitals with every indication of great interest. She bends over to let Mike finger her pink bottom, the sign of estrus.

Rachel finds herself standing at the wire mesh, making low moaning noises. She can see Mike's erection, hear his grunting cries. He squats on the floor of Susie's cage, gesturing to the female. Rachel's feelings are mixed: she is fascinated, fearful, confused. She keeps thinking of the description of sex in the *Love Confessions* story: When Alice feels Danny's lips on hers, she is swept away by the passion of the moment. He takes her in his arms and her skin tingles as if she were consumed by an inner fire.

Susie bends down and Mike penetrates her with a loud grunt, thrusting violently with his hips. Susie cries out shrilly and suddenly leaps up, knocking Mike away. Rachel watches, overcome with fascination. Mike, his penis now limp, follows Susie slowly to the corner of the cage, where he begins grooming her carefully. Rachel finds that the wire mesh has cut her hands where she gripped it too tightly.

It is night, and the door at the end of the corridor creaks open. Rachel is immediately alert, peering through the wire mesh and trying to see down to the end of the corridor. She bangs on the wire mesh. As Jake comes closer, she waves a greeting.

When Jake reaches for the lever that will raise the door to Rachel's cage, Johnson charges toward him, howling and waving his arms above his head. He hammers on the wire mesh with his fists, howling and grimacing at Jake. Rachel ignores Johnson and hurries after Jake.

Again Rachel helps Jake clean. In the laboratory, she greets the old chimp, but the animal is more interested in the banana that Jake has brought than in conversation. The chimp will not reply to her questions, and after several tries, she gives up.

While Jake vacuums the carpeted corridors, Rachel empties the trash, finding a magazine called *Modern Romance* in the same wastebasket that had provided *Love Confessions*.

Later, in the janitor's lounge, Jake smokes a cigarette, sips whiskey, and flips through one of his own magazines. Rachel reads love stories in *Modern Romance*.

Every once in a while, she looks over Jake's shoulder at grainy pictures of naked women with their legs spread wide apart. Jake looks for a long time at a picture of a blonde woman with big breasts, red fingernails, and purple-painted eyelids. The woman lies on her back and smiles as she strokes the pinkness between her legs. The picture on the next page shows her caressing her own breasts, pinching the dark nipples. The final picture shows her looking back over her shoulder. She is in the position that Susie took when she was ready to be mounted.

Rachel looks over Jake's shoulder at the magazine, but she does not ask questions. Jake's smell began to change as soon as he opened the magazine; the scent of nervous sweat mingles with the aromas of tobacco and whiskey. Rachel suspects that questions would not be welcome just now.

At Jake's insistence, she goes back to her cage before dawn.

Over the next week, she listens to the conversations of the men who come and go, bringing food and hosing out the cages. From the men's conversation, she learns that the Primate Research Center is primarily a breeding facility that supplies researchers with domestically bred apes and monkeys of several species. It also maintains its own research staff. In indifferent tones, the men talk of horrible things. The adolescent chimps at the end of the corridor are being fed a diet high in cholesterol to determine cholesterol's effects on the circulatory system. A group of pregnant females are being injected with male hormones to determine how that will affect the female offspring. A group of infants are being fed a low protein diet to determine adverse effects on their brain development.

The men look through her as if she were not real, as if she were a part of the wall, as if she were no one at all. She cannot speak to them; she cannot trust them.

Each night, Jake lets her out of her cage and she helps him clean. He brings treats: barbecued potato chips, fresh fruit, chocolate bars, and cookies. He treats her fondly, as one would treat a precocious child. And he talks to her.

At night, when she is with Jake, Rachel can almost forget the terror of the cage, the anxiety of watching Johnson pace to and fro, the sense of unreality that accompanies the simplest act. She would be content to stay with Jake forever, eating snack food and reading confessions magazines. He seems to like her company. But each morning, Jake insists that she must go back to the cage and the terror. By the end of the first week, she has begun plotting her escape.

Whenever Jake falls asleep over his whiskey, something that happens three nights out of five, Rachel prowls the center alone, surreptitiously gathering things that she will need to survive in the desert: a plastic jug filled with water, a plastic bag of food pellets, a large beach towel that will serve as a blanket on the cool desert nights, a discarded plastic shopping bag in which she can carry the other things. Her best find is a road map on which the Primate Center is marked in red. She knows the address of Aaron's ranch and finds it on the map. She studies the roads and plots a route home. Cross-country, assuming that she does not get lost, she will have to travel about fifty miles to reach the ranch. She hides these things behind one of the shelves in the janitor's storeroom.

Her plans to run away and go home are disrupted by the idea that she is in love with Jake, a notion that comes to her slowly, fed by the stories in the confessions magazines. When Jake absentmindedly strokes her, she is filled with a strange excitement. She longs for his company and misses him on the weekends when he is away. She is happy only when she is with him, following him through the halls of the center, sniffing the aroma of tobacco and whiskey that is his own perfume. She steals a cigarette from his pack and hides it in her cage, where she can savor the smell of it at her leisure.

She loves him, but she does not know how to make him love her back. Rachel knows little about love: she remembers a high-school crush where she mooned after a boy with a locker near hers, but that came to nothing. She reads the confessions magazines and Ann Landers's column in the newspaper that Jake brings with him each night, and from these sources, she learns about romance. One night, after Jake falls asleep, she types a badly punctuated, ungrammatical letter to Ann. In the letter, she explains her situation and asks for advice on how to make Jake love her. She slips the letter into a sack labeled "Outgoing Mail," and for the next week she reads Ann's column with increased interest. But her letter never appears.

Rachel searches for answers in the magazine pictures that seem to fascinate Jake. She studies the naked women, especially the big-breasted woman with the purple smudges around her eyes.

One night, in a secretary's desk, she finds a plastic case of eyeshadow. She steals it and takes it back to her cage. The next evening, as soon as the center is quiet, she upturns her metal food dish and regards her reflection in the shiny bottom. Squatting, she balances the eyeshadow case on one knee and examines its contents: a tiny makeup brush and three shades of eyeshadow—Indian Blue, Forest Green, and Wildly Violet. Rachel chooses the shade labeled Wildly Violet.

Using one finger to hold her right eye closed, she dabs her eyelid carefully with the makeup brush, leaving a gaudy orchid-colored smudge on her brown skin. She studies the smudge critically, then adds to it, smearing the color beyond the corner of her eyelid until it disappears in her brown fur. The color gives her eye a carnival brightness, a lunatic gaiety. Working with great care, she matches the effect on the other side, then smiles at herself in the glass, blinking coquettishly.

In the other cage, Johnson bares his teeth and shakes the wire mesh. She ignores him.

When Jake comes to let her out, he frowns at her eyes. — Did you hurt yourself? he asks.

— No, she says. Then, after a pause, — Don't you like it?

Jake squats beside her and stares at her eyes. Rachel puts a hand on his knee and her heart pounds at her own boldness. — You are a very strange monkey, he signs.

Rachel is afraid to move. Her hand on his knee closes into a fist; her face folds in on itself, puckering around the eyes.

Then, straightening up, he signs, — I liked your eyes better before.

He likes her eyes. She nods without taking her eyes from his face. Later, she washes her face in the women's rest room, leaving dark smudges the color of bruises on a series of paper towels.

Rachel is dreaming. She is walking through the Painted Desert with her hairy brown mother, following a red rock canyon that Rachel somehow knows will lead her to the Primate Research Center. Her mother is lagging behind: she does not want to go to the center; she is afraid. In the shadow of a rock outcropping, Rachel stops to explain to her mother that they must go to the center because Jake is at the center.

Rachel's mother does not understand sign language. She watches Rachel with mournful eyes, then scrambles up the canyon wall, leaving Rachel behind. Rachel climbs after her mother, pulling herself over the edge in time to see the other chimp loping away across the windblown red cinder-rock and sand.

Rachel bounds after her mother, and as she runs she howls like an abandoned infant chimp, wailing her distress. The figure of her mother wavers in the distance, shimmering in the heat that rises from the sand. The figure changes. Running away across the red sands is a pale blonde woman wearing a purple sweatsuit and jogging shoes, the sweet-smelling mother that Rachel remembers. The woman looks back and smiles at Rachel. "Don't howl like an ape, daughter," she calls. "Say Mama."

Rachel runs silently, dream running that takes her nowhere. The sand burns her feet and the sun beats down on her head. The blonde woman vanishes in the distance, and Rachel is alone. She collapses on the sand, whimpering because she is alone and afraid.

She feels the gentle touch of fingers grooming her fur, and for a moment, still half asleep, she believes that her hairy mother has returned to her. She opens her eyes and looks into a pair of dark brown eyes, separated from her by wire mesh. Johnson. He has reached through a gap in the fence to groom her. As he sorts through her fur, he makes soft cooing sounds, gentle comforting noises.

Still half asleep, she gazes at him and wonders why she was so fearful. He does not seem so bad. He grooms her for a time, and then sits nearby, watching her through the mesh. She brings a slice of apple from her dish of food and offers it to him. With her free hand, she makes the sign for apple. When he takes it, she signs again: apple. He is not a particularly quick student, but she has time and many slices of apple.

All Rachel's preparations are done, but she cannot bring herself to leave the center. Leaving the center means leaving Jake, leaving potato chips and whiskey, leaving security. To Rachel, the thought of love is always accompanied by the warm taste of whiskey and potato chips.

Some nights, after Jake is asleep, she goes to the big glass doors that lead to the outside. She opens the doors and stands on the steps, looking down into the desert. Sometimes a jackrabbit sits on its haunches in the rectangles of light that shine through the glass doors. Sometimes she sees kangaroo rats, hopping through the moonlight like rubber balls bouncing on hard pavement. Once, a coyote trots by, casting a contemptuous glance in her direction.

The desert is a lonely place. Empty. Cold. She thinks of Jake snoring softly in the janitor's lounge. And always she closes the door and returns to him.

Rachel leads a double life: janitor's assistant by night, prisoner and teacher by day. She spends her afternoons drowsing in the sun and teaching Johnson new signs.

On a warm afternoon, Rachel sits in the outside run, basking in the sunlight. Johnson is inside, and the other chimps are quiet. She can almost imagine she is back at her father's ranch, sitting in her own yard. She naps and dreams of Jake.

She dreams that she is sitting in his lap on the battered old couch. Her hand is on his chest: a smooth pale hand with red-painted fingernails. When she looks at the dark screen of the television set, she can see her reflection. She is a thin teenager with blonde hair and blue eyes. She is naked.

Jake is looking at her and smiling. He runs a hand down her back and she closes her eyes in ecstasy.

But something changes when she closes her eyes. Jake is grooming her as her mother used to groom her, sorting through her hair in search of fleas. She opens her eyes and sees Johnson, his diligent fingers searching through her fur, his intent brown eyes watching her. The reflection on the television screen shows two chimps, tangled in each other's arms.

Rachel wakes to find that she is in heat for the first time since she came to the center. The skin surrounding her genitals is swollen and pink.

For the rest of the day, she is restless, pacing to and fro in her cage. On his side of the wire mesh wall, Johnson is equally restless, following her when she goes outside, sniffing long and hard at the edge of the barrier that separates him from her.

That night, Rachel goes eagerly to help Jake clean. She follows him closely, never letting him get far from her. When he is sweeping, she trots after him with the dustpan and he almost trips over her twice. She keeps waiting for him to notice her condition, but he seems oblivious.

As she works, she sips from a cup of whiskey. Excited, she drinks more than usual, finishing two full cups. The liquor leaves her a little disoriented, and she sways as she follows Jake to the janitor's lounge. She curls up close beside him on the couch. He relaxes with his arms resting on the back of the couch, his legs stretching out before him. She moves so that she presses against him.

He stretches, yawns, and rubs the back of his neck as if trying to rub away stiffness. Rachel reaches around behind him and begins to gently rub his neck, reveling in the feel of his skin, his hair against the backs of her hands. The thoughts that hop and skip through her mind are confusing. Sometimes it seems that the hair that tickles her hands is Johnson's; sometimes, she knows it is Jake's. And sometimes it doesn't seem to matter. Are they really so different? They are not so different.

She rubs his neck, not knowing what to do next. In the confessions magazines, this is where the man crushes the woman in his arms. Rachel climbs into Jake's lap and hugs him, waiting for him to crush her in his arms. He blinks at her sleepily. Half asleep, he strokes her, and his moving hand brushes near her genitals. She presses herself against him, making a soft sound in her throat. She rubs her hip against his crotch, aware now of a slight change in his smell, in the tempo of his breathing. He blinks at her again, a little more awake now. She bares her teeth in a smile and tilts her head back to lick his neck. She can feel his hands on her shoulders, pushing her away, and she knows what he wants. She slides from his lap and turns, presenting him with her pink genitals, ready to be mounted, ready to have him penetrate her. She moans in anticipation, a low inviting sound.

He does not come to her. She looks over her shoulder and he is still sitting on the couch, watching her through half-closed eyes. He reaches over and picks up a magazine filled with pictures of naked women. His other hand drops to his crotch and he is lost in his own world.

Rachel howls like an infant who has lost its mother, but he does not look up. He is staring at the picture of the blonde woman.

Rachel runs down dark corridors to her cage, the only home she has. When she reaches her corridor, she is breathing hard and making small lonely whimpering noises. In the dimly lit corridor, she hesitates for a moment, staring into Johnson's cage. The male chimp is asleep. She remembers the touch of his hands when he groomed her.

From the corridor, she lifts the gate that leads into Johnson's cage and enters. He wakes at the sound of the door and sniffs the air. When he sees Rachel, he stalks toward her, sniffing eagerly. She lets him finger her genitals, sniff deeply of her scent. His penis is erect and he grunts in excitement. She turns and presents herself to him and he mounts her, thrusting deep inside. As he penetrates, she thinks, for a moment, of Jake and of the thin blonde teenage girl named Rachel, but then the moment passes. Almost against her will she cries out, a shrill exclamation of welcoming and loss.

After he withdraws his penis, Johnson grooms her gently, sniffing her genitals and softly stroking her fur. She is sleepy and content, but she knows that she cannot delay.

Johnson is reluctant to leave his cage, but Rachel takes him by the hand and leads him to the janitor's lounge. His presence gives her courage. She listens at the door and hears Jake's soft breathing. Leaving Johnson in the hall, she slips into the room. Jake is lying on the couch, the magazine draped over his legs. Rachel takes the equipment that she has gathered and stands for a moment, staring at the sleeping man. His baseball cap hangs on the arm of a broken chair, and she takes that to remember him by.

Rachel leads Johnson through the empty halls. A kangaroo rat, collecting seeds in the dried grass near the glass doors, looks up curiously as Rachel leads Johnson down the steps. Rachel carries the plastic shopping bag slung over her shoulder. Somewhere in the distance, a coyote howls, a long yapping wail. His cry is joined by others, a chorus in the moonlight.

Rachel takes Johnson by the hand and leads him into the desert.

A cocktail waitress, driving from her job in Flagstaff to her home in Winslow, sees two apes dart across the road, hurrying away from the bright beams of her headlights. After wrestling with her conscience (she does not want to be accused of drinking on the job), she notifies the county sheriff.

A local newspaper reporter, an eager young man fresh out of journalism school, picks up the story from the police report and interviews the waitress. Flattered by his enthusiasm for her story and delighted to find a receptive ear, she tells him details that she failed to mention to the police: one of the apes was wearing a baseball cap and carrying what looked like a shopping bag.

The reporter writes up a quick humorous story for the morning edition, and begins researching a feature article to be run later in the week. He knows that the newspaper, eager for news in a slow season, will play a human-interest story up big—kind of *Lassie, Come Home* with chimps.

Just before dawn, a light rain begins to fall, the first rain of spring. Rachel searches for shelter and finds a small cave formed by three tumbled boulders. It will keep off the rain and hide them from casual observers. She shares her food and water with Johnson. He has followed her closely all night, seemingly intimidated by the darkness and the howling of distant coyotes. She feels protective toward him. At the same time, having him with her gives her courage. He knows only a few gestures in ASL, but he does not need to speak. His presence is comfort enough.

Johnson curls up in the back of the cave and falls asleep quickly. Rachel sits in the opening and watches dawn-light wash the stars from the sky. The rain rattles against the sand, a comforting sound. She thinks about Jake. The baseball cap on her head still smells of his cigarettes, but she does not miss him. Not really. She fingers the cap and wonders why she thought she loved Jake.

The rain lets up. The clouds rise like fairy castles in the distance and the rising sun tints them pink and gold and gives them flaming red banners. Rachel remembers when she was younger and Aaron read her the story of Pinocchio, the little puppet who wanted to be a real boy. At the end of his adventures, Pinocchio, who has been brave and kind, gets his wish. He becomes a real boy.

Rachel had cried at the end of the story and when Aaron asked why, she had rubbed her eyes on the backs of her hairy hands. — I want to be a real girl, she signed to him. — A real girl.

"You are a real girl," Aaron had told her, but somehow she had never believed him.

The sun rises higher and illuminates the broken rock turrets of the desert. There is a magic in this barren land of unassuming grandeur. Some cultures send their young people to the desert to seek visions and guidance, searching for true thinking spawned by the openness of the place, the loneliness, the beauty of emptiness.

Rachel drowses in the warm sun and dreams a vision that has the clarity of truth. In the dream, her father comes to her. "Rachel," he says to her, "it doesn't matter what anyone thinks of you. You're my daughter."

— I want to be a real girl, she signs.

"You *are* real," her father says. "And you don't need some two-bit drunken janitor to prove it to you." She knows she is dreaming, but she also knows that her father speaks the truth. She is warm and happy and she doesn't need Jake at all. The sunlight warms her and a lizard watches her from a rock, scurrying for cover when she moves. She picks up a bit of loose rock that lies on the floor of the cave. Idly, she scratches on the dark red sandstone wall of the cave. A lopsided heart shape. Within it, awkwardly printed: Rachel and Johnson. Between them, a plus sign. She goes over the letters again and again, leaving scores of fine lines on the smooth rock surface. Then, late in the morning, soothed by the warmth of the day, she sleeps.

Shortly after dark, an elderly rancher in a pickup truck spots two apes in a remote corner of his ranch. They run away and lose him in the rocks, but not until he has a good look at them. He calls the police, the newspaper, and the Primate Center.

The reporter arrives first thing the next morning, interviews the rancher, and follows the men from the Primate Center as they search for evidence of the chimps. They find monkey shit near the cave, confirming that the runaways were indeed nearby. The news reporter, an eager and curious young man, squirms on his belly into the cave and finds the names scratched on the cave wall. He peers at it. He might have dismissed them as the idle scratchings of kids, except that the names match the names of the missing chimps. "Hey," he calls to his photographer, "take a look at this."

The next morning's newspaper displays Rachel's crudely scratched letters. In a brief interview, the rancher mentioned that the chimps were carrying bags. "Looked like supplies," he said. "They looked like they were in for a long haul."

On the third day, Rachel's water runs out. She heads toward a small town, marked on the map. They reach it in the early morning—thirst forces them to travel by day. Beside an isolated ranch house, she finds a faucet. She is filling her bottle when Johnson grunts in alarm.

A dark-haired woman watches from the porch of the house. She does not move toward the apes, and Rachel continues filling the bottle. "It's all right, Rachel," the woman, who has been following the story in the papers, calls out. "Drink all you want."

Startled, but still suspicious, Rachel caps the bottle and, keeping her eyes on the woman, drinks from the faucet. The woman steps back into the house. Rachel motions Johnson to do the same, signaling for him to hurry and drink. She turns off the faucet when he is done.

They are turning to go when the woman emerges from the house carrying a plate of tortillas and a bowl of apples. She sets them on the edge of the porch and says, "These are for you."

The woman watches through the window as Rachel packs the food into her bag. Rachel puts away the last apple and gestures her thanks to the woman. When the woman fails to respond to the sign language, Rachel picks up a stick and writes in the sand of the yard. "Thank you," Rachel scratches, then waves good-bye and sets out across the desert. She is puzzled, but happy.

The next morning's newspaper includes an interview with the dark-haired woman. She describes how Rachel turned on the faucet and turned it off when she was through, how the chimp packed the apples neatly in her bag and wrote in the dirt with a stick.

The reporter also interviews the director of the Primate Research Center. "These are animals," the director explains angrily. "But people want to treat them like they're small hairy people." He describes the center as "primarily a breeding center with some facilities for medical research." The reporter asks some pointed questions about their acquisition of Rachel.

But the biggest story is an investigative piece. The reporter reveals that he has tracked down Aaron Jacobs's lawyer and learned that Jacobs left a will. In this will, he bequeathed all his possessions—including his house and surrounding land—to "Rachel, the chimp I acknowledge as my daughter."

The reporter makes friends with one of the young women in the typing pool at the research center, and she tells him the office scuttlebutt: people suspect that the chimps may have been released by a deaf and drunken janitor, who was subsequently fired for negligence. The reporter, accompanied by a friend who can communicate in sign language, finds Jake in his apartment in downtown Flagstaff.

Jake, who has been drinking steadily since he was fired, feels betrayed by Rachel, by the Primate Center, by the world. He complains at length about Rachel: they had been friends, and then she took his baseball cap and ran away. He just didn't understand why she had run away like that.

"You mean she could talk?" the reporter asks through his interpreter.

— Of course she can talk, Jake signs impatiently. — She is a smart monkey.

The headlines read: "Intelligent chimp inherits fortune!" Of course, Aaron's bequest isn't really a fortune and she isn't just a chimp, but close enough. Animal rights activists rise up in Rachel's defense. The case is discussed on the national news. Ann Landers reports receiving a letter from a chimp named Rachel; she had thought it was a hoax perpetrated by the boys at Yale. The American Civil Liberties Union assigns a lawyer to the case.

By day, Rachel and Johnson sleep in whatever hiding places they can find: a cave; a shelter built for range cattle; the shell of an abandoned car, rusted from long years in a desert gully. Sometimes Rachel dreams of jungle darkness, and the coyotes in the distance become a part of her dreams, their howling becomes the cries of fellow apes.

The desert and the journey have changed her. She is wiser, having passed through the white-hot love of adolescence and emerged on the other side. She dreams, one day, of the ranch house. In the dream, she has long blonde hair and pale white skin. Her eyes are red from crying and she wanders the house restlessly, searching for something that she has lost. When she hears coyotes howling, she looks through a window at the darkness outside. The face that looks in at her has jug-handle ears and shaggy hair. When she sees the face, she cries out in recognition and opens the window to let herself in.

By night, they travel. The rocks and sands are cool beneath Rachel's feet as she walks toward her ranch. On television, scientists and politicians discuss the ramifications of her case, describe the technology uncovered by investigation of Aaron Jacobs's files. Their debates do not affect her steady progress toward her ranch or the stars that sprinkle the sky above her.

It is night when Rachel and Johnson approach the ranch house. Rachel sniffs the wind and smells automobile exhaust and strange humans. From the hills, she can see a small camp beside a white van marked with the name of a local television station. She hesitates, considering returning to the safety of the desert. Then she takes Johnson by the hand and starts down the hill. Rachel is going home.

Game Night at the Fox and Goose

KAREN JOY FOWLER

The reader will discover that my reputation, wherever I have lived, is endorsed as that of a true and pure woman.

LAURA D. FAIR

Alison called all over the city trying to find a restaurant that served blowfish, but there wasn't one. She settled for Chinese. She would court an MSG attack. And if none came, then she'd been craving red bean sauce anyway. On the way to the restaurant, Alison chose not to wear her seat belt.

Alison had been abandoned by her lover, who was so quick about it, she hadn't even known she was pregnant yet. She couldn't ever tell him now. She sat pitifully alone, near the kitchen at a table for four. *You've really screwed up this time,* her fortune cookie told her. *Give up.* And in small print: *Chin's Oriental Palace.*

The door from the kitchen swung open, so the air around her was hot for a moment, then cold when the door closed. Alison drank her tea and looked at the tea leaves in the bottom of her cup. They were easy to read. *He doesn't love you,* they said. She tipped them out onto the napkin and tried to rearrange them. *You fool.* She covered the message with the one remaining wonton, left the cookie for the kitchen god, and decided to walk all by herself in the dark, three blocks up Hillside Drive, past two alleyways, to have a drink at the Fox and Goose. No one stopped her.

Alison had forgotten it was Monday night. Sometimes there was music in the Fox and Goose. Sometimes you could sit in a corner by yourself listening to someone with an acoustic guitar singing "Killing Me Softly." On Monday nights the television was on and the bar was rather crowded. Mostly men. Alison swung one leg over the only empty bar stool and slid forward. The bar was made of wood, very upscale.

"What can I get the pretty lady?" the bartender asked without taking his eyes off the television screen. He wore glasses, low on his nose.

Alison was not a pretty lady and didn't feel like pretending she was. "I've been used and discarded," she told the bartender. "And I'm pregnant. I'd like a glass of wine."

"You really shouldn't drink if you're pregnant," the man sitting to Alison's left said.

"Two more downs and they're already in field goal range again." The bartender set the wine in front of Alison. He was shaking his head. "Pregnant women aren't supposed to drink much," he warned her.

"How?" the man on her left asked.

"How do you think?" said Alison.

"Face-mask," said the bartender.

"Turn it up."

Alison heard the amplified *thwock* of football helmets hitting together. "Good coverage," the bartender said.

"No protection," said the man on Alison's right.

Alison turned to look at him. He was dressed in a blue sweater with the sleeves pushed up. He had dark eyes and was drinking a dark beer. "I asked him to wear a condom," she said quietly. "I even brought one. He couldn't."

"He *couldn't?*"

"I really don't want to discuss it." Alison sipped her wine. It had the flat, bitter taste of House White. She realized the bartender hadn't asked her what she wanted. But then, if he had, House White was what she would have requested. "It just doesn't seem fair." She spoke over her glass, unsure that anyone was listening, not really caring if they weren't. "All I did was fall in love. All I did was believe someone who said he loved me. *He* was the liar. But nothing happens to him."

"Unfair is the way things are," the man on her right told her. Three months ago Alison would have been trying to decide if she were attracted to him. Not that she would necessarily have wanted to do anything about it. It was just a question she'd always asked herself, dealing with men, interested in the answer, interested in those times when the answer changed abruptly, one way or another. But it was no longer an issue. Alison was a dead woman these days. Alison was attracted to no one.

Two men at the end of the bar began to clap suddenly. "He hasn't missed from thirty-six yards yet this season," the bartender said.

Alison watched the kickoff and the return. Nothing. No room at all. "Men handle this stuff so much better than women. You don't know what heartbreak is," she said confrontationally. No one responded. She backed off anyway. "Well, that's how it looks." She drank and watched an advertisement for trucks. A man bought his wife the truck she'd always wanted. Alison was afraid she might cry. "What would you do," she asked the man on her right, "if you were me?"

"Drink, I guess. Unless I was pregnant."

"Watch the game," said the man on her left.

"Focus on your work," said the bartender.

"Join the foreign legion." The voice came from behind Alison. She swiveled around to locate it. At a table near a shuttered window a very tall woman sat by herself. Her face was shadowed by an Indiana Jones–type hat, but the candle on the table lit up the area below her neck. She was wearing a black T-shirt with a picture on it that Alison couldn't make out. She spoke again. "Make new friends. See distant places." She gestured for Alison to join her. "Save two galaxies from the destruction of the alien armada."

Alison stood up on the little ledge that ran beneath the bar, reached over the counter, and took an olive, sucking the pimiento out first, then eating the rest. She picked up her drink, stepped down, and walked over to the woman's table. Elvis. That was Elvis's face on the T-shirt right between the woman's breasts. ARE YOU LONESOME TONIGHT? the T-shirt asked.

"That sounds good." Alison sat down across from the woman. She could see her face better now; her skin was pale and a bit rough. Her hair was long, straight, and brown. "I'd rather time travel, though. Back just two months. Maybe three months. Practically walking distance."

"You could get rid of the baby."

"Yes," said Alison. "I could."

The woman's glass sat on the table in front of her. She had finished whatever she had been drinking; the maraschino cherry was all that remained. The woman picked it up and ate it, dropping the stem onto the napkin under her glass. "Maybe he'll come back to you. You trusted him. You must have seen something decent in him."

Alison's throat closed so that she couldn't talk. She picked up her drink, but she couldn't swallow, either. She set it down again, shaking her head. Some of the wine splashed over the lip and onto her hand.

"He's already married," the woman said.

Alison nodded, wiping her hand on her pant leg. "God." She searched in her pockets for a Kleenex. The woman handed her the napkin from beneath the empty glass. Alison wiped her nose with it and the cherry stem fell out. She did not dare look up. She kept her eyes focused on the napkin in her hand, which she folded into four small squares. "When I was growing up," she said, "I lived on a block with lots of boys. Sometimes I'd come home and my knees were all scraped up because I'd fallen or I'd taken a ball in the face or I'd gotten kicked or punched, and I'd be crying and my mother would always say the same thing. 'You play with the big boys and you're going to get hurt,' she'd say. Exasperated." Alison unfolded the napkin, folded it diagonally instead. Her voice shrank. "I've been so stupid."

"The universe is shaped by the struggle between two great forces," the woman told her.

It was not really responsive. It was not particularly supportive. Alison felt just a little bit angry at this woman who now knew so much about her. "Good and evil?" Alison asked, slightly nastily. She wouldn't meet the woman's eyes. "The Elvis and the anti-Elvis?"

"Male and female. Minute by minute, the balance tips one way or the other. Not just here. In every universe. There are places"—the woman leaned forward—"where men are not allowed to gather and drink. Places where football is absolutely illegal."

"England?" Alison suggested and then didn't want to hear the woman's answer. "I like football," she added quickly. "I like games with rules. You can be stupid playing football and it can cost you the game, but there are penalties for fouls, too. I like games with rules."

"You're playing one now, aren't you?" the woman said. "You haven't hurt this man, even though you could. Even though he's hurt you. He's not playing by the rules. So why are you?"

"It doesn't have anything to do with rules," Alison said. "It only has to do with me, with the kind of person I think I am. Which is not the kind of person he is." She thought for a moment. "It doesn't mean I wouldn't like to see him get hurt," she added. "Something karmic. Justice."

" 'We must storm and hold Cape Turk before we talk of social justice.' " The woman folded her arms under her breasts and leaned back in her chair. "Did Sylvia Townsend Warner say that?"

"Not to me."

Alison heard more clapping at the bar behind her. She looked over her shoulder. The man in the blue sweater slapped his hand on the wooden bar. "Good call. Excellent call. They won't get another play in before the half."

"Where I come from she did." Alison turned back to the woman. "And she was talking about women. No one gets justice just by deserving it. No one ever has."

Alison finished off her wine. "No." She wondered if she should go home now. She knew when she got there that the apartment would be unbearably lonely and that the phone wouldn't ring and that she would need immediately to be somewhere else. No activity in the world could be more awful than listening to a phone not ring. But she didn't really want to stay here and have a conversation that was at worst too strange, and at best too late. Women usually supported you more when they talked to you. They didn't usually make you defensive or act as if they had something to teach you, the way this woman did. And anyhow, justice was a little peripheral now, wasn't it? What good would it really do her? What would it change?

She might have gone back and joined the men at the bar during the half. They were talking quietly among themselves. They were ordering fresh drinks and eating beer nuts. But she didn't want to risk seeing cheerleaders. She didn't want to risk the ads with the party dog and all his women, even though she'd read in a magazine that the dog was a bitch. Anywhere she went, there she'd be. Just like she was. Heartbroken.

The woman was watching her closely. Alison could feel this, though the woman's face remained shadowed and she couldn't quite bring herself to look back at her directly. She looked at Elvis instead and the way his eyes wavered through her lens of candlelight and tears. *Lonesome tonight*? "You really have it bad, don't you?" the woman said. Her tone was sympathetic. Alison softened again. She decided to tell this perceptive woman everything. How much she'd loved him. How she'd never loved anyone else. How she felt it every time she took a *breath,* and had for weeks now.

"I don't think I'll ever feel better," she said. "No matter what I do."

"I hear it takes a year to recover from a serious loss. Unless you find someone else."

A year. Alison could be a mother by then. How would she find someone else, pregnant like she was or with a small child? Could she spend a year hurting like this? Would she have a choice?

"Have you ever heard of Laura D. Fair?" the woman asked.

Alison shook her head. She picked up the empty wineglass and tipped it to see if any drops remained. None did. She set it back down and picked up the napkin, wiping her eyes. She wasn't crying. She just wasn't exactly not crying.

"Mrs. Fair killed her lover," the woman told her. Alison looked at her own fingernails. One of them had a ragged end. She bit it off shorter while she listened. "He was a lawyer. A. P. Crittenden. She shot him on the ferry to Oakland in November of 1870 in front of his whole family because she saw him kiss his wife. He'd promised to leave her and marry Mrs. Fair instead, and then he didn't, of course. She pleaded a transient insanity known at that time as *emotional* insanity. She said she was incapable of killing Mr. Crittenden, who had been the only friend she'd had in the world." Alison examined her nail. She had only succeeded in making it more ragged. She bit it again, too close to the skin this time. It hurt and she put it back in her mouth. "Mrs. Fair said she had no memory of the murder, which many people, not all of them related to the deceased, witnessed. She was the first woman sentenced to hang in California."

Loud clapping and catcalls at the bar. The third quarter had started with a return all the way to the fifty-yard line. Alison heard it. She did not turn around, but she took her finger out of her mouth and picked up the napkin. She folded it again. Four small squares. "Rules are rules," Alison said.

"But then she didn't hang. Certain objections were made on behalf of the defense and sustained, and a new trial was held. This time she was acquitted. By now she was the most famous and the most hated woman in the country."

Alison unfolded the napkin and tried to smooth out the creases with the side of her palm. "I never heard of her."

"Laura D. Fair was not some little innocent." The woman's hat brim dipped decisively. "Mrs. Fair had been married four times, and each had been a profitable venture. One of her husbands killed himself. She was not pretty, but she was passionate. She was not smart, but she was clever. And she saw, in her celebrity, a new way to make money. She announced a new career as a public speaker. She traveled the country with her lectures. And what was her message? She told women to murder the men who seduced and betrayed them."

"I never heard of her," said Alison.

"Mrs. Fair was a compelling speaker. She'd had some acting and elocution experience. Her performance in court showed training. On the stage she was even better. 'The act will strike a terror to the hearts of sensualists and libertines.' " The woman stabbed dramatically at her own breast with her fist, hitting Elvis right in the eye. Behind her hand, Elvis winked at Alison in the candlelight. "Mrs. Fair said that women throughout the world would glory in the revenge exacted by American womanhood. Overdue. Long overdue. Thousands of women heard her. Men, too, and not all of them entirely unsympathetic. Fanny Hyde and Kate Stoddart were released in Brooklyn. Stoddart never even stood trial. But then there was a backlash. The martyred Marys were hanged in Philadelphia. And then . . ." The woman's voice dropped suddenly in volume and gained in intensity. Alison looked up at her quickly. The woman was staring back. Alison looked away. "And then a group of women hunted down and dispatched Charles S. Smith in an alley near his home. Mr. Smith was a married man and his victim, Edith Wilson, was pregnant, an invalid, and eleven years old. But this time the women wore sheets and could not be identified. Edith Wilson was perhaps the only female in Otsego County, New York, who could not have taken part."

Alison folded her napkin along the diagonal.

"So no one could be tried. It was an inspiring and purging operation. It was copied in many little towns across the country. God knows, the women had access to sheets."

Alison laughed, but the woman was not expecting it, had not paused to allow for laughter. "And then Annie Oakley shot Frank Butler in a challenge match in Cincinnati."

"Excuse me," said Alison. "I didn't quite hear you." But she really had and the woman continued anyway, without pausing or repeating.

"She said it was an accident, but she was too good a shot. They hanged her for it. And then Grover Cleveland was killed by twelve sheeted women on the White House lawn. At teatime," the woman said.

"Wait a minute." Alison stopped her. "Grover Cleveland served out two terms. Nonconsecutively. I'm sure."

The woman leaned into the candlelight, resting her chin on a bridge she made of her hands. "You're right, of course," she said. "That's what happened here. But in another universe where the feminine force was just a little stronger in 1872, Grover Cleveland died in office. With a scone in his mouth and a child in New York."

"All right," said Alison accommodatingly. Accommodation was one of Alison's strengths. "But what difference does that make to us?"

"I could take you there." The woman pushed her hat back so that Alison could have seen her eyes if she wanted to. "The universe right next door. Practically walking distance."

The candle flame was casting shadows which reached and withdrew and reached at Alison over the table. In the unsteady light, the woman's face flickered like a silent film star's. Then she pulled back in her chair and sank into the darkness beyond the candle. The ball was on the ten-yard line and the bar was quiet. "I knew you were going to say that," Alison said finally. "How did I know you were going to say that? Who would say that?"

"Some lunatic?" the woman suggested.

"Yes."

"Don't you want to hear about it anyway? About my universe?" The woman smiled at her. An unperturbed smile. Nice even teeth. And a kind of confidence that was rare among the women Alison knew. Alison had noticed it immediately without realizing she was noticing. The way the woman sat back in her chair and didn't pick at herself. Didn't play with her hair. Didn't look at her hands. The way she lectured Alison.

"All right," Alison said. She put the napkin down and fit her hands together, forcing herself to sit as still. "But first tell me about Laura Fair. *My* Laura Fair."

"Up until 1872 the two histories are identical," the woman said. "Mrs. Fair married four times and shot her lover and was convicted and the conviction was overturned. She just never lectured. She planned to. She was scheduled to speak at Platt's Hotel in San Francisco on November 21, 1872, but a mob of some two thousand men gathered outside the hotel and another two thousand surrounded the apartment building she lived in. She asked for police protection, but it was refused and she was too frightened to leave her home. Even staying where she was proved dangerous. A few men tried to force their way inside. She spent a terrifying night and never attempted to lecture again. She died in poverty and obscurity.

"Fanny Hyde and Kate Stoddart were released anyway. I can't find out what happened to the Marys. Edith Wilson was condemned by respectable people everywhere and cast out of her family."

"The eleven-year-old child?" Alison said.

"In *your* universe," the woman reminded her. "Not in mine. You don't know much of your own history, do you? Name a great American woman."

The men at the bar were in an uproar. Alison turned to look. "Interception," the man in the blue sweater shouted to her exultantly. "Did you see it?"

"Name a great American woman," Alison called back to him.

"Goddamn interception with goal to go," he said. "Eleanor Roosevelt?"

"Marilyn Monroe," said a man at the end of the bar.

"The senator from California?" the woman asked. "Now that's a good choice."

Alison laughed again. "Funny," she said, turning back to the woman. "Very good."

"We have football, too," the woman told her. "Invented in 1873. Outlawed in 1950. No one ever got paid to play it."

"And you have Elvis."

"No, we don't. Not like yours. Of course not. I got this here."

"Interception," the man in the blue sweater said. He was standing beside Alison, shaking his head with the wonder of it. "Let me buy you ladies a drink." Alison opened her mouth and he waved his hand. "Something nonalcoholic for you," he said. "Please. I really want to."

"Ginger ale, then," she agreed. "No ice."

"Nothing for me," said the woman. They watched the man walk back to the bar, and then, when he was far enough away not to hear, she leaned forward toward Alison. "You like men, don't you?"

"Yes," said Alison. "I always have. Are they different where you come from? Have they learned to be honest and careful with women, since you kill them when they're not?" Alison's voice was sharper than she intended, so she softened the effect with a sadder question. "Is it better there?"

"Better for whom?" The woman did not take her eyes off Alison. "Where I come from the men and women hardly speak to each other. First of all, they don't speak the same language. They don't here, either, but you don't recognize that as clearly. Where I come from there's men's English and there's women's English."

"Say something in men's English."

" 'I love you.' Shall I translate?"

"No," said Alison. "I know the translation for that one." The heaviness closed over her heart again. Not that it had ever gone away. Nothing made Alison feel better, but many things made her feel worse. The bartender brought her ginger ale. With ice. Alison was angry, suddenly, that she couldn't even get a drink with no ice. She looked for the man in the blue sweater, raised the glass at him, and rattled it. Of course he was too far away to hear even if he was listening, and there was no reason to believe he was.

"Two-minute warning," he called back. "I'll be with you in two minutes."

Men were always promising to be with you soon. Men could never be with you now. Alison had only cared about this once, and she never would again. "Football has the longest two minutes in the world," she told the woman. "So don't hold your breath. What else is different where you come from?" She sipped at her ginger ale. She'd been grinding her teeth recently; stress, the dentist said, and so the cold liquid made her mouth hurt.

"Everything is different. Didn't you ask for no ice? Don't drink that," the woman said. She called to the bartender. "She didn't want ice. You gave her ice."

"Sorry." The bartender brought another bottle and another glass. "Nobody told me no ice."

"Thank you," Alison said. He took the other glass away. Alison thought he was annoyed. The woman didn't seem to notice.

"Imagine your world without a hundred years of adulterers," she said. "The level of technology is considerably depressed. Lots of books never written because the authors didn't live. Lots of men who didn't get to be president. Lots of passing. Although it's illegal. Men dressing as women. Women dressing as men. And the dress is more sexually differentiated. Codpieces are fashionable again. But you don't have to believe me," the woman said. "Come and see for yourself. I can take you there in a minute. What would it cost you to just come and see? What do you have here that you'd be losing?"

The woman gave her time to think. Alison sat and drank her ginger ale and repeated to herself the things her lover had said the last time she had seen him. She remembered them all, some of them surprisingly careless, some of them surprisingly cruel, all of them surprising. She repeated them again, one by one, like a rosary. The man who had left was not the man she had loved. The man she had loved would never have said such things to her. The man she had loved did not exist. She had made him up. Or he had. "Why would you want me to go?" Alison asked.

"The universe is shaped by the struggle between two great forces. Sometimes a small thing can tip the balance. One more woman. Who knows?" The woman tilted her hat back with her hand. "Save a galaxy. Make new friends. Or stay here where your heart is. Broken."

"Can I come back if I don't like it?"

"Yes. Do you like it here?"

She drank her ginger ale and then set the glass down, still half full. She glanced at the man in the blue sweater, then past him to the bartender. She let herself feel just for a moment what it might be like to know that she could finish this drink and then go home to the one person in the world who loved her.

Never in this world. "I'm going out for a minute. Two minutes," she called to the bartender. One minute to get back. "Don't take my drink."

She stood and the other woman stood, too, even taller than Alison had thought. "I'll follow you. Which way?" Alison asked.

"It's not hard," the woman said. "In fact, I'll follow you. Go to the back. Find the door that says Women and go on through it. I'm just going to pay for my drink and then I'll be right along."

Vixens, was what the door actually said, across the way from the one marked Ganders. Alison paused and then pushed through. She felt more than a little silly, standing in the small bathroom that apparently fronted two universes. One toilet, one sink, one mirror. Two universes. She went into the stall and closed the door. Before she had finished she heard the outer door open and shut again. "I'll be right out," she said. The toilet paper was small and unusually rough. The toilet wouldn't flush. It embarrassed her. She tried three times before giving up.

The bathroom was larger than it had been, less clean, and a row of urinals lined one wall. The woman stood at the sink, looking into the mirror, which was smaller. "Are you ready?" she asked and removed her breasts from behind Elvis, tossing them into a wire wastebasket. She turned. "Ready or not."

"No," said Alison, seeing the face under the hat clearly for the first time. "Please, no." She began to cry again, looking up at his face, looking down at his chest. ARE YOU LONESOME TONIGHT?

"You lied to me," she said dully.

"I never lied," he answered. "Think back. You just translated wrong. Because you're that kind of woman. We don't have women like you here now. And anyway, what does it matter whose side you play on? All that matters is that no one wins. Aren't I right? Aren't I?" He tipped his hat to her.

Tiny Tango

JUDITH MOFFETT

I

I've been encouraged (read: ordered) by my friend, a Hefn called Godfrey, to make this recording. I'm not sure why. It's to be the story of my life, and frankly, a lot of my life's been kind of grim. Godfrey tells me he values the story as an object lesson, but to whom and for what purpose he's not saying. It isn't news anymore that the Hefn don't think like we do.

I made an important choice at twenty-two. Because of that choice I'm alive right now, but I'm still wondering: was it a wise choice, given that the next twenty-five years turned out to be a kind of living death? I hoped that if I did this recording, thought it all through in one piece, I'd be able to answer that question. I need to understand my life better than I do. I'm about to be put to sleep for a long time—forever if things go badly—and I need to know . . . well, what Godfrey thinks *he* knows. What it's meant. What it's all been *for*.

I can't really say that this review has worked, because I still don't think I know. But who can tell? Maybe you listeners in the archive will see something in it I can't see. (Godfrey's betting that you will.)

I recall a certain splendid June morning between the two accidents, mine and Peach Bottom's—a bright, cool morning after a spell of sticky weather. I'd hobbled out to the patio in robe and slippers with my breakfast tray, and loitered over my homegrown whole-grain honey and raisin muffins and strawberry-soy milkshake, browsing through a new copy of *Rodale's Organic Gardening* magazine (featuring an article I'd written on ways to discourage squirrels in the orchard and corn patch). Then, after a while, I'd taken my cane and gimped out in a leisurely way to inspect the crops. I'd broken an ankle bone that was taking its time about healing; to be forbidden my exercise routines was distressing, but also kind of a relief.

Because the kitchen garden provided my entire supply of vegetables and fruit, my interest in it was like a gardening hobbyist's crossed with a frontier homesteader's. If a crop failed I knew I wouldn't, or needn't, starve. On the other hand, since I never—ever—bought any produce for home consumption, if a crop failed it *would* almost certainly mean doing without something for a whole year. The daily tour of the kitchen garden was therefore always deeply interesting; and if the tour of the field-test plots was even more so, theirs was an interestingness of a less intimate type.

Something serious had happened to the Kennebec potatoes; I noticed it at once. Yesterday at dusk the plants had been bushy and green, bent out of their beds on water-filled stalks by last week's storm of rain but healthy, thriving, beginning to put out the tiny flowers that meant I could soon steal a few small tubers from under the mulch to eat with the new peas. Now the leaves of several plants were rolled and mottled with yellow. I pulled these up right away, doubting it would do any good, sick at heart as always to see my pampered children fail, however often failure struck them down.

The biggest threat to crops in an organic garden like mine is always disease spread by insects, aphids or leafhoppers in this case, which had all but certainly passed this disease on to other potato plants by now. The mottling and leaf-rolling meant that the bugs—probably aphids, the flightless sort I'd been taught to call "ant cows" in grade school—had infected my Kennebecs with a virus. At least one virus, maybe more. The ants would soon have moved their dairy herd all through the patch, if they hadn't already. Plants still symptom-free would not remain so for long. When Eric showed up I would get him to spray the patch with a Rotenone solution but it was probably too late to save the crop by killing the carriers, the vector. These potatoes already had a virus, incurable and potentially lethal.

I remember that I thought: Well, that makes some more of us then.

I left the heap of infected plants for Eric to cart to the incinerator; they must be not composted but burned, and at once, or there'd be no chance at all of saving the crop and I could look forward to a potatoless year.

Destroy the infected to protect the healthy. The AIDS witch-hunts of the late nineties, the vigilante groups that had broken into testing and treatment facilities all over the country in order to find out who the infected people were, had been acting from a similar principle: Identify! Destroy! They wanted not just the ones with the acute form of the disease, but also those who'd tested positive to HIV-I, II, and/or III. I'd been lucky; workers in the Task Force office where my records were kept had managed to stand off the mob while a terrified volunteer worked frantically to erase the computer records and two others burned the paper files in the lavatory sink. The police arrived in time to save those brave people, thank God, but in other cities, workers were shot and, in that one dreadful incident in St. Louis, barricaded in their building while somebody shattered the window with a firebomb.

My luck hadn't stopped there, no sirree. I had the virus right enough, but not—still not, after twenty-five long years—the disease itself. (These two facts have shaped my life. I mean my adult life; I'd just turned twenty-two, and was about to graduate from college in the spring of 1985, when my Western Blot came back positive and everything changed.)

Even the sporadic persecutions ended in 2001, when they got the Lowenfels vaccine. That took care of the general public; but nobody looked for a cure, or expected that a way would ever be found to eliminate the virus from the bodies of those of us who'd already been exposed to it. The best *we* could hope for was a course of treatment to improve our chances of not developing full-blown AIDS, at least not for a long, long time. The peptide vaccine that had become the standard therapy by 1994, which worked with the capsid protein in the cells of the virus, was ineffective with too many patients, as were the GMSC factor injections; and zidovudine and its cousins were just too toxic. A lot more research still needed to be done. We hoped that it would be, that we would not be forgotten; but we didn't think it a very realistic hope.

The bone punch, and especially the Green Monkey vaccine, which quickly supplanted that radical and rather painful procedure, meant the end of terror for the unsmitten; for the less fortunate it meant at least the end of persecution, as I said, and so for us, too, the day when the mass inoculations began was a great day. A lot of us were also suicidally depressed. Imagine how people crippled from childhood with polio must have felt when they started giving out the Salk vaccine to school kids on those little cubes of sugar, and the cripples had to stand around on their braces and crutches and try to be glad.

It didn't do to think too much about it.

The Test Site clinician who gave me the news had steered me into a chair right afterwards and said, "When the results came in I made you an appointment for tonight with a counselor. She'll help you more than you'd ever believe, and I don't care what other commitments you've got to break: you be there." And he wrote the address and the time on a piece of paper, and I went.

The counselor was a woman in her thirties, sympathetic but tough, and she told me things that evening while I sat and was drenched in wave after icy wave of terror and dread. "We don't know why some people seem to resist the virus better than others, and survive much longer, or why some of those that are AB-positive develop the disease fairly quickly, while others can have a latency period of five or six years," Elizabeth said. "We don't know for sure what triggers the development of the acute disease, if and when it does develop, or what percentage of infected people will eventually develop it.

"But there's a lot of research going on right now into what they call 'cofactors,' variables that may influence the behavior of the virus in individual cases. Cofactors are things like general health, stress levels lifestyle. We think—we're pretty sure—that it's extremely important for people like you, who've been exposed, to live as healthfully and calmly as you possibly can. The HIV-I virus is linked to the immune system. You get the flu, your immune system kicks in to fight the flu virus, the AIDS virus multiplies; so the trick is to give your immune system as little to do as possible and buy yourself some time.

"Now, what that means in practical terms is: take care of yourself. Get lots of sleep and exercise. Don't get overtired or too stressed out. Pay attention to your nutrition. Meditate. Above all, try not to fall into a despairing frame of mind! There's a good chance they'll find an effective treatment in four or five years, and if that happens and you're still symptom-free, you should be able to live a normal life with a normally functioning immune system, so long as you keep up your treatments."

That was the gist of her talk, and some of it sank in. She was wrong about the treatment, of course. In those days everybody expected it would be the vaccine that would prove impossible to make, that a drug to control the course of infection seemed much likelier. We were better off not knowing. Even with treatments to hope for, in those days it was fairly unusual to survive as long as four or five years after infection.

Elizabeth suggested a therapy group of people like myself that I might like to join, a group that had volunteered for a research project being done by a team of psychoneuroimmunologists, though we didn't know that's what they were. They were the hope-givers, that was enough. During the weeks that followed, with help from Elizabeth and the group, I began to work out a plan—to impose my own controls over my situation, in accordance with the research team's wish to explore the effects of an extraordinarily healthful lifestyle on symptom-free HIV-I carriers.

My undergraduate work in biology had been good enough to get me accepted into the graduate program at Cornell with a research assistantship. Until the test results came back, I'd been excited by the challenge and the prospect of a change of scene; afterwards, and after a few sessions with Elizabeth and her group, I began instead to feel apprehensive about the effort it would take to learn the ropes of a new department, new university community, new city famous for its six annual months of winter. It seemed better to stick to familiar surroundings and to continue with the same counselor and therapy group. So I made late application to my own university's graduate department and was admitted, and I stayed on: my first major life decision to be altered, the first of many times I was to choose a less challenging and stressful alternative over one that in every other way looked like the more attractive choice.

I'd caught the virus from my major professor; he'd been my only lover, so there could be no doubt of that. While I was still nerving myself up to tell him about the blood test he died in an accident on Interstate 95. Distressingly enough, I'm afraid I felt less grieved than relieved. The death let me off the hook and, more importantly, cleared the way for me to stay, for Bill's presence would have been a difficulty. I'd felt from the first instant that I wanted *no one*, apart from the Task Force people, to know. Not my Fundamentalist family, certainly. Not my friends, from whom I now found myself beginning to withdraw (and since, like me, most of these were graduating seniors, this was easier than it sounds). Overnight my interests had grown utterly remote from theirs. They were full of parties and career plans; I was fighting for my life, and viewed the lot of them from across the chasm of that absolute unlikeness.

I strolled, more or less, through graduate school, working competently without distinguishing myself. I wasn't in a hurry, either. Distinction and rapid progress would have meant a greater commitment and a lot more work, and these were luxuries I could no longer afford, for my first commitment, and first responsibility, now, were to keeping myself alive.

As for how I was to use this life, a picture had gradually begun to form.

First of all it was necessary to divest myself of desire. The yuppiedom I had only recently looked forward to with so much confidence—the dazzling two-career marriage and pair of brilliant children, the house in the suburbs, the cabin in the Poconos, and the vacations in Europe—had become, item by item, as unavailable to me as a career in space exploration or ballet. Children, obviously, were out. So was marriage. So, it seemed, was sex in any form; sex had been my nemesis, scarcely discovered before it had blighted me forever. The prestigious high-pressure career in research, which my undergraduate record had made seem a reasonable ambition, had become anything but. I was not after all going to be one of those remarkable professional mothers, making history in the lab, putting in quality time with the kids every day, keeping the lines of communication with my husband open and clear at every level no matter what. I built up the picture of the life I had aspired to for my counselor and my group—and looked at it long and well—and said good-bye to it, as I believed, forever. All that was over.

The next step was to create an alternate picture of a life that *would* be possible. We discussed my abilities and my altered wish list. I toyed briefly with the idea of a career in AIDS research—but AIDS research in the late eighties was about as calm and unstressful a line of work as leading an assault on the North Face of the Eiger in winter, and I had no yearning for martyrdom, then or ever. Through the hours and hours of therapy it emerged that what I wanted most was simple: just to survive, until the other scientists working that field had found a drug that would control the virus and make a normal life possible again. It wasn't hard to work this out in group, because we all wanted the same thing: to hang on until the day—not too far away now—when some hero in a white coat, mounted on a white charger, came galloping up to the fort, holding a beaker of Miracle Formula high like a banner.

But *how* to hang on? For each of us the answer, if different in particulars, was also the same. We wanted to be able to support ourselves (and our families, if we had them) in reasonable comfort, and to keep our antibody status secret. Achieving this, for some of us—the older ones—meant giving up practices in law or medicine, or business careers, or staying in but lowering our sights. Some of us quit struggling to save troubled marriages or get custody of children.

For me the obvious course seemed to be a teaching job in an academic backwater, preferably one in that same metropolitan area. Accordingly—at a time in my life when I'd expected to be at Cornell, cultivating a mentor, working with keen zest and keener ambition at my research, developing and pursuing a strategy for landing a classy position at a prestigious eastern university—I quietly looked into the several nearby branch campuses of the Pennsylvania State University Commonwealth Campus System and made a choice.

My personal style altered a lot during graduate school. I'd done some acting in high school and college, and that made it easier—though you mustn't suppose it was *easy*—to put my new persona over by turning down invitations ("too busy") and so on. Before long my department, which had been so delighted to keep me, had lumped me in with that breed of student that fizzles out after a promising undergraduate takeoff, and the rest of the RAs had given up on me too.

My therapy group speedily became my complete social universe. Nobody in the Bio Department could possibly have shared the intensity of common concern *we* shared within what we came to call the Company (after the thing Misery loves best). When as time went by one or another of us would lose the battle for wellness, the rest would push aside our own fears and rally round the ailing boon Companion, doing our best to make the final months as comfortable as we could. That wasn't easy either, let me tell you. But we did it. We were like a church family, all in all to one another. Elizabeth, who had given her life to helping us and the researchers at Graduate Hospital—she was our pastor and our friend, and yet, even so, a little bit of an outsider. When she asked what I meant to do for *fun*—since life could not consist entirely of the elimination of challenges and risks—I could only reply that just staying alive and well seemed like plenty of fun for the present, and think privately that no true Companion would ever need to have *that* explained to him or her.

We never told our real names, not in a quarter of a century, and stubbornly refused all that time to evolve from a collective into an assembly of intimates, but we knew each other inside out.

But to the people in my department, who did know my name, I appeared by the age of twenty-nine to have contracted into a prematurely middle-aged schoolmarmish and spinsterish recluse, and nobody there seemed surprised when I accepted a job for which I was grossly overqualified, teaching basic biology and botany at a two-year branch of the Penn State System, fifteen miles out in the suburbs of Delaware County.

My parents in Denver were also unsurprised. Neither had known how to read between the lines of my decision to stay put rather than go to Cornell. To them all college teaching seemed equally prestigious, and equally fantastic. They liked telling their friends about their daughter the future biology professor, but they knew too little about the life I would lead for the particulars to interest them much or invite their judgment. After the first grandchild came they'd been more incurious than ever about my doings, which had seemed less and less real to them anyway ever since I left the church. My new church was the Company, and of this they knew nothing, ever.

My job was a dull one made duller by my refusal to be drawn into the school's social web. But it was tolerable work, adequately paid. I stayed in character as the reliable but lackluster biologist; I did what was necessary, capably, without zest or flair. My pretenure years were a balancing act, filled but not overfilled. I prepared and taught my classes, swam a mile or ran five every day, meditated for half an hour each morning and evening, carefully shopped for and cooked my excruciatingly wholesome and balanced meals, and took the train into the city one night a week to meet with the Company, and one afternoon a month for my aptly named gag p24 treatments. Every summer for five years I would spend some leisurely hours in the lab, then sit in my pleasant apartment and compose a solid, economical, careful paper developing one aspect or another of my Ph.D. research, which had dealt with the effects of stress on the immune system in rats. One after another these papers were published in perfectly respectable scientific journals, and were more than enough to satisfy the committee that in due course awarded me tenure.

By the time they had approved me, in the fateful year 1999, my medical records had been destroyed. No document or disk anywhere in the world existed to identify me by name as a symptom-free carrier of the HIV-I virus, though no other personal fact spoke as eloquently about the drab thing I had become.

The fourteen years had thinned the ranks of Companions, but a fair number of us were still around. Just about all of us survivors had faithfully—often fanatically—followed the prescribed fitness/nutrition/stress management regimen, and it was about then that our team of doctors began to congratulate us and each other that we were beating the bejeezus out of the odds. If you're wondering about the lost Companions, whether they too hadn't stuck to the routines and rules, the answer is that they usually *said* they had; but it was easy enough for us to see (or suppose) how this or that variable made their cases different from ours.

I myself hardly ever fell ill, hardly had colds or indigestion, so extremely careful was I of myself. My habits, athletics aside, were those of a fussy old maid—Miss Dove or Eleanor Rigby or W. H. Auden's Miss Edith Gee. They were effective though. When a bug did get through my defenses despite all my care—as some inevitably did, for student populations have always harbored colds and flus of the most poisonous volatility—I would promptly put myself to bed and stay there, swallowing aspirins, liquids by the bucket, and one-gram vitamin C tablets, copious supplies of which were always kept on hand. No staggering in with a fever to teach a class through the raging snowstorm—no sirree, not on your life. Not this survivor.

After tenure I bought a little house in a pleasant development of modest brick tract homes on half-acre lots near the campus, and settled in for the long haul. For years I'd subscribed to the health magazine *Prevention,* published by the Rodale press; now at last I'd be able to act on their advice to grow my own vegetables instead of buying the toxin-doused produce sold in the supermarkets. I mailed off my subscription to *Organic Gardening,* had the soil tested, bought my first spade, hoe, trowel, and rake, and some organic fertilizers, spaded up a corner of the backyard, and began.

That first posttenure summer I made a garden and wrote no paper. My mood was reflective but the reflections led nowhere much. The next year of teaching was much the same: I did my job, steered clear of controversy, kept in character. But as the following spring came on—spring of the year 2000—I became restless and vaguely uneasy. Even as I loosened the soil in my raised beds and spread over them the compost I had learned to make, I had dimly begun to know that the cards I'd been playing thus far were played out, that it was time for a new deal.

What I felt, I know now, were the perfectly ordinary first stirrings of a midlife crisis, probably initiated by the "marker event" of successfully securing my means of support for the foreseeable future. Ordinary it may have been, but it scared me badly. Uneasiness is stressful; stress is lethal.

I've stopped to read over what I've written to this point. It all seems true and correct, but it leaves too much out, and I think what it mainly leaves out is the terror. I don't mean the obvious terror of the Terror, the riots of 1998–99, when I might have been killed outright had the mob that stormed the Alternate Test Site on Walnut Street gotten its talons into my file and learned my name, when the Company met for months in church basements kept dark, when threatening phone calls woke Elizabeth night after night and she didn't dare come to meetings because the KKK was shadowing her in hopes of being led to us. I certainly don't deny we were scared to death while that nightmare lasted, but it *was* like a nightmare, born of hysteria and short-lived. In a while, we woke up from it. I'm talking about something else.

It's true that we all know we're going to die. Whether we're crunched by a truck tomorrow while crossing the street or expire peacefully in our sleep at ninety, we know it'll happen.

Now, as long as one fate seems no more likely than the other, most people manage to live fairly cheerfully with the awareness that one day they will meet their death for sure. But knowing that your chances of dying young, and soon, and not pleasantly, are many percentage points higher than other people's, changes your viewpoint a lot. Some of the time my radically careful way of life kept the demons at bay, but some of the time I would get up and run my five miles and shower and dress and meditate and drive to school and teach my classes and buy cabbages and oranges at the market and drive home and grade quizzes and meditate and eat supper and go to bed, all in a state of anxiety so intense I could scarcely control it at all.

There were drugs that helped some, but the best were addictive so you couldn't take those too often. The only thing that made years of such profound fear endurable was the Companionship of my fellow travelers. Together we could keep our courage up, we could talk out (or scream or sob out) our helpless rage at the medical establishment as years went by without producing the miracle drugs they'd been more or less promising, that would lift this bane of uncertainty from us and make us like everybody else—mortal, but with equal chances. Now, terror and rage are extremely stressful. Stress is lethal. I had said so over and over in print, my white rats and I had demonstrated it in the lab, statistics of every sort bore out the instinctive conviction that we had more to fear from fear itself than from just about anything else; and so our very terrors terrified us worst of all. But we bore it better together than we possibly could have borne it alone.

A few of my Companions in these miseries took the obvious next step and paired off. One or two probably told each other their real names. I wasn't even tempted. But sexual denial is stressful too; so on Saturday afternoons I used to rent a pornographic video or holo. A lot of these were boring, but trial and error taught me which brands showed some imagination in concept or direction, and voyeurism in that sanitary form did turn me on, it worked, it took care of the problem. Miniaturized in two or three dimensions, the shape-shifting penises of the actors seemed merely fascinating and the spurting semen innocent. No matter that a few spurts of semen had destroyed my life, and that a penis, the only real one I'd ever had to do with, had been the murder weapon; these facts did not feel relevant to the moaning and slurping of the young folks—certified AB-Negatives every one—who provided my weekly turn-on.

For a very long time I was content to release my sexuality, for hygienic reasons, into its narrow run for an hour or so each weekend, like some dangerous animal at the zoo. A few of the guys in the Company were straight, and maybe even willing, but a real relationship—a business as steamy and complicated as that—would have been out of the question for me. Others might have the skills; I lacked them. How much safer and less demanding the role of voyeur in the age of electronics, able to fast-forward through the dull bits and play the best ones over!

The Company, directed by Elizabeth, seemed to understand the force of these feelings. At any rate I wasn't pushed to try to overcome them.

Well, as I was saying: the beginning of my thirty-seventh summer, one year after receiving tenure at the two-year college where I seemed doomed to spend the rest of my life, however long that proved to be, and a year after the worst of the rioting ended—the beginning of that summer found me jittery and depressed, and very worried about being jittery and depressed. Probably I wouldn't have acted even so; but at about the same time, or a bit earlier, I'd begun to exhibit a piece of obsessive-compulsive behavior that until then I'd only heard about at Company gatherings: one morning, toweling down after my shower, I caught myself scrutinizing the skin of my thighs and calves for the distinctive purplish blotches of Kaposi's sarcoma, the form of skin cancer, previously rare, whose appearance is a diagnostic sign of the acute form of AIDS.

How long I'd been doing this half-consciously I couldn't have told you, but from that morning I was never entirely free of the behavior. I'd reached an age when my skin had begun to have its share of natural blotches and keratoses, and I gave myself heart failure more times than I can count, thinking some innocent bruise or lesion meant *this was finally it*. After several weeks, growing desperate, I gave up shaving my legs—and shorts and skirts in consequence—and suffered through the hot weather in loose overalls, just to avoid the chronic anxiety of seeing my own skin. I nearly drove myself nuts.

The Company assaulted this symptom with shrewd concern and a certain amount of relish. Your unconscious is trying to tell you something, dummy, one or another of them would say; I used to do that when I got so freaked out in the riots—sloppy about doing my Yoga—too busy chasing the bucks—into a bad way after I lost my mother—upset because I couldn't afford to keep the house but didn't want to sell. Remember when *I* did that? they'd say. Just figure out what you're doing wrong and fix *that*, then you'll be okay. For starters, try deciding whether it's something you need to work into your life, or something you need to get rid of.

I didn't see how it could very well be the latter, since my present life had been stripped to the bare essentials already. But what they said made sense. It was this sort of counsel that made us so necessary to one another.

Elizabeth, moreover, had a concrete suggestion. On her advice I rented a condo in the Poconos near the Delaware Water Gap—almost the vacation spot of my former Yuppie dreams—for a couple of weeks. The Appalachian Trail, heavily used in summer unfortunately, passes through the Gap. I spent the two weeks of my private retreat hiking the Trail, canoeing on the river, and assessing the state of my life.

So how was I doing?

Well, on the plus side, *I was still alive*. Half the original Company of sixteen years before, when I'd just come into it, were not, most from having developed the disease, though in a few cases more than a decade after seroconverting. In the early days it had been hoped that if a person with HIV-I antibodies hadn't fallen ill after six or eight years or so he probably never would, but it hadn't turned out like that. So far, the longer we survived, the more of the virus we had in us; to be alive at all after such a long time was pretty remarkable. I tried to feel glad.

I'd chosen a suitable job and fixed things so I could keep it; I'd also managed my money intelligently during the years before getting tenure. My salary, while not great, was adequate for a single person who hardly went anywhere and whose expensive tastes ran to top-of-the-line exercise equipment and holographic projectors. Raises would be regular, I would be able to manage my house payments easily. I'd already bought nearly all the furniture I needed, and had assembled a solid reference library of books, tapes, and disks on nutrition, fitness, stress management, and diseases, especially my own; and the gardening and preserving shelf was getting there. In short, all the details of the plan I had devised for myself sixteen years before were in place. And it had worked out: here I was.

So how come I felt so lousy?

At first, when I tried to tot up the negatives, it was hard to think of any at all. I was alive, wasn't I? Didn't that cancel out all the minuses right there?

As a matter of fact, it didn't. Once I got started the list went on and on.

As a bright college senior I had planned to make something really dazzling and grand of my life. That dream had been aborted; but I began to see that all these years I had been secretly grieving for it as for an aborted child. However obvious this looks now, at the time the recognition was a terrific shock. Years and years had lapsed since my last conscious fantasy of knocking the Cornell Biology Department on its collective ear, and I really believed I had ritualistically said good-bye to all that, early in my therapy.

Just what was it I'd wanted to do after Cornell, apart from becoming rich and famous? I could hardly remember. But after a while (and an hour of stony trail, with magnificent views of New Jersey) I had called back into being a sense of outward-directedness, of largesse bestowed upon a grateful world, that differed absolutely from the intense and cautious self-preoccupation which had governed my life from the age of twenty-two. Once, I had craved to be a leader in an international scientific community of intellectual exchange. Now, I thought, planned, and worked for the well-being of just one individual, myself—for what was the Company but just myself, multiplied by fifteen or eleven or nine? I'd hardly given a thought to *normal* people, people not afflicted as we were, for a long, long time, and certainly I had given them nothing else—not even a halfway decent course in botany.

It was an awful shock, remembering what it had been like to take engagement with the great world for granted. I turned aside from the Trail and its traffic to climb a gray boulder shaggy with mountain laurel, and sat staring out over the summery woods, remembering the hours I'd spent talking with Bill—my professor, the one who'd exposed me to the virus—about world population control and sustainable agriculture. No details came back; but the sheer energy and breadth of vision, the ability to imagine tackling issues of such complexity and social import, now seemed unbelievable. How had I shrunk so small?

At that moment on the mountain my triumph of continuing to live looked paltry and mean. I'd died anyway, hadn't I? Wasn't this death-in-life a kind of unwitting suicide? But I knew at bottom that it was no ignoble thing to have gone on living where so many had died. My fit of self-loathing ran its course, and I climbed down from the rock and started back down the Trail toward the Water Gap, three miles below, where I'd left my car.

I pondered as I went. What was missing from my life now seemed clearer. Meaningful work, first and foremost. Engagement. Self-respect, if that wasn't asking too much—not simply for having survived, but for contributing something real to society; and perhaps even the respect of others.

And last of all I let myself remember, really remember, those springtime afternoons in Bill's sunny office with its coffee machine and little refrigerator and daybed, and added one more thing: intimacy, social and sexual. Not the Company, that bunch of neutered and clairvoyant clones, but I and Thou: intimacy with the Other.

It was a list of things necessary to a fulfilled and happy life, and it bristled like a porcupine with potential stresses.

The trail was rough and steep, and I was wiped out from both my journeys, the inner more than the outer. When I let myself back into the condo the sun had set, and I thought with a fierce rush of resentment how *nice* it would be, just for once, to microwave a box of beans and franks and open a Coke, like a normal American citizen on holiday, instead of having to boil the goddamned homemade pasta and cook the spaghetti sauce from scratch. The strength of this resentment astounded me all over again: how long had I been sitting on the powder keg of so much rage *against the virus itself*?

Enlightenment came early in the first week of my retreat, so I had plenty of time left to process my insights and form conclusions.

About personal intimacy first. Essential or not, I found that I still just didn't feel able to risk it. The potential trouble seemed bigger than the potential payoff; as I've mentioned, I lacked the skills.

About engagement. More promising. The thought of connecting myself in a meaningful way to society by some means that didn't threaten my own stability appealed to me a lot. I could *teach* in a more engaged fashion, but that felt far too personal, too exposed and risky. Then I thought of something else, something actually quite perfect: I could volunteer to work with AIDS patients. This may sound uniquely stressful for someone in my position, but the prospect oddly wasn't. I already knew everything about the progression of the disease (I'd been through it half a dozen times with dying Companions, so could not be shocked); I needn't fear infection (being infected already); and I felt certain my powers of detachment would be adequate.

Then about meaningful work. I pondered that one for the whole ten days remaining, pretty much all the time.

In the end it was a dream—the holo of the unconscious—that showed me what to do. I dreamed of Gregor Mendel, the Austrian monk who invented modern genetics while serving obscurely in a monastery. In my dream Mendel had the mild wide face with its little round-lensed spectacles of the photograph in the college biology text I used. Sweating and pink-faced in his heavy cassock, he bent tenderly over a bed of young peas, helping them find the trellis of strings and begin to climb. I stood at a little distance and watched, terribly moved to see how carefully he tucked the delicate tendrils around the strings. As I approached, he looked up and smiled as if to say, "Ah, so *there* you are at last!"—a smile brimful of love—and handed me his notebook and pen. When I hung back, reluctant somehow to accept them, he straightened up slowly—his back was stiff—and moving closer drew me into an embrace so warm and protective that it seemed fatherly; yet at once I was aware of his penis where it arched against me through the folds of cloth, and of his two firm breasts pressed above my own. He kissed the top of my head. Then he was gone, striding away through the gate, and I stood alone among the peas, the pen and notebook in my hands somehow after all—in my own garden, my own backyard.

It had been a long time, literally years, since I'd last cried about anything; but when I woke that dawn my soaked pillow and clogged sinuses showed that I'd been weeping in my sleep, evidently for quite a while. Not since childhood had I felt such powerful love; not since childhood had anyone loved *me*, or held me, in just that way. To be reminded broke my heart, yet there was something healing in the memory too, and in the luxury of crying.

I lay in my dampness and thought about Mendel—how, having failed to qualify as a teacher, he had returned to the monastery; and there, in that claustrophobic place, in that atmosphere of failure, without the approval or maybe even the knowledge of his bishop, he planned his experiments and planted his peas.

In its way Mendel's life was as circumscribed, and presumably as monastic, as my own. Yet instead of whining and bitching he'd turned his hand to what was possible and done something uniquely fine.

Me, I'd written off further research because the campus lab facilities were so limited and so public, and applying for funding or the chance to work for a summer or two in a better-equipped lab seemed incautious. It was also true that I'd done about as much in the area of stress and the immune system as I cared to do, and that white rats got more expensive every year and the administration more grudging each spring when my latest requisition forms went in. But if I could change directions completely—

Well, the Company had a perfect field day with that dream. You can imagine. They were all sure I'd been telling myself to do exactly that: *shift directions,* devise some experiments for my own backyard garden and publish the results. About the symbolism of the hermaphroditic monk, opinion was divided; one person thought him a fused father/mother figure, breasts and gownlike cassock muddling his obvious identity as *Father* Mendel. ("Monks are called *Brother,*" a lapsed-

Catholic Companion protested.) Others suggested variously that the dream message concerned repressed bisexuality, incest, plain old sexual frustration, even religious longings. They all seemed to have a clearer idea of that part of what it meant than I had myself. But I thought they were right about the other part: that I seemed to want to turn my garden to scientific account in some way, then write up the results (the pen and notebook, both anachronistic types) and disseminate them.

II

This was the year 2000, when four separate strains of HIV virus had been isolated and more than a million people had died. There was a desperate need for qualified volunteer help, for the hospital wings, hastily thrown up by the newly organized National Health, were bursting with AIDS patients. The great majority of new cases now were addicts and the spouses and infants of addicts, and most of these were poor people. Except among the poor, sexual transmission of the virus had become much less common for a variety of reasons. So there were far fewer groups like ours being formed by then, but still plenty of old cases around—people exposed years ago who had survived a long time but whose luck had finally run out. As mine might any day.

Perhaps I secretly believed that by caring for such people I could somehow propitiate or suborn the Fates—"magical thinking" this is called—or perhaps my bond with them, which I refused to *feel*, demanded some other expression of solidarity. I don't know. I told myself that this was my debt to society, due and payable now.

So, soon after returning from my retreat, I attended an Induction Day for volunteers at the AIDS Task Force office in the city. The experience wrung me out and set me straight. I'd vaguely pictured myself helping in the wards, carrying lunch trays and cleaning bedpans, but it was plain from what the speakers told us that I would find this sort of work more emotionally demanding than I'd expected and more than I'd be at all able to handle. I had already known better than to offer myself as a counselor or a "buddy" assigned to a particular patient; I'd been "buddy" to too many Companions already, with more of this bound to come, and even in that collective and defended context it was hard. That left the dull but essential clerical work: getting new patients properly registered and identified within the bureaucracy of the National Health, processing and filing information, explaining procedures, taking medical histories.

I signed up for that, one afternoon a week. Compared to the burdens other volunteers were shouldering, I felt like a coward, but within the Company itself I was a sort of hero, though resented also for what my action made the rest face anew: their fear. Several of the gay men who had gone to Induction Days in years past, but had not felt able to sign up for anything at all, felt especially put down; but *everyone* reported a sense of being implicitly criticized. "You're, like, the teetotaler at the cocktail party," said one of the gays, making us all laugh.

We were no band of activists and saints, the nine of us left of the original Company. Nobody new had joined us for a long time. When the National Health was chartered by Congress, the mandatory anonymous universal blood tests establishing who was and who was not a carrier had brought in a few fresh faces for a time, but those just-identified AB-Positives had mostly preferred to form groups of their own. The rigors of psychoneuroimmunology didn't appeal to everybody, nor did the medical profession agree unanimously that avoiding stress should be a First Principle for the infected. But it was ours; and by making my Companions feel guilty, I was guilty myself of stressing them. I understood their resentment perfectly.

At the same time I did feel a first small flush of self-respect to find that none of the others could face this work, relatively undemanding though it was, and that I could.

And almost at once I had my reward. The obsessive blotch-hunting stopped, I could again bear with composure the sight of my own skin; but a stranger and funnier reward was to follow. One day in the hospital outlet shop, on an errand for a busier volunteer, my eye fell by chance upon an object invented to make life easier for diabetic women: a hard plastic device molded to be tucked between the legs, with a spout designed to project a stream of urine forward, the more conveniently to be tested with litmus strips. In a flash a bizarre idea sprang fully developed into my head, exactly like one of those toads that lie buried in dried-up mudholes in the desert, patiently waiting out the years for the rains that tell it the time had come to emerge and mate. I bought the thing.

Back home I dug out an old electric dildo whose motor had long since burned out—a flexible rod with a "skin" of pink rubber. This I castrated, or rather circumcised. I then glued the three inches of amputated rubber foreskin snugly to the base of the plastic spout and snipped a hole in the tip.

I now had an implement capable of letting female plumbing mimic male plumbing, at least from a short distance, unless the observer were very sharp-eyed or very interested.

Inspired, my next step was to go out and buy myself a complete set of men's clothing: socks and underwear, trousers generously tailored, shirt, sweater, tie, and loosely fitting sport jacket, all of rather conservative cut and color and good quality. I even bought a pair of men's shoes. I'm quite a tall woman—five feet ten and a half inches—with a large-boned face, a flat chest, and the muscular arms and shoulders you build up through years at the rowing machine. And I found that the proverb Clothes make the man is true, for my full-length bathroom mirror confirmed that I made a wholly creditable one. Last of all, into the pouch of my brand-new jockey shorts, right behind the zipper of my new slacks, I tucked the plastic-and-rubber penis. The hard thing pressed against my pubic bone, none too comfortably.

Dress rehearsals went on for a whole weekend. By Monday, based on comparisons with certain water-sports videos I had seen, I thought the effect hilariously realistic. *Where Brother Mendel leads,* I said to myself with reckless glee, *I follow!* I can tell you for sure that this entire undertaking—making my dildo, buying my disguises, learning to fish out the fake penis suavely and snug it in place and let fly—was altogether the most fun I'd had in years. The only fun, really, the only bursting out of bounds. The thought of beans and franks was nothing to this.

When I felt ready for a trial run, I put on my reverse-drag costume and drove to a shopping mall in a neighboring state, where for three hours I practiced striding confidently into the men's rooms of different department stores. I would hit the swinging door with a straight arm, swagger up to a urinal, plant my feet wide apart . . . I kind of overacted the role, but I could do this much with a flourish anyway. What I could *not* do was unclench my sphincter; I was all style and no substance in the presence of authentic (urinating) men. So I flunked that final test.

But my first purpose all along had been voyeuristic, and in this I was wildly, immediately successful. It was a mild day in early autumn. Lots of guys in shirtsleeves, with no bulky outer clothing to hinder the eager voyeur, came in and struck a pose at urinals near mine. For three hours I stole furtive glances at exposed penises from within a disguise that no one appeared even to question, let alone see through. It was *marvelous.* I drove home exhilarated quite as much by my own daring as by what I'd managed to see. To have infiltrated that bastion of male privilege and gotten away with it! What a triumph! What an actor!

All that year, the year 2000, I worked by fits and starts on my role of male impersonator, adding outfits to suit the different seasons and practicing body control (roll of shoulders, length of stride) like a real actor training for a part. I cruised the men's rooms less often than I'd have liked, since it seemed only prudent to avoid those near home, and I was kept fairly busy. But over time, by trial and error, I gained confidence. I learned that large public men's rooms in bus and train stations, airports, interstate rest areas and the like, were best—that men visiting these were usually in a hurry and the rooms apt to be fairly crowded, so that people were least likely to take notice of me there. It was in one such place that I was at last able to perfect my role by actually relieving myself into the porcelain bowl, and after that time I could usually manage it, a fact which made me smug as a cat.

Every cock I sneaked a look at that year seemed beautiful to me. The holos were so much less interesting than this live show that I all but stopped renting them. I also made some fascinating observations. For instance, young gay men no longer rash enough to pick somebody up in a bus station or whatever would sometimes actually stand at adjacent urinals, stare at one another, and stroke themselves erect. Wow! I felt a powerful affinity with these gays, whose motives for being there were so much like my own. Alas, they also made me nervous, for my prosthesis couldn't hold up to fixed regard, and sometimes, if I lingered too long, someone would show more interest than was safe.

The Company had been three-fourths gay men in the beginning, five of whom were still around, yet not one had ever said a word to the rest of us about mutual exhibitionism in public toilets, and it seemed possible that most straight men had never noticed. After sixteen years of weekly group therapy I'd have sworn none of us could possibly have any secrets left; but perhaps the gay Companions simply preferred not to offer up this behavior to the judgment of the straights—even now, and even us. Perhaps it was humiliating for them, even a bit sordid. I could see that. This behavior of mine had its sordid side. The recreational/adventurous side outweighed that twenty to one; but I took my cue from the gays, and kept my weird new hobby to myself—learning in this way that withholding a personal secret from the Company, retaining one exotic scrap of privacy, exhilarated me nearly as much as having live penises to admire after all the dreary years of admiring them on tape.

But if the dream image of Gregor-Mendel-as-hermaphrodite was present to me through much of this experience—for I knew that in some deep way they were connected—Mendel was a still more potent icon in the garden that summer. At first thought, backyard research seemed very small beer. I knew as well as anyone that the day had long since passed when a single white-coated scientist, working alone amid the test tubes in his own basement laboratory, could do important research. Mendel himself had had a larger plot of ground at his disposal.

Yet examining the unfamiliar literature of this field, and browsing in *Biological Abstracts,* forced me to revise my view: there were some very useful experiments within the scope even of a backyard researcher. Some of the published papers that interested me most had been written by amateurs. It appeared that master gardeners, like amateur archeologists and paleontologists, had long been making substantial contributions to the fields of plant breeding, pest control, cultivation practices, and the field trials of new varieties. Organic methods of gardening and farming, which were what interested me, were particularly open to contributions from gardeners and farmers, nonscientists who had taught themselves to run valid trials and keep good records. Genetic engineering and chemical warfare were clearly not the only ways to skin the cat of improved crop yields.

The more I looked into it, the more impressed I was, and correspondingly the more hopeful. Though but a beginning gardener, I was a trained scientist; if these other people could do something useful in their modest way, I should certainly be able to.

I'd lost my first two crops of melons to bacterial wilt and/or mosaic virus, I wasn't sure which, and both years my cucumbers had also died of wilt. (The first couple of seasons in an organic garden are tough sledding.) The striped cucumber beetle was the probable vector for both diseases. God knows I had enough of the little bastards. Now, you can grow *Cucurbita*—the vining crops, including all melons, squashes, cucumbers, and gourds—under cheesecloth or spun-bonded floating row covers, which exclude the bugs, but you have to uncover the plants when the female flowers appear so the bees can get at them, and if the bees can, so can the beetles. Besides, half the fun of gardening is watching the crops develop, and how can you do that if they're shrouded under a white web of Ultramay?

No, the thing was to produce a cultivar with resistance, or at least tolerance, to one or more of the insect-borne diseases. After reading everything I could get my hands on about bacterial wilt and cucumber mosaic virus, I concluded that a project of trying to breed a really flavorful variety of muskmelon strongly resistant to bacterial wilt would make the most sense. Wilt was a bigger problem in our area, and some hybridization for wilt resistance in muskmelons had already been done. But I was much more powerfully attracted to the mosaic problem. It took the Company about half a minute to point out, once they'd understood the question, that cucumber mosaic is caused by a *virus*. There's no cure for mosaic; once it infects a plant, the plant declines, leaf by leaf and vine by vine, until it dies. (Just like you-know-who.)

There's no cure for bacterial wilt, either, but I couldn't help myself: I began to plan an experiment focusing on mosaic.

I didn't want to waste time duplicating the research of others, so I made several trips that summer to Penn State's main campus at University Park to extract from their excellent library everything that was known about all previous efforts to breed virus resistance into muskmelons. These trips were fun. For one thing it pleased me a lot to be doing research again. For another I did the trips in undrag, stopping at every highway rest area on the Pennsylvania Turnpike between Valley Forge and Harrisburg to investigate men's rooms—and in fact simply to use them too, as this was, prosthesis and all, easier, quicker, and less grubby than using the ladies'.

It turned out that the breeders had never made much headway against virus disease in muskmelons, and since the introduction of row covers and beetle traps the subject had been generally slighted. Commercial growers had been getting around the problem of pollination for quite a while by constructing great tents of Ultramay over their fields and putting a hive of honeybees inside with the melons. As this was hardly practical for the home gardener, the state agricultural extension services recommended several pesticides for use on the beetles (and aphids, another serious virus vector for cucurbits) during the two or three weeks when the plants would have to come out from under cover to be pollinated. Spraying at dusk was suggested, to spare the bees. But these were persistent toxins, and I doubted all the bees would be spared, though they might pollinate the vines before they died.

I also read up on the life cycle of the striped cucumber beetle, then built a clever cage in which to rear as many generations of virus-bearing beetles as necessary to carry the critters through the winter —they hibernate in garden trash, but I wanted to guarantee my supply. When the cage was ready I rigged a shelf-and-fluorescent-tube setup in which to raise a sequence of zucchini plants to feed the beetles— nothing grows faster than a zucchini, and nothing's easier to grow, and the beetles love them. As each plant in turn began to sicken, I would transplant a new, healthy seedling into the soil on the bottom of the rearing cage, then cut through the stem of the sick zucchini, shake off the beetles, and remove the plant. The roots had to be left undisturbed, because the soil around them contained eggs, feeding larvae, and pupae, but by the time the space was needed for a new transplant the roots would have died or been eaten up.

It worked beautifully. My quarter-inch black-and-yellow beetles spent that winter, and the next four winters, living the life of Riley.

And throughout that hard late winter of 2001 I spent all my spare time thinking out my project, its objectives and procedures, until I knew exactly what I wanted to do. By April a small ranked and labeled army of cantaloupe seedlings stood waiting in my basement, under lights, for the day when they could safely be set out in their carefully prepared beds and tucked under Ultramay. Assuming no spectacular early success, the plan would organize my summers for the next five years. Plant breeding is not an enterprise for impatient people. It *is* a gesture of faith in the (personal) future.

In early May, just as the azaleas were at their peak of bloom, a week before the last frost date in Delaware County, Jacob Lowenfels and his team of American and French researchers announced their discovery of the AIDS vaccine.

The announcement threw me, and the rest of the Company with me, into a profound funk. Except for us and several thousand dying people, the whole city seemed to rejoice around us; even the war news yielded pride of place. Thank God the spring quarter had ended, except for some finals I could grade with one hand tied behind me. Watering cantaloupe seedlings before turning in, on the night of May 15, I came within a hair of wrenching the table over and dumping the lot of them, *smash,* onto the concrete floor. Why should these frivolous *Cucurbita* live when so many innocents were dead?

I know, I know: the Lowenfels vaccine was of enormous importance even to us—even, for that matter, to those who had developed the disease but would not begin dying seriously for months or years; for overnight the fear of discovery and persecution ended. We were no longer lepers. People could acquire immunity to us now. Only those already in the final stages of dying from AIDS benefited not at all, so that the AIDS wings of the hospitals lay for weeks beneath a pall of sorrow.

And of course I knew all this really, even at the time. I carried out my trays of cantaloupes and honeydews on the sixteenth after all, and planted them on schedule. The beds beneath their Ultramay covers looked so peculiar that I decided to fence the yard, discourage the neighbors' curiosity. I planted with a leaden heart that day, but the melons didn't seem to mind; in their growing medium of compost, peat moss, and vermiculite dug well into my heavy clay soil they soon sent out runners and began to produce male flowers. When the female flowers appeared about ten days later I pulled the Ultramay off of some beds just long enough to rub the anthers of the male flowers against the pistils of the female ones. At other beds I sent in the beetle troops. At the same time I was growing a year's supply of vegetables in my kitchen garden. My computer kept daily records for both garden and field trials. In August I gave my control melons away by the car-trunkload to the Companions, ate tons of them myself, froze some, saved the rest to rot peacefully till they could be blended with autumn leaves into a giant compost tower. (The vines that died of mosaic, and the malformed fruit they produced, if any, went out with the trash.) And I preserved, packaged, labeled, and froze my hybrid seeds.

None of the varieties I'd inoculated with the virus that first year had resisted it worth a damn. I saved seed from only one mosaic-stunted hybrid cultivar, a *Cucumis melo* called "Mi ting tang," which had shown good resistance to cucumber mosaic (plus gummy stem blight and downy mildew) in field trials in Japan. That one had managed to struggle to maturity and produce a crop despite its illness. The fruit, though dwarfed, had a fair flavor and good thick flesh, and I thought I might backcross and then cross it with other varieties after I saw the results of my hybridizing the following year. Resistance in the Ano strains of muskmelon appeared to vary according to the weather; I wanted to find out more about that, too.

Between times I canned and froze and dried my garden produce as one after another the overlapping crops came in. Once I'd gotten over the shock of the vaccine, it was a wonderful summer, the best of my life, full of pleasurable outdoor work; and the four that followed resembled it pretty closely.

Each fall and winter I would overhaul my records and revise my schedules; compost plant residues; treat the soil of the inoculated beds to kill any leftover beetles; care for the next year's beetle crop and manage their supply of zucchini plants; clean and oil my tools; consume my preserved stock of organically grown, squeaky-clean food; teach my classes and run my labs; put in my afternoon at the hospitals every week; meet with the Company; and take my treatments. In a small way I'd also begun to write for gardening magazines, mainly Rodale's and *National Gardening*, though occasionally for *Horticulture* or even *Harrowsmith*. I'd never been so busy nor interested nor free of anxiety, and I think now that unconsciously I'd come to believe that I was safe. "Magical thinking," sure—but it *was* a much healthier and better-rounded way of life, no question.

It was the fifth year of the research, the spring of 2006, that two events occurred to shatter the even tenor of my days. The arrival of the ship from outer space was the big news; but the Hefn delegation was still in England, and in the daily headlines, when devastating news broke upon us in the Company: for our counselor Elizabeth had developed the bodily wasting and red-rimmed eyes of AIDS-Related Complex, and confessed at last that all this while she had been keeping a secret of her own.

One and all we were stricken anew with terror, my eight surviving Companions and I. Elizabeth, who had been our mother, our guardian, our stay against destruction, who had held us together and wedged the door shut against the world's cruelty, could not be dying—for if she were dying, we could none of us feel safe. Our reaction was infantile and total: we were furious. Who would take care of us when she was dead? When an accountant who called himself "Phil" promptly developed skin lesions, we all blamed Elizabeth.

"Phil's" symptoms turned out to be hysterical; his apparent defeat had been the medium through which we had collectively expressed our virulently reactivated panic and dread. After that episode we pulled ourselves together and stopped whining long enough to think a little of Elizabeth, and not so much about our miserable selves.

She had been admitted to Graduate Hospital, the one our psychoneuroimmunology team was affiliated with. I sat with her for a while one afternoon, a sulky, resentful child and her mortally ill mother. When I apologized for my behavior, Elizabeth smiled tiredly. "Oh, I know how you all feel, you're reacting exactly like I thought you would. Listen, Sandy, this had to happen sometime. You folks have all been much too dependent and you know it. Now's your chance to stand on your own, ah, eighteen feet—but I'm sorry you feel let down." She grimaced. "I feel pretty bad about that myself."

Her generosity dissolved my fretful resentment; and love, shocking as the dream-love of Gregor Mendel, flooded into the vacancy. I choked and burst into wrenching tears; Elizabeth patted my arm, which made me cry harder; in a moment I was crouching beside her bed, my hot, wet face pressed against her shoulder, the first time in twenty years that I had touched another human being intimately. A surreal moment. It was glorious, to tell the truth, though I felt as if my chest would burst with grief.

When I forced myself to report this scene on Company time, the story was received in a glum silence tinged with embarrassment. Finally "Larry," a balding, thickening physical therapist I'd known since he was a skinny teenager, puffed out a breath and said disgustedly,

"Well, don't feel like the Lone Ranger, Sandy. I never touch anybody either, except on the job. Hell, we *all* love Elizabeth! But I never let myself know that. I haven't taken an emotional risk in so many years I literally can't remember when the last time was, and you people aren't any better than me."

"I've often thought," said "Phil," "that it's funny we don't love each other. I mean, as much as we need each other, you'd think . . ."

He trailed off, and we glanced obliquely (and guiltily) at one another, except for the two couples present—who naturally couldn't help looking a little smug—and the one father who blurted defensively, "I love my kids!"

"Elizabeth knows we love her," said "Sherry," over against the far wall.

"Maybe she does," "Larry" growled, "but *we* need to know it. That's my point, goddammit."

"Other groups do better. Some of them are really close," I put in. "Maybe we fuss over ourselves so much we can't connect, except to spot weaknesses."

"Other groups don't have our survival rate either," "Mitch" reminded me.

Breaking the gloomy silence, "Phil" roused himself to say, "What about these spacemen, anything doing in that direction?"

When the Hefn first arrived, half the world's people had recoiled in panicky dismay; the other half had seemed to expect them to provide a magical cure for all our ills: war, cancer, pollution, overpopulation, famine, AIDS. So far they had shown no interest in us whatever. The landing party was presently in London because the mummified corpse of one of their relations, stranded here hundreds of years ago, had been discovered in a Yorkshire bog; but suggestions that they set up some sort of cultural and scientific exchange with humanity had been politely ignored, and I doubted there was any chance at all that Elizabeth's life was going to be saved by ET intervention. The AIDS Task Force in New York had already sent them a long, pleading letter, but had received no reply. We were all aware of these facts. Nobody bothered to answer "Phil," and after a while the hour was over and we broke up; and when the Hefn ship took off from the moon a few weeks later, having neither helped nor harmed us by their visit, we weren't surprised. It was what we'd expected.

Just as we'd expected Elizabeth to waste and decline, and finally die, and she did—leaving the Companions rudderless and demoralized. At least we'd rallied and borne up pretty well throughout the last weeks of her dying. We must have done her, and ourselves, a little good.

Surprisingly, despite even this trauma none of the rest of us became ill. Apparently we who were still alive were the hardiest of the lot, or at least the ones who had taken the best care of ourselves. But the emotional jolt of Elizabeth's death—the one death we had *not* protected ourselves from being badly hurt by—showed me, as the dream of Mendel had shown me all those years ago, that something was still wrong with my life. It was still a loveless life, and just when I seemed to need it least, it now appeared that I was no longer willing to do without love. I'd failed to acknowledge Elizabeth alive; now that she was dead I wanted at least to keep alive the emotion—the capacity for feeling and showing emotion—that she had released in me at the end.

It didn't have to be romantic love, in fact I rather thought that any other sort would probably be preferable, though I was still determined not to *teach* lovingly. It seems odd now that I never thought of getting a pet—or maybe the image of a dog wouldn't readily superimpose itself upon the image of a backyard carpeted with melon vines? And I'm allergic to cat dander . . . anyway, whatever the reasons, the idea never crossed my mind. The months glided by as usual, and became years, before anything changed.

III

What happened was that I broke a small bone in my left ankle in a common type of running accident: one foot came down at the edge of a pothole and twisted beneath me as I fell. The X ray showed a hairline fracture. They put me in a cast and crutches and ordered me off the foot for a month, and this was May.

May 2010; Year Four of my second five-year plan. With the whole season's research at stake I had no choice but to hire some help.

A bright, possibly talented sophomore in my botany course took the job. His name was Eric Meredith, and he was the first person other than my unobservant parents, a dishwasher repairer, and the water meter reader to have entered my house in the ten years I had owned it. I bitterly resented the need that had brought him there; but I knew the source of this bitterness (apprehension: what other infirmities would be violating my privacy in future summers?) and made a perfunctory effort not to work it out on Eric.

He seemed not to take my unfriendliness personally—I had a certain reputation at the college as a grump—and willingly did what I told him to without trying to chat me up. I showed him *once* how to handle the transplants, how big and how far apart to make the holes, how to work fertilizer and compost into the loose earth, dump in a liter of water, and firm the soil around the stem. He never forgot, never did it wrong, even beneath my jealous eye; he seemed to discover a knack for the work in the process of performing it that pleased him as much as it mollified me. He was scrupulously careful with the labeling and weighed the Ultramay at the beds' edges with earth, leaving no gaps for wandering bees or beetles to find. In a week the entire lot of transplants was in the ground. I recorded the data myself—I could sit at a keyboard, anyway—but Eric did everything else.

He grew so earnestly interested in the experiment, what's more, that after the second week he couldn't help asking questions; and I found his interest so irresistible that before I knew it I'd invited him to review the records.

For I did, finally, really appear to be getting someplace. Several hybrids of the "Mi ting tang" (Ano II) strain had done unusually well the previous year; I thought I knew now which of their parents to cross with Perfection and Honey Dew to produce at least one variety which would show exceptional tolerance to mosaic in the field. Immunity now looked impossible, resistance unlikely; but I felt I would be more than satisfied with a strain that could *tolerate* the presence of the virus in its system without being killed or crippled too much—that could go on about its business of making a pretty good crop of sweet, firm-fleshed melons in spite of the disease.

Eric sat for an hour while the screen scrolled through the records of a near-decade. I jumped when he spoke. "This whole thing is just *beautifully* conceived." His amazement was understandable; why expect anything good from a professor as mediocre in class as I? "You're just about there, aren't you?"

He had a plain, narrow face, much improved by enthusiasm. I felt my own face growing warm. "Mm-hm, I think so. One more season. Of course, this isn't a very exciting experiment—not like what they do in the labs, genetic manipulation, that sort of thing."

"Well," said Eric, "but it's not so much the experiment itself as the experimental model. Heck, you could apply this model to any traits you were trying to select for. Did you work it out yourself?" I suspected that this was doubt, but when I nodded, he did too. "I thought so, I never came across this system of notation before and I bet everybody'll be using it after you publish."

I'd been working in isolation a long time, without admiration, and the traitorous balloon of gratitude that swelled my chest undid me. "Come have something cold to drink," I offered gruffly, and as I went before him into the kitchen the rubber tip of my crutch slipped on a wet patch of linoleum and I fell, whacking my head hard on the corner of a shelf on the way down.

For a few seconds the pain in both ankle and scalp was blinding. Then as I struggled to rise, embarrassed and angry, and as Eric leaned over me to help, I saw the drops of blood on the floor, brilliant against the pale tiles. "Get away!" I shouted, shoving him so hard he stumbled against the counter and I fell flat on my back. In rage I hauled myself upright, holding to the counter, and managed to rip off some paper toweling to blot my head with. Again Eric moved instinctively to help, and again I snapped, "No, get back I said, keep away from me. *Did you get any blood on yourself?*"

"Unh unh," said Eric, looking at his hands and arms, bewildered and then—bright student—suddenly comprehending. "Oh, hey, it's okay—I'm vaccinated."

I froze and stared at him, my head singing. "*What did you say?*"

"I'm *vaccinated* against AIDS. A bone punch in the sixth grade, see?" He pulled down the neck of his T-shirt and showed me the little V-shaped scar on his collarbone.

Vaccinated. Immune. Of course he was. *Everybody* was vaccinated nowadays. Eric had been in no danger from me—but in my instinctive panic I'd given myself away. For exactly the third time that decade I burst into tears, and I couldn't have told you which of the two of us was the more embarrassed.

I don't remember how I got him out of the house. I spent that evening raging at myself, my situation, the plague that had blighted my life, aborted my career, turned me into a time bomb of thwarted need. So what if it came out that I was a carrier of the virus? Nobody gave a damn anymore. During the past few years, the deadly micro-organisms that had built up strength in my system throughout the first ten had begun to decline. I might never die of AIDS now, might not even be infectious, nobody knew. Even if I were, the world had been immunized against me. Yet I *felt* infectious, consumed with longing for something that would certainly be destroyed if I tried to possess it. No amount of rational certainty that this was *not* so acted to defuse a conviction which had for so long been the central emotional truth, the virtual mainspring, of my life. For the past nine years I had abstained from sex for my own reasons of stress-avoidance, not to protect others; I had known this and not-known it, both.

The truth was, I had lived as a leper too long to change my self-concept. Now here was this boy, who had guessed my guilty secret just like that and spoken it aloud without batting an eye. He would have to be replaced, possibly bribed . . . no, that was crazy thinking. Yet the thought of facing him was unendurable. I'd pay him off in the morning and dismiss him. The pain of this thought astonished me; yet I couldn't doubt it must be done.

I had not, however, factored in Eric's own attitudes and wishes. The next day he showed up at the usual time and went straight to work in the kitchen garden, spreading straw mulch on the tomato and pepper beds, whistling the noble theme from the second movement of Beethoven's Seventh. From the kitchen window I watched his tall, bony frame fold and unfold, gather the straw from the cart in armfuls and heap it carefully around the bases of the plants; and gradually I became aware that here was the only living being, not one of the Company, who knew The Truth. Gradually, it even began to seem a wonderful thing that somebody knew. Eric dragged the empty cart across the yard for more straw bales, then back to the nightshade beds. I regarded his back in its sweat-soaked T-shirt, the play of the shoulder muscles, the stretching tendons at the sides of his knees as he folded and straightened—and something fluttered and turned over in my middle-aged insides. "Eric," I murmured in wonderment; and as if he had heard he turned his head, saw me at the window, waved, and grinned. Then he stooped to gather another armful of straw, and I fell back out of view.

That grin . . . I dropped onto a stool, hearing in my head the incongruous voice of my best high-school friend: "He looked over at me from the other side of the class and it just really boinged me." Boinged, I'd been boinged! By Eric's cheerfulness, the wave of his long arm with its brown work glove at the end. I knew by then, I guess, that I wasn't going to fire him; but I couldn't see how to do anything else with him either.

At noon Eric came to the house to wash up under the spigot before leaving, in his khaki shorts and old running shoes. He had taken off his shirt, and dust and bits of straw had stuck to the sweaty skin of his chest and back, and in the curly golden hairs of his legs and the blond mop on his head. He was a very lanky guy, pretty well put together, not a bit handsome. I regarded his long body with awe.

"I'll be late tomorrow, got a dentist appointment," he said. "Listen, I wanted you to know I'm not going to say anything to anybody else about yesterday. In case you were worrying about it. I mean, I don't go in for gossip much anyway, and even if I did I wouldn't spread stuff around about you."

I managed to reply, "Thanks, I'd appreciate it if you wouldn't."

Eric started to say something else but instead stuck his head under the faucet for a minute, dried himself on his shirt, and slipped away around the house. There was a paperback novel crammed into the back pocket of his shorts, its title *Sowbug!* scrawled diagonally across the cover in screaming colors, and water droplets spangled his bare shoulders.

And so we went on as before, but nothing was as it had been for me. Once again I became an actor, for I found myself against all sense and expectation carrying a blazing torch for a boy considerably less than half my age: a clever, nice, probably not terribly remarkable boy who (as the Companions agreed) was serving now as representative object of the pent-up love of half a lifetime. Eric, the wick for this deep reservoir of flammable fuel, became "Lampwick" in Company nomenclature: Lampwick, the boy who went to Pleasure Island with Pinocchio and turned into a braying jackass before the puppet's horrified eyes.

I felt like the jackass, let me tell you. *Knowing* the passion that so rocked me to be symbolic and categorical, hardly about Eric-the-singular-individual at all, made exactly zero difference to my experience of it. In the Company we'd been talking and thinking more about love since Elizabeth's death, and they all thought it was great. *All* loves are part personal, part associational, the more worldly among them assured me. Go for it! Get it out of your system. Wasn't your primary sexual involvement in the past with a teacher? Hey, the unconscious is a tidy bastard; naturally yours would think it fitting to pass the baton to the next generation by making you fall for a student of your own.

And I have to admit that even the hopeless misery of *this* passion was, in a weird way, kind of fun. It rejuvenated my libido, for one thing. It took me out of myself. I no longer feared the lethal effects of stress so much, and in any case this stress was salutary, too.

I did take enormous care to protect myself from the humiliation of letting Eric catch me out, as he had caught me out about my antibody status. He never dreamed I seethed with lust for him, I feel quite sure of that. I think he did regret my aloofness—he was a sociable boy, and truly admired my work—but not so much as to be pained by it; and in any event Eric had other fish to fry that summer.

My ankle had healed well enough by late July for me to take over the kitchen garden, and a bit later the processing of its produce, when that began to roll in; but I pretended a greater disability than I really had just to keep Eric around. And when my old mother in Denver had a stroke, making a visit unavoidable, I was happy to leave him in charge of both kitchen garden and melon plots. The special hybrids were looking great, but records on rainfall and hours of sunlight during this crucial month would have to be kept. I asked Eric to come live in the house while I was away, and promised him a bonus if he did a meticulous job of keeping the records.

I decided not to fly, and drove west in an erotically supercharged state of psyche, sleeping in the carbed, peeing in the men's rooms of seven states, feasting my eyes on hundreds of penises and fantasizing that this or that one could be Eric's. . . . I hadn't done much of this recently and suspect I made a less convincing man as I grew older but I had a terrific time for a while, although to tell the truth I rather wore my imagination out. My mother was feeling better and received my attentions with gratified complacency; but the five grandchildren had become her life, and we regarded one another, benignly enough, through a glaze of mutual incomprehension. It seemed likely that I would see her next when I flew out for the funeral.

All the same I stayed a week before returning by easy stages across the hot, dry, dusty plains, eager to get back but pleased to think of Eric still holding the fort in my stead. No point in pretending I couldn't handle the work now, not after a drive like this. Anyway, the term would be starting soon. When I got back, I'd have to let him go; and so I dawdled and fantasized across Kansas and Missouri, and late in the afternoon of August 30 was approaching Indianapolis when I told the radio to turn itself on and was informed that early that same morning there had been a meltdown at the nuclear power plant at Peach Bottom, on the Susquehanna River downstream from Three Mile Island.

Luckily traffic was light. I managed to pull off the road without smashing up and sat gripping the wheel while the radio filled me in. The disaster was unprecedented, making even Chernobyl look paltry. The Peach Bottom plant was fifty years old and overdue to be shut down for good. It *had* been shut down in the eighties, then reopened in 1993, when improved decontamination technology had reduced its radioactivity to acceptable levels. Though the plant had a history of scandalously inept management, technicians asleep on duty and so on, stretching back a long way, it didn't appear that the meltdown had been caused by human error.

From the standpoint of damage to nearby populations, the weather could not have been much worse, given that it was summer. A storm system with a strong south-southwest wind had pushed the enormous radioactive plume across the fertile Amish farmland of Lancaster

County; then a westerly shift had carried the plume over the continuous urban sprawl of Wilmington, Philadelphia, and Trenton. Heavy rains had dumped the hot stuff on the ground across that whole area. The storm had also put out the fire at the plant; damage was therefore horrific but, so far, highly localized.

The plume had been washed to earth before it could enter the upper atmosphere—but in one of the most densely populated regions of the world. A very high death count from acute radiation poisoning was expected; the Amish farmers, working in the fields without radios to warn them, were especially at risk. *Eight million people,* more or less, had to be evacuated and relocated, probably permanently, for the Philadelphia-Wilmington area would be a wasteland for at least a decade to come, perhaps much longer.

Terry Carpenter's name was mentioned again and again. A moderate Republican Congressman from Delaware County, Carpenter was being described by reporters as a miracle worker. His understanding and the speed of his response suggested that Carpenter had planned carefully for just this sort of emergency. Because of him, the cost in human lives would be far less, though no one person could cope with every aspect of a disaster as great as this one. . . . (I'd crossed over and voted for the guy myself, last election. Good move.)

People who had not yet left their homes had been urged to keep doors and windows shut and air conditioners turned off, to reduce inhalation uptake, which would be reduced somewhat anyway by the rain, and to draw water in their bathtubs and sinks before the runoff from the storm could contaminate the supply. Each was to pack a small bag . . .

The radio went on and on as I sat by the highway, shocked beyond thought. My house, my garden, the campus, the hospital where I worked and the one where I had my monthly treatments, the Company, the experiment—all the carefully assembled infrastructure of my unnatural life—had melted down with the power plant. What in the world was I going to do? My trip had saved me from radiation poisoning, and from being evacuated and stuck in a Red Cross camp someplace; my car and I were clean. But my life was in ruins.

And all the while, still in shock, I thought about Eric, whom I'd left to mind the store, who might be in my house right now with the doors and windows shut, waiting to be evacuated. Abruptly snapping out of it, I drove back onto the road and went off at the next exit, where I found a pay phone that worked and put the call through.

But the phone in my house rang and rang, and finally I hung up and stood shaking in the already-sweltering morning, unable to think what to do now, stranded. Impossible to go back to Denver. Impossible to go home. Impossible also to find Eric, at least until things settled down. Eric, of course, would go to his parents' house—only what if they lived in the evacuation zone? A lot of our students were local kids; it was that kind of college.

I knew not even that much about Eric's personal life, I realized with a furious rush of shame, and at this moment all my uncertainty and powerlessness fused into a desperate need to find him, see him, make sure he was all right. Of all the desperately threatened people I knew in the area of contamination, only this one boy mattered to me.

I got back in my car and started driving. I drove all night, stopped at a western Pennsylvania sleepyside for a nap the following morning, drove on again. The radio kept me posted on developments. All that way I thought about Eric. Half of my mind was sure he was fine, safe in his parents' (grandparents'?) home in Pittsburgh or Allentown; the other half played the Eric-tape over and over, his longness and leanness, the grown-up way he'd handled my breaking down, his careful tenderness with the melon seedlings (like Mendel's!), his reliability, his frank, unstudied admiration of my trial model, his schlock horror novel *Sowbug!* Why hadn't I been *nicer* to him while I'd had the chance? Why had I played it safe? My house and garden were lost, my experimental records doubtless ruined by fallout, the work of the past decade all gone for nothing, yet worse by far was the fact that I had squandered my one God-given chance to come close to another person, thrown it away, out of fear. I beat on the steering wheel and sobbed. Eric, Eric, if only I hadn't been so scared.

Whatever happened now, I knew I would never again watch him fold that long body up like a folding ruler to tend the crops or sic the virus-loaded striped cucumber beetles onto a melon cultivar. That life was finished. There was nothing to connect us now, because I had wasted my one chance and would never get another. I was hardly thinking straight, of course; I was in shock. I'd heard my colleagues speak often enough, and wistfully enough, of promising former students from whom they rarely or never heard anymore. Students go away and teachers stay—that's the way it's always been, they'd say. Put not your faith in students. A card at Christmas for a year or two after they leave, then zip.

But I wasn't thinking of what Eric might or might not have done in some hypothetical future time; I was thinking of what I myself had failed to do and now could never do. I cried, off and on, for hours, being forced once by uncontrollable weeping to stop the car. I shed far more tears during that nightmarish trip than in my whole previous life since childhood. If I'd only put my arms around him, just one time, just held him for a minute, not even saying anything—if I'd just managed to do that— As the hours and miles went by my grief became more and more inconsolable, as if all the tragedy of the meltdown, and even of my life, were consolidated into this one spurned chance to become human. It didn't matter whether Eric wanted to be befriended (let alone held) by me, diseased middle-aged spinsterish schoolmarm and part-time pervert that I had become; what mattered, beyond measure or expression, was that I'd been too cowardly even to consider the possibility of closeness with another person and now it was too late.

I drove and wept, wept and drove. Gradually traffic going the opposite direction began to build up. Just west of Harrisburg a bunch of state troopers were turning the eastbound cars back. Beyond the roadblock only two lanes were open; the other two, and the four going west, were full of cars fleeing the contaminated zone. I pulled over, cleaned my blotchy face as best I could with a wet cloth, and got out. A trooper was directing U-turns at the head of a line of creeping cars. I walked up to him. "Excuse me, do you know how I can find out where somebody is?"

The trooper turned, gray-faced with exhaustion. "You from Philadelphia?" I nodded. "I dunno, bud," he replied—reminding me that I was still in my traveling costume of undrag. "In a coupla days they'll know where everybody's at, but it's a madhouse back there right now, there's eight million people they're trying to evacuate. You had your radio on?"

"Yeah, but—"

"Maybe it's too far to pick it up out here." He took off his cap and rubbed his hand over his face. "Everybody that's got someplace to go, that has a car, is supposed to go there. Relatives, whatever. That's what all these people are doing. These are the ones from Lancaster and thereabouts—Philadelphia people were supposed to take the Northeast Extension or else head down into south Jersey or Delaware along with the Wilmington people. The ones that don't have noplace to go, they're all being sent to camps up in the Poconos or down around Baltimore. The Army's bringing in tents and cots."

"For eight million people?"

"Naaah, most of 'em'll have somebody they can stay with for a while. They figure a million and a half, two million, tops. Still a hell of a lot of campers. Who ya looking for?"

"A student of mine, he was house-sitting for me."

"Local kid?"

"I don't know, actually."

The trooper looked me over, red swollen eyes and rumpled, slept-in clothes, and drew his own conclusions but was too tired to care. "Probably went home to his folks if they don't live around Philly. They're telling everybody to call in with the info of where they're at as soon as they get to wherever it is they're going. There's a phone number for every letter of the alphabet. A couple more days, if the kid does like he's supposed to, you'll be able to track him down."

"Sounds pretty well worked out," I said vaguely. A couple of days, IF he was okay, and no way to find out if he wasn't.

"It's a goddamn miracle is what it is," said the trooper fervently. "That goddamn Congressman, Terry Carpenter, that son of a bitch was just waiting for something like this to happen, I swear to God, must of been. He had everything all thought out and ready to go. He commandeered the suburban trains in Philly, the buses, all the regular Amtrak trains and the freight trains, too, that were anywheres around, and had 'em all rolling within a couple hours of the accident, got the hospitals and so forth emptied out, and look at this here"—he waved at the six lanes of cars contracting into four, but moving along pretty well, at about forty—"it's the same back in Philadelphia except at the ramps and like that." The trooper put his cap back on. "I got to get back to work here. Don't worry about your little pal, he'll be okay. You got someplace to go? I can give you directions to a refugee camp."

"No thanks, I'm fine." It was stupid to resent the trooper for what he was thinking but I did all the same.

I edged my car into the stream of traffic being guided back the way it had come, but at the first exit slid out of formation and onto a little road that headed off into the mountains. I drove along for several miles, looking for a town with a phone; but when I finally found one, in front of a closed-up shop in a closed-up town, there was still no answer.

That was crisis time, there and then. I don't know how long I stood beside that phone kiosk while the battle raged. At one point several busloads of Amish families went by, probably headed for relatives in Ohio; they stared out, faces blank and stony; for them, too, it was the end of the world. The wind had only held SSW a little while before shifting to southwest, but that was long enough.

Finally I got back into the car, turned it around, reentered the turnpike by the eastbound ramp, drove back to the roadblock, and found my trooper. He stood still and watched me walk up to him, too beat to show surprise. "Look," I said, "I'd like to go in and help search for the people that got missed. They must need volunteers. I'm volunteering."

Very slowly he nodded. "If that's what you want. Go on into Harrisburg and talk to somebody there. Get off at the Capitol, there's a trooper station set up around there somewheres, you'll see it. Maybe they'll take you. I'll radio ahead so they know you're comin'." I thanked him and started to leave; he called after me, "Listen up a minute, bud. Later on it might be too late to change your mind. We might be moving people out of York and Harrisburg if the wind shifts again."

"I understand," I called back, and felt him watch for a minute before moving to his car to use the radio.

In Harrisburg I talked fast and they took me—took me also, at face value, for a youthfully middle-aged man. They issued me a radiation suit, and minimal instructions, and flew me into the contaminated zone along with a batch of other volunteers, a few Quakers and some workers from Three Mile Island.

We were dropped in Center City, fifteen miles from where I needed to be. They didn't like to spare any people for the suburbs, but emergency volunteers are hard to control and some of the others were looking for friends or relatives, too. In the end they let each of us take a police vehicle with a loudspeaker and told us to make a mad dash for home, then drive back slowly into the city, keeping the siren on and picking up stragglers as we came.

I'd only made it a little more than halfway home when I ran out of gas. The damned van burned ethanol and I'd been driving some kind of electric or solar car for thirteen years, but even so . . . I tore off on foot in my radiation suit to find a filling station, looking I'm sure exactly like a space invader in a B-grade flick, trying to run along the deserted street—not deserted enough, though: when I got back with a can of ethanol half an hour later, streaming with sweat and nearly suffocated, the van was gone. Like an idiot I hadn't taken the keys. I heaved the can into a hedge and started walking.

I was seven miles from home, give or take half a mile. Just as I set off, the sun came out. I had to pee badly and didn't know how (or whether) to open the suit, and I was already terribly thirsty.

That walk was no fun at all. I had to rest a lot. I also had decided that wetting the suit was preferable to the consequences of any alternative I could think of, which made the hike even more unpleasant than it would have been in any case. It was more than three hours from the time I'd left the van when I finally got home. The key was in my pocket but I couldn't get to it; I ended up breaking my own basement window to get in.

Eric wasn't there.

I knew the house was empty the instant I got inside. In the basement I leaned against the cool wall, overcome with exhaustion and letdown. After a while I fumbled with the suit till something came unfastened, and crawled out of it, drenched and reeking; I left the suit in the basement with all my seed-starting equipment and insect cages and dragged myself on wobbling knees upstairs, shutting the door behind me.

The kitchen sink was full of water. So were both bathroom sinks and the tub. My feeling of letdown lifted; he'd followed instructions then, that probably meant he'd gotten safely away. Good old Eric. I drank a couple of liters of water from the sink before stripping off my vile clothes and plunging into the full, cool tub. Might as well die clean.

Almost instantly I went to sleep. When I woke an hour or so later with a stiff neck I took a thorough bath, got dressed again (this time in my "own" clothes, some shorts and a shirt), realized I was famished, and raided the refrigerator for a random sampling of Eric's abandoned provisions: cold chicken, supermarket bread, a banana, a tomato from the garden. The power was off, but the doors had been kept shut and nothing had spoiled. I drank a can of Eric's Coke, my first in nearly thirty years. It was delicious. In a cabinet I found a bag of potato chips and ate them all with deliberate relish: exquisite! There were half a dozen boxes of baked beans in there—and pickled herring—and a box of cheese. . . . Irrationally I began to feel terrific, as if the lost chance with Eric were somehow being made up for by his unintended gifts, the last meals I expected ever to eat. I meant to enjoy them, and I did.

Sated at last, I wandered into my airless bedroom and fell across the bed. Strange as it may sound, I never thought to switch on the transistor, so wholly had I crossed over into a realm governed by the certainty of my own imminent death. I had been fleeing my death for so long that on one level I actually felt relief to believe I could give in to it now, stop twisting and doubling and trying to give it the slip. Nor, still stranger, did I even glance into the garden.

The house was stifling, must have been shut up for many hours. It had been many hours, too, since people had been told not to run any more water or flush their toilets, though both of mine were flushed and clean. These things pointed to Eric's safe escape and relieved my mind of its last burden. I sank like a stone into sleep. When I woke it was dark, and the house was being battered by the amazing racket of the helicopter landing in the little park a block away.

They'd caught the person who had pinched my van as he was trying to cross the Commodore Barry Bridge into New Jersey. A police van is a conspicuous object to steal, but he'd been offered no alternatives and didn't mind being apprehended at all, so long as his captors took him out of danger. He'd seen me stop and leave the van, waited till I was gone, then poured fuel from some cans in his landlady's garage into the tank and taken off, while I'd still been hoofing it up the road. Inside the helmet I hadn't heard the engine start. It seemed less reasonable to steal the van outright than to beg a lift, but people act oddly when their lives are at stake, and that was how he'd chosen to play it—a white man in his fifties, no family, a night-shift worker who had somehow slept through the evacuation. In fact, the very sort of person I'd been sent to pick up. All this I learned later.

It had taken time to trace the van, and everybody was plenty busy enough without coming to rescue the would-be rescuer, and they didn't even know my name. But I'd mentioned the name of my development to one of the other volunteers, and its general location near the campus, and eventually they sent the helicopter out to find me. It wasn't till I was out of my suit again that anybody realized the man they'd come to find had metamorphosed into a woman.

The rest is all aftermath, but I may as well set it down anyway.

I lived for a month in a refugee camp near Kutztown, Pennsylvania, on land owned by the Rodale Research Center; I chose it for that reason. By month's end it was obvious that Greater Philadelphia was going to be uninhabitable for years—maybe a decade, maybe more.

A month to the day after the accident they sighted the returning Hefn ship.

I took a pretty high dose of radiation. My chances of developing leukemia in fifteen or twenty years aren't bad at all. However, I don't expect to be around that long unless I accept the Hefn's offer (of which more later).

One day in the camp they paged me, and when I got to the admin tent, who should be standing there in pack, T-shirt, and shorts but Eric Meredith. I'd found out, quite quickly, that he had indeed gone to relatives in Erie with the first wave of the evacuation, and had sent him a letter saying how relieved I was that he'd gotten away safely. I'd mentioned that I would be staying at the Rodale Camp for a while. Eric had come all that way, not to collect his bonus (as I thought at first), but to deliver the contents of his backpack: a complete printout of the records of my experiment, this season's preliminary notes on disk, and six seriously overripe cantaloupes containing the seeds of *Cucumis melo reticulatus* var. Milky Tango, the hybrid melon I'd had the highest hopes for, saved by his quick thinking from the radioactive rain. "I didn't know how to get the tough disk out of the computer," he apologized.

I stared at the bagful of smelly spheres on the table before us with the oddest emotion. For part of a day not long before I'd surrendered, I'd given up my life. By purest luck my life had been restored to me; but I had crossed some psychic boundary that day, and had never crossed back again. And Eric and the experiment both belonged to the time before the accident, when fighting viral diseases had been most of what I cared to do.

It only took one step to close the distance. I took it, put my arms around that bony, sinewy, beanpole torso and held myself against it for a moment out of time. Eric stood stiff as a tomato stake, and about as responsive, but I didn't mind. "Eric, do me a favor," I said, letting go of him and stepping back. "I'll take half of these, you keep the others. Plant them in your grandparents' backyard next summer. Finish the experiment for me."

A coughing fit made me break off, and Eric unstiffened enough to say, "Are you okay? That cough sounds terrible."

"I'm fine now. I had a cold, then bronchitis. Listen: the soil at my place will be contaminated for years, and God knows when I'll get another yard to grow things in. The college may reorganize, but it hasn't been decided whether or where. Not in Delaware County, though. Will you be going on down to University Park?"

He nodded. "Next week. They're letting us start late."

"Good, then you just have time to collect yourself a supply of cucumber beetles. You can expose them to mosaic later if they haven't already picked it up." The poor kid was staring, unable to believe what was happening. "I'm perfectly serious. Look: *you* saved the data and the seed. I was in the house for eight hours or so myself and it never crossed my mind to try to rescue either one." This was true. The only thing *I'd* thought to rescue, when the helicopter came, had been my fake penis. "You've earned the right to finish the work. But don't feel you have to, either; the Rodale people will be glad to take over, or a seed company would."

"Oh no, I *want* to! Really!" he protested. "If you don't that is—but you could make money from this. It isn't right."

"Tell you what. For safety's sake, let's have another copy of these records made and print out the ones from this summer. I'll hang on to half the seed, as I said. If you don't produce salable results I'll see that somebody who might gets my copy and the seed; and if you do get results we'll split the money down the middle. How does that sound?"

The camp had several notaries. We wrote up an agreement and got one of them to notarize our signatures. I wasn't even sure it was legal—Eric was only nineteen or twenty—but never mind, I thought, never mind!

I walked him back to his car. Still bedazzled by the turn of events, he let the window down to say earnestly, "Nobody *ever* gave me anything this important before. I don't know what to say."

"You gave me something important too."

"*I* did? When? What was it?"

I thought of trying to tell him just what, thought better of it. "Cold chicken. Potato chips. Baked beans. Coke."

It took him a minute to realize what I was talking about, but then he objected, "That's different! That's not the same thing at all!"

"Less different than you know. Think about it, eh?" And then, a bit rashly, "Think about *me* once in a while."

Last month I attended Eric's graduation from Penn State: *Magna cum laude* in biology and a graduate fellowship to Cornell. For a boy from the nether regions of academe, not bad at all. Maybe he'll do with his life what I'd have done with mine if things had been different. Eric's final proof of Milky Tango's tolerance to mosaic under a wide variety of growing conditions earned him his classy degree, though he gave me full credit for my own work, to which his was only the capstone—but a beautifully cut and polished capstone, every bit as good as the one I might have cut myself. I wore a long-sleeved shirt to the commencement, too warm for such a sunny day, to cover the Kaposi's lesions that have spread now over much of my body.

My own research has taken an unexpected turn.

Early last summer I donned a radiation suit and went back home to see my abandoned garden and my field-trial beds. Everything was a disheartening mess, but that wasn't what I'd come to see. Eric had ripped loose the Ultramay cover on the Milky Tango beds to harvest those six melons. Remnants of the stuff flapped around me as I knelt to look, imagining his haste and fright as he'd scrabbled frantically among the vines while behind him in the house the printer pipped and pinged. But such thoughts weren't what I'd come for either.

The rest of the Milky Tango seedcrop had eventually rotted where it lay, and the seeds had been directly exposed to the elements all these months. I'd been reading a lot about using fast neutrons, X rays, and gamma rays to induce desirable mutations in plants, including disease resistance, and had begun to wonder what effect the fallout might have had on my own already highly resistant muskmelons. I wanted to know whether any of the accidentally irradiated seed had made it through the winter and germinated, and so did my new bosses at the Rodale Press, who were paying for this expedition. Our Hefn observer was interested too—enough to come along and help.

Sure enough, there were about two dozen volunteer seedlings growing in the Milky Tango plots. Some leaves showed signs of moderate beetle damage but not enough to set the plants back much. With Godfrey's help I transplanted each seedling, radioactive soil and all, into its own large peat pot brought along for the purpose. Back at the Research Center we planted the lot of them at a special site set apart from the other trials and waited to see what would happen.

While we were waiting, I got sick. Before that, the eighteen months between the Peach Bottom accident and my illness were my happiest ever.

When Penn State made the decision to disband the Delaware County Campus, they offered to try to place the tenured faculty at other branches of the system; but by then the Rodale Press had offered me a job. I'd been writing for their magazines for years and knew a number of Rodale editors and writers through correspondence, so it was natural enough that they should think of me when an editorial slot opened up that September at *Backyard Researcher* magazine, the newest member of the Rodale family of publications.

I can remember when all this part of Pennsylvania was farmland, and Kutztown a tiny college town with one main street, one bad motel, and one decent restaurant. But high-tech industry like AT&T and Xerox had moved in, changing the character of the area completely. When I came here to live, the Research Center had become a green island in a sea of development. I moved into one of the old farm buildings at the Center and commuted to my job in Emmaus, where the Press was located. Living out at the Center made it easier to keep an eye on my new experimental garden. No more battling with diseases now; the project I devised had to do with increasing yields in several kinds of potatoes. No more hyperpure living, either: the potato chip and I were strangers no longer. No more Companions; we were scattered to the winds, but the new friends I made here knew about my condition. No more celibacy: for a while, one of these friends became my lover.

When the Hefn returned and decided to take charge of us, they looked around for pockets of sanity and right action in the general balls-up we'd made of things, and so they were interested in the Rodale enterprise and in sustainable agriculture generally—enough to assign us a permanent observer/adviser, and that was Godfrey. He moved into the farmhouse with me. When I got sick he knew about it; when the lesions appeared he asked about them, and the disease they meant I had. It's because of Godfrey that the search for a "cure"—fallen on very thin times since the numbers of still-living victims had dropped below ten thousand—has taken off again.

It looks pretty promising, actually. They've found a way to paralyze the enzyme that the virus uses to replicate in the cell—not like zidovudine and its kindred, which only slowed the enzyme down, but a drug that stops it cold. There's no way I'd still be alive by the time they finish sanding the side effects off the stuff, not in the natural course of things. But Godfrey's had another idea.

You know that, like cucumber beetles, the Hefn hibernate—and that their bodies use chemicals pretty much the same way ours do? Well, Godfrey figures it should be possible to synthesize a drug—using a chipmunk or woodchuck model in conjunction with a Hefn model—that would put the ninety-five-hundred-odd AIDS patients and AB-positives to sleep for a couple of years, until the cure can be perfected. There's a problem about testing the stuff if we *all* take the cold sleep, because of course the bosses, the Gafr, won't let them use animals. So we might be asleep for quite a while—or forever—or be damaged by the procedure. But the Gafr have given the go-ahead, and I'm thinking seriously about it. The Kaposi's can only be treated effectively with radiation, and I've had much more than my fair share of that already. I'll die of cancer anyway, probably sooner than later; in a month I'll be forty-nine. But I'm thinking about it. I wish they'd come up with this before, is all.

I have to tell you something funny. One of my irradiated melon plants turned out to be one hundred percent *immune* to mosaic! It's peculiar in other ways that make it useless for commercial purposes at this point, but the Rodale breeders are sure to keep working on improvements. I mentioned before that like all cucurbits melons produce separate male and female flowers, the male flowers bearing the pollen-producing stamens, the female flowers the pistil and ovary. Ordinarily it's easy to tell which is which, because the ovary behind the female blossom is a large hairy structure and the male flower has nothing behind it but a stem.

Well, the immune melon bears male and female flowers that look exactly alike! You can't tell them apart, except by peering closely at the inner structures or tearing off the petals, because the ovary is tiny, and concealed entirely within the flower. The fruit is correspondingly tiny, about the size of a small orange—much too small to appeal to growers, though I'd think home gardeners might raise it as a novelty.

I've given this new cultivar the official name of Tiny Tango, a name to please the seed catalog writers. Privately I think of it as Male Impersonator (or sometimes—a pun—Atomic Power Plant). Its rind is tan and thin, netted like the rind of an ordinary cantaloupe, and its flesh is a beautiful deep salmon-orange, as sweetly, intensely delicious as any I ever tasted.

At the Rialto

CONNIE WILLIS

"Seriousness of mind was a prerequisite for understanding Newtonian physics. I am not convinced it is not a handicap in understanding quantum theory."

Excerpt from Dr. Gedanken's keynote address to the 1989 International Congress of Quantum Physicists Annual Meeting, Hollywood, California

I got to Hollywood around one-thirty and started trying to check into the Rialto.

"Sorry, we don't have any rooms," the girl behind the desk said. "We're all booked up with some science thing."

"I'm with the science thing," I said. "Dr. Ruth Baringer. I reserved a double."

"There are a bunch of Republicans here, too, and a tour group from Finland. They told me when I started work here that they got all these movie people, but the only one so far was that guy who played the friend of that other guy in that one movie. You're not a movie person, are you?"

"No," I said. "I'm with the science thing. Dr. Ruth Baringer."

"My name's Tiffany," she said. "I'm not actually a hotel clerk at all. I'm just working here to pay for my transcendental posture lessons. I'm really a model/actress."

"I'm a quantum physicist," I said, trying to get things back on track. "The name is Ruth Baringer."

She messed with the computer for a minute. "I don't show a reservation for you."

"Maybe it's in Dr. Mendoza's name. I'm sharing a room with her."

She messed with the computer some more. "I don't show a reservation for her either. Are you sure you don't want the Disneyland Hotel? A lot of people get the two confused."

"I want the Rialto," I said, rummaging through my bag for my notebook. "I have a confirmation number. W37420."

She typed it in. "Are you Dr. Gedanken?" she asked.

"Excuse me," an elderly man said.

"I'll be right with you," Tiffany told him. "How long do you plan to stay with us, Dr. Gedanken?" she asked me.

"*Excuse* me," the man said, sounding desperate. He had bushy white hair and a dazed expression, as if he had just been through a horrific experience or had been trying to check into the Rialto.

He wasn't wearing any socks. I wondered if *he* was Dr. Gedanken. Dr. Gedanken was the main reason I'd decided to come to the meeting. I had missed his lecture on wave/particle duality last year, but I had read the text of it in the *ICQP Journal,* and it had actually seemed to make sense, which is more than you can say for most of quantum theory. He was giving the keynote address this year, and I was determined to hear it.

It wasn't Dr. Gedanken. "My name is Dr. Whedbee," the elderly man said. "You gave me the wrong room."

"All our rooms are pretty much the same," Tiffany said. "Except for how many beds they have in them and stuff."

"My room has a *person* in it!" he said. "Dr. Sleeth. From the University of Texas at Austin. She was changing her clothes." His hair seemed to get wilder as he spoke. "She thought I was a serial killer."

"And your name is Dr. Whedbee?" Tiffany asked, fooling with the computer again. "I don't show a reservation for you."

Dr. Whedbee began to cry. Tiffany got out a paper towel, wiped off the counter, and turned back to me. "May I help you?" she said.

Thursday, 7:30–9 P.M. *Opening Ceremonies*. Dr. Halvard Onofrio, University of Maryland at College Park, will speak on the topic, "Doubts Surrounding the Heisenberg Uncertainty Principle." Ballroom.

I finally got my room at five after Tiffany went off duty. Till then I sat around the lobby with Dr. Whedbee, listening to Abey Fields complain about Hollywood.

"What's wrong with Racine?" he said. "Why do we always have to go to these exotic places, like Hollywood? And St. Louis last year wasn't much better. The Institut Henri Poincaré people kept going off to see the arch and Busch Stadium."

"Speaking of St. Louis," Dr. Takumi said, "have you seen David yet?"

"No," I said.

"Oh, really?" she said. "Last year at the annual meeting you two were practically inseparable. Moonlight riverboat rides and all."

"What's on the programming tonight?" I said to Abey.

"David was just here," Dr. Takumi said. "He said to tell you he was going out to look at the stars in the sidewalk."

"That's exactly what I'm talking about," Abey said. "Riverboat rides and movie stars. What do those things have to do with quantum theory? Racine would have been an appropriate setting for a group of physicists. Not like this . . . this . . . do you realize we're practically across the street from Grauman's Chinese Theatre? And Hollywood Boulevard's where all those gangs hang out. If they catch you wearing red or blue, they'll—"

He stopped. "Is that Dr. Gedanken?" he asked, staring at the front desk.

I turned and looked. A short roundish man with a mustache was trying to check in. "No," I said. "That's Dr. Onofrio."

"Oh, yes," Abey said, consulting his program book. "He's speaking tonight at the opening ceremonies. On the Heisenberg uncertainty principle. Are you going?"

"I'm not sure," I said, which was supposed to be a joke, but Abey didn't laugh.

"I must meet Dr. Gedanken. He's just gotten funding for a new project."

I wondered what Dr. Gedanken's new project was—I would have loved to work with him.

"I'm hoping he'll come to my workshop on the wonderful world of quantum physics," Abey said, still watching the desk. Amazingly enough, Dr. Onofrio seemed to have gotten a key and was heading for the elevators. "I think his project has something to do with understanding quantum theory."

Well, that let me out. I didn't understand quantum theory at all. I sometimes had a sneaking suspicion nobody else did either, including Abey Fields, and that they just weren't willing to admit it.

I mean, an electron is a particle except it acts like a wave. In fact, a neutron acts like two waves and interferes with itself (or each other), and you can't really measure any of this stuff properly because of the Heisenberg uncertainty principle, and that isn't the worst of it. When you set up a Josephson junction to figure out what rules the electrons obey, they sneak past the barrier to the other side, and they don't seem to care much about the limits of the speed of light either, and

Schrödinger's cat is neither alive nor dead till you open the box, and it all makes about as much sense as Tiffany's calling me Dr. Gedanken.

Which reminded me, I had promised to call Darlene and give her our room number. I didn't have a room number, but if I waited much longer, she'd have left. She was flying to Denver to speak at C.U. and then coming on to Hollywood sometime tomorrow morning. I interrupted Abey in the middle of his telling me how beautiful Racine was in the winter and went to call her.

"I don't have a room yet," I said when she answered. "Should I leave a message on your answering machine or do you want to give me your number in Denver?"

"Never mind all that," Darlene said. "Have you seen David yet?"

"To illustrate the problems of the concept of wave function, Dr. Schrödinger imagines a cat being put into a box with a piece of uranium, a bottle of poison gas, and a Geiger counter. If a uranium nucleus disintegrates while the cat is in the box, it will release radiation which will set off the Geiger counter and break the bottle of poison gas. Since it is impossible in quantum theory to predict whether a uranium nucleus will disintegrate while the cat is in the box, and only possible to calculate uranium's probable half-life, the cat is neither alive nor dead until we open the box."

From "The Wonderful World of Quantum Physics," a seminar presented at the ICQP Annual Meeting by A. Fields, Ph.D., University of Nebraska at Wahoo

I completely forgot to warn Darlene about Tiffany, the model-slash-actress.

"What do you mean you're trying to avoid David?" she had asked me at least three times. "Why would you do a stupid thing like that?"

Because in St. Louis I ended up on a riverboat in the moonlight and didn't make it back until the conference was over.

"Because I want to attend the programming," I said the third time around, "not a wax museum. I am a middle-aged woman."

"And David is a middle-aged man who, I might add, is absolutely charming. In fact, he may be the last charming man left in the universe."

"Charm is for quarks," I said and hung up, feeling smug until I remembered I hadn't told her about Tiffany. I went back to the front desk, thinking maybe Dr. Onofrio's success signaled a change. Tiffany asked, "May I help you?" and left me standing there.

After a while I gave up and went back to the red-and-gold sofas.

"David was here again," Dr. Takumi said. "He said to tell you he was going to the wax museum."

"There *are* no wax museums in Racine," Abey said.

"What's the programming for tonight?" I said, taking Abey's program away from him.

"There's a mixer at six-thirty and the opening ceremonies in the ballroom and then some seminars." I read the descriptions of the seminars. There was one on the Josephson junction. Electrons were able to somehow tunnel through an insulated barrier even though they didn't have the required energy. Maybe I could somehow get a room without checking in.

"If we were in Racine," Abey said, looking at his watch, "we'd already be checked in and on our way to dinner."

Dr. Onofrio emerged from the elevator, still carrying his bags. He came over and sank down on the sofa next to Abey.

"Did they give you a room with a semi-naked woman in it?" Dr. Whedbee asked.

"I don't know," Dr. Onofrio said. "I couldn't find it." He looked sadly at the key. "They gave me 1282, but the room numbers only go up to seventy-five."

"I think I'll attend the seminar on chaos," I said.

"The most serious difficulty quantum theory faces today is not the inherent limitation of measurement capability or the EPR paradox. It is the lack of a paradigm. Quantum theory has no working model, no metaphor that properly defines it."

Excerpt from Dr. Gedanken's keynote address

I got to my room at six, after a brief skirmish with the bellboy-slash-actor who couldn't remember where he'd stored my suitcase, and unpacked. My clothes, which had been permanent press all the way from MIT, underwent a complete wave function collapse the moment I opened my suitcase, and came out looking like Schrödinger's almost-dead cat.

By the time I had called housekeeping for an iron, taken a bath, given up on the iron, and steamed a dress in the shower, I had missed the "Mixer with Munchies" and was half an hour late for Dr. Onofrio's opening remarks.

I opened the door to the ballroom as quietly as I could and slid inside. I had hoped they would be late getting started, but a man I didn't recognize was already introducing the speaker. "—and an inspiration to all of us in the field."

I dived for the nearest chair and sat down.

"Hi," David said. "I've been looking all over for you. Where were you?"

"Not at the wax museum," I whispered.

"You should have been," he whispered back. "It was great. They had John Wayne, Elvis, and Tiffany the model-slash-actress with the brain of a pea-slash-amoeba."

"Shh," I said.

"—the person we've all been waiting to hear, Dr. Ringgit Dinari."

"What happened to Dr. Onofrio?" I asked.

"Shhh," David said.

Dr. Dinari looked a lot like Dr. Onofrio. She was short, roundish, and mustached, and was wearing a rainbow-striped caftan. "I will be your guide this evening into a strange new world," she said, "a world where all that you thought you knew, all common sense, all accepted wisdom, must be discarded. A world where all the rules have changed and it sometimes seems there are no rules at all."

She sounded just like Dr. Onofrio, too. He had given this same speech two years ago in Cincinnati. I wondered if he had undergone some strange transformation during his search for Room 1282 and was now a woman.

"Before I go any farther," Dr. Dinari said, "how many of you have already channeled?"

"Newtonian physics had as its model the machine. The metaphor of the machine, with its interrelated parts, its gears and wheels, its causes and effects, was what made it possible to think *about Newtonian physics."*

Excerpt from Dr. Gedanken's keynote address

"You *knew* we were in the wrong place," I hissed at David when we got out to the lobby.

When we stood up to leave, Dr. Dinari had extended her pudgy hand in its rainbow-striped sleeve and called out in a voice a lot like Charlton Heston's, "O Unbelievers! Leave not, for here only is reality!"

"Actually, channeling would explain a lot," David said, grinning.

"If the opening remarks aren't in the ballroom, where are they?"

"Beats me," he said. "Want to go see the Capitol Records Building? It's shaped like a stack of records."

"I want to go to the opening remarks."

"The beacon on top blinks out Hollywood in Morse code."

I went over to the front desk.

"Can I help you?" the clerk behind the desk said. "My name is Natalie, and I'm an—"

"Where is the ICQP meeting this evening?" I said.

"They're in the ballroom."

"I'll bet you didn't have any dinner," David said. "I'll buy you an ice-cream cone. There's this great place that has the ice-cream cone Ryan O'Neal bought for Tatum in *Paper Moon*."

"A channeler's in the ballroom," I told Natalie. "I'm looking for the ICQP."

She fiddled with the computer. "I'm sorry. I don't show a reservation for them."

"How about Grauman's Chinese?" David said. "You want reality? You want Charlton Heston? You want to see quantum theory in action?" He grabbed my hands. "Come with me," he said seriously.

In St. Louis I had suffered a wave function collapse a lot like what had happened to my clothes when I opened the suitcase. I had ended up on a riverboat halfway to New Orleans that time. It happened again, and the next thing I knew I was walking around the courtyard of Grauman's Chinese Theatre, eating an ice-cream cone and trying to fit my feet in Myrna Loy's footprints.

She must have been a midget or had her feet bound as a child. So, apparently, had Debbie Reynolds, Dorothy Lamour, and Wallace Beery. The only footprints I came close to fitting were Donald Duck's.

"I see this as a map of the microcosm," David said, sweeping his hand over the slightly irregular pavement of printed and signed cement squares. "See, there are all these tracks. We know something's been here, and the prints are pretty much the same, only every once in a while you've got this," he knelt down and pointed at the print of John Wayne's clenched fist, "and over here," he walked toward the box office and pointed to the print of Betty Grable's leg, "and we can figure out the signatures, but what is this reference to 'Sid' on all these squares? And what does this mean?"

He pointed at Red Skelton's square. It said, "Thanks Sid We Dood It."

"You keep thinking you've found a pattern," David said, crossing over to the other side, "but Van Johnson's square is kind of sandwiched in here at an angle between Esther Williams and Cantinflas, and who the hell is May Robson? And why are all these squares over here empty?"

He had managed to maneuver me over behind the display of

Academy Award winners. It was an accordionlike wrought-iron screen. I was in the fold between 1944 and 1945.

"And as if that isn't enough, you suddenly realize you're standing in the courtyard. You're not even in the theater."

"And that's what you think is happening in quantum theory?" I said weakly. I was backed up into Bing Crosby, who had won for Best Actor in *Going My Way*. "You think we're not in the theater yet?"

"I think we know as much about quantum theory as we can figure out about May Robson from her footprints," he said, putting his hand up to Ingrid Bergman's cheek (Best Actress, *Gaslight*) and blocking my escape. "I don't think we understand anything *about* quantum theory, not tunneling, not complementarity." He leaned toward me. "Not passion."

The best movie of 1945 was *Lost Weekend*. "Dr. Gedanken understands it," I said, disentangling myself from the Academy Award winners and David. "Did you know he's putting together a new research team for a big project on understanding quantum theory?"

"Yes," David said. "Want to see a movie?"

"There's a seminar on chaos at nine," I said, stepping over the Marx Brothers. "I have to get back."

"If it's chaos you want, you should stay right here," he said, stopping to look at Irene Dunne's handprints. "We could see the movie and then go have dinner. There's this place near Hollywood and Vine that has the mashed potatoes Richard Dreyfus made into Devil's Tower in *Close Encounters*."

"I want to meet Dr. Gedanken," I said, making it safely to the sidewalk. I looked back at David. He had gone back to the other side of the courtyard and was looking at Roy Rogers's signature.

"Are you kidding? He doesn't understand it any better than we do."

"Well, at least he's trying."

"So am I. The problem is, how can one neutron interfere with itself, and why are there only two of Trigger's hoofprints here?"

"It's eight fifty-five," I said. "I am going to the chaos seminar."

"If you can find it," he said, getting down on one knee to look at the signature.

"I'll find it," I said grimly.

He stood up and grinned at me, his hands in his pockets. "It's a great movie," he said.

It was happening again. I turned and practically ran across the street.

"*Benji Nine* is showing," he shouted after me. "He accidentally exchanges bodies with a Siamese cat."

Thursday, 9–10 P.M. "The Science of Chaos." I. Durcheinander, University of Leipzig. A seminar on the structure of chaos. Principles of chaos will be discussed, including the Butterfly Effect, fractals, and insolid billowing. Clara Bow Room.

I couldn't find the chaos seminar. The Clara Bow Room, where it was supposed to be, was empty. A meeting of vegetarians was next door in the Fatty Arbuckle Room, and all the other conference rooms were locked. The channeler was still in the ballroom. "Come!" she commanded when I opened the door. "Understanding awaits!" I went upstairs to bed.

I had forgotten to call Darlene. She would have left for Denver already, but I called her answering machine and told it the room number in case she picked up her messages. In the morning I would have to tell the front desk to give her a key. I went to bed.

I didn't sleep well. The air conditioner went off during the night, which meant I didn't have to steam my suit when I got up the next morning. I got dressed and went downstairs. The programming started at nine o'clock with Abey Fields's Wonderful World workshop in the Mary Pickford Room, a breakfast buffet in the ballroom, and a slide presentation on "Delayed Choice Experiments" in Cecil B. DeMille A on the mezzanine level.

The breakfast buffet sounded wonderful, even though it always turns out to be urn coffee and donuts. I hadn't had anything but an ice-cream cone since noon the day before, but if David were around, he would be somewhere close to the food, and I wanted to steer clear of him. Last night it had been Grauman's Chinese. Today I was likely to end up at Knott's Berry Farm. I wasn't going to let that happen, even if he was charming.

It was pitch-dark inside Cecil B. DeMille A. Even the slide on the screen up front appeared to be black. "As you can see," Dr. Lvov said, "the laser pulse is already in motion before the experimenter sets up the wave or particle detector." He clicked to the next slide, which was dark gray. "We used a Mach-Zender interferometer with two mirrors and a particle detector. For the first series of tries we allowed the experimenter to decide which apparatus he would use by whatever method he wished. For the second series, we used that most primitive of randomizers—"

He clicked again, to a white slide with black polka dots that gave off enough light for me to be able to spot an empty chair on the aisle ten rows up. I hurried to get to it before the slide changed, and sat down.

"—a pair of dice. Alley's experiments had shown us that when the particle detector was in place, the light was detected as a particle, and when the wave detector was in place, the light showed wavelike behavior, no matter when the choice of apparatus was made."

"Hi," David said. "You've missed five black slides, two gray ones, and a white with black polka dots."

"Shh," I said.

"In our two series, we hoped to ascertain whether the consciousness of the decision affected the outcome." Dr. Lvov clicked to another black slide. "As you can see, the graph shows no effective difference between the tries in which the experimenter chose the detection apparatus and those in which the apparatus was randomly chosen."

"You want to go get some breakfast?" David whispered.

"I already ate," I whispered back, and waited for my stomach to growl and give me away. It did.

"There's a great place down near Hollywood and Vine that has the waffles Katharine Hepburn made for Spencer Tracy in *Woman of the Year*."

"Shh," I said.

"And after breakfast, we could go to Frederick's of Hollywood and see the bra museum."

"Will you please be quiet? I can't hear."

"Or see," he said, but he subsided more or less for the remaining ninety-two black, gray, and polka-dotted slides.

Dr. Lvov turned on the lights and blinked smilingly at the audience. "Consciousness had no discernible effect on the results of the experiment. As one of my lab assistants put it, 'The little devil knows what you're going to do before you know it yourself.' "

This was apparently supposed to be a joke, but I didn't think it was very funny. I opened my program and tried to find something to go to that David wouldn't be caught dead at.

"Are you two going to breakfast?" Dr. Thibodeaux asked.

"Yes," David said.

"No," I said.

"Dr. Hotard and I wished to eat somewhere that is *vraiment* Hollywood."

"David knows just the place," I said. "He's been telling me about this great place where they have the grapefruit James Cagney shoved in Mae Clark's face in *Public Enemy*."

Dr. Hotard hurried up, carrying a camera and four guidebooks. "And then perhaps you would show us Grauman's Chinese Theatre," he asked David.

"Of course he will," I said. "I'm sorry I can't go with you, but I promised Dr. Verikovsky I'd be at his lecture on Boolean logic. And after Grauman's Chinese, David can take you to the bra museum at Frederick's of Hollywood."

"And the Brown Derby?" Thibodeaux asked. "I have heard it is shaped like a *chapeau*."

They dragged him off. I watched till they were safely out of the lobby and then ducked upstairs and into Dr. Whedbee's lecture on information theory. Dr. Whedbee wasn't there.

"He went to find an overhead projector," Dr. Takumi said. She had half a donut on a paper plate in one hand and a Styrofoam cup in the other.

"Did you get that at the breakfast buffet?" I asked.

"Yes. It was the last one. And they ran out of coffee right after I got there. You weren't in Abey Fields's thing, were you?" She set the coffee cup down and took a bite of the donut.

"No," I said, wondering if I should try to take her by surprise or just wrestle the donut away from her.

"You didn't miss anything. He raved the whole time about how we should have had the meeting in Racine." She popped the last piece of donut in her mouth. "Have you seen David yet?"

Friday, 9–10 P.M. "The Eureka Experiment: A Slide Presentation." J. Lvov, Eureka College. Descriptions, results, and conclusions of Lvov's delayed conscious/randomed choice experiments. Cecil B. DeMille A.

Dr. Whedbee eventually came in carrying an overhead projector, the cord trailing behind him. He plugged it in. The light didn't go on.

"Here," Dr. Takumi said, handing me her plate and cup. "I have one of these at Caltech. It needs its fractal basin boundaries adjusted." She whacked the side of the projector.

There weren't even any crumbs left of the donut. There was about a millimeter of coffee in the bottom of the cup. I was about to stoop to new depths when she hit the projector again. The light came on. "I learned that in the chaos seminar last night," she said, grabbing the cup away from me and draining it. "You should have been there. The Clara Bow Room was packed."

"I believe I'm ready to begin," Dr. Whedbee said. Dr. Takumi and I sat down. "Information is the transmission of meaning," Dr. Whedbee said. He wrote "meaning" or possibly "information" on the screen with a green Magic Marker. "When information is randomized, meaning cannot be transmitted, and we have a state of entropy." He wrote it under "meaning" with a red Magic Marker. His handwriting appeared to be completely illegible.

"States of entropy vary from low entropy, such as the mild static on your car radio, to high entropy, a state of complete disorder, of randomness and confusion, in which no information at all is being communicated."

Oh, my God, I thought. I forgot to tell the hotel about Darlene. The next time Dr. Whedbee bent over to inscribe hieroglyphics on the screen, I sneaked out and went down to the desk, hoping Tiffany hadn't come on duty yet. She had.

"May I help you?" she asked.

"I'm in Room 663," I said. "I'm sharing a room with Dr. Darlene Mendoza. She's coming in this morning, and she'll be needing a key."

"For what?" Tiffany said.

"To get into the room. I may be in one of the lectures when she gets here."

"Why doesn't she have a key?"

"Because she isn't here yet."

"I thought you said she was sharing a room with you."

"She *will* be sharing a room with me. Room 663. Her name is Darlene Mendoza."

"And your name?" she asked, hands poised over the computer.

"Ruth Baringer."

"We don't show a reservation for you."

"We have made impressive advances in quantum physics in the ninety years since Planck's constant, but they have by and large been advances in technology, not theory. We can only make advances in theory when we have a model we can visualize."

Excerpt from Dr. Gedanken's keynote address

I high-entropied with Tiffany for a while on the subjects of my not having a reservation and the air conditioning and then switched back suddenly to the problem of Darlene's key, in the hope of catching her off guard. It worked about as well as Alley's delayed choice experiments.

In the middle of my attempting to explain that Darlene was not the air-conditioning repairman, Abey Fields came up.

"Have you seen Dr. Gedanken?"

I shook my head.

"I was sure he'd come to my Wonderful World workshop, but he didn't, and the hotel says they can't find his reservation," he said, scanning the lobby. "I found out what his new project is, incidentally, and I'd be perfect for it. He's going to find a paradigm for quantum theory. Is that him?" he said, pointing at an elderly man getting in the elevator.

"I think that's Dr. Whedbee," I said, but he had already sprinted across the lobby to the elevator.

He nearly made it. The elevator slid to a close just as he got there. He pushed the elevator button several times to make the door open again, and when that didn't work, tried to readjust its fractal basin boundaries. I turned back to the desk.

"May I help you?" Tiffany said.

"You may," I said. "My roommate, Darlene Mendoza, will be arriving sometime this morning. She's a producer. She's here to cast the female lead in a new movie starring Robert Redford and Harrison Ford. When she gets here, give her her key. And fix the air-conditioning."

"Yes, ma'am," she said.

"The Josephson junction is designed so that electrons must obtain additional energy to surmount the energy barrier. It has been found, however, that some electrons simply tunnel, as Heinz Pagels put it, 'right through the wall.'"

From "The Wonderful World of Quantum Physics,"
A. Fields, UNW

Abey had stopped banging on the elevator button and was trying to pry the elevator doors apart. I went out the side door and up to Hollywood Boulevard. David's restaurant was near Hollywood and Vine. I turned the other direction, toward Grauman's Chinese, and ducked into the first restaurant I saw.

"I'm Stephanie," the waitress said. "How many are there in your party?"

There was no one remotely in my vicinity. "Are you an actress-slash-model?" I asked her.

"Yes," she said. "I'm working here part-time to pay for my holistic hairstyling lessons."

"There's one of me," I said, holding up my forefinger to make it perfectly clear. "I want a table away from the window."

She led me to a table in front of the window, handed me a menu the size of the macrocosm, and put another one down across from me. "Our breakfast specials today are papaya stuffed with salmon-berries and nasturtium/radicchio salad with a balsamic vinaigrette. I'll take your order when your other party arrives."

I stood the extra menu up so it hid me from the window, opened the other one, and read the breakfast entrees. They all seemed to have cilantro or lemongrass in their names. I wondered if radicchio could possibly be Californian for donut.

"Hi," David said, grabbing the standing-up menu and sitting down. "The sea urchin pâté looks good."

I was actually glad to see him. "How did you get here?" I asked.

"Tunneling," he said. "What exactly is extra-virgin olive oil?"

"I wanted a donut," I said pitifully.

He took my menu away from me, laid it on the table, and stood up. "There's a great place next door that's got the donut Clark Gable taught Claudette Colbert how to dunk in *It Happened One Night*."

The great place was probably out in Long Beach someplace, but I was too weak with hunger to resist him. I stood up. Stephanie hurried over.

"Will there be anything else?" she asked.

"We're leaving," David said.

"Okay, then," she said, tearing a check off her pad and slapping it down on the table. "I hope you enjoyed your breakfast."

"Finding such a paradigm is difficult, if not impossible. Due to Planck's constant the world we see is largely dominated by Newtonian mechanics. Particles are particles, waves are waves, and objects do not suddenly vanish through walls and reappear on the other side. It is only on the subatomic level that quantum effects dominate."

Excerpt from Dr. Gedanken's keynote address

The restaurant was next door to Grauman's Chinese, which made me a little nervous, but it had eggs and bacon and toast and orange juice and coffee. And donuts.

"I thought you were having breakfast with Dr. Thibodeaux and Dr. Hotard," I said, dunking one in my coffee. "What happened to them?"

"They went to Forest Lawn. Dr. Hotard wanted to see the church where Ronald Reagan got married."

"He got married at Forest Lawn?"

He took a bite of my donut. "In the Wee Kirk of the Heather. Did you know Forest Lawn's got the World's Largest Oil Painting Incorporating a Religious Theme?"

"So why didn't you go with them?"

"And miss the movie?" He grabbed both my hands across the table. "There's a matinee at two o'clock. Come with me."

I could feel things starting to collapse. "I have to get back," I said, trying to disentangle my hands. "There's a panel on the EPR paradox at two o'clock."

"There's another showing at five. And one at eight."

"Dr. Gedanken's giving the keynote address at eight."

"You know what the problem is?" he said, still holding on to my hands. "The problem is, it isn't really Grauman's Chinese Theatre, it's Mann's, so Sid isn't even around to ask. Like, why do some pairs like Joanne Woodward and Paul Newman share the same square and other pairs don't? Like Ginger Rogers and Fred Astaire?"

"You know what the problem is?" I said, wrenching my hands free. "The problem is you don't take anything seriously. This is a conference, but you don't care anything about the programming or hearing Dr. Gedanken speak or trying to understand quantum theory!" I fumbled in my purse for some money for the check.

"I thought that was what we were talking about," David said, sounding surprised. "The problem is, where do those lion statues that guard the door fit in? And what about all those empty spaces?"

> Friday, 2–3 P.M. *Panel Discussion on the EPR Paradox.* I. Takumi, moderator, R. Iverson, L. S. Ping. A discussion of the latest research in singlet-state correlations including nonlocal influences, the Calcutta proposal, and passion. Keystone Kops Room.

I went up to my room as soon as I got back to the Rialto to see if Darlene was there yet. She wasn't, and when I tried to call the desk, the phone wouldn't work. I went back down to the registration desk. There was no one there. I waited fifteen minutes and then went into the panel on the EPR paradox.

"The Einstein-Podolsky-Rosen paradox cannot be reconciled with quantum theory," Dr. Takumi was saying. "I don't care what the experiments seem to indicate. Two electrons at opposite ends of the universe can't affect each other simultaneously without destroying the entire theory of the space-time continuum."

She was right. Even if it were possible to find a model of quantum theory, what about the EPR paradox? If an experimenter measured one of a pair of electrons that had originally collided, it changed the cross-correlation of the other instantaneously, even if the electrons were light-years apart. It was as if they were eternally linked by that one collision, sharing the same square forever, even if they were on opposite sides of the universe.

"If the electrons *communicated* instantaneously, I'd agree with you," Dr. Iverson said, "but they don't, they simply influence each other. Dr. Shimony defined this influence in his paper on passion, and my experiment clearly—"

I thought of David leaning over me between the best pictures of 1944 and 1945, saying, "I think we know as much about quantum theory as we do about May Robson from her footprints."

"You can't explain it away by inventing new terms," Dr. Takumi said.

"I completely disagree," Dr. Ping said. "Passion at a distance is not just an invented term. It's a demonstrated phenomenon."

It certainly is, I thought, thinking about David taking the macrocosmic menu out of the window and saying, "The sea urchin pâté looks good." It didn't matter where the electron went after the collision. Even if it went in the opposite direction from Hollywood and Vine, even if it stood a menu in the window to hide it, the other electron would still come and rescue it from the radicchio and buy it a donut.

"A demonstrated phenomenon!" Dr. Takumi said. "Ha!" She banged her moderator's gavel for emphasis.

"Are you saying passion doesn't exist?" Dr. Ping said, getting very red in the face.

"I'm saying one measly experiment is hardly a demonstrated phenomenon."

"One measly experiment! I spent five years on this project!" Dr. Iverson said, shaking his fist at her. "I'll show you passion at a distance!"

"Try it, and I'll adjust your fractal basin boundaries!" Dr. Takumi said, and hit him over the head with the gavel.

"Yet finding a paradigm is not impossible. Newtonian physics is not a machine. It simply shares some of the attributes of a machine. We must find a model somewhere in the visible world that shares the often bizarre attributes of quantum physics. Such a model, unlikely as it sounds, surely exists somewhere, and it is up to us to find it."

Excerpt from Dr. Gedanken's keynote address

I went up to my room before the police came. Darlene still wasn't there, and the phone and air-conditioning still weren't working. I was really beginning to get worried. I walked up to Grauman's Chinese to find David, but he wasn't there. Dr. Whedbee and Dr. Sleeth were behind the Academy Award Winners folding screen.

"You haven't seen David, have you?" I asked.

Dr. Whedbee removed his hand from Norma Shearer's cheek.

"He left," Dr. Sleeth said, disentangling herself from the Best Movie of 1929–30.

"He said he was going out to Forest Lawn," Dr. Whedbee said, trying to smooth down his bushy white hair.

"Have you seen Dr. Mendoza? She was supposed to get in this morning."

They hadn't seen her, and neither had Drs. Hotard and Thibodeaux, who stopped me in the lobby and showed me a postcard of Aimee Semple McPherson's tomb. Tiffany had gone off duty. Natalie couldn't find my reservation. I went back up to the room to wait, thinking Darlene might call.

The air-conditioning still wasn't fixed. I fanned myself with a Hollywood brochure and then opened it up and read it. There was a map of the courtyard of Grauman's Chinese on the back cover. Deborah Kerr and Yul Brynner didn't have a square together either, and Katharine Hepburn and Spencer Tracy weren't even on the map. She had made him waffles in *Woman of the Year,* and they hadn't even given them a square. I wondered if Tiffany the model-slash-actress had been in charge of assigning the cement. I could see her looking blankly at Spencer Tracy and saying, "I don't show a reservation for you."

What exactly was a model-slash-actress? Did it mean she was a model *or* an actress or a model *and* an actress? She certainly wasn't a hotel clerk. Maybe electrons were the Tiffanys of the microcosm, and that explained their wave-slash-particle duality. Maybe they weren't really electrons at all. Maybe they were just working part-time at being electrons to pay for their singlet-state lessons.

Darlene still hadn't called by seven o'clock. I stopped fanning myself and tried to open a window. It wouldn't budge. The problem was, nobody knew anything about quantum theory. All we had to go on were a few colliding electrons that nobody could see and that couldn't be measured properly because of the Heisenberg uncertainty principle. And there was chaos to consider, and entropy, and all those empty spaces. We didn't even know who May Robson was.

At seven-thirty the phone rang. It was Darlene.

"What happened?" I said. "Where are you?"

"At the Beverly Wilshire."

"In Beverly Hills?"

"Yes. It's a long story. When I got to the Rialto, the hotel clerk, I think her name was Tiffany, told me you weren't there. She said they were booked solid with some science thing and had had to send the overflow to other hotels. She said you were at the Beverly Wilshire in Room 1027. How's David?"

"Impossible," I said. "He's spent the whole conference looking at Deanna Durbin's footprints at Grauman's Chinese Theatre and trying to talk me into going to the movies."

"And are you going?"

"I can't. Dr. Gedanken's giving the keynote address in half an hour."

"He is?" Darlene said, sounding surprised. "Just a minute." There was a silence, and then she came back on and said, "I think you should go to the movies. David's one of the last two charming men in the universe."

"But he doesn't take quantum theory seriously. Dr. Gedanken is hiring a research team to design a paradigm, and David keeps talking about the beacon on top of the Capitol Records Building."

"You know, he may be on to something there. I mean, seriousness was all right for Newtonian physics, but maybe quantum theory needs a different approach. Sid says—"

"Sid?"

"This guy who's taking me to the movies tonight. It's a long story. Tiffany gave me the wrong room number, and I walked in on this guy in his underwear. He's a quantum physicist. He was supposed to be staying at the Rialto, but Tiffany couldn't find his reservation."

"The major implication of wave/particle duality is that an electron has no precise location. It exists in a superposition of probable locations. Only when the experimenter observes the electron does it 'collapse' into a location."

"The Wonderful World of Quantum Physics,"
A. Fields, UNW

Forest Lawn had closed at five o'clock. I looked it up in the Hollywood brochure after Darlene hung up. There was no telling where he might have gone: the Brown Derby or the La Brea Tar Pits or some great place near Hollywood and Vine that had the alfalfa sprouts John Hurt ate right before his chest exploded in *Alien*.

At least I knew where Dr. Gedanken was. I changed my clothes and got in the elevator, thinking about wave/particle duality and fractals and high entropy states and delayed choice experiments. The problem was, where could you find a paradigm that would make it possible to visualize quantum theory when you had to include Josephson junctions and passion and all those empty spaces? It wasn't possible. You had to have more to work with than a few footprints and the impression of Betty Grable's leg.

The elevator door opened, and Abey Fields pounced on me. "I've been looking all over for you," he said. "You haven't seen Dr. Gedanken, have you?"

"Isn't he in the ballroom?"

"No," he said. "He's already fifteen minutes late, and nobody's seen him. You have to sign this," he said, shoving a clipboard at me.

"What is it?"

"It's a petition." He grabbed it back from me. " 'We the undersigned demand that annual meetings of the International Congress of Quantum Physicists henceforth be held in appropriate locations.' Like Racine," he added, shoving the clipboard at me again. "*Unlike* Hollywood."

Hollywood.

"Are you aware it took the average ICQP delegate two hours and thirty-six minutes to check in? They even sent some of the delegates to a hotel in Glendale."

"And Beverly Hills," I said absently. Hollywood. Bra museums and the Marx Brothers and gangs that would kill you if you wore red or blue and Tiffany/Stephanie and the World's Largest Oil Painting Incorporating a Religious Theme.

"Beverly Hills," Abey muttered, pulling an automatic pencil out of his pocket protector and writing a note to himself. "I'm presenting the petition during Dr. Gedanken's speech. Well, go on, sign it," he said, handing me the pencil. "Unless you want the annual meeting to be here at the Rialto next year."

I handed the clipboard back to him. "I think from now on the annual meeting might be here every year," I said, and took off running for Grauman's Chinese.

"When we have that paradigm, one that embraces both the logical and the nonsensical aspects of quantum theory, we will be able to look past the colliding electrons and the mathematics and see the microcosm in all its astonishing beauty."

Excerpt from Dr. Gedanken's keynote address

"I want a ticket to *Benji Nine,*" I told the girl at the box office. Her name tag said, "Welcome to Hollywood. My name is Kimberly."

"Which theater?" she said.

"Grauman's Chinese," I said, thinking, This is no time for a high entropy state.

"Which theater?"

I looked up at the marquee. *Benji IX* was showing in all three theaters, the huge main theater and the two smaller ones on either side. "They're doing audience reaction surveys," Kimberly said. "Each theater has a different ending."

"Which one's in the main theater?"

"I don't know. I just work here part-time to pay for my organic breathing lessons."

"Do you have any dice?" I asked, and then realized I was going about this all wrong. This was quantum physics, not Newtonian. It didn't matter which theater I chose or which seat I sat down in. This was a delayed choice experiment and David was already in flight.

"The one with the happy ending," I said.

"Center theater," she said.

I walked past the stone lions and into the lobby. Rhonda Fleming and some Chinese wax figures were sitting inside a glass case next to the door to the rest rooms. There was a huge painted screen behind the concessions stand. I bought a box of Raisinets, a tub of popcorn, and a box of jujubes and went inside the theater.

It was bigger than I had imagined. Rows and rows of empty red chairs curved between the huge pillars and up to the red curtains where the screen must be. The walls were covered with intricate drawings. I stood there, holding my jujubes and Raisinets and popcorn, staring at the chandelier overhead. It was an elaborate gold sunburst surrounded by silver dragons. I had never imagined it was anything like this.

The lights went down, and the red curtains opened, revealing an inner curtain like a veil across the screen. I went down the dark aisle and sat down in one of the seats. "Hi," I said, and handed the Raisinets to David.

"Where have you been?" he said. "The movie's about to start."

"I know," I said. I leaned across him and handed Darlene her popcorn and Dr. Gedanken his jujubes. "I was working on the paradigm for quantum theory."

"And?" Dr. Gedanken said, opening his jujubes.

"And you're both wrong," I said. "It isn't Grauman's Chinese. It isn't movies either, Dr. Gedanken."

"Sid," Dr. Gedanken said. "If we're all going to be on the same research team, I think we should use first names."

"If it isn't Grauman's Chinese or the movies, what is it?" Darlene asked, eating popcorn.

"It's Hollywood."

"Hollywood," Dr. Gedanken said thoughtfully.

"Hollywood," I said. "Stars in the sidewalk and buildings that look like stacks of records and hats, and radicchio and audience surveys and bra museums. And the movies. And Grauman's Chinese."

"And the Rialto," David said.

"Especially the Rialto."

"And the ICQP," Dr. Gedanken said.

I thought about Dr. Lvov's black and gray slides and the disappearing chaos seminar and Dr. Whedbee writing "meaning" or possibly "information" on the overhead projector. "And the ICQP," I said.

"Did Dr. Takumi really hit Dr. Iverson over the head with a gavel?" Darlene asked.

"Shh," David said. "I think the movie's starting." He took hold of my hand. Darlene settled back with her popcorn, and Dr. Gedanken put his feet up on the chair in front of him. The inner curtain opened, and the screen lit up.

Midnight News

LISA GOLDSTEIN

Stevens and Gorce sat at the hotel bar, watching television. Helena Johnson's face nearly filled the entire screen. Snow drifted across her face and then covered the screen, and five or six people in the bar raised their voices. The bartender quickly switched the channel, and Helena Johnson's face came on again, shot from the same angle.

She had told the reporters she was eighty-four, but Stevens thought she looked older. Her face was covered with a soft down and her right cheek discolored with liver-colored age spots, and the white of one eye had turned as yellow as an egg yolk. The hairdressers had dyed her hair a full, rich white, but Stevens remembered from earlier interviews that it had been dull gray, and that a lot of it had fallen out.

"I lived at home for a long, long time," Helena Johnson was saying in her slow scratchy voice. The reporters sat at the bar or at round tables scattered throughout the room and watched her raptly. The bar, which the hotel called a "lobby lounge," had once been elegant, but two months of continuous occupancy by the reporters had changed it into something quite different. Cigarette butts had been ground into the lush carpet, drinks had been spilled, glasses broken. "Well, it was the Depression, you know, and I couldn't move out," the old woman said. "And girls weren't supposed to live on their own back then—only loose girls lived by themselves. My father had been laid off, and I got a job as a stenographer. I was lucky to get it. I supported my family for two years, all by myself."

She stopped for a moment, unwilling or unable to go on. The camera pulled back to show her seated on the bed, then cut to the small knot of reporters standing in her hotel room. Stevens saw himself and Gorce and all the rest of them. He remembered how tense he'd been, how worried that she wouldn't call on him. One of the reporters raised his hand.

"Yes, Mr.—Mr.—" Helena Johnson said.

"Look at that," Stevens said in the bar. "She's senile, on top of everything else. How can she forget his name after two months?"

"Shhh," Gorce said.

"Capelli, ma'am," the reporter said. "I wondered how you felt while you were supporting your family. Didn't it make you feel proud?"

"Objection," Gorce said in the bar. "He's leading the witness."

"Shhh," Stevens said.

"Well, of course I was proud," Helena Johnson said. "I was putting my younger brother through college, too. He had to stop after two years, though, because I lost my job."

Her manner was poised, regal. She reminded Stevens of nothing so much as Queen Victoria. And yet she hadn't even finished grade school. "Look at her," he said in disgust. He raised his glass in a toast. "This is the woman who's going to save the world."

No one knew how the aliens had chosen Helena Johnson. A month after they had appeared, their round ships like gold coins above the seven largest cities in the world, they had jammed radio frequencies and announced their terms for a meeting. One ship would land outside of Los Angeles, and only twenty reporters would be allowed to board.

Stevens's first surprise was that they looked human, or at least humanoid. (After the meeting scientists would speculate endlessly about androids and holograms and parallel biology.) Stevens sat on an ordinary folding chair and watched closely as the alien stepped up to the front of the room. Near him he saw reporters looking around for clues to the aliens' technology, but the room was bare except for the chairs and made of something that might have been steel.

"Good afternoon," the alien said. Its voice sounded amplified, but Stevens could see no microphone anywhere. "Hello. We are your judges. We have judged you and found you wanting. Some of us were of the opinion that you should be destroyed immediately. We have decided not to do this. We have found a representative of your species. She will make the decision. At midnight on your New Year's Eve she will tell you if you are to live or die."

No one spoke. Then a bony young woman, her thin black hair brushed back and away from her face, jumped up from her seat. It was the first time Stevens saw Gorce in person, though he had heard of her from his colleagues. He held his breath without knowing it. "Why do you feel you have the right to sit in judgment over us?" she asked. Her voice was level.

"No questions," the alien said. "We will give you the name of the woman who is to represent you. Her name is Helena Johnson. She lives in Phoenix, Arizona. And there is one more thing. Brian Capelli, will you stand please?"

Capelli stood. His face was as white as his shirt. The alien made no motion that Stevens could see, but suddenly there was a sharp noise like a backfire and Capelli's chair burst into flames. Capelli moaned a little and then seemed to realize where he was and stopped.

"We have power and we will use it," the alien said.

Not surprisingly, with every state and federal organization mobilized to look for her, Helena Johnson was found within two hours. She lived in a state-sponsored nursing home. She was asleep when the FBI agent found her and when she woke she seemed unable to answer the simplest question. "What is your name?" the agent asked. Helena Johnson gave no sign that she had heard him.

But within a month she seemed to have accepted the situation as her due. The government put her up in the best hotel in Washington and hired nurses, hairdressers, manicurists, companions. She had an ulcer on her leg that had never been seen to at the home, and the government sent out a highly paid specialist to treat it. Another specialist discovered that she wasn't so much disoriented as hard of hearing, and she was fitted with a hearing aid.

She granted interviews with the twenty reporters daily, then screened the tapes and deleted anything she didn't like. The world discovered to its dismay that Helena Johnson's life hadn't been an easy one, and everything possible was done to make it easier. Television programs now played for an audience of one: stations showed *The Nutcracker* over and over again because she had talked about being taken to see it as a child. Newspapers stopped reporting crime and wars—crime and wars had, in fact, nearly disappeared—and ran headlines about the number of kittens adopted. She got an average of ten thousand letters a day: most of them came with a gift and about a third were marriage proposals.

"So my co-worker, Doris, she said the boss would let you stay on if you would, well, do favors for him," Helena Johnson was saying. "You know what I mean. And I decided that I'd rather starve. But then the next day I thought, well, it's not just me that's depending on the money I earn. It's my parents, and my brother who I was putting through college—did I tell you about that?—and I decided that if he asked me I'd do it. I'm not ashamed to tell you that that's what I thought." The camera cut to the reporters again. Most of them were nodding sympathetically. "So the next day I was called into his office. I was called alone, so I thought, here it comes. Usually when he fired you he called you in in a group. He was standing behind his desk—I can see it now, as clear as day—and he opened his mouth to say something. And then he shook his head, like this, and he said, 'Forget it, girl, go home. You're too ugly.' "

"I wonder if that guy's still alive," Stevens said in the bar.

"I hope for his sake he's dead."

"Gone to the grave never knowing he doomed the world with one sentence."

"She doesn't seem too bitter."

"Who knows what she seems? Who knows what she's thinking? Look at her—she looks like the cat that ate the canary. She's going to play this for all it's worth."

"I got married at the beginning of the war," Helena Johnson said. "World War Two, that was. I was thirty, a bit old for those days. My husband met one of those female soldiers over there in Europe, one of those WACs, and left me for her. Left me and our baby son."

"Is that when you went back to your maiden name?" Gorce asked.

"Yes, and that's a very sharp question, young lady," Helena Johnson said.

"I don't see why," Stevens said, in the bar.

"Because she wants to talk about herself, that's why," Gorce said.

"My husband's name was Furnival," Helena Johnson said. "Isn't that a dreadful name? It sounds just like a funeral, that's what I always thought. I went back to my maiden name as soon as I heard about him and that WAC. They tell me he's dead now. Died in 1979. I lost track of him a long time ago."

"And then you had to raise your baby all by yourself," Gorce said.

"That's right, I did," Helena Johnson said, smiling at her. "And he left me too, soon as he could get a job. He was about seventeen. Seventeen, that's right."

"Have they found him yet?" Stevens asked in the bar.

"They traced him to that trailer camp in Florida," Gorce said. "He left last April, and they haven't been able to pick him up from there. Probably on the run."

"You'd be too."

"I don't know. This could be just what she needs, an emotional reunion with the prodigal son. Make great television."

"The prodigal son has a record as long as your arm—assault, armed robbery, breaking and entering. . . ."

"Do you think the Feds will grant him that pardon?"

"Probably."

On the screen the interview was coming to an end. "Anything else you want to say, Miss Johnson?" the hired companion asked.

"No, I'm feeling a little tired," she said. "Oh, I did want to thank—what was his name? Oh, dear, I can't remember it. A young man in Texas who sent me this ring." She held the back of her hand to the camera. The diamond caught the light and sparkled. "Thank you so much."

Her face faded. "The Dance of the Sugar-Plum Fairies" came on over the credits and several people in the bar groaned loudly. The bartender turned the sound down and then turned it back up for the nightly news.

"Good evening," the anchorman said. "Our top story today concerns the daily interview with Helena Johnson. During the course of the interview Miss Johnson spoke once again about her childhood and growing up during the Depression, about her marriage and son. She had this to say about her husband."

"Good God, she's the most boring woman in the world!" Stevens said. "Why do we have to sit through this drivel again?"

"You know why," Gorce said. "In case she's watching."

"In other news, the government reported that the number of survivors of the Denver fire-bombing stands at two," the anchorman said. "Both the survivors are listed in stable condition. Both have burns over fifty percent of their bodies. Skin grafts are scheduled to begin tomorrow."

"God, that was stupid," Gorce said. "I wonder whose idea it was to attack that ship."

"Well, how the hell could we know? All we'd seen them do was burn a chair, and any special-effects man could have done that. What if they were just bluffing?"

"And now we know," Gorce said.

"Now we know."

"Government sources say the bombs were not nuclear weapons," the anchorman said. "There is no radioactive fallout at all from the bombing. Miss Johnson has sent both the survivors a telegram expressing her wishes for their speedy recovery."

"Bully for her," Stevens said.

"Come off it," Gorce said. "She's not that bad."

"She's a horror. She hasn't called on me once the last three days, and you know why? It's because I accidentally called her Ms."

"I feel sorry for her. What a hard life she's had."

"Sure you do—she loves you. Look at the way she beamed at you all through the interview today. But I guess you're right. I guess she's been lonely. She was only married a year before her husband was called up."

"I didn't mean just her marriage—"

"Now don't go giving me that feminist look," Stevens said, though in fact Gorce's steady gaze hadn't changed. "You know what I meant. If they're not married they usually have a career, something they're interested in. Like you. But this woman had nothing."

"Were you ever married, Stevens?"

"No." He looked at her, surprised by the question. "Relationships don't work out for me. Too much traveling, I guess. How about you?"

"No," she said.

On the screen a scientist was summarizing the latest attempt to communicate with the ships, and then the news ended. "Stay tuned for *Cinderella* following tonight's news," the announcer said over the credits.

"*Cinderella!*" Stevens said, disgusted. "Come on, guys. She can't be awake this late."

"Shhh."

"What—you think she'll hear me? She's on the top floor."

The bartender turned the television off. Stevens and Gorce ordered another round. "You know what I was thinking?" Gorce said. "Have you thought about these aliens? I mean really thought about them?"

"Sure," Stevens said. "Like everyone else in America. I've got a new theory, too. I bet it's a test."

"A what?"

"A test. It doesn't matter what the old bitch chooses, whether she wants us destroyed or not. It's like a laboratory experiment. They're watching us to see how we act under pressure. If we do okay, if we don't all go nuts, we'll be asked to join some kind of galactic federation."

She said nothing for a while. The dim light in the bar made her face look sallow, darkened the hollows under her eyes. "You ever read comic books when you were a kid, Stevens?"

"Huh? No."

"That's what it always turned out to be in the comic books. Some kind of test. All these weird things would happen—the super-hero might even die—but in the end everything returned to normal. Because the kids reading the comics never liked it when things changed too much. The only explanation the writers could come up with was that it had all been a test. But I don't think these tests happen outside of comic books."

"Okay, so what's your theory?"

"Well, think about what's happening here. These guys have set themselves up as the final law, judge, jury, and executioner all rolled into one. Sure, they picked the old woman, but that's just the point—*they* picked her. They probably know how she's going to vote, or they have a good idea. What kind of people would do something like that?"

"I don't know."

"Pretty sadistic people, I'd say. If there was some kind of galactic federation, wouldn't they just observe us and contact us when we were ready? I mean, we were on our way to blowing ourselves up without any outside help at all. Maybe these people travel around the galaxy getting their jollies from watching helpless races cower for months before someone makes the final decision. These aliens are probably outlaws, some kind of renegades. They're so immoral no galactic federation would have them."

"That's a cheerful thought."

Gorce looked around. "Hey, where's Nichols?"

"I don't know. He said something this morning—"

"What?"

"He was going to try to talk to her alone."

"He can't do that."

"You're damn right he can't. Look at all the security they've got posted around her."

"No, I mean he can't get a story the rest of us don't have. We've got to go up there."

"Forget it."

"Come on. We can stop by for a visit or something. Play a game of cards. She'll be happy to see us."

"You're crazy."

"All right, you stay here. I'm going up and talk to her. She won't mind—she likes me."

"Gorce—"

Gorce stood up. "Gorce, don't do that! For God's sake—*Melissa!*"

He wouldn't have remembered her first name if they hadn't done interviews with each other for their respective news stations. "This is Melissa Gorce, reporting from Washington," she'd said, and he'd thought that he couldn't have come up with a name less like her.

Using it seemed to work. She stopped, and the mad light in her eyes went out. "Okay," she said. "Maybe you're right."

The next day, at the daily interview, Stevens found out how right he'd been. The number of FBI guards at the door had been doubled, and when his ID had been checked and he'd finally been let in he saw that Nichols was gone.

"He tried to get inside her room last night," Capelli said. "The guards said they were reaching for their guns when they saw this bright flash of light go off. He was practically unrecognizable—they had to check his dental records to make sure it was him."

"He'd been Denverized," another reporter said, trying to laugh.

"He wanted to commit suicide, you ask me," Capelli said. His hands were shaking.

"You see?" Stevens couldn't resist saying to Gorce. "You see what I mean?"

The two cameramen finished setting up, and Helena Johnson's companion opened the floor to questions. No one brought up the dead reporter and Helena Johnson didn't mention him; maybe, Stevens thought, she didn't know. To Stevens's relief she called on him for the first time in four days.

"I was wondering," he said, "how you spend your time. What are your hobbies?"

She smiled at him almost flirtatiously. He was surprised at how much hatred he felt for her at that moment. "Oh, I keep busy," she said. "I look through my mail, though of course I don't have time to answer all my correspondence. And I watch some television, I watch videotapes people send me, I have my hair done . . . I enjoy mealtimes especially, though there's a lot of food my stomach can't take. Do you know, I'd never eaten lobster in my life until last week."

Gorce was right, he thought. She does like talking about herself. If they survived New Year's Eve, he'd have to keep in contact with Gorce—she was one smart woman.

Someone asked Helena Johnson a question about her father, and the old woman droned on. She's already told us this story, Stevens thought. There were a few more questions, and then Gorce raised her hand. Helena Johnson smiled at her. "Yes, dear?"

"What do you think of the aliens, Miss Johnson?"

"Gorce!" Capelli whispered behind her. The other reporters thought he'd lost his nerve at the first press conference, when his chair had burst into flames behind him.

"I suppose I'm grateful to them," Helena Johnson said. "If it wasn't for them I'd still be in that dreadful old age home."

"But what do you think of the way they've interfered with us? Of the way they want to make our decisions for us?"

Capelli wasn't the only reporter who became visibly nervous at this question. Stevens felt he could have cheerfully strangled her.

"I don't know, dear. You mean they want to tell us what to do?"

"They want to tell you what to do. They want to force you to make a choice."

"Oh, I don't mind making the choice. In fact—"

Oh, Lord, Stevens thought. She's going to tell us right now.

The companion stepped forward. "Our hour with Miss Johnson is almost up," she said smoothly. "Do you have anything else you want to say, Miss Johnson?"

"Yes, I do," the old woman said. "I wanted to say— Oh, dear, I've forgotten."

The companion moved to the desk and brought her a slip of paper. "Oh yes, that's right," Helena Johnson said, looking at it. "I wanted to tell everyone not to get me a Christmas present. I know a lot of people have been worrying about what to get me, and I just want to tell them I have everything I need."

So give a contribution to charity instead, Stevens thought, but Helena Johnson seemed to have finished. Did she neglect to mention charity because she knew there would be no charities, or anything else, in a few weeks? It was amazing how paranoid they had all become, how they analyzed her slightest gesture.

The companion ushered everyone out of the room. The reporters went downstairs to stand in front of the hotel and tape a short summary of the interview for their stations. Upstairs, Stevens knew, Helena Johnson and the cameramen were going over the footage, editing out parts where she thought she looked too old, too vulnerable, or too uncertain.

He felt depressed by the interview, by Nichols's death. The old lady hadn't given them any hope at all this time. What would he be doing a few weeks from now? If she said no, he could probably have his pick of assignments. But if she said yes he'd be charred bones and ashes, like poor Nichols, like all the people in Denver. God, what a horrible way to die. She had to say no, she had to.

On New Year's Eve everyone was either watching television, getting drunk, or doing both at once. The last show would be broadcast live.

Stevens had taken a sedative for the final interview, and he knew he wasn't the only one. There had been no commercials on any network for the last five hours; if the old lady said no, Stevens had heard, there would be commercials every three minutes.

They were let into the room for the last time at exactly midnight. "Hello," Helena Johnson said, smiling at all of them. The smell of fear was very strong.

"I have been chosen by the aliens to decide Earth's future," she said. "I don't understand why I was chosen, and neither does anyone else. But I have taken the responsibility very seriously, and I feel I have been conscientious in doing my duty."

Get on with it, Stevens thought. Yes or no.

"I have to say I have enjoyed my stay here at the hotel," she said. "But it is impossible not to think that all of you must consider me very stupid indeed." Oh, God, Stevens thought. Here it comes. The old lady's revenge. "I know very well that none of you were interested in me, in Helena Hope Johnson. If the aliens hadn't chosen me I would probably be at the nursing home right now, if not dead of neglect. My leg would be in constant pain, and the nurses would think I was senile because I couldn't hear the questions they asked me.

"So, at first, I thought I would say yes. I would say that Earth deserves to be destroyed, that its people are cruel and selfish and will only show kindness if there's something in it for them. And sometimes not even then. Why do you think my son hasn't come to visit me?" The yellow eye had filled with tears.

Oh, shit, Stevens thought. I knew it would come to this. He had heard her son was dead, killed in a bar fight.

"But then I remembered what this young lady had said," Helena Johnson said. "Miss Gorce. She asked me what I thought about the aliens interfering with our lives, with my life. Well, I thought about it, and I didn't like what I came up with. They have no right to decide whether we will live or die, whoever they are. All my life, people have decided for me, my parents, my teachers, my bosses. But that's all over with now. My answer is—no answer. I will not give them an answer."

No one moved for a long moment. Then one of the agents stationed outside the door ran into the room. "The ships are leaving!" he said. "They're taking off!"

Suddenly everyone was cheering. Stevens hugged Gorce, hugged Capelli, hugged the FBI agent. The reporters lifted Gorce and threw her into the air until she yelled at them to stop. I hope the camera's getting all this, Stevens thought. It's great television.

The reporters, quieter now, came over to Helena Johnson to thank her. Stevens saw Gorce kiss the old woman carefully on the cheek. "You'd better leave now," the companion said. "She gets tired so easily."

One by one the reporters went downstairs to the bar. Helena Johnson and Gorce were left alone together. Stevens went outside and waited for Gorce near the door. He wanted to tell her she'd been right to ask that question.

Gorce seemed pleased to see him when she came out. "What'd she want to talk to you about?" he asked.

"She wanted me to ghostwrite her autobiography."

Stevens laughed. "No one would read it," he said. "We know far too much about her as it is."

"It don't matter—they've already given her a million dollar contract."

"So what'd you say?"

"Well, she offered me ten percent. What do you think I said? I said yes."

"Congratulations," he said, happy for her. Outside he heard police sirens and what sounded like firecrackers.

"Thanks," she said. "Do you want t-t-to go out somewhere and celebrate?"

He looked at her with surprise. He had never known her to stutter before. She wasn't bad-looking, he thought, but too bony, and her chin and forehead were too long. She had to have gotten her job through her mad bravery and sharp common sense, because she sure didn't look like a blow-dried TV reporter. "Sorry," he said. "I told my girlfriend I'd call her when this whole thing was over."

"You never told me you had a girlfriend."

"Yeah, well, it never came up," he said. "See you, Gorce."

She looked at him a long time. "You know, Stevens, you better start being nicer to me," she said. "What if the aliens pick me to save the world next time?"

And Wild for to Hold

NANCY KRESS

The demon came to her first in the long gallery at Hever Castle. She had gone there to watch Henry ride away, magnificent on his huge charger, the horse's legs barely visible through the summer dust raised by the king's entourage. But Henry himself was visible. He rose in his stirrups to half turn his gaze back to the manor house, searching its sun-glazed windows to see if she watched. The spurned lover, riding off, watching over his shoulder the effect he himself made. She knew just how his eyes would look, small blue eyes under the curling red-gold hair. Mournful. Shrewd. Undeterred.

Anne Boleyn was not moved. Let him ride. She had not wanted him at Hever in the first place.

As she turned from the gallery window a glint of light in the far corner caught her eye, and there for the first time was the demon.

It was made all of light, which did not surprise her. Was not Satan himself called Lucifer? The light was square, a perfectly square box such as no light had ever been before. Anne crossed herself and stepped forward. The box of light brightened, then winked out.

Anne stood perfectly still. She was not afraid; very little made her afraid. But nonetheless she crossed herself again and uttered a prayer. It would be unfortunate if a demon took residence at Hever. Demons could be dangerous.

Like kings.

Lambert half turned from her console toward Culhane, working across the room. "Culhane—they said she was a witch."

"Yes? So?" Culhane said. "In the fifteen hundreds they said any powerful woman was a witch."

"No, it was more. They said it before she became powerful." Culhane didn't answer. After a moment Lambert said quietly, "The Rahvoli equations keep flagging her."

Culhane grew very still. Finally he said, "Let me see."

He crossed the bare small room to Lambert's console. She steadied the picture on the central square. At the moment the console appeared in this location as a series of interlocking squares mounting from floor to ceiling. Some of the squares were solid real-time alloys; some were holosimulations; some were not there at all, neither in space nor in time, although they appeared to be. The Project Focus Square, which *was* there, said:

TIME RESCUE PROJECT
UNITED FEDERATION OF UPPER SLIB, EARTH
FOCUS: ANNE BOLEYN
HEVER CASTLE, KENT, ENGLAND, EUROPE
1525:645:89:3
CHURCH OF THE HOLY HOSTAGE TEMPORARY PERMIT
#4592

In the time-jump square was framed a young girl, dark hair just visible below her coif, her hand arrested at her long slender neck in the act of signing the cross.

Lambert said, as if to herself, "She considered herself a good Catholic."

Culhane stared at the image. His head had been freshly shaved, in honor of his promotion to Project Head. He wore, Lambert thought, his new importance as if it were a fragile implant, liable to be rejected. She found that touching.

Lambert said, "The Rahvoli probability is .798. She's a definite key."

Culhane sucked in his cheeks. The dye on them had barely dried. He said, "So is the other. I think we should talk to Brill."

The servingwomen had finally left. The priests had left, the doctors, the courtiers, the nurses, taking with them the baby. Even Henry had left, gone . . . where? To play cards with Harry Norris? To his latest mistress? Never mind—at last they had all left her alone.

A girl.

Anne rolled over in her bed and pounded her fists on the pillow. A girl. Not a prince, not the son that England needed, that *she* needed . . . a girl. And Henry growing colder every day, she could feel it, he no longer desired her, no longer loved her. He would bed with her—oh, that, most certainly, if it would get him his boy, but her power was going. Was gone. That power she had hated, despised, but had used nonetheless because it was there and Henry should feel it, as he had made her feel his power over and over again . . . her power was going. She was Queen of England but her power was slipping away like the Thames at ebb tide, and she just as helpless to stop it as to stop the tide itself. The only thing that could have preserved her power was a son. And she had borne a girl. Strong, lusty, with Henry's own red curling hair . . . but a girl.

Anne rolled over on her back, painfully. Elizabeth was already a month old, but everything in Anne hurt. She had contracted white leg, so much less dreaded than childbed fever but still weakening, and for the whole month had not left her bedchamber. Servants and ladies and musicians came and went, while Anne lay feverish, trying to plan. . . . Henry had as yet made no move. He had even seemed to take the baby's sex well: "She seems a lusty wench. I pray God will send her a brother in the same good shape." But Anne knew. She always knew. She had known when Henry's eye first fell upon her. Had known to a shade the exact intensity of his longing during the nine years she had kept him waiting: nine years of celibacy, of denial. She had known the exact moment when that hard mind behind the small blue eyes had decided: *It is worth it. I will divorce Catherine and make her queen.* Anne had known before he did when he decided it had all been a mistake. The price for making her queen had been too high. She was not worth it. Unless she gave him a son.

And if she did not . . .

In the darkness Anne squeezed her eyes shut. This was but an attack of childbed vapors, it signified nothing. She was never afraid, not she. This was only a night terror, and when she opened her eyes it would pass, because it must. She must go on fighting, must get herself heavy with son, must safeguard her crown. And her daughter. There was no one else to do it for her, and there was no way out.

When she opened her eyes, a demon, shaped like a square of light, glowed in the corner of the curtained bedchamber.

Lambert dipped her head respectfully as the High Priest passed.

She was tall, and wore no external augments. Eyes, arms, ears, shaved head, legs under the gray-green ceremonial robe—all were her own, as required by the charter of the Church of the Holy Hostage. Lambert had heard a rumor that before her election to High Priest she had had brilliant violet augmented eyes and gamma-strength arms, but on her election had had both removed and the originals restored. The free representative of all the hostages in the solar system could not walk around enjoying high-maintenance augments. Hostages could, of course, but the person in charge of their spiritual and material welfare must appear human to any hostage she chose to visit. A four-handed Spacer held in a free-fall chamber on Mars must find the High Priest as human as did a genetically altered flyer of Ipsu being held hostage by the New Trien Republic. The only way to do that was to forego external augments.

Internals, of course, were a different thing.

Beside the High Priest walked the Director of the Time Research Institute, Toshio Brill. No ban on externals for *him:* Brill wore gold-plated sensors in his shaved black head, a display Lambert found slightly ostentatious. Also puzzling: Brill was not ordinarily a flamboyant man. Perhaps he was differentiating himself from Her Holiness. Behind Brill his Project Heads, including Culhane, stood silent, not speaking unless spoken to. Culhane looked nervous: he was ambitious, Lambert knew. She sometimes wondered why she was not.

"So far I am impressed," the High Priest said. "Impeccable hostage conditions on the material side."

Brill murmured, "Of course, the spiritual is difficult. The three hostages are so different from each other, and even for culture specialists and historians . . . the hostages arrive here very upset."

"As would you or I," the High Priest said, not smiling, "in similar circumstances."

"Yes, Your Holiness."

"And now you wish to add a fourth hostage, from a fourth time stream."

"Yes."

The High Priest looked slowly around at the main console; Lambert noticed that she looked right past the time-jump square itself. Not trained in peripheral vision techniques. But she looked a long time at the stasis square. They all did; outsiders were unduly fascinated by the idea that the whole building existed between time streams. Or maybe Her Holiness merely objected to the fact that the Time Research Institute, like some larger but hardly richer institutions, was exempt from the all-world taxation that supported the Church. Real estate outside time was also outside taxation.

The High Priest said, "I cannot give permission for such a political disruption without understanding fully every possible detail. Tell me again."

Lambert hid a grin. The High Priest did not need to hear it again. She knew the whole argument, had pored over it for days, most likely, with her advisers. And she would agree; why wouldn't she? It could only add to her power. Brill knew that. He was being asked to explain only to show that the High Priest could force him to do it, again and again, until she—not he—decided the explanation was sufficient and the Church of the Holy Hostage issued a permanent hostage permit to hold one Anne Boleyn, of England Time Delta, for the altruistic purpose of preventing a demonstrable Class One war.

Brill showed no outward recognition that he was being humbled. "Your Holiness, this woman is a fulcrum. The Rahvoli equations, developed in the last century by—"

"I know the Rahvoli equations," the High Priest said. And smiled sweetly.

"Then Your Holiness knows that any person identified by the equations as a fulcrum is directly responsible for the course of history. Even if he or she seems powerless in local time. Mistress Boleyn was the second wife of Henry VIII of England. In order to marry her, he divorced his first wife, Catherine of Aragon, and in order to do that, he took all of England out of the Catholic Church. Protestantism was—"

"And what again was that?" Her Holiness said, and even Culhane glanced sideways at Lambert, appalled. The High Priest was playing. With a *Research Director*. Lambert hid her smile. Did Culhane know that high seriousness opened one to the charge of pomposity? Probably not.

"Protestantism was another branch of 'Christianity,'" the director said patiently. So far, by refusing to be provoked, he was winning. "It was warlike, as was Catholicism. In 1642 various branches of Protestantism were contending for political power within England, as was a Catholic faction. King Charles was Catholic, in fact. Contention led to civil war. Thousands of people died fighting, starved to death, were hanged as traitors, were tortured as betrayers. . . ."

Lambert saw Her Holiness wince. She must hear this all the time, Lambert thought, what else was her office for? Yet the wince looked genuine.

Brill pressed his point. "Children were reduced to eating rats to survive. In Cornwall, rebels' hands and feet were cut off, gibbets were erected in market squares and men hanged on them alive and—"

"Enough," the High Priest said. "This is why the Church exists. To promote the Holy Hostages that prevent war."

"And that is what we wish to do," Brill said swiftly, "in other time streams, now that our own has been brought to peace. In Stream Delta, which has only reached the sixteenth century—Your Holiness knows that each stream progresses at a different relative rate—"

The High Priest made a gesture of impatience.

"—the woman Anne Boleyn is the fulcrum. If she can be taken hostage after the birth of her daughter Elizabeth, who will act throughout a very long reign to preserve peace, and before Henry declares the Act of Supremacy that opens the door to religious divisiveness in England, we can prevent great loss of life. The Rahvoli equations show a 79.8 percent probability that history will be changed in the direction of greater peace, right up through the following two centuries. Religious wars often—"

"There are other, bloodier religious wars to prevent than the English civil war."

"True, Your Holiness," the director said humbly. At least it looked like humility to Lambert. "But ours is a young science. Identifying other time streams, focusing on one, identifying historical fulcra—it is such a new science. We do what we can, in the name of Peace."

Everyone in the room looked pious. Lambert kept her face blank. In the name of Peace—and of prestigious scientific research, attended by rich financial support and richer academic reputations.

"And it is Peace we seek," Brill pressed, "as much as the Church itself does. With a permanent permit to take Anne Boleyn hostage, we can save countless lives in this other time stream, just as the Church preserves peace in our own."

The High Priest played with the sleeve of her robe. Lambert could not see her face. But when she looked up, she was smiling.

"I'll recommend to the All-World Forum that your hostage permit be granted, Director. I will return in two months to make an official check on the Holy Hostage."

Brill, Lambert saw, didn't quite stop himself in time from frowning. "Two months? But with the entire solar system of hostages to supervise—"

"Two months, Director," Her Holiness said. "The week before the All-World Forum convenes to vote on revenue and taxation."

"I—"

"Now I would like to inspect the three Holy Hostages you already hold for the altruistic prevention of war."

Later, Culhane said to Lambert, "He did not explain it very well. It could have been made so much more urgent . . . it *is* urgent. Those bodies rotting in Cornwall . . ." He shuddered.

Lambert looked at him. "You care. You genuinely do."

He looked back at her, in astonishment. "And you don't? You must, to work on this project!"

"I care," Lambert said. "But not like that."

"Like what?"

She tried to clarify it for him, for herself. "The bodies rotting . . . I see them. But it's not our own history—"

"What does that matter? They're still human!"

He was so earnest. Intensity burned on him like skin tinglers. Did Culhane even use skin tinglers, Lambert wondered? Fellow researchers spoke of him as an ascetic, giving all his energy, all his time, to the project. A woman in his domicile had told Lambert he even lived chaste, doing a Voluntary Celibacy Mission for the entire length of his research grant. Lambert had never met anyone who actually did that. It was intriguing.

She said, "Are you thinking of the priesthood once the project is over, Culhane?"

He flushed. Color mounted from the dyed cheeks, light blue since he had been promoted to Project Head, to pink on the fine skin of his shaved temples.

"I'm thinking of it."

"And doing a Celibacy Mission now?"

"Yes. Why?" His tone was belligerent: a Celibacy Mission was slightly old-fashioned. Lambert studied his body: tall, well-made, strong. Augmented? Muscular, maybe. He had beautiful muscles.

"No reason," she said, bending back to her console until she heard him walk away.

The demon advanced. Anne, lying feeble on her curtained bed, tried to call out. But her voice would not come, and who would hear her anyway? The bedclothes were thick, muffling sound; her ladies would all have retired for the night, alone or otherwise; the guards would be drinking the ale Henry had provided all of London to celebrate Elizabeth's christening. And Henry . . . he was not beside her. She had failed him of his son.

"Be gone," she said weakly to the demon. It moved closer.

They had called her a witch. Because of her little sixth finger, because of the dog named Urian, because she had kept Henry under her spell so long without bedding him. But if I were really a witch, she thought, I could send this demon away. More: I could hold Henry, could keep him from watching that whey-faced Jane Seymour, could keep him in my bed. . . . She was not a witch.

Therefore, it followed that there was nothing she could do about this demon. If it was come for her, it was come. If Satan Master of Lies was decided to have her, to punish her for taking the husband of another woman, and for . . . how much could demons know?

"This was all none of my wishing," she said aloud to the demon. "I wanted to marry someone else." The demon continued to advance.

Very well, then, let it take her. She would not scream. She never had—she prided herself on it. Not when they had told her she could not marry Harry Percy. Not when she had been sent home from the Court, peremptorily and without explanation. Not when she had discovered the explanation: Henry wished to have her out of London so he could bed his latest mistress away from Catherine's eyes. She had not screamed when a crowd of whores had burst into the palace where she was supping, demanding Nan Bullen, who they said was one of them. She had escaped across the Thames in a barge, and not a cry had escaped her lips. They had admired her for her courage: Wyatt, Norris, Weston, Henry himself. She would not scream now.

The box of light grew larger as it approached. She had just time to say to it, "I have been God's faithful and true servant, and my husband the king's," before it was upon her.

"The place where a war starts," Lambert said to the faces assembled below her in the Hall of Time, "is long before the first missile, or the first bullet, or the first spear."

She looked down at the faces. It was part of her responsibilities as an intern researcher to teach a class of young, some of whom would become historians. The class was always taught in the Hall of Time. The expense was enormous: keeping the Hall in stasis for nearly an hour, bringing the students in through the force field, activating all the squares at once. Her lecture would be replayed for them later, when they could pay attention to it: Lambert did not blame them for barely glancing at her now. Why should they? The walls of the circular room, which were only there in a virtual sense, were lined with squares, which were not really there at all. The squares showed actual local-time scenes from wars that had been there, were there now, somewhere, in someone's reality.

Men died writhing in the mud, arrows through intestines and necks and groins, at Agincourt.

Women lay flung across the bloody bodies of their children at Cawnpore.

In the hot sun the flies crawled thick upon the split faces of the heroes of Marathon.

Figures staggered, their faces burned off, away from Hiroshima.

Breathing bodies, their perfect faces untouched and their brains turned to mush by spekaline, sat in orderly rows under the ripped dome on Io-One.

Only one face turned toward Lambert, jerked as if on a string, a boy with wide violet eyes brimming with anguish. Lambert obligingly began again.

"The place where a war starts is long before the first missile, or the first bullet, or the first spear. There are always many forces causing a war: economic, political, religious, cultural. Nonetheless, it is the great historical discovery of our time that if you trace each of these back—through the records, through the eyewitness accounts, through the entire burden of data only Rahvoli equations can handle—you come to a fulcrum. A single event or act or person. It is like a decision tree with a thousand thousand generations of decisions: somewhere there was one first yes/no. The place where the war started, and where it could have been prevented.

"The great surprise of time-rescue work has been how often that place was female.

"Men fought wars, when there were wars. Men controlled the gold and the weapons and the tariffs and sea rights and religions that have caused wars, and the men controlled the bodies of other men that did the actual fighting. But men are men. They acted at the fulcrum of history, but often what tipped their actions one way or another was what they loved. A woman. A child. She became the passive, powerless weight he chose to lift, and the balance tipped. She, not he, is the branching place, where the decision tree splits and the war begins."

The boy with the violet eyes was still watching her. Lambert stayed silent until he turned to watch the squares—which was the reason he had been brought here. Then she watched him. Anguished, passionate, able to feel what war meant—he might be a good candidate for the time-rescue team, when his preliminary studies were done. He reminded her a little of Culhane.

Who right now, as Project Head, was interviewing the new hostage, not lecturing to children.

Lambert stifled her jealousy. It was unworthy. And shortsighted: she remembered what this glimpse of human misery had meant to her three years ago, when she was a historian candidate. She had had nightmares for weeks. She had thought the event was pivotal to her life, a dividing point past which she would never be the same person again. How could she? She had been shown the depths to which humanity, without the Church of the Holy Hostage and the All-World

Concordance, could descend. Burning eye sockets, mutilated genitals, a general who stood on a hill and said, "How I love to see the arms and legs fly!" It had been shattering. She had been shattered, as the Orientation intended she should be.

The boy with the violet eyes was crying. Lambert wanted to step down from the platform and go to him. She wanted to put her arms around him and hold his head against her shoulder . . . but was that because of compassion, or was that because of his violet eyes?

She said silently to him, without leaving the podium, *You will be all right. Human beings are not as mutable as you think. When this is over, nothing permanent about you will have changed at all.*

Anne opened her eyes. Satan leaned over her.

His head was shaved, and he wore strange garb of an ugly blue-green. His cheeks were stained with dye. In one ear metal glittered and swung. Anne crossed herself.

"Hello," Satan said, and the voice was not human.

She struggled to sit up; if this be damnation, she would not lie prone for it. Her heart hammered in her throat. But the act of sitting brought the Prince of Darkness into focus, and her eyes widened. He looked like a man. Painted, made ugly, hung around with metal boxes that could be tools of evil—but a man.

"My name is Culhane."

A man. And she had faced men. Bishops, nobles, Chancellor Wolsey. She had outfaced Henry, Prince of England and France, Defender of the Faith.

"Don't be frightened, Mistress Boleyn. I will explain to you where you are and how you came to be here."

She saw now that the voice came not from his mouth, although his mouth moved, but from the box hung around his neck. How could that be? Was there then a demon in the box? But then she realized something else, something real to hold on to.

"Do not call me Mistress Boleyn. Address me as Your Grace. I am the queen."

The something that moved behind his eyes convinced her, finally, that he was a mortal man. She was used to reading men's eyes. But why should this one look at her like that—with pity? With admiration?

She struggled to stand, rising off the low pallet. It was carved of good English oak. The room was paneled in dark wood and hung with tapestries of embroidered wool. Small-paned windows shed brilliant light over carved chairs, table, chest. On the table rested a writing desk and a lute. Reassured, Anne pushed down the heavy cloth of her night shift and rose.

The man, seated on a low stool, rose too. He was taller than Henry—she had never seen a man taller than Henry—superbly muscled. A soldier? Fright fluttered again, and she put her hand to her throat. This man, watching her—watching her *throat*. Was he then an executioner? Was she under arrest, drugged and brought by some secret method into the Tower of London? Had someone brought evidence against her—or was Henry that disappointed that she had not borne a son that he was eager already to supplant her?

As steadily as she could, Anne walked to the window.

The Tower bridge did not lay beyond in the sunshine. Nor the river, nor the gabled roofs of Greenwich Palace. Instead there was a sort of yard, with huge beasts of metal growling softly. On the grass naked young men and women jumped up and down, waving their arms, running in place and smiling and sweating as if they did not know either that they were uncovered or crazed.

Anne took firm hold of the windowsill. It was slippery in her hands and she saw that it was not wood at all, but some material made to resemble wood. She closed her eyes, then opened them. She was a queen. She had fought hard to become a queen, defending a virtue nobody believed she still had, against a man who claimed that to destroy that virtue was love. She had won, making the crown the price of her virtue. She had conquered a king, brought down a Chancellor of England, outfaced a pope. She would not show fear to this executioner in this place of the damned, whatever it was.

She turned from the window, her head high. "Please begin your explanation, Master . . ."

"Culhane."

"Master Culhane. We are eager to hear what you have to say. And we do not like waiting."

She swept aside her long nightdress as if it were Court dress and seated herself in the not-wooden chair carved like a throne.

"I am a hostage," Anne repeated. "In a time that has not yet happened."

From beside the window, Lambert watched. She was fascinated. Anne Boleyn had, according to Culhane's report, listened in silence to the entire explanation of the time rescue, that explanation so carefully drafted and revised a dozen times to fit what the sixteenth-century mind could understand of the twenty-second. Queen Anne had not become hysterical. She had not cried, nor fainted, nor professed disbelief. She had asked no questions. When Culhane had finished, she had requested, calmly and with staggering dignity, to see the ruler of this place, with his ministers. Toshio Brill, watching on monitor because the wisdom was that at first new hostages would find it easier to deal with one consistent researcher, had hastily summoned Lambert and two others. They had all dressed in the floor-length robes used for grand academic ceremonies and never else. And they had marched solemnly into the ersatz sixteenth-century room, bowing their heads.

Only their heads. No curtsies. Anne Boleyn was going to learn that no one curtsied anymore.

Covertly Lambert studied her, their fourth time hostage, so different from the other three. She had not risen from her chair, but even seated she was astonishingly tiny. Thin, delicate bones, great dark eyes, masses of silky black hair loose on her white nightdress. She was not pretty by the standards of this century; she had not even been counted pretty by the standards of her own. But she was compelling. Lambert had to give her that.

"And I am prisoner here," Anne Boleyn said. Lambert turned up her translator; the words were just familiar, but the accent so strange she could not catch them without electronic help.

"Not prisoner," the director said. "Hostage."

"Lord Brill, if I cannot leave, then I am a prisoner. Let us not mince words. I cannot leave this castle?"

"You cannot."

"Please address me as 'Your Grace.' Is there to be a ransom?"

"No, Your Grace. But because of your presence here thousands of men will live who would have otherwise died."

With a shock, Lambert saw Anne shrug; the deaths of thousands of men evidently did not interest her. It was true, then. They really were moral barbarians, even the women. The students should see this. That small shrug said more than all the battles viewed in squares. Lambert felt her sympathy for the abducted woman lessen, a physical sensation like the emptying of a bladder, and was relieved to feel it. It meant she, Lambert, still had her own moral sense.

"How long must I stay here?"

"For life, Your Grace," Brill said bluntly.

Anne made no reaction; her control was awing.

"And how long will that be, Lord Brill?"

"No person knows the length of his or her life, Your Grace."

"But if you can read the future, as you claim, you must know what the length of mine would have been."

Lambert thought: We must not underestimate her. This hostage is not like the last one.

Brill said, with the same bluntness that honored Anne's comprehension—did she realize that?—"If we had not brought you here, you would have died May 19, 1536."

"How?"

"It does not matter. You are no longer part of that future, and so now events there will—"

"How?"

Brill didn't answer.

Anne Boleyn rose and walked to the window, absurdly small, Lambert thought, in the trailing nightdress. Over her shoulder she said, "Is this castle in England?"

"No," Brill said. Lambert saw him exchange glances with Culhane.

"In France?"

"It is not in any place on the Earth," Brill said, "although it can be entered from three places on Earth. It is outside of time."

She could not possibly have understood, but she said nothing, only went on staring out the window. Over her shoulder Lambert saw the exercise court, empty now, and the antimatter power generators. Two technicians crawled over them with a robot monitor. What did Anne Boleyn make of them?

"God knows if I had merited death," Anne said. Lambert saw Culhane start.

Brill stepped forward. "Your Grace—"

"Leave me now," she said, without turning.

They did. Of course she would be monitored constantly—everything from brain scans to the output of her bowels. Although she would never know this. But if suicide was in that life-defying mind, it would not be possible. If Her Holiness ever learned of the suicide of a time hostage . . . Lambert's last glimpse before the door closed was of Anne Boleyn's back, still by the window, straight as a spear as she gazed out at antimatter power generators in a building in permanent stasis.

"Culhane, meeting in ten minutes," Brill said. Lambert guessed the time lapse was to let the director change into working clothes. Toshio Brill had come away from the interview with Anne Boleyn somehow diminished. He even looked shorter, although shouldn't her small stature have instead augmented his?

Culhane stood still in the corridor outside Anne's locked room (would she try the door?). His face was turned away from Lambert's.

She said, "Culhane . . . you jumped a moment in there. When she said God alone knew if she had merited death."

"It was what she said at her trial," Culhane said. "When the verdict was announced. Almost the exact words."

He still had not moved so much as a muscle of that magnificent body. Lambert said, probing, "You found her impressive, then. Despite her scrawniness, and beyond the undeniable pathos of her situation."

He looked at her then, his eyes blazing: Culhane, the research engine. "I found her magnificent."

She never smiled. That was one of the things she knew they remarked upon among themselves: she had overheard them in the walled garden. Anne Boleyn never smiles. Alone, they did not call her Queen Anne, or Her Grace, or even the Marquis of Rochford, the title Henry had conferred upon her, the only female peeress in her own right in all of England. No, they called her Anne Boleyn, as if the marriage to Henry had never happened, as if she had never borne Elizabeth. And they said she never smiled.

What cause was there to smile, in this place that was neither life nor death?

Anne stitched deftly at a piece of amber velvet. She was not badly treated. They had given her a servant, cloth to make dresses—she had always been clever with a needle, and the skill had not deserted her when she could afford to order any dresses she chose. They had given her books, the writing Latin but the pictures curiously flat, with no raised ink or painting. They let her go into any unlocked room in the castle, out to the gardens, into the yards. She was a Holy Hostage.

When the amber velvet gown was finished, she put it on. They let her have a mirror. A lute. Writing paper and quills. Whatever she asked for, as generous as Henry had been in the early days of his passion, when he had divided her from her love Harry Percy, and had kept her loving hostage to his own fancy.

Cages came in many sizes. Many shapes. And, if what Master Culhane and the Lady Mary Lambert said was true, in many times.

"I am not a lady," Lady Lambert had protested. She needn't have bothered. Of course she was not a lady—she was a commoner, like the others, and so perverted was this place that the woman sounded insulted to be called a lady. Lambert did not like her, Anne knew, although she had not yet found out why. The woman was unsexed, like all of them, working on her books and machines all day, exercising naked with men, who thus no more looked at their bodies than they would those of fellow soldiers in the roughest camp. So it pleased Anne to call Lambert a lady when she did not want to be one, as Anne was now so many things she had never wanted to be. "Anne Boleyn." Who never smiled.

"I will create you a lady," she said to Lambert. "I confer on you the rank of baroness. Who will gainsay me? I am the queen, and in this place there is no king."

And Mary Lambert had stared at her with the unsexed bad manners of a common drab.

Anne knotted her thread and cut it with silver scissors. The gown was finished. She slipped it over her head and struggled with the buttons in the back, rather than call the stupid girl who was her servant. The girl could not even dress hair. Anne smoothed her hair herself, then looked critically at her reflection in the fine mirror they had brought her.

For a woman a month and a half from childbed, she looked strong. They had put medicines in her food, they said. Her complexion, that creamy dark skin that seldom varied in color, was well set off by the amber velvet. She had often worn amber, or tawny. Her hair, loose, since she had no headdress and did not know how to make one, streamed over her shoulders. Her hands, long and slim despite the tiny extra finger, carried a rose brought to her by Master Culhane. She toyed with the rose, to show off the beautiful hands, and lifted her head high.

She was going to have an audience with Her Holiness, a female pope. And she had a request to make.

"She will ask, Your Holiness, to be told the future. Her future, the one Anne Boleyn experienced in our own time stream, after the point we took her hostage from hers. And the future of England." Brill's face had darkened; Lambert could see that he hated this. To forewarn his political rival that a hostage would complain about her treatment. A *hostage,* that person turned sacred object through the sacrifice of personal freedom to global peace. When Tullio Amaden Koyushi had been hostage from Mars Three to the Republic of China, he had told the Church official in charge of his case that he was not being allowed sufficient exercise. The resulting intersystem furor had lost the Republic of China two trade contracts, both important. There was no other way to maintain the necessary reverence for the hostage political system. The Church of the Holy Hostage was powerful because it must be, if the solar system was to stay at peace. Brill knew that.

So did Her Holiness.

She wore full state robes today, gorgeous with hundreds of tiny mirrors sent to her by the grateful across all worlds. Her head was newly shaved. Perfect synthetic jewels glittered in her ears. Listening to Brill's apology-in-advance, Her Holiness smiled. Lambert saw the smile, and even across the room she felt Brill's polite, concealed frustration.

"Then if this is so," Her Holiness said, "why cannot Lady Anne Boleyn be told her future? Hers and England's?"

Lambert knew that the High Priest already knew the answer. She wanted to make Brill say it.

Brill said, "It is not thought wise, Your Holiness. If you remember, we did that once before."

"Ah, yes, your last hostage. I will see her, too, of course, on this visit. Has Queen Helen's condition improved?"

"No," Brill said shortly.

"And no therapeutic brain drugs or electronic treatments have helped? She still is insane from the shock of finding herself with us?"

"Nothing has helped."

"You understand how reluctant I was to let you proceed with another time rescue at all," Her Holiness said, and even Lambert stifled a gasp. The High Priest did not make those determinations; only the All-World Forum could authorize or disallow a hostage-taking—across space *or* time. The Church of the Holy Hostage was responsible only for the inspection and continuation of permits granted by the Forum. For the High Priest to claim political power she did not possess—

The director's eyes gleamed angrily. But before he could reply, the door opened and Culhane escorted in Anne Boleyn.

Lambert pressed her lips together tightly. The woman had sewn herself a gown, a sweeping ridiculous confection of amber velvet so tight at the breasts and waist she must hardly be able to breathe. How had women conducted their lives in such trappings? The dress narrowed her waist to nearly nothing; above the square neckline her collarbones were delicate as a bird's. Culhane hovered beside her, huge and protective. Anne walked straight to the High Priest, knelt, and raised her face.

She was looking for a ring to kiss.

Lambert didn't bother to hide her smile. A High Priest wore no jewelry except earrings, ever. The pompous little hostage had made a social error, no doubt significant in her own time.

Anne smiled up at Her Holiness, the first time anyone had seen her smile at all. It changed her face, lighting it with mischief, lending luster to the great dark eyes. A phrase came to Lambert, penned by the poet Thomas Wyatt to describe his cousin Anne: *"And wild for to hold, though I seem tame."*

Anne said, in that sprightly yet aloof manner that Lambert was coming to associate with her, "It seems, Your Holiness, that we have reached for what is not there. But the lack is ours, not yours, and we hope it will not be repeated in the request we come to make of you."

Direct. Graceful, even through the translator and despite the ludicrous imperial plural. Lambert glanced at Culhane, who was gazing down at Anne as at a rare and fragile flower. How could he? That skinny body, without muscle tone let alone augments, that plain face, the mole on her neck . . . This was not the sixteenth century. Culhane was a fool.

As Thomas Wyatt had been. And Sir Harry Percy. And Henry, King of England. All caught not by beauty but by that strange elusive charm.

Her Holiness laughed. "Stand up, Your Grace. We don't kneel to officials here." *Your Grace*. The High Priest always addressed hostages by the honorifics of their own state, but in this case it could only impede Anne's adjustment.

And what do I care about her adjustment? Lambert jeered at herself. Nothing. What I care about is Culhane's infatuation, and only because he rejected me first. Rejection, it seemed, was a great whetter of appetite—in any century.

Anne rose. Her Holiness said, "I'm going to ask you some questions, Your Grace. You are free to answer any way you wish. My function is to ensure that you are well treated, and that the noble science of the prevention of war, which has made you a Holy Hostage, is also well served. Do you understand?"

"We do."

"Have you received everything you need for your material comfort?"

"Yes," Anne said.

"Have you received everything you've requested for your mental comfort? Books, objects of any description, company?"

"No," Anne said. Lambert saw Brill stiffen.

Her Holiness said, "No?"

"It is necessary for the comfort of our mind—and for our material comfort as well—to understand our situation as fully as possible. Any rational creature requires such understanding to reach ease of mind."

Brill said, "You have been told everything related to your situation.

What you ask is to know about situations that now, because you are here, will never happen."

"Situations that *have* happened, Lord Brill, else no one could know of them. You could not."

"In *your* time stream they will not happen," Brill said. Lambert could hear the suppressed anger in his voice, and wondered if the High Priest could. Anne Boleyn couldn't know how serious it was to be charged by Her Holiness with a breach of hostage treatment. If Brill was ambitious—and why wouldn't he be?—such charges could hurt his future.

Anne said swiftly, "Our time is now your time. *You* have made it so. The situation was none of our choosing. And if your time is now ours, then surely we are entitled to the knowledge that accompanies our time." She looked at the High Priest. "For the comfort of our mind."

Brill said, "Your Holiness—"

"No, Queen Anne is correct. Her argument is valid. You will designate a qualified researcher to answer any questions she has—any at all—about the life she might have had, or the course of events England took when the queen did not become a sacred hostage."

Brill nodded stiffly.

"Good-bye, Your Grace," Her Holiness said. "I shall return in two weeks to inspect your situation again."

Two weeks? The High Priest was not due for another inspection for six months. Lambert glanced at Culhane to see his reaction to this blatant political fault-hunting, but he was gazing at the floor, to which Anne Boleyn had sunk in another of her embarrassing curtsies, the amber velvet of her skirts spread around her like gold.

They sent a commoner to explain her life to her, the life she had lost. A commoner. And he had as well the nerve to be besotted with her. Anne always knew. She tolerated such fellows, like that upstart musician Smeaton, when they were useful to her. If this Master Culhane dared to make any sort of declaration, he would receive the same sort of snub Smeaton once had. Inferior persons should not look to be spoken to as noblemen.

He sat on a straight-backed chair in her Tower room, looking humble enough, while Anne sat in the great carved chair with her hands tightly folded to keep them from shaking.

"Tell me how I came to die in 1536." God's blood! Had ever before there been such a sentence uttered?

Culhane said, "You were beheaded. Found guilty of treason." He stopped, and flushed.

She knew, then. In a queen, there was one cause for a charge of treason. "He charged me with adultery. To remove me, so he could marry again."

"Yes."

"To Jane Seymour."

"Yes."

"Had I first given him a son?"

"No," Culhane said.

"Did Jane Seymour give him a son?"

"Yes, Edward VI. But he died at sixteen, a few years after Henry."

There was vindication in that, but not enough to stem the sick feeling in her gut. Treason. And no son . . . There must have been more than desire for the Seymour bitch. Henry must have hated her. Adultery . . .

"With whom?"

Again the oaf flushed. "With five men, Your Grace. Everyone knew the charges were false, created merely to excuse his own adultery—even your enemies admitted such."

"Who were they?"

"Sir Henry Norris. Sir Francis Weston. William Brereton. Mark Smeaton. And . . . and your brother George."

For a moment she thought she would be sick. Each name fell like a blow, and the last like the ax itself. George. Her beloved brother, so talented at music, so high-spirited and witty . . . Henry Norris, the king's friend. Weston and Brereton, young and light-hearted but always, to her, respectful and careful . . . and Mark Smeaton, the oaf made courtier because he could play the virginals.

The long beautiful hands clutched the sides of the chair. But the moment passed, and she could say with dignity, "They denied the charges?"

"Smeaton confessed, but he was tortured into it. The others denied the charges completely. Henry Norris offered to defend your honor in single combat."

Yes, that was like Harry: so old-fashioned, so principled. She said, "They all died." It was not a question: if she had died for treason, they would have, too. And not alone; no one died alone. "Who else?"

Culhane said, "Maybe we should wait for the rest of this, Your—"

"Who else? My father?"

"No. Sir Thomas More, John Fisher—"

"More? For my . . ." She could not say *adultery*.

"Because he would not swear to the Oath of Supremacy, which made the king and not the pope head of the Church in England. That act opened the door to religious dissension in England."

"It did not. The heretics were already strong in England. History cannot fault that to me!"

"Not as strong as they would become," Culhane said, almost apologetically. "Queen Mary was known as Bloody Mary for burning heretics who used the Act of Supremacy to break from Rome— Your Grace! Are you all right . . . Anne!"

"Do not touch me," she said. Queen Mary. Then her own daughter Elizabeth had been disinherited, or killed. . . . Had Henry become so warped that he would kill a child? His own child? Unless he had come to believe . . .

She whispered, "Elizabeth?"

Comprehension flooded his eyes. "Oh, no, Anne! No! Mary ruled first, as the elder, but when she died heirless, Elizabeth was only twenty-five. Elizabeth became the greatest ruler England had ever known! She ruled for forty-four years, and under her England became a great power."

The greatest ruler. Her baby Elizabeth. Anne could feel her hands unknotting on the ugly artificial chair. Henry had not repudiated Elizabeth, nor had her killed. She had become the greatest ruler England had ever known.

Culhane said, "This is why we thought it best not to tell you all this."

She said coldly, "I will be the judge of that."

"I'm sorry." He sat stiffly, hands dangling awkwardly between his knees. He looked like a plowman, like that oaf Smeaton. . . . She remembered what Henry had done, and rage returned.

"I stood accused. With five men . . . with George. And the charges were false." Something in his face changed. Anne faced him steadily. "Unless . . . were they false, Master Culhane? You who know so much of history—does history say—" She could not finish. To beg for history's judgment from a man like this . . . no humiliation had ever been greater. Not even the Spanish ambassador, referring to her as "the Concubine," had ever humiliated her so.

Culhane said carefully, "History is silent on the subject, Your Grace. What your conduct was . . . would have been . . . is known only to you."

"As it should be. It was . . . would have been . . . mine," she said viciously, mocking his tones perfectly. He looked at her like a wounded puppy, like that lout Smeaton when she had snubbed him. "Tell me this, Master Culhane. You have changed history as it would have been, you tell me. Will my daughter Elizabeth still become the greatest ruler England has ever seen—in *my* 'time stream'? Or will that be altered, too, by your quest for peace at any cost?"

"We don't know. I explained to you. . . . We can only watch your time stream now as it unfolds. It had only reached October, 1533, which is why after analyzing our own history we—"

"You have explained all that. It will be sixty years from now before you know if my daughter will still be great. Or if you have changed that as well by abducting me and ruining my life."

"Abducting! You were going to be killed! Accused, beheaded—"

"And you have prevented that." She rose, in a greater fury than ever she had been with Henry, with Wolsey, with anyone. "You have also robbed me of my remaining three years as surely as Henry would have robbed me of my old age. And you have mayhap robbed my daughter as well, as Henry sought to do with his Seymour-get prince. So what is the difference between you, Master Culhane, that you are a saint and Henry a villain? He held me in the Tower until my soul could be commended to God; you hold me here in this castle you say I can never leave where time does not exist, and mayhap God neither. Who has done me the worse injury? Henry gave me the crown. You—all you and my Lord Brill have given me is a living death, and then given my daughter's crown a danger and uncertainty that without you she would not have known! Who has done to Elizabeth and me the worse turn? And in the name of preventing war! *War!* You have made war upon *me!* Get out, get out!"

"Your—"

"Get out! I never want to see you again! If I am in hell, let there be one less demon!"

Lambert slipped from her monitor to run down the corridor. Culhane flew from the room; behind him the sound of something heavy struck the door. Culhane slumped against it, his face pasty around his cheek dye. Almost Lambert could find it in herself to pity him. Almost.

She said softly, "I told you so."

"She's like a wild thing."

"You knew she could be. It's documented enough, Culhane. I've put a suicide watch on her."

"Yes. Good. I . . . she was like a wild thing."

Lambert peered at him. "You still want her! After that!"

That sobered him; he straightened and looked at her coldly. "She is a Holy Hostage, Lambert."

"I remember that. Do you?"

"Don't insult me, Intern."

He moved angrily away; she caught his sleeve. "Culhane—don't be angry. I only meant that the sixteenth century was so different from our own, but s—"

"Do you think I don't know that? I was doing historical research while you were learning to read, Lambert. Don't instruct *me*."

He stalked off. Lambert bit down hard on her own fury and stared at Anne Boleyn's closed door. No sound came from behind it. To the soundless door she finished her sentence: "—but some traps don't change."

The door didn't answer. Lambert shrugged. It had nothing to do with her. She didn't care what happened to Anne Boleyn, in this century or that other one. Or to Culhane, either. Why should she? There were other men. She was no Henry VIII, to bring down her world for passion. What was the good of being a time researcher, if you could not even learn from times past?

She leaned thoughtfully against the door, trying to remember the name of the beautiful boy in her Orientation lecture, the one with the violet eyes.

She was still there, thinking, when Toshio Brill called a staff meeting to announce, his voice stiff with anger, that Her Holiness of the Church of the Holy Hostage had filed a motion with the All-World Forum that the Time Research Institute, because of the essentially reverent nature of the time-rescue program, be removed from administration by the Forum and placed instead under the direct control of the Church.

She had to think. It was important to think, as she had thought through her denial of Henry's ardor, and her actions when that ardor waned. Thought was all.

She could not return to her London, to Elizabeth. They had told her that. But did she know beyond doubt that it was true?

Anne left her apartments. At the top of the stairs she usually took to the garden she instead turned and opened another door. It opened easily. She walked along a different corridor. Apparently even now no one was going to stop her.

And if they did, what could they do to her? They did not use the scaffold or the rack; she had determined this from talking to that oaf Culhane and that huge ungainly woman, Lady Mary Lambert. They did not believe in violence, in punishment, in death. (How could you not believe in death? Even *they* must one day die.) The most they could do to her was shut her up in her rooms, and there the female pope would come to see she was well-treated.

Essentially they were powerless.

The corridor was lined with doors, most set with small windows. She peered in: rooms with desks and machines, rooms without desks and machines, rooms with people seated around a table talking, kitchens, still rooms. No one stopped her. At the end of the corridor she came to a room without a window and tried the door. It was locked, but as she stood there, her hand still on the knob, the door opened from within.

"Lady Anne! Oh!"

Could no one in this accursed place get her name right? The woman who stood there was clearly a servant, although she wore the same ugly gray-green tunic as everyone else. Perhaps, like Lady Mary, she was really an apprentice. She was of no interest, but behind her was the last thing Anne expected to see in this place: a child.

She pushed past the servant and entered the room. It was a little boy, his dress strange but clearly a uniform of some sort. He had dark eyes, curling dark hair, a bright smile. How old? Perhaps four. There was an air about him that was unmistakable; she would have wagered her life this child was royal.

"Who are you, little one?"

He answered her with an outpouring of a language she did not know. The servant scrambled to some device on the wall; in a moment Culhane stood before her.

"You said you didn't want to see me, Your Grace. But I was closest to answer Kiti's summons. . . ."

Anne looked at him. It seemed to her that she looked clear through him, to all that he was: desire, and pride of his pitiful strange learning, and smugness of his holy mission that had brought her life to wreck. Hers, and perhaps Elizabeth's as well. She saw Culhane's conviction, shared by Lord Director Brill and even by such as Lady Mary, that what they did was right because they did it. She knew that look well: it had been Cardinal Wolsey's, Henry's right-hand man and Chancellor of England, the man who had advised Henry to separate Anne from Harry Percy. And advised Henry against marrying her. Until she, Anne Boleyn, upstart Tom Boleyn's powerless daughter, had turned Henry against Wolsey and had the cardinal brought to trial. *She.*

In that minute, she made her decision.

"I was wrong, Master Culhane. I spoke in anger. Forgive me." She smiled, and held out her hand, and she had the satisfaction of watching Culhane turn color.

How old was he? Not in his first youth. But neither had Henry been.

He said, "Of course, Your Grace. Kiti said you talked to the tsarevich."

She made a face, still smiling at him. She had often mocked Henry thus. Even Harry Percy, so long ago, a lifetime ago . . . No. Two lifetimes ago. "The what?"

"The tsarevich." He indicated the child.

Was the dye on his face permanent, or would it wash off?

She said, not asking, "He is another time hostage. He, too, in his small person, prevents a war."

Culhane nodded, clearly unsure of her mood. Anne looked wonderingly at the child, then winningly at Culhane. "I would have you tell me about him. What language does he speak? Who is he?"

"Russian. He is—was—the future emperor. He suffers from a terrible disease: you called it the bleeding sickness. Because his mother the empress was so driven with worry over him, she fell under the influence of a holy man who led her to make some disastrous decisions while she was acting for her husband the emperor, who was away at war."

Anne said, "And the bad decisions brought about another war."

"They made more bloody than necessary a major rebellion."

"You prevent rebellions as well as wars? Rebellions against a monarchy?"

"Yes, it—history did not go in the direction of monarchies."

That made little sense. How could history go other than in the direction of those who were divinely anointed, those who held the power? Royalty won. In the end, they always won.

But there could be many casualties before the end.

She said, with that combination of liquid dark gaze and aloof body that had so intrigued Henry—and Norris, and Wyatt, and even presumptuous Mark Smeaton, God damn his soul—"I find I wish to know more about this child and his country's history. Will you tell me?"

"Yes," Culhane said. She caught the nature of his smile: relieved, still uncertain how far he had been forgiven, eager to find out. Familiar, all so familiar.

She was careful not to let her body touch his as they passed through the doorway. But she went first, so he would catch the smell of her hair.

"Master Culhane—you are listed on the demon machine as 'M. Culhane.' "

"The . . . oh, the computer. I didn't know you ever looked at one."

"I did. Through a window."

"It's not a demon, Your Grace."

She let the words pass; what did she care what it was? But his tone told her something. He liked reassuring her. In this world where women did the same work as men and female bodies were to be seen uncovered in the exercise yard so often that even turning your head to look must become a bore, this oaf nonetheless liked reassuring her.

She said, "What does the *M* mean?"

He smiled. "Michael. Why?"

As the door closed, the captive royal child began once more to wail.

Anne smiled, too. "An idle fancy. I wondered if it stood for Mark."

"What argument has the Church filed with the All-World Forum?" a senior researcher asked.

Brill said irritably, as if it were an answer, "Where is Mahjoub?"

Lambert spoke up promptly. "He is with Helen of Troy, Director, and the doctor. The queen had another seizure last night." Enzio Mahjoub was the unfortunate Project Head for their last time rescue.

Brill ran his hand over the back of his neck. His skull needed shaving, and his cheek dye was sloppily applied. He said, "Then we will begin without Mahjoub. The argument of Her Holiness is that the primary function of this Institute is no longer pure time research, but practical application, and that the primary practical application is time rescue. As such, we exist to take hostages, and thus should come under direct control of the Church of the Holy Hostage. Her secondary argument is that the time hostages are not receiving treatment up to intersystem standards as specified by the All-World Accord of 2154."

Lambert's eyes darted around the room. Cassia Kohambu, Project Head for the Institute's greatest success, sat up straight, looking outraged. "Our hostages aren't—on what are these charges allegedly based?"

Brill said, "No formal charges as yet. Instead, she has requested an investigation. She claims we have hundreds of potential hostages pinpointed by the Rahvoli equations, and the ones we have chosen do not meet standards for either internal psychic stability or benefit accrued to the hostages themselves, as specified in the All-World Accord. We have chosen to please ourselves, with flagrant disregard for the welfare of the hostages."

"Flagrant disregard!" It was Culhane, already on his feet. Beneath the face dye his cheeks flamed. Lambert eyed him carefully. "How can Her Holiness charge flagrant disregard when without us the Tsarevich Alexis would have been in constant pain from hemophiliac episodes, Queen Helen would have been abducted and raped, Herr Hitler blown up in an underground bunker, and Queen Anne Boleyn beheaded!"

Brill said bluntly, "Because the tsarevich cries constantly for his mother, the Lady Helen is mad, and Mistress Boleyn tells the Church she has been made war upon!"

Well, Lambert thought, that still left Herr Hitler. She was just as appalled as anyone at Her Holiness's charges, but Culhane had clearly violated both good manners and good sense. Brill never appreciated being upstaged.

Brill continued, "An investigative committee from the All-World Forum will arrive here next month. It will be small: Delegates Soshiru, Vlakhav, and Tullio. In three days the Institute staff will meet again at 0700, and by that time I want each project group to have prepared an argument in favor of the hostage you hold. Use the prepermit justifications, including all the mathematical models, but go far beyond that in documenting benefits to the hostages themselves since they arrived here. Are there any questions?"

Only one, Lambert thought. She stood. "Director—were the three delegates who will investigate us chosen by the All-World Forum or requested by Her Holiness? To whom do they already owe their allegiance?"

Brill looked annoyed. He said austerely, "I think we can rely upon the All-World delegates to file a fair report, Intern Lambert," and Lambert lowered her eyes. Evidently she still had much to learn. The question should not have been asked aloud.

Would Mistress Boleyn have known that?

Anne took the hand of the little boy. "Come, Alexis," she said. "We walk now."

The prince looked up at her. How handsome he was, with his thick curling hair and beautiful eyes almost as dark as her own. If she had given Henry such a child . . . She pushed the thought away. She spoke to Alexis in her rudimentary Russian, without using the translator box hung like a peculiarly ugly pendant around her neck. He answered with a stream of words she couldn't follow, and she waited for the box to translate.

"Why should we walk? I like it here in the garden."

"The garden is very beautiful," Anne agreed. "But I have something interesting to show you."

Alexis trotted beside her obediently then. It had not been hard to win his trust—had no one here ever passed time with children? Wash off the scary cheek paint, play for him songs on the lute—an instrument he could understand, not like the terrifying sounds coming without musicians from yet another box—learn a few phrases of his language. She had always been good at languages.

Anne led the child through the far gate of the walled garden, into the yard. Machinery hummed; naked men and women "exercised" together on the grass. Alexis watched them curiously, but Anne ignored them. Servants. Her long full skirts, tawny silk, trailed on the ground.

At the far end of the yard, she started down the short path to that other gate, the one that ended at nothing.

Queen Isabella of Spain, Henry had told Anne once, had sent an expedition of sailors to circumnavigate the globe. They were supposed to find a faster way to India. They had not done so, but neither had they fallen off the edge of the world, which many had prophesied for them. Anne had not shown much interest in the story, because Isabella had after all been Catherine's mother. The edge of the world.

The gate ended with a wall of nothing. Nothing to see, or smell, or taste—Anne had tried. To the touch the wall was solid enough, and faintly tingly. A "force field," Culhane said. Out of time as we experience it; out of space. The gate, one of three, led to a place called Upper Slib, in what had once been Egypt.

Anne lifted Alexis. He was heavier than even a month ago; since she had been attending him every day, he had begun to eat better, play more, cease crying for his mother. Except at night. "Look, Alexis, a gate. Touch it."

The little boy did, then drew back his hand at the tingling. Anne laughed, and after a moment Alexis laughed, too.

The alarms sounded.

"Why, Your Grace?" Culhane said. "Why *again*?"

"I wished to see if the gate was unlocked," Anne said coolly. "We both wished to see." This was a lie. She knew it—did he? Not yet, perhaps.

"I told you, Your Grace, it is not a gate that can be left locked or unlocked, as you understand the terms. It must be activated by the stasis square."

"Then do so; the prince and I wish for an outing."

Culhane's eyes darkened; each time, he was in more anguish. And each time, he came running. However much he might wish to avoid her, commanding his henchmen to talk to her most of the time, he must come when there was an emergency because he was her gaoler, appointed by Lord Brill. So much had Anne discovered in a month of careful trials. He said now, "I told you, Your Grace, you can't move past the force field, no more than I could move into your palace at Greenwich. In the time stream beyond that gate—*my* time stream—you don't exist. The second you crossed the force field you'd disintegrate into nothingness."

Nothingness again. To Alexis she said sadly in Russian, "He will never let us out. Never, never."

The child began to cry. Anne held him closer, looking reproachfully at Culhane, who was shifting toward anger. She caught him just before the shift was complete, befuddling him with unlooked-for wistfulness: "It is just that there is so little we can do here, in this time where we do not belong. You can understand that, can you not, Master Culhane? Would it not be the same for you, in my Court of England?"

Emotions warred on his face. Anne put her free hand gently on his arm. He looked down: the long slim fingers with their delicate tendons, the tawny silk against his drab uniform. He choked out, "Anything in my power, anything within the rules, Your Grace . . ."

She had not yet gotten him to blurt out "Anne," as he had the day she'd thrown a candlestick after him at the door.

She removed her hand, shifted the sobbing child against her neck, spoke so softly he could not hear her.

He leaned forward, toward her. "What did you say, Your Grace?"

"Would you come again tonight to accompany my lute on your guitar? For Alexis and me?"

Culhane stepped back. His eyes looked trapped.

"Please, Master Culhane?"

Culhane nodded.

Lambert stared at the monitor. It showed the hospital suite, barred windows and low white pallets, where Helen of Troy was housed. The queen sat quiescent on the floor, as she usually did, except for the brief and terrifying periods when she erupted, shrieking and tearing at her incredible hair. There had never been a single coherent word in the eruptions, not since the first moment Helen had awoken as hostage and had been told where she was, and why. Since that day Queen Helen had never responded in the slightest to anything said to her. Or maybe that fragile mind, already quivering under the strain of her affair with Paris, had snapped too completely to even hear them. Helen, Lambert thought, was no Anne Boleyn.

Anne sat close to the mad Greek queen, her silk skirts overlapping Helen's white tunic, her slender body leaning so far forward that her hair, too, mingled with Helen's, straight black waterfall with masses of springing black curls. Before she could stop herself, Lambert had run her hand over her own shaved head.

What was Mistress Anne trying to say to Helen? The words were too low for the microphones to pick up, and the double curtain of hair hid Anne's lips. Yet Lambert was as certain as death that Anne was talking. And Helen, quiescent—was she nonetheless hearing? What could it matter if she *were*, words in a tongue that from her point of view would not exist for another two millennia?

Yet the Boleyn woman visited her every day, right after she left the tsarevich. How good was Anne, from a time almost as barbaric as Helen's own, at nonverbal coercion of the crazed?

Culhane entered, glanced at the monitor, and winced.

Lambert said levelly, "You're a fool, Culhane."

He didn't answer.

"You go whenever she summons. You—"

He suddenly strode across the room, two strides at a time. Grabbing Lambert, he pulled her from her chair and yanked her to her feet. For an astonished moment she thought he was actually going to hit her—two researchers *hitting* each other. She tensed to slug him back. But abruptly he dropped her, giving a little shove so that she tumbled gracelessly back into her chair.

"You feel like a fat stone."

Lambert stared at him. Indifferently, he activated his own console and began work. Something rose in her, so cold the vertebrae of her back felt fused in ice. Stiffly she rose from the chair, left the room, and walked along the corridor.

A *fat stone*. Heavy, stolid yet doughy, the flesh yielding like a slug, or a maggot. Bulky, without grace, without beauty, almost without individuality, as stones were all alike. A fat stone.

Anne Boleyn was just leaving Helen's chamber. In the corridor, back to the monitor, Lambert faced her. Her voice was low, like a subterranean growl. "Leave him alone."

Anne looked at her coolly. She did not ask whom Lambert meant.

"Don't you know you are watched every minute? That you can't so much as use your chamber pot without being taped? How do you ever expect to get him to your bed? Or to do anything with poor Helen?"

Anne's eyes widened. She said loudly, "Even when I use the chamber pot? Watched? Have I not even the privacy of the beasts in the field?"

Lambert clenched her fists. Anne was acting. Someone had already told her, or she had guessed, about the surveillance. Lambert could *see* that she was acting—but not *why*.

A part of her mind noted coolly that she had never wanted to kill anyone before. So this, finally, was what it felt like, all those emotions she had researched throughout time: fury and jealousy and the desire to destroy. The emotions that started wars.

Anne cried, even more loudly, "I had been better had you never told me!" and rushed toward her own apartments.

Lambert walked slowly back to her work area, a fat stone.

Anne lay on the grass between the two massive power generators. It was a poor excuse for grass; although green enough, it had no smell. No dew formed on it, not even at night. Culhane had explained that it was bred to withstand disease, and that no dew formed because the air had little moisture. He explained, too, that the night was as man-bred as the grass; there was no natural night here. Henry would have been highly interested in such things; she was not. But she listened carefully, as she listened to everything Michael said.

She lay completely still, waiting. Eventually the head of a researcher thrust around the corner of the towering machinery: a purposeful thrust. "Your Grace? What are you doing?"

Anne did not answer. Getting to her feet, she walked back toward the castle. The place between the generators was no good: the woman had already known where Anne was.

The three delegates from the All-World Forum arrived at the Time Research Institute looking apprehensive. Lambert could understand this; for those who had never left their own time-space continuum, it probably seemed significant to step through a force field to a place that did not exist in any accepted sense of the word. The delegates looked at the ground, and inspected the facilities, and asked the same kinds of questions visitors always asked, before they settled down to actually investigate anything.

They were given an hour's overview of the time-rescue program, presented by the director himself. Lambert, who had not helped write this, listened to the careful sentiments about the prevention of war, the nobility of hostages, the deep understanding the Time Research

Institute held of the All-World Accord of 2154, the altruistic extension of the Holy Mission of Peace into other time streams. Brill then moved on to discuss the four time-hostages, dwelling heavily on the first. In the four years since Herr Hitler had become a hostage, the National Socialist Party had all but collapsed in Germany. President Paul von Hindenburg had died on schedule, and the new moderate chancellors were slowly bringing order to Germany. The economy was still very bad and unrest was widespread, but no one was arresting Jews or gypsies or homosexuals or Jehovah's Witnesses or . . . Lambert stopped listening. The delegates knew all this. The entire solar system knew all this. Hitler had been a tremendous popular success as a hostage, the reason the Institute had obtained permits for the next three. Herr Hitler was kept in his locked suite, where he spent his time reading power-fantasy novels whose authors had not been born when the bunker under Berlin was detonated.

"Very impressive, Director," Goro Soshiru said. He was small, thin, elongated, a typical free-fall Spacer, with a sharp mind and a reputation for incorruptibility. "May we now talk to the hostages, one at a time?"

"Without any monitors. That is our instruction," said Anna Vlakhav. She was the senior member of the investigative team, a sleek, gray Chinese who refused all augments. Her left hand, Lambert noticed, trembled constantly. She belonged to the All-World Forum's Inner Council and had once been a hostage herself for three years.

"Please," Soren Tullio smiled. He was young, handsome, very wealthy. Disposable, added by the Forum to fill out the committee, with few recorded views of his own. Insomuch as they existed, however, they were not tinged with any bias toward the Church. Her Holiness had not succeeded in naming the members of the investigative committee—if indeed she had tried.

"Certainly," Brill said. "We've set aside the private conference room for your use. As specified by the Church, it is a sanctuary: there are no monitors of any kind. I would recommend, however, that you allow the bodyguard to remain with Herr Hitler, although of course you will make up your own minds."

Delegate Vlakhav said, "The bodyguard may stay. Herr Hitler is not our concern here."

Surprise, Lambert thought. Guess who *is*?

The delegates kept Hitler only ten minutes, the catatonic Helen only three. They said the queen did not speak. They talked to the little tsarevich a half hour. They kept Anne Boleyn in the sanctuary/conference room four hours and twenty-three minutes.

She came out calm, blank-faced, and proceeded to her own

apartments. Behind her the three delegates were tight-lipped and silent. Anna Vlakhav, the former hostage, said to Toshio Brill, "We have no comment at this time. You will be informed."

Brill's eyes narrowed. He said nothing.

The next day, Director Toshio Brill was subpoenaed to appear before the All-World Forum on the gravest of all charges: mistreating Holy Hostages detained to keep Peace. The tribunal would consist of the full Inner Council of the All-World Forum. Since Director Brill had the right to confront those who accused him, the investigation would be held at the Time Research Institute.

How, Lambert wondered? They would not take her unsupported word. How had the woman done it?

She said to Culhane, "The delegates evidently make no distinction between political hostages on our own world and time hostages snatched from shadowy parallel ones."

"Why should they?" coldly said Culhane. The idealist. And where had it brought him?

Lambert was assigned that night to monitor the tsarevich, who was asleep in his crib. She sat in her office, her screen turned to Anne Boleyn's chambers, watching her play on the lute and sing softly to herself the songs written for her by Henry VIII when his passion was new and fresh, six hundred years before.

Anne sat embroidering a sleeve cover of cinnamon velvet. In strands of black silk she worked intertwined *H* and *A:* Henry and Anne. Let their spying machines make of that what they would.

The door opened, and without permission, Culhane entered. He stood by her chair and looked down into her face. "Why, Anne? Why?"

She laughed. He had finally called her by her Christian name. Now, when it could not possibly matter.

When he saw that she would not answer, his manner grew formal. "A lawyer has been assigned to you. He arrives tomorrow."

A lawyer. Thomas Cromwell had been a lawyer, and Sir Thomas More. Dead, both of them, at Henry's hand. So had Master Culhane told her, and yet he still believed that protection was afforded by the law.

"The lawyer will review all the monitor records. What you did, what you said, every minute."

She smiled at him mockingly. "Why tell me this now?"

"It is your right to know."

"And you are concerned with rights. Almost as much as with death."

She knotted the end of her thread and cut it. "How is it that you command so many machines and yet do not command the knowledge that every man must die?"

"We know that," Culhane said evenly. His desire for her had at last been killed; she could feel its absence, like an empty well. The use of her name had been but the last drop of living water. "But we try to prevent death when we can."

"Ah, but you *can't*. 'Prevent death'—as if it were a fever! You can only postpone it, Master Culhane, and you never even ask if that is worth doing."

"I only came to tell you about the lawyer," Culhane said stiffly. "Good night, Mistress Boleyn."

"Good night, Michael," she said, and started to laugh. She was still laughing when the door closed behind him.

The Hall of Time, designed to hold three hundred, was packed.

Lambert remembered the day she had given the Orientation lecture to the history candidates, among them what's-his-name of the violet eyes. Twenty young people huddled together against horror in the middle of squares, virtual and simulated, but not really present. Today the squares were absent and the middle of the floor was empty, while all four sides were lined ten-deep with All-World Inner Council members on high polished benches, archbishops and lamas and shamans of the Church of the Holy Hostage, and reporters from every major newsgrid in the solar system. Her Holiness the High Priest sat among her followers, pretending she wanted to be inconspicuous. Toshio Brill sat in a chair alone, facing the current Premier of the All-World Council, Dagar Krenya of Mars.

Anne Boleyn was led to a seat. She walked with her head high, her long black skirts sweeping the floor.

Lambert remembered that Anne had worn black to her trial for treason, in 1536.

"This investigation will begin," Premier Krenya said. He wore his hair to his shoulders; fashions must have changed again on Mars. Lambert looked at the shaved heads of her colleagues, at the long loose black hair of Anne Boleyn. To Culhane, seated beside her, she whispered, "We'll be growing our hair again soon." He looked at her as if she were crazy.

It *was* a kind of crazy, to live everything twice: once in research, once in the flesh. Did it seem so to Anne Boleyn? Lambert knew her frivolity was misplaced, and she thought of the frivolity of Anne in the

Tower, awaiting execution: "They will have no trouble finding a name for me. I shall be Queen Anne Lackhead." At the memory, Lambert's hatred burst out fresh. She had the memory, and now Anne never would. But in bequeathing it forward in time to Lambert, the memory had become secondhand. That was Anne Boleyn's real crime, for which she would never be tried: She had made this whole proceeding, so important to Lambert and Brill and Culhane, a mere reenactment. Prescripted. Secondhand. She had robbed them of their own, unused time.

Krenya said, "The charges are as follows: That the Time Research Institute has mistreated the Holy Hostage Anne Boleyn, held hostage against war. Three counts of mistreatment are under consideration this day: First, that researchers willfully increased a hostage's mental anguish by dwelling on the pain of those left behind by the hostage's confinement, and on those aspects of confinement that cause emotional unease. Second, that researchers failed to choose a hostage that would truly prevent war. Third, that researchers willfully used a hostage for sexual gratification."

Lambert felt herself go very still. Beside her, Culhane rose to his feet, then sat down again slowly, his face rigid. Was it possible he had . . . no. He had been infatuated, but not to the extent of throwing away his career. He was not Henry, any more than she had been over *him*.

The spectators buzzed, an uneven sound like malfunctioning equipment. Krenya rapped for order. "Director Brill—how do you answer these charges?"

"False, Premier. Every one."

"Then let us hear the evidence against the Institute."

Anne Boleyn was called. She took the chair in which Brill had been sitting. *"She made an entry as though she were going to a great triumph and sat down with elegance"* . . . but that was the other time, the *first* time. Lambert groped for Culhane's hand. It felt limp.

"Mistress Boleyn," Krenya said—he had evidently not been told that she insisted on being addressed as a queen, and the omission gave Lambert a mean pleasure—"in what ways was your anguish willfully increased by researchers at this Institute?"

Anne held out her hand. To Lambert's astonishment, her lawyer put into it a lute. At an official All-World Forum investigation—a *lute*. Anne began to play, the tune high and plaintive. Her unbound black hair fell forward; her slight body made a poignant contrast to the torment in the words:

Defiled is my name, full sore,
Through cruel spite and false report,
That I may say forever more,
Farewell to joy, adieu comfort.

O death, rock me asleep,
Bring on my quiet rest,
Let pass my very guiltless ghost
Out of my careful breast.

Ring out the doleful knell,
Let its sound my death tell,
For I must die,
There is no remedy,
For now I die!

The last notes faded. Anne looked directly at Krenya. "I wrote that, my Lords, in my other life. Master Culhane of this place played it for me, along with death songs written by my . . . my brother. . . ."

"Mistress Boleyn . . ."

"No, I recover myself. George's death tune was hard for me to hear, my Lords. Accused and condemned because of *me*, who always loved him well."

Krenya said to the lawyer whose staff had spent a month reviewing every moment of monitor records, "Culhane made her listen to these?"

"Yes," the lawyer said. Beside Lambert, Culhane sat unmoving.

"Go on," Krenya said to Anne.

"He told me that I was made to suffer watching the men accused with me die. How I was led to a window overlooking the block, how my brother George knelt, putting his head on the block, how the ax was raised—" She stopped, shuddering. A murmur ran over the room. It sounded like cruelty, Lambert thought—but *whose*?

"Worst of all, my Lords," Anne said, "was that I was told I had bastardized my own child. I chose to sign a paper declaring no valid marriage had ever existed because I had been precontracted to Sir Henry Percy, so my daughter Elizabeth was illegitimate and thus barred from her throne. I was taunted with the fact that I had done this, ruining the prospects of my own child. He said it over and over, Master Culhane did. . . ."

Krenya said to the lawyer, "Is this in the visuals?"

"Yes."

Krenya turned back to Anne. "But, Mistress Boleyn—these are

things that, because of your time rescue, did *not* happen. *Will* not happen, in your time stream. How can they thus increase your anguish for relatives left behind?"

Anne stood. She took one step forward, then stopped. Her voice was low and passionate. "My good Lord—do you not understand? It is because you took me here that these things did not happen. Left to my own time, I *would have been responsible for them all.* For my brother's death, for the other four brave men, for my daughter's bastardization, for the torment in my own music . . . I have escaped them only because of *you.* To tell me them in such detail, not the mere provision of facts that I myself requested but agonizing detail of mind and heart—is to tell me that *I* alone, in my own character, am evil, giving pain to those I love most. And that in this time stream you have brought me to, I *did* these things, felt them, feel them still. You have made me guilty of them. My Lord Premier, have you ever been a hostage yourself? Do you know, or can you imagine, the torment that comes from imagining the grief of those who love you? And to know you have *caused* this grief, not merely loss but death, blood, the pain of disinheritance—that you have caused it, and are now being told of the anguish you cause? Told over and over? In words, in song even—can you imagine what that feels like to one such as I, who cannot return at will and comfort those hurt by my actions?"

The room was silent. Who, Lambert wondered, had told Anne Boleyn that Premier Krenya had once served as Holy Hostage?

"Forgive me, my Lords," Anne said dully, "I forget myself."

"Your testimony may take whatever form you choose," Krenya said, and it seemed to Lambert that there were shades and depths in his voice.

The questioning continued. A researcher, said Anne, had taunted her with being spied on even at her chamber pot—Lambert leaned slowly forward—which had made Anne cry out, "I had been better had you never told me!" Since then, modesty had made her reluctant to even answer nature, "so that there is every hour a most wretched twisting and churning in my bowels."

Asked why she thought the Institute had chosen the wrong hostage, Anne said she had been told so by my Lord Brill. The room exploded into sound, and Krenya rapped for quiet. "That visual now, please." On a square created in the center of the room, the visuals replayed on three sides:

"My Lord Brill . . . Was there no other person you could take but I to prevent this war you say is a hundred years off? This civil war in England?"

"The mathematics identified you as the best hostage, Your Grace."

"The best? Best for what, my Lord? If you had taken Henry himself, then he could not have issued the Act of Supremacy. His supposed death would have served the purpose as well as mine."

"Yes. But for Henry VIII to disappear from history while his heir is but a month old . . . We did not know if that might not have started a civil war in itself. Between the factions supporting Elizabeth and those for Queen Catherine, who was still alive."

"What did your mathematical learning tell you?"

"That it probably would not," Brill said.

"And yet choosing me instead of Henry left him free to behead yet another wife, as you yourself have told me, my cousin Catherine Howard!"

Brill shifted on his chair. "That is true, Your Grace."

"Then why not Henry instead of me?"

"I'm afraid Your Grace does not have sufficient grasp of the science of probabilities for me to explain, Your Grace."

Anne was silent. Finally she said, "I think that the probability is that you would find it easier to deal with a deposed woman than with Henry of England, whom no man can withstand in either a passion or a temper."

Brill did not answer. The visual rolled—ten seconds, fifteen—and he did not answer.

"Mr. Premier," Brill said in a choked voice, "Mr. Premier —"

"You will have time to address these issues soon, Mr. Director," Krenya said. "Mistress Boleyn, this third charge—sexual abuse—"

The term had not existed in the sixteenth century, thought Lambert. Yet Anne understood it. She said, "I was frightened, my Lord, by the strangeness of this place. I was afraid for my life. I didn't know then that a woman may refuse those in power, may—"

"That is why sexual contact with hostages is universally forbidden," Krenya said. "Tell us what you think happened."

Not what did happen—what you *think* happened. Lambert took heart.

Anne said, "Master Culhane bade me meet him at a place . . . it is a small alcove beside a short flight of stairs near the kitchens. . . . He bade me meet him there at night. Frightened, I went."

"Visuals," Krenya said in a tight voice.

The virtual square reappeared. Anne, in the same white nightdress in which she had been taken hostage, crept from her chamber, along the corridor, her body heat registering in infrared. Down the stairs, around to the kitchens, into the cubbyhole formed by the flight of steps, themselves oddly angled as if they had been added, or altered, after the main structure was built, after the monitoring system installed . . . Anne dropped to her knees and crept forward beside the isolated stairs. And disappeared.

Lambert gasped. A time hostage was under constant surveillance, that was a basic condition of their permit, there was no way the Boleyn bitch could escape constant monitoring. But she had.

"Master Culhane was already there," Anne said in a dull voice. "He . . . he used me ill there."

The room was awash with sound. Krenya said over it, "Mistress Boleyn—there is no visual evidence that Master Culhane was there. He has sworn he was not. Can you offer any proof that he met you there? Anything at all?"

"Yes. Two arguments, my Lord. First: How would I know there were not spying devices in but this one hidden alcove? I did not design this castle; it is not mine."

Krenya's face showed nothing. "And the other argument?"

"I am pregnant with Master Culhane's child."

Pandemonium. Krenya rapped for order. When it was finally restored, he said to Brill, "Did you know of this?"

"No, I . . . it is a hostage's right by the Accord to refuse intrusive medical treatment . . . she has been healthy. . . ."

"Mistress Boleyn, you will be examined by a doctor immediately."

She nodded assent. Watching her, Lambert knew it was true. Anne Boleyn was pregnant, and had defeated herself thereby. But she did not know it yet.

Lambert fingered the knowledge, seeing it as a tangible thing, cold as steel.

"How do we know," Krenya said, "that you were not pregnant before you were taken hostage?"

"It was but a month after my daughter Elizabeth's birth, and I had the white leg. Ask one of your doctors if a woman would bed a man then. Ask a woman expert in the women of my time. Ask Lady Mary Lambert."

Heads in the room turned; ask whom? Krenya said, "Ask whom?" An aide leaned toward him and whispered something. He said, "We will have her put on the witness list."

Anne said, "I carry Michael Culhane's child. I, who could not carry a prince for the king."

Krenya said, almost powerlessly, "That last has nothing to do with this investigation, Mistress Boleyn."

She only looked at him.

They called Brill to testify, and he threw up clouds of probability equations that did nothing to clarify the choice of Anne over Henry as Holy Hostage. Was the woman right? Had there been a staff meeting to choose between the candidates identified by the Rahvoli applications, and had someone said of two very close candidates, "We should think about the effect on the Institute as well as on history. . . ." Had someone been developing a master theory based on a percentage of women influencing history? Had someone had an infatuation with the period, and chosen by that what should be altered? Lambert would never know. She was an intern.

Had been an intern.

Culhane was called. He denied seducing Anne Boleyn. The songs on the lute, the descriptions of her brother's death, the bastardization of Elizabeth—all done to convince her that what she had been saved from was worse than where she had been saved to. Culhane felt so much that he made a poor witness, stumbling over his words, protesting too much.

Lambert was called. As neutrally as possible she said, "Yes, Mr. Premier, historical accounts show that Queen Anne was taken with white leg after Elizabeth's birth. It is a childbed illness. The legs swell up and ache painfully. It can last from a few weeks to months. We don't know how long it lasted—would have lasted—for Mistress Boleyn."

"And would a woman with this disease be inclined to sexual activity?"

" 'Inclined'—no."

"Thank you, Researcher Lambert."

Lambert returned to her seat. The committee next looked at visuals, hours of visuals—Culhane, flushed and tender, making a fool of himself with Anne. Anne with the little tsarevich, an exile trying to comfort a child torn from his mother. Helen of Troy, mad and pathetic. Brill, telling newsgrids around the solar system that the time-rescue program, savior of countless lives, was run strictly in conformance with the All-World Accord of 2154. And all the time, through all the visuals, Lambert waited for what was known to everyone in that room except Anne Boleyn: that she could not pull off in this century what she might have in Henry's. That the paternity of a child could be genotyped in the womb.

Who? Mark Smeaton, after all? Another miscarriage from Henry, precipitately gotten and unrecorded by history? Thomas Wyatt, her most faithful cousin and cavalier?

After the committee had satisfied itself that it had heard enough, everyone but Forum delegates was dismissed. Anne, Lambert saw, was led away by a doctor. Lambert smiled to herself. It was already over. The Boleyn was defeated.

The All-World Forum investigative committee deliberated for less than a day. Then it issued a statement: The child carried by Holy Hostage Anne Boleyn had not been sired by Researcher Michael Culhane. Its genotypes matched no one's at the Time Research Institute. The Institute, however, was guilty of two counts of hostage mistreatment. The Institute charter as an independent tax-exempt organization was revoked. Toshio Brill was released from his position, as were Project Head Michael Culhane and intern Mary Lambert. The Institute stewardship was reassigned to the Church of the Holy Hostage under the direct care of Her Holiness the High Priest.

Lambert slipped through the outside door to the walled garden. It was dusk. On a seat at the far end a figure sat, skirts spread wide, a darker shape against the dark wall. As Lambert approached, Anne looked up without surprise.

"Culhane's gone. I leave tomorrow. Neither of us will ever work in time research again."

Anne went on gazing upward. Those great dark eyes, that slim neck, so vulnerable . . . Lambert clasped her hands together hard.

"Why?" Lambert said. "Why do it all again? Last time use a king to bring down the power of the Church, this time use a Church to—before, at least you gained a crown. Why do it here, when you gain nothing?"

"You could have taken Henry. He deserved it; I did not."

"But we didn't take Henry!" Lambert shouted. "So why?"

Anne did not answer. She put out one hand to point behind her. Her sleeve fell away, and Lambert saw clearly the small sixth finger that had marked her as a witch. A tech came running across the half-lit garden. "Researcher Lambert—"

"What is it?"

"They want you inside. Everybody. The queen—the other one, Helen—she's killed herself."

The garden blurred, straightened. "How?"

"Stabbed with a silver sewing scissors hidden in her tunic. It was so quick, the researchers saw it on the monitor but couldn't get there in time."

"Tell them I'm coming."

Lambert looked at Anne Boleyn. "You did this."

Anne laughed. *This lady,* wrote the Tower constable, *hath much joy in death.* Anne said, "Lady Mary—every birth is a sentence of death. Your age has forgotten that."

"Helen didn't need to die yet. And the Time Research Institute didn't need to be dismantled—it *will* be dismantled. Completely. But somewhere, sometime, you *will* be punished for this. I'll see to that!"

"Punished, Lady Mary? And mayhap beheaded?"

Lambert looked at Anne: the magnificent black eyes, the sixth finger, the slim neck. Lambert said slowly, "You *want* your own death. As you had it before."

"What else did you leave me?" Anne Boleyn said. "Except the power to live the life that is mine?"

"You will never get it. We don't kill, here!"

Anne smiled. "Then how will you 'punish' me—'sometime, somehow'?"

Lambert didn't answer. She walked back across the walled garden, toward the looming walls gray in the dusk, toward the chamber where lay the other dead queen.

Immaculate

STORM CONSTANTINE

For Pat Cadigan

Donna can feel computers dreaming: they reach out and touch her mind, or so she says. In the dark of her room, as the white noise tide of day goes out, and the glowing sky rises, the machines begin to meditate, or so she says. It makes Reeb think of dogs twitching in their sleep, the tongues of slumbering cats licking at invisible bowls of milk; human signs.

"You always have to look for human signs in everything," says Donna. She's a star, she's a nobody. She sells things.

Reeb is a director, a creative of sufficient reputation to currently work for Say! Play!, a company specializing in leisure software. This is the man who configured the footage that sold the product that juiced the data-suit that excited the customer who paid the cash that went into the accounts of Say! Play! He would not dare to call himself an artist, although his previous campaigns have done much to increase the sales of Say! Play!; his mind is the company's, he can find no other. Donna is their hot package of the moment. In studio, she is a child, innocent and trusting. As a warming light image on your retina, a sound effect between your ears, a grind and stroke of vibro-fabric, she can be your unforbidden lover. Is there such a thing as the girl next door nowadays? Who lives next door, or next floor, another tuned-up commodity? Marketing-wise, Donna is perfection. How young is she: thirteen? Sixteen? Twenty? She also hears voices; there's a market for that, but is she the right product? She can hardly be termed normal. Once, she had a strange pain in her side and when the medics examined her, they found a tiny six-sided die in her liver. Donna was not surprised; she said the People had put it there. The People advise her often, although fortunately for everyone concerned they appear to have a fairly favorable view of her occupation. Neither does Donna punish herself. She has no conscience that Reeb can detect.

Today, she is pouting and blinking at the scanners, sighing softly in a provocative and exciting way. "Oh! Oh!" Reeb supervises laconically. Later, he will tinker with the footage and, combined with a graphics package, will produce some hard-core delight for the consumer. Donna doesn't have to be too explicit, not like it's the real thing. Reeb can shoot a few limb movements tomorrow, some dildonics the next day; the software overdubs stock effects. Donna puts her tiny hands on either side of her face and grimaces. It is not part of the script.

"What is it?" Reeb asks from the other side of the observation panel.

"Oh, they are speaking to me," Donna says, putting shaking fingers to her forehead, where the skin is almost translucent and has a damp sheen to it. Today, that suggestion of delicacy repulses Reeb; on other days, it has seemed attractive. She is a child, in mind if not in flesh. Reeb has a desire to tweak her smug piety with a burst of power; he can do that, but he doesn't.

"Who is speaking to you?" He adjusts one of the scan controls, still shooting.

She shrugs, hand flopping into her lap. "My People. They're gone now."

"What did they say?"

"Something about an elevator."

She's making this up; she has to be. "What?"

"I don't remember."

She can be convincing when she wants to be. That's why she's here in his studio. Dice and elevators, computers dreaming. Young lips wetted with the tip of a nervous tongue, wide eyes. Donna lives in another world.

If Donna has her aspects of freakishness, Reeb has his own, too. Nearly two years ago, he lost half of his body. The accident itself was freakish, like getting hit by lightning. Relaxing in his data-suit at home, living out a hi-res dream, the suit had suddenly turned on him like a swarm of deadly insects, cooking his right side to a frazzle, eating away at his groin and gut. The prostheticians had been delighted by him. (We can redesign this man, they had announced proudly, and proceeded to do so.) Medics could not rebuild his apartment or resurrect the other victim of the accident, his dog.

"You called it to you, that power," Donna once said. He hated her the day she said that, the very first time he worked with her. For a while, after his therapy had proved so successful, he'd been a reluctant media star himself. Donna had recognized him instantly. "Electricity is alive, too; it's what makes the machines dream," she told him. His prosthetics are more sensitive than his meat ever was, but there is still a seam, a sense of unreality, a sense that outsiders have moved into his body and might, one day, take over.

"The machines are alive," Donna says, casting a meaningful glance at Reeb's right side. He puts his hand on his leg; squeezes. It feels like flesh, but slightly rubbery; perhaps like some kind of tough mollusk. This is his first commission since he came out of therapy.

Donna has been one of the company's products for six months—one of Reeb's for three weeks. Her face is burned into a million consumers' dreams. She might have been a little crazy for years and kept it quiet, only now she wants to tell people about her Voices and Visions, her People. She has mentioned them in interviews. People have conjectured whether her peculiarities are the result of how she was conceived. Donna was one of the first of the homegrown "virgin births." This fact must be significant, surely? Some people are not only prepared to believe it, but desperate to do so. These people are a cult the media tagged The Immaculates. To Reeb, they are a sad group of crazies that grew up around the virgin birth kick, desperate underachievers trying to populate the steamed-up, fucked-up world with little messiahs. At the end of the twentieth century the Goddess of Love had tended to stride around with a scythe in her hand, more often than not, and the fear of fatal disease had not only launched the suddenly respectable software porn industry, but had also estranged many people from the desire for human contact. Through artificial insemination, women gave birth who had never known a man's touch, or indeed a woman's. At first, it was just the single women, then the gay women; later, the cult of the Immaculates grew up. Men can be Immaculate too. Reeb thinks the Immaculates should all be locked up, even though he knows the phenomenon is merely a reaction against the fear of death, the delustifying of sexuality. There's no need for that anymore, but the vein runs deep in human consensus. Too many died back then. The Immaculates were a fringe group wanting to turn it all into a religion. Mercifully, they had never progressed beyond a minority, but they still gushed warmly about Donna in their cult magazines. The company have kept an eye on the media and now wonder whether this is an angle of Donna worth exploiting. After all, if the rumors circulating on the networks are true, Donna is not unique. Many people, whatever their background, are stepping forward to talk about Voices and Visions. Donna, being public property, could very easily be turned into a spearhead for this movement. Her family is totally devoid of fevered religion-mongerers looking for a place to hang their beliefs, but she does have two mothers; hers was a conception of convenience rather than conviction. Alexis, the woman who carried her, is now her agent and manager. Alexis is probably the opposite of anyone's vision of a Madonna. It is doubtful whether her hands have ever met beneath her chin in prayer. She is an eternal teenager, lankily attractive with razor-cut hair and slept-in-look anti-fashion gear. That she could have spawned an angel like Donna is in itself, Reeb supposes, a kind of miracle. And, if your child really does look like an angel, and fulfills everybody's dreams, then you exploit it; in the best possible sense. Especially when your girlfriend is obsessed by graffiti art and the photographic medium; nobody's into anything less than 3-D nowadays, so somebody has to see to the family income. Alexis brings Donna over to the studio four days a week, for Reeb to record her. Reeb is also interviewing the girl about her Visions and Voices. Donna is pleased to comply, because she likes to talk. She is one of those pale, tiny people who sometimes become attractive under the right lighting, the right conditions of the mind. Sometimes Reeb likes her very much and is convinced she has a startling clear-sightedness. Sometimes, she irritates him and he thinks she's stupid. He used to feel the same way about his dog, when he had one.

Reeb went back to live with his mother after the accident. It was supposed to be a temporary arrangement—he's still paying rent on his own apartment—but somehow he doesn't have the will to move back home yet. He knows there couldn't be a smell of burning flesh there anymore, and the block domestics would have cleaned everything up, but . . . His mother's apartment is spacious, she's never there, she never bothers him. He likes the view, and it's nearer to the studio than his old place. Occasionally, he thinks about ending his lease with the property agency, although it seems a little ungrateful, seeing as they compensated him so heavily for the accident.

Sometimes, he goes over to Alexis and Meriel's for dinner; he has become friendly with them since working with Donna. "When are you going to let go of Mommy's apron strings?" Alexis says, smiling. They are worried about him. Meriel points a camera at him.

"And when are you going to strip for me?" she says.

He's not sure whether that's an offer or a request.

He goes to the studio early. Alexis and Donna are late today. The trains were down again. "Someone died, I expect," Alexis says when she finally arrives, scraping back her artfully ragged black hair. "Jumpers!

I hate 'em. Why do I have to be inconvenienced by their inadequacy? It's so selfish!" Her eyes skitter nervously away from Reeb's body as if she wonders whether she's touched on taboo. "I can't bear to be held up!" she says.

In the office, after her mother has left, Donna leans demurely against the desktop. Reeb cannot imagine her living with Alexis and Meriel; she is an anachronism, a time-child from years past. She wears a white dress, but that is part of her costume wardrobe. The primness exists in the fabric of the dress, but is it a part of Donna? Reeb doesn't know yet. Is she an example of her mothers' artistic experiments? He would not put it past them. They never talk about Donna to him, and neither is she ever present at the dim-lit, smoky evenings Reeb enjoys in their company. It is as if the women lock her away in a cupboard when she's not working. Once, he tried to talk to Alexis about Donna's problem. "She's imaginative," Alexis said. "That's all. She makes things up."

"She believes it," Reeb said.

Alexis rolled her eyes. "You think so?"

He hadn't meant the Voices and Visions; the problem, in his opinion, was that Donna had a reality all to herself. Her home, the studio, A to B, and anything in between, like other people, her parents, street bums, commuters, interviewers, even himself, seemed only to touch her awareness on a superficial level. Her only contact with the world outside her own was through performance. And in her room, what did she do in her room? Reeb cannot ask Alexis questions like that; she is clearly not maternal material. The procedure was all the rage back then, of course. New legislation meant women could claim it as a right. Perhaps all Alexis's friends were having children that way. A public statement about her chosen way of life, her chosen lover.

Over the past two weeks, Reeb has been studying the phenomenon that is Donna. There has to be a new angle on her as a product, something the company can use; that's his brief. Has she always heard the Voices, had these experiences, and not spoken about them, or are they a more recent phenomenon? Donna cannot remember. She wrinkles her nose, pulls a face. "One night Merry's laptop dreamed to me," she says, "but I don't remember when."

And what does a computer's dream look like?

She doesn't have the words to describe it; she has grown up that much. "I could think it to you," she says, "but that's all."

He would dismiss it as fantasy, if it wasn't for the die. The slap-marks which had appeared instantaneously on her arm one day could be explained away as being psychologically self-induced. At the time, when it happened, Donna had told him one of the People had got angry with her.

"So, what are you going to do with this material?" Alexis asks him, through the cloud of smoke she has just exhaled. He is over for dinner again, but only has Alexis's company because Meriel's been called out; a rare offer of work, she can't refuse. Reeb is surprised Alexis wants to discuss it now. Usually, she talks to him about himself.

"Donna is not unique," he says. "There are others like her, increasing all the time. They make a market. Understand?"

"A market for what?" Alexis swings her booted feet up on the table, kicking a plate out of the way.

"I'm supposed to be thinking that one up." He considers the next question before he speaks. "Aren't you worried about her?"

"She's quite happy," Alexis says. "She's always been happy. Completely alien to me, of course, but always happy. I think she gets on better with Merry." She pulls a face and offers him her joint.

Reeb shakes his head; some things are just too anachronistic.

"I tried to be specific about what kind of donor I wanted when she was conceived. I think they lied to me, don't you?" She grins. "Sometimes I wonder whether anything of mine went into her at all." If she feels wistful about that, she hides it.

"Where is Donna?" Reeb asks. "She's never around when I call."

"She's in her playroom. All the things she likes are in there."

Reeb thinks Donna is too old to have a playroom. She should be hanging out with kids her own age, learning to live. Is that discouraged? He can't believe so. Alexis and Merry wouldn't be that enthusiastic about Donna seeing guys, he thinks, but they would never force their lifestyle on someone else, not even if that someone was their daughter.

"What's she get up to in there, anyway?" Reeb asks, jerking his head in the direction of the closed door that is Donna's.

Alexis shrugs. "Who knows? She doesn't like us going in there, so we don't. We all respect each other's privacy."

Reeb frowns at the door. Hasn't Donna any friends at all?

"Donna will be okay," Alexis says. "Don't you worry about her; she's a survivor. Now, you"—she stabs a finger in his direction—"you, I worry about."

She hardly knows him; she hadn't met him before he began working with Donna. He ought to be annoyed at her interference, and would be, if he didn't enjoy it so much. Is that what he wants, motherly concern? Becka, his own mother, doesn't know how to deal with emotional crises; she organized his life and then left him to deal with the burned-out mess of his self-image and feelings. Perhaps that's why he hardly ever sees her. She isn't busy exactly; just busy avoiding him.

"I ought to find myself a place," he says.

"What's wrong with the one you've got?"

"It's my mother's. I cramp her style."

"I meant the one you pay for, stupid. Are you never going to go back there?"

He shrugs.

"What reason is there not to?" Alexis demands. "Your body probably performs now better than it ever did. . . ." She drops her eyes, actually blushes. "Oh, I'm sorry . . ."

More than an arm and leg had been burned away. But they can fix that. They can fix everything. He didn't believe it.

"It's okay," he says. "You're right. I just feel . . . I don't know. It's as if someone died in there."

"You had a dog, didn't you?"

"I didn't mean him. Someone else."

"Oh." Alexis shrugs awkwardly. "I think I understand that. It's terrible." She brightens and pours him another glass of wine. "Tell you what. We'll look for a new apartment for you this week, shall we? Somewhere near here, so we can keep an eye on you."

Reeb is glad he has met these women. He is happy to lean on them.

"Yeah. Fine."

"I heard you talking to Alexis last night," Donna says, when she arrives at Reeb's studio the following day.

"Oh?" Reeb tries to recall what he said, what Alexis might have said. But Donna isn't interested in what she might have heard about herself.

"You've *never* been back to your apartment?" she says, round-eyed.

Reeb is taken aback. He smiles, laughs unconvincingly. "Not yet."

"What are you afraid of?"

"Nothing. Just, well, bad memories." I lost half my life there, he thinks, half myself, perhaps more than half. A demon hive in the walls had swarmed into his data-suit and sucked away his juice. He feels the place is haunted, perhaps by himself.

"Your dog died there," Donna says.

"Yeah. Now, tell me what you've been experiencing since I last spoke with you."

Donna reaches out and puts a delicate hand on his arm, the right arm. "I want to experience your old apartment," she says.

"Why? What for?"

She smiles an adult smile. "The People want me to."

"And what do they want to do that for?" He smiles back at her, although he feels nervous. He is thinking about the place, his collection of old books, his wall paintings, the way the morning light comes into the main living space, the color of the floor. He sees himself standing in the kitchenette, mixing an old-style martini for a shadowy ghost sitting on the couch, out by the hearth. The whole apartment is lit by the flicker of holographic flames. He can hear a body shifting impatiently. The air is full of perfume. The owner of these shadows, these subtle noises, this perfume was, in Reeb's memory, nothing but a human template. Later, he re-created this person as Elna, creature of dreams, modified to his taste. Elna never had to go home, live its own life, but the dream had existed only in the artificial world of re-creation and had burned out along with his data-suit.

Donna's small, pale fingers dig into his artificial flesh. He winces a little, brought back to the present. "When are you going to confront this problem, Reeb?" she asks, in a voice very much like Meriel's. "Until you confront the dark things inside you, they make you helpless. They are your weaknesses." She stands up straight, arms folded, and, for a moment, she is a young woman wearing a child's dress. "Please, take me there."

He doesn't want to go, even though he's sure the place will be cleaned up. He doesn't want to see that place again and yet, paradoxically, he does. Some of his life is still there.

Donna seems to sense his indecision. She doesn't argue with him as Alexis would. She simply breathes some words at him. "Please, oh pleeeese, Reeb. I have to go there. I have to see. Let me help you. I can do that. Really I can. Take me there."

The door is familiar yet strange. He puts his lock-card in the slot and, as if he's never been away, the door opens. Donna steps past, steps inside. He stands on the threshold staring, his right side tingling, his heart beating quickly. He can't go in. He can't. It stinks too much. The smell comes out in a wave of sharp remembrance. Blinking, he watches as Donna goes to the far side of the living room and raises the blind, opens the window. The city comes inside; noise below. The only smell is of disuse, a kind of staleness harboring memories, but not reeking. The girl turns round, a silhouette against the light.

"I like it," she says.

The walls have been repainted in a creamy color. The sofa has been replaced, an inoffensive yet nondescript piece of furniture. Reeb would not have chosen it himself, but he can see Becka hurriedly and distastefully ordering it from the mail-order channel. As he looks at it, a memory resurfaces: frantic barking, teeth closing on the fabric of his suit, pulling desperately, the deadly current passed on. He looks away quickly. Everything else is just the same. His equipment, surprisingly, doesn't even look slightly damaged, although the data-suit has gone. Most of it was burned into him; the medics removed it along with his ruined flesh. Reeb feels sick, yet detached.

Donna crosses the room on light feet and puts her childlike hands on his arms. "You must come inside," she says.

"I don't think I . . ."

She pulls him over the threshold. "You think it's haunted here?" she says, breathlessly.

He doesn't answer. Now he's here, he might as well pack some of his stuff together. The kid can poke around if she wants to. He can see into the small bedroom, the disarray which was caused by his mother throwing things around, looking for the items he asked her to bring him. It isn't too bad for him here. He should have come before. He feels he's been trying to spray plastic skin over a rotten wound. He might as well face reality.

Donna stands in the middle of the room with her eyes closed, humming to herself. One hand is held out toward the far wall, against which the couch rests. Her face is frowning in concentration. Reeb shakes his head and goes into his bedroom. This is where the ghosts would lie, not back in the other room, or splayed out on the floor, but here, healthy and whole. He looks at himself in the smoky mirror behind the bed, pulls down the collar of his shirt, scrapes back his hair. It is impossible to see the join between what is human and what is not human. The two materials have meshed invisibly. He has been told by the medics that his synthetic cells are no less part of him than the cells he had before; if anything, the new ones are more efficient and durable. There is no reason why he shouldn't simply forget half of him is synthetic. He wishes he could. Turning away from the mirror, he opens a wall cupboard, but finds it difficult to summon any interest for his possessions inside. Perhaps he should throw everything away. Begin again.

"Reeb?" Donna is standing in the doorway. "You're still in the wires." She looks small, hugging herself. Her words make his spine crawl with unease. Why did he let her talk him into bringing her here? What was the point? There's nothing left for him here.

"Let's go, then."

She shakes her head. "No. You need that part of yourself. You need to connect with it again."

Alexis and Meriel should have done something about her a long time ago. Computers dreaming? She's out of her mind.

"Don't look at me like that," she says. "I know what you're thinking, but it's true. Part of you is in the wires here."

"We're going, Donna," he says. "Come on. Don't scare yourself."

"I'm not scared." She submits passively as he tries to lead her out of the apartment. Before they reach the door, she says, "You were in a dark red room, like a womb. The light was red. Someone was with you. They were very dark. Their hair felt like feathers under your hands. They were like a shellfish, like a cat, like a bird. The name was Elna."

Reeb drops the girl's arm as if it has burned him. A hi-res dream, a ghost's dream. How can she know the last thing that was playing in his mind before the swarm came down the line? Donna looks troubled. "I don't want to invade you," she says, "but I have to make you see I know what I'm talking about. I'm not mad."

"How do you know that?"

She shrugs. "It's in the walls, your leisure-station, the heating ducts. It's all there, and the People thought it all to me."

"What *are* the People, Donna?" He wonders whether they could actually be real. Has she been telling the truth?

Donna turns away from him. "Oh, the People are only parts of me, that's all. I call them People because I want it to be like a movie, or like having friends. I'm friends with all the parts of myself, and they speak to me. Some are smarter than others." She holds out her hands to him, as if she wants to touch him. "Your data-suit's been replaced, Reeb. It's in the drawer under the monitor. You can take back what you lost, if you want to."

"I can't take back the flesh," he says sharply.

"That is replaceable, it doesn't matter about that," Donna replies. "You've left stuff behind, though, that does matter. Feedback."

He feels awkward putting the suit on in front of Donna, he feels vulnerable. She is quite familiar with the equipment, which surprises him. "I have stuff like this in my room at home," she says.

Is that all? Reeb hadn't imagined her secret playthings would be anything as mundane as data-suits.

"There are two suits here," she says.

"There shouldn't be."

Donna pulls a face and shakes out the wired fabric. "But here it is. For me. I need it, so here it is." She smiles. "You see?"

It's only further compensation, Reeb thinks. Two suits left in the apartment to replace the one that fried him. Most people would never think of putting one of the damn things on again. If the suits are a gift from the property agency, it's in the worst taste.

"Ready?" says Donna. For a moment, Reeb wonders whether he is afraid. Not of being hurt again, but of Donna herself. There's something too eager about her. The hood goes over his eyes.

"Relax," Donna murmurs. "You're on your way."

He feels claustrophobic for a few seconds until Donna connects him. At first, it is all fuzzy; black-and-white static, noise-sight. He is hooked into nothing but the main power system. The program they are running is the daytime purr of appliances ticking over, the nowhere hiss of mindless, directionless, formless energy. This is crazy. The girl is crazy. There's nothing here. Nothing.

Then, out of nowhen, he is aware but dreaming, jacking into a tactile visualization. The light is red around him. His body throbs in anticipation and there are feathers beneath his hand. For the first time since the accident, he senses a feeling of desire, his body is waking up, but this is only a dream, isn't it? He is in a dark place, surrounded by a sense of breathing, perhaps his own. There is also a feeling of confinement. Reeb flexes his arms, his fingers, breathes in through his nose. He does not know where he is. "In the wires," says Donna, close by, yet far away. This is not real, Reeb thinks and attempts to extend his awareness. He feels the presence of Elna, his animal-human companion, but cannot see it. Part of him can sense the touch, but it is incomplete. There is no sound, no chirrup of welcome, no sensuous brush of fur. Red light pulses swiftly round him, and for an instant he is back fully in the old dream: that of feathers and sex, warmth and envelopment. He sees Elna's slanted slitted eyes, open mouth, small pointed teeth. The eyes blink in greeting, the velvety throat purrs. Then it has flashed past him, just a fragment, like an echo of a cry.

"Come to *me*," Donna says.

"Where are you?" Reeb gropes blindly, fighting vertigo, nausea. He has never experienced anything like this before. He is nowhere. What if he can't return? That is ridiculous. All he has to do is disconnect, press the stud in his arm, which in reality will end the program run. But there is no program. He's hooked into nothing.

"Here!" He blinks and Donna is standing beside him.

"How did you get in here?" he asks. A stupid question. Donna knows what she is doing. He is aware of that.

She holds out her hand. "Come to my room," she says. "My playroom. All my things are there, the things that I like."

Ahead of them is a plain white door. It could be any door, but Reeb knows it is the one that leads to Donna's playroom. As they approach it, it swings open and a strong light pours out.

"Here we are," Donna says, gripping Reeb's hand. "Home again."

The room is full of things. Things and people. Creatures like automatons, beautiful dolls. Puppets hang from the ceiling, which is a blue sky, the impossible blue of childhood memories. The puppets swing on invisible strings. They are objects of human desire: cars, gleaming household goods, jewelry, expensive consumables, silk and real leather, but at the same time they are effigies of people. There are no walls to this room, only a ceaseless rush of color and visual noise; scenes flashing by. Reeb sees dark forests, beaches, cityscapes, alien lands, the interiors of immense houses.

"Look," Donna says, pulling on his hand, pulling him out of a stunned stasis. "I have something of yours here, too."

They push their way through the dangling feet of the puppets and Reeb sees two yellow eyes glowing from the darkness of a forest. There is a throaty purr and a sinuous shape slinks toward him, dragging its landscape with it.

"Elna," he says. "You reconstructed her."

Donna shakes her head. "Oh no," she says. "No need to. I have the dreams of all the machines here, the computer dreams. I collect them. I bring them through."

Elna drops to its belly in front of them.

"Part of you," Donna says. "Take it back now."

Reeb has to fight to escape Donna's tight-fingered grip. His hand is damp. So real. It feels so real in here. He could almost believe she's somehow flipped them out of his apartment into her own surreal world. He never doubted it wasn't real for her. Is it possible to share a dream?

"Open the door." Donna's voice has become hard. She is holding the hand that Reeb wrenched himself away from to her breast, as if he has hurt her. "Open the door, and you'll find Merry and Alex getting stoned, as usual. You doubt me, don't you?" She smiles at him and walks toward the door, which is closed.

"Don't open it," he says. "Donna, get me out of here. It's too crazy. Take me back."

"You are back," she says. "Stupid. I let you into my world and you're too stupid to believe it."

He knows, if she opens the door, and he steps out into reality as she described it, he will go mad. If he walks out into Merry and Alex's apartment, the shock could kill him, because it wouldn't be possible. It isn't possible. Why even be afraid that might happen? Even if it did, it couldn't be true reality, but only further evidence of Donna's virtuosity in programming leisure software. She's always been on the wrong side of the camera, he realizes, but perhaps this is all too weird for public consumption, too detailed to be comfortable. Elna has curled a fingered paw around his ankle. Instinctively, he extends a hand to caress the feathered head. Elna has never felt so real to him before.

"Do I open the door or not?" Donna asks.

He shakes his head. "No, I believe you."

She relaxes, folds her arms. "Good. Now, fuck your animal-person. Do you mind if I watch?"

"Donna!"

"Oh, you're not shy are you? It's easy. I can do it, so can you. I only want to help you, Reeb. Take back what you lost. Be a man again."

"I'm not into this, Donna." He feels for the disconnect stud, the bump on his non-real arm that corresponds to the button on the datasuit, back in the apartment. He tries to concentrate on the fact that he never left there: this is just an illusion. No need to be worried.

"Don't bother doing that," Donna says. "It won't work. I brought you here, down the wires. To my playroom. I collect the dreams of machines here. I collected the dreams of your machines. Aren't you pleased? You thought Elna was dead, didn't you?"

Reeb puts his hands against his eyes, shakes his head. Donna makes a sound of distress and hurries toward him on her tiny feet. "Oh, I've scared you. I'm sorry. I was showing off. Silly. Like a kid. I'm not that, I don't want you to think I'm that. Look, the animal has gone. I made it go. But there's me. There's me!" She leans against him, a Reeb that is not real, that cannot be flesh and blood, a dream icon. He closes his eyes and she puts her arms around him. She feels warm and solid against his body.

"Whatever is given to you here can be taken back," she says, and kisses him. "I promise."

Child-woman, dream lover of a multitude of leisure sleepers, at home in her true medium; the non-real, the fantastic. There are no feathers beneath his hands.

Donna can feel computers dreaming, or so she says. She collects the dreams of machines, or so she thinks. The dreams of people are in the machines, a planet network of active imaginations hooked into their made-up, make-believe worlds. Artificial reality is taking over; it has its own children. Donna feels the dreams of people. There are others like her. She is not unique.

Farming in Virginia

REBECCA ORE

Su'ranchingal's scales stepped down the human sun wave frequencies. Heat. His brain sizzled until he hallucinated humans turning into *zr'as*. Already they had thin hornlike sheets on their toes and fingers as if nature, beginning at the extremities, was working scales over them. Two million years from now, they'd have scaled hands; then a million years later . . .

It's not just the heat, it's the *ti'if*, Su'ranchingal thought, the drug the ship machine used to sedate him and Hu'rekhi, the other ship specimen. The humans kept feeding it to him.

But Hu'rekhi had stopped, pulled the pills out of her throat sac with her double-pointed tongue. She drank isopropyl alcohol, the skin under her scales turgid from it. Hu'rekhi hated everyone. Being locked with Hu'rekhi in the research labs reminded Su'ranchingal of the way humans kept birds and fish in small arenas, no choice of mates, no escape from constant bickering. Being housed with Hu'rekhi in Virginia was more tolerable, more two birds who hated each other sharing a three-hundred-square-meter aviary.

Yesterday the human Culpepper told him they were going to send him and Hu'rekhi back to the descendants of the *zr'a*. But I'm so harmless and addicted, Su'ranchingal thought, and Hu'rekhi's a drunk. I grow the human's food. I'm useful. And the *zr'as* sent us away. Hu'rekhi thought that going back was more than stupid. She hated the *zr'as*.

Visions of glass hot-towers with another sun going through them, and *zr'as* walking always at a distance, through the tubes connecting the hot-towers, among the vats and sleeping ledges.

If I don't cool off, I'll die, Su'ranchingal realized. He checked to see if his human neighbors were watching, then frothed on his belly, tongue lashing out gobs of cooling saliva. His genitals felt heavier than usual. He touched a tingle into them. Then he leaned down and tasted the sour dirt he'd hoed, with the iron in it.

Su'ranchingal saw the tracks—cloven hooves: deer, huge herbivores—and wondered if the locals down at the store would tell him what cured gardens of deer.

C'yanginthu, w'yanamthi, th'yamgi—now just alien sounds—murmured through his head, meanings vaguely smeared between Spanyol and Amerish. Su'ranchingal hugged his toes, suddenly a child again, with another child, chilled, sleeping five years away, tended by a machine with speech cones murmuring Spanyol and Amerish at them both, warping and drugging their baby brains.

I'm still too hot, Su'ranchingal thought as he walked out toward the faucet with the coiled hose attached. He turned on the water and sprayed himself. Humans preferred that he did that rather than use his own froth. *Ohna'a,* the alien word rose in his mind, "rain on the grass."

He raised the scales over his belly and lungs while he played the hose against the blood-gorged skin. When he was almost dizzy, he thrilled a pitch too high for the humans. The neighbor's cat slouched across the garden to see if Su'ranchingal would feed it. Up in a hanging basket on the porch, Su'ranchingal kept a carton of cat snacks he suspected were addictive to cats. High-order sapients tended to addict their underlings with something.

"Mee-ow," the cat went in its funny little voice, meaning, *I like you, but don't tease,* according to the program Su'ranchingal had seen on the television. Not language, signal. Not sophont, but sapient.

"Would you eat a deer if it was finely minced?" Su'ranchingal asked the cat. He fed the cat a lump of the cat snack and rubbed its flesh over the skull behind the ears. "Is it legal to kill a deer for eating in your garden?"

The cat could eat a whole deer, frozen and thawed in chunks. His house had a freezer—it had been explained as though the house was capable of ownership, he thought at first. *The house has a freezer. I have a deer problem.*

Can Hu'rekhi and I have children?

The human scientists had been very interested in that. They told Su'ranchingal he was male genetically and Hu'rekhi female. Gave them pronouns, genders: he, she, male, female. Su'ranchingal had heard nothing about matings when young in the crèche.

Crèche was the word the humans gave it.

Have. Gave. Possessive mammals sparsely coated with almost invisible hair except on some arms and legs, male chests, and major joint inner surfaces. They smelled each other but weren't aware of doing it. Su'ranchingal wondered if he and Hu'rekhi did things to each other that they weren't aware of.

"Me-ow," went the cat again, breaking through his mind thoughts and images.

"Ah, cat," he said, giving it another morsel, "do people plan to send you back to your original home, too?"

He had to put on overalls before he went looking for Hu'rekhi, who was probably drinking too much again with human males. Hu'rehki . . . Thinking about Hu'rehki made him terribly anxious, suddenly.

The human intelligence agent Culpepper had always come to the store about three minutes after Su'ranchingal—that human tracked his every move. *A boring job for poor Culpepper,* Su'ranchingal decided as he fastened his overall suspenders and slipped on foot covers to keep them free of road tar, watching mismatched creatures from space. As he was walking by the old Morgan place, Su'ranchingal wondered why Culpepper and Josephine Vann, Hu'rekhi's watcher, didn't share the house with Hu'rekhi and him.

And Su'ranchingal was jealous of Hu'rekhi with the human men. *Jealous—possessive. I'm mentally humanized,* he thought as he walked down the hot asphalt and rock that keep brush from blocking people and cars. He wondered again why he and Hu'rekhi were sent here, why the humans wanted to send them back.

Vann was at the store instead of Culpepper when Su'ranchingal got there. She came up to him, eyes wobbling in their sockets, avoiding his own eyes as he bought a Dr Pepper.

Su'ranchingal said, "I thought you watched Hu'rekhi. Where's Culpepper?"

Her eye muscles went rigid. Finally eye to eye, she said, "Culpepper went to Washington to brief the new man."

Secretly thrilled that Vann finally gave him eye contact, Su'ranchingal asked, "New human watcher for me?"

"Yes," she said. "Culpepper asked to be taken off your case when the results on Hu'rekhi came in. He'd believed you."

"Culpepper told me yesterday you wanted to send Hu'rekhi and me into space."

"Where is Hu'rekhi?"

"Drinking isopropyl with your ethanol-drinking men. If I had not been a crèche baby, I think I would be lonelier." Hu'rekhi was strange company—and the local humans were aloof, with flabby eyelids that blinked so slowly you saw the flesh go up and down. Vann looked away now, eyes twisted back slightly to look at him again. Suddenly he missed the days when Hu'rekhi and he had landed into a midst of questioning, touching humans, patchy hair concealed under white clothes. Then they'd acted as though he were important, so he had thought so, too. But he knew now he'd just been novel.

"We will send you back," Vann said, "even if we never find Hu'rekhi."

"There is no back in space-time," Su'ranchingal said.

She sighed. "You're sure you don't know where Hu'rekhi is?"

"I haven't seen Hu'rekhi since you checked her blood and excretory crystals," Su'ranchingal told Vann.

"Her hormones changed. We think she's pregnant."

"We have no idea of how to raise our reproductions."

"Say children, it's less weird," Vann suggested.

Su'ranchingal thought *children* was for humans as *fawn* was for deer, but since he and Hu'rekhi had been treated as honorary humans, then *children* made sense. Up until yesterday, when Culpepper told him about the plans to return him to the *zr'as*, he thought he was an honorary human. "*Children, child* for young language users, then?"

Jo Vann said, "Better not to have *any* children. They'd be so isolated growing up. And any matings would be genetically dangerous."

"We'd have to reproduce heavily for fifty generations to threaten your biomass," Su'ranchingal said. He felt, in waves, alternately close to the humans and distant from them, as if alternating pulses of caffeine cleared the *ti'if* from his head, then washed more from his digestive web to his brains. He tried to pinpoint which pulse left him feeling close, the clearing one or the muzzy one. "We don't have enough genetic material. Within a few generations, we'd be clones of each other from inbreeding, as your cheetahs were before gene splicing." His back tongue flap twitched the *ng* toward a *zr'a* phoneme, but the woman's face went cold—if cold was a rigid adjective, as cold water went rigid itself into ice.

"Gene splicing?" Vann said.

Su'ranchingal realized he'd said too much about gene splicing and yet knew so little about it. "I don't remember giving Hu'rekhi genetic material."

"Maybe you fuck in your sleep?"

"And sleepwalk to the other side of the house? Pretty obscure sex," Su'ranchingal slurred, back flap instead of front trying to make the *t* sounds. Su'ranchingal, fighting the *ti'if* as best he could, "I am anxious more than usual, now that Culpepper is gone. Why is your posture so stiff?"

She said, "You make us nervous."

"How can I force you to be nervous? I'm so helpless I have sex I can't remember with a female who hates me," Su'ranchingal said. "But I can grow you lettuce, make you a crop, not nervous. Are the *zr'as* still . . . are you still getting radio signals?"

"Still sending."

"You can't possibly know that. They are two hundred light-years away." The whole confusion of whens and wheres hit Su'ranchingal like more *ti'if*. "I've been most of my waking life here." His eyes felt dusty, so he rolled them back into his head a few times before remembering humans loathed seeing his eye moistening. *Well, they blink their flabby eyelids disgustingly slow.*

"But you didn't evolve here," Vann said as if that mattered.

"You evolved in Africa—why are you here?" Su'ranchingal asked. "You don't send cats back to the Libyan Desert. You don't—"

"It's the planet we evolved on."

"Your people tried to terraform Venus."

"Our solar system, then, when that becomes habitable."

Su'ranchingal remembered how drugged the *zr'as* had kept him in space, ungrowing, perpetually chilled. "Are you going to send me alone?"

"You are worried about her, aren't you? We want to terminate the pregnancy. We're not going to be inhumane about this. We don't think alcohol or *ti'if* could be good for genetic material. You'd probably spawn monsters."

"In-humane?"

"Cruel."

Something vaguely reptilian—archaic shock instincts—screech of scale or fingernail on slate, a zr'a *vowel we can't use.* Su'ranchingal felt too numb. "You should have scales, thin fast eyelids."

She shuddered faintly, the same muscle recoil vibrations he'd seen in others who braced against a flight reaction. "I'm sorry I feel the way I do. You are a very social creature, aren't you?"

"Humanized. Not with Hu'rekhi."

"You do seem a bit shocked. Hu'rekhi lost, probably pregnant, and your flight back coming up." She bought him another Dr Pepper. "But we'd appreciate a little more honesty, not the farming pseudo-yokel shtick."

"I don't remember . . ." He took the bottle from her and up-ended it, tongue flaps directing the fluid to his digestive web. "I remember space." He looked at her evasive eyes. "It was extremely inhumane."

"Your people were the cruel ones."

"I don't remember doing sex with Hu'rekhi. I used to hear about times when sexual tissue was swollen." He remembered touching his genitals in the garden, feeling them tingle. Vann's eyes swiveled down. Su'ranchingal's fingers twitched around his waist—where humans had their nonfunctional navels.

"It must be cleaner than our fucking," Vann said when he drew his fingers up toward his mouth. "Your sex isn't between piss and shit."

"But it's unimportant if I did it without noticing." Su'ranchingal felt very strange. "Can someone help me with a deer that interferes with my vegetable-growing duties?" He stared to wobble and added, "I don't think I can take another Dr Pepper."

Vann stared at the clerk, who switched the cash-register screen on and off; then they both looked at Su'ranchingal and hissed breath around their teeth.

The next morning a message chip arrived, a chip for an obsolete computer. Su'ranchingal finally found one with mud daubers' nests on it in the basement. The loading port had been sealed with plastic that now shredded to his touch while the disturbed wasps vainly tried to sting him through his scales, eyesheaths, and thicker-than-human skin. He cleaned it, brought it upstairs, and plugged it into the house circuits—the receptacles still took the same plugs—then nervously turned the computer on. *Uk ka, a self-boot,* tongue flaps alternating. He looked at the package the chip arrived in and found a brittle yellow paper with odd-shaped alphabetics on it—"Call up vis.inf once you get the c prompt."

Nervously he typed in VIS.INF and the return key; he'd seen visual of these archaic Terran computers in the archives, but working on one by hand was strange.

Pixtels. He strained to make out the image, to read it as a three-dimensional visual of a woman, and wondered how the *zr'as* originally learned to decipher this code of colored dots. Finally he worked on the focus and contrast to make the image more appropriate to his brain's visual centers. And the woman was talking:

> My name was Alice Maxwell. I arranged for friends to deliver these tapes to you to assure you that some humans are your allies. I'm dead now, but I lived long enough to hear the first signals.

Su'ranchingal froze the picture and looked at the woman, trying to imagine why a dying human would want to tell him this. *What had she been? And why am I only now getting this message tape?* He started the image and the sound moving again.

> Did you first decide to send to us because of our radio signals, TV signals? Or those nuclear blasts? Will you help us? I didn't find out when I was alive, and now I'll never know.

He waited while the woman on the tape drank a glass of water, throat muscles working, but no lump bobbing up and down as in the male humans. She seemed sick; she was dead many years now. Then she said, "You have friends among us. I started an organization. This is their contact with you."

Random light hashes bounced on the screen. Su'ranchingal knew the message was really for another kind of alien and turned the computer off, pulled the chip and destroyed it, his digestive web burning itself slightly.

Culpepper came walking out of the deer's path into the garden while Su'ranchingal was wrestling with the Rototiller. "You aren't my watcher anymore," Su'ranchingal said to the human. "You resigned."

"Do you want to go back?"

"I grew up in Annapolis. I don't understand when my original language speaks to me. And if I went to the planet I was born on, I would be an alien all over again. And there is no way back in time to where I was. My immune system is not as evolved as the germs on that planet now."

"But no one would be afraid of you."

"That's stupid," Su'ranchingal said. "Why should humans fear me? I'm a drugged addict. Do you fear me?"

"No, I don't fear you. But when Hu'rekhi turned up pregnant, I thought you'd lied to me. But now I think I know what you are."

"I don't remember inseminating her."

"You're the experimental chimp, not the guys who sent you. You could inseminate while you were asleep."

"Or drugged," Su'ranchingal said primly.

"There are people who want to help you. You're still a sapient, but I suspect it would go better for you if you stayed with us."

"Sophont, linguist. And you want me to go back to those people who called me . . . made me . . ." A concept lurked in alien sounds that he had almost forgotten—*sr'arrXch,* not of full quality/dignity. His bottom tongue flap spasmed with the stop that the humans lettered X. "They took away what you would call my dignity."

"Dignity? That's important to you? I don't believe we've ever discussed that. Bizarre, considering. I wonder if the people we think may try to help would be so interested if they knew you weren't the inventor of your ship."

He is still a watcher, Su'ranchingal realized, hearing Culpepper's voice shift tones and cadences, seeing the human's body stiffened as though he'd sighted a deer or a space-going chimpanzee. Su'ranchingal said, "A word, *sr'arrXch.* I didn't be brought up to it, but when I first arrived, you gave it to me." He realized the idiomatic thing to have said was *didn't get brought up to it,* human possession again: *getting, having, holding.*

"All you want to do is stay here?"

Su'ranchingal imitated with his rounded shoulder blades a human shrug and looked like he was drawing his head into his body. When he realized Culpepper looked perplexed, he said, "I like to trick plants in a garden."

"Hu'rekhi escaped."

"Escaped? To where?"

"Someone helped her out before we could a—"

Before humans could abort her babies, Su'ranchingal realized.

Culpepper said, "Help us find her before she gets hurt."

"We were not close friends." Human talk, *close* metaphorized as if two mental lives brushed up against each other, closely. "We were thrown together without testing."

"You got her pregnant."

"We must have a truly occult sex life," Su'ranchingal said. "Did you sent me the old lady's visu-chip?"

"What visu-chip?"

"Laser erratics, not a message, just the picture of an old woman." Su'ranchingal felt hot and pulled the hose from the reel and sprayed under his belly scales, the tiny erectile muscles aching like a thousand pins from both cold and tension. He wondered if he'd really fooled Culpepper or if the human tested him.

Culpepper leaned away from the water as if wetness could damage him. "Su'ranchingal, give me the visu-chip. If you still have it."

The possessive human language seemed to melt in Su'ranchingal's mind, oozing over all the images of his past stored there. "Culpepper, I've never been socially normal—I was raised to send me here. I want to be socially normal for my own kind, but now that's impossible. Return for me is degrading." He was angry that Culpepper had believed humans rather than him about his closeness to Hu'rekhi. To disgust the human, Su'ranchingal frothed on his belly, lashing out at himself with his tongue. Now, an instant after he hated Culpepper, he hated himself for being so inhuman. At the corner of his vision, he saw Culpepper go back to his car and sit down in it, talking into a microphone.

"You missing a friend?" an old man whispered to Su'ranchingal while the new watcher, Baxter, paid the clerk, who began bantering about the new visual chips dispenser that let you program endings, mix actors who'd never shared realtime.

"No," Su'ranchingal said.

"A friend," the old man said fiercely. "You know, like a mate?"

"Hu'rekhi?"

"We . . ."

Baxter, as he walked by them to the chip machine, stared at the old man. He programmed a chip with fast jabs of an old message spike, saying, "Su'ranchingal, you know you're a chip character?"

"Message," the old man whispered, shoving a scrap of plastic at Su'ranchingal. *Lose him.*

Baxter popped recorder contacts onto his eyeballs and stared at Su'ranchingal, then at the old man, then at a girl walking back from the toilet.

The old man stiffened. Su'ranchingal saw him force limpness into each muscle, waves of human muscle bunching, then mentally pressed loose.

"I'm not brave like Hu'rekhi," Su'ranchingal said to everyone in the store. Memories Su'ranchingal had repressed, of human horror films, jagged through his vision centers so hard they blurred the air world beyond his eyes. "I don't want to see my own kind ever again. Under the circumstances."

The old man stayed put, his muscles twitching gently under his thin wrinkled skin, his eyes unfocused but occasionally flicking toward Baxter, never quite engaging in eye-to-eye contact with the watcher. Su'ranchingal stared, fascinated, at the man. Then he realized the man was scared. He said, "Baxter, we must go."

Baxter paid for the drinks and the chip and said, "Let's go, then."

The clerk handed Su'ranchingal the bag. Su'ranchingal felt the cold bottles through the bag, the four-inch-square case housing the tiny movie chip. He felt very small himself—deer bit away his bean pods and no human would help him stop them. He touched his dewlaps with the bottles, cooling the blood surging there.

The old man disappeared. Baxter looked around as though he'd left something behind, then popped off his lenses—finger squeezes to either side of each lens and a moist suck of lens released from eyeball. Su'ranchingal remembered an array of other lenses in a tube, pointed at his eyes—somewhere, on Earth, on *Za'aga*—while he was pinned down with drugs or straps, he didn't remember now. Baxter dropped the lenses in a case and they walked out of the store.

"Do the lenses record?" Su'ranchingal asked.

"You betcha," Baxter said. "You've been approached. We'd like you to cooperate with them."

"No."

"Pretend."

"I don't understand pretending. My mind . . ."

"Relax and just do what I say, Ranch, boy."

Ranch? Unsure as to whether he'd been insulted or not, Su'ranchingal's head jerked back and his head scales flared. He stopped walking. Baxter took his elbow and pulled. *I'm just a specimen. I can take insults as well as examinations.* "So you want to call me Ranch?"

"We all call you Ranch."

"Oh. What do you call Hu'rekhi?"

"The Wreck."

"And she's missing, presumed pregnant, and not dead?"

"Yeah. We never thought . . ." Su'ranchingal could almost feel the man's thoughts creep around his speech centers, down to the vocal instruments . . . *never thought a pregnant alien could get away, and with ideas about gene recombination.* A cheetah walked through Su'ranchingal's visual centers, overlaid on what he was perceiving of Baxter's face, a guy who wanted to expell him and Hu'rekhi from this planet. He wondered if he would ever stop hallucinating or if what he saw was normal.

"What do you want me to do?"

"A man approaches you—go with him. I'll get lost. Try your best to lose me."

Su'ranchingal and Baxter watched a holographic movie of Su'ranchingal and a small woman in a white lab coat. Su'ranchingal's tiny image plotted the force lines of a ramscoop on a computer screen the width and height of a man's thumbnail. "But I don't know anything about ramscoops," Su'ranchingal said.

"You'd cooperate with your return?"

"I'm helpless," Su'ranchingal said, pouring himself another *ti'if*-spiked Dr Pepper. His visual focus wavered. "You'll send me to strangers, just like the *zr'a* did."

"Go down to the store tomorrow and see if anyone approaches you again. Then lose me. Go with them. Maybe we'll let you stay."

A roadfuser was moving slowly down the left half of State Road 696 by the store, the road surface hot and smooth behind it, too hot to walk on, so Su'ranchingal walked through blue chicory blooms the state bush hog would slice down after the roadfuser did its work. Three guys sat on a short length of sidewalk that ran thigh high above the street, talking about the inches in the rain gauge—archaic, Su'ranchingal thought, since the rain gauges were now electronic, the raindrops themselves measured for velocity and volume as they fell. They hushed when he came within three feet of them as though he couldn't have heard them before.

"Good morning," Su'ranchingal said.

"Um," one answered, then another murmured, "Munnin."

After he passed, the talk shifted to how some kid buried automatic plow guide stobs either side of a hardtop road and the tractor just sliced the hell out of the road until the chisel popped. Su'ranchingal wondered if humans always changed their conversations when he passed, tried to remember other occasions. They shifted topics as though his ears polluted the gist of the earlier sound.

A small boy sitting on the back of an old-fashioned driven tractor, behind the Plexiglas cab on an air conditioner hump, hissed like a cat at Su'ranchingal, who felt ashamed, as though he had frightened the boy deliberately.

The boy hissed again. Su'ranchingal remembered that humans, unlike cats, rarely hissed in fright. He went up to the tractor.

"Follow me and get up in the cab from their blind side." The boy nodded at the men sitting on the sidewalk. "Cab's rigged to show false image in the glass, looks real. I'll take you to see some people who want to meet you."

"Hu'rekhi?"

"Sho-o-sh." The boy swung off the air conditioner apparatus behind the cab, climbed in the tractor cab, closed the door, and turned into a man who started the tractor. Su'ranchingal wondered if the cab windows played a distortion of the boy driving it or a hologram utterly unrelated to what was happening inside the cab. *Will what shows in the glass when I'm in the cab be human enough to fool Baxter?* He wished he could live the rest of his life behind such glass if it would make him look human.

Su'ranchingal walked around the store to the back, then raced for the tractor, flung open the right-hand-side door, and jumped in. The window appeared tinted with tiny flecks of various colors that squirmed in the thick glass.

The boy handed Su'ranchingal a note: TAKE OFF YOUR CLOTHES.

Su'ranchingal was relieved to be out of his overalls, but wondered how the boy would react to seeing his belly, his excretion glands along his groin. The boy grabbed the overalls, swerved the tractor in front of the roadfuser, threw out the overalls, and swerved back. The roadfuser ran over the clothes with a spurt of greasy smoke. A fan blew the ashes aside. The roadfuser, sensing an irregularity, backed up and remelted the road.

The boy giggled, then said, "We didn't know until yesterday that the fuser was going to be working, but it sure took care of any fed gear in your stuff."

Su'ranchingal pried up a scale and scratched out an aspirin-sized capsule. "This too."

"Damn." The boy swerved in front of the fuser again and tossed the capsule out. "The feds got my voice."

"Have your voice? What do people see when they look in at your tractor windows?" *Remember they're possessive.*

"Bastards got voiceprints on me now, damn. Oh, they see two guys in a drive tractor. We'll cruise around for a couple hours."

"Out in the open. What if Baxter searches the tractor?"

"They'll expect you to try a long fast run out of the area. And we're not running, you know, just plowing a field or two. No place *in* the tractor to hide something as big as you, and the visual stuff playing the window ain't a loop. From out there, we're two grown men plowing."

"I want a suit of this glass."

"The Wreck's around. Spacer freaks helping her."

"Are you a saucer freak?" Su'ranchingal knew that some humans felt he and Hu'rekhi were gods who'd reveal themselves only to true believers. Obviously, these people were insane.

"Not religious saucer freaks, okay. We're spacer freaks. Jesus, they have my voice." The boy, face crumpled by rigorously contracted muscles, turned the tractor up into a field and lowered gang plows into the soil. He muttered again, "My voice."

About five o'clock, the boy drove the tractor back through the village and down a dirt road, the tractor bumping on ruts, Su'ranchingal feeling oddly soothed as though the computer glass transformed him into a real human on both sides of the graphics. The planet was kind, rocking them both. The boy didn't say anything, just pulled at Su'ranchingal until he climbed out of the cab and followed the boy into a pine forest with scrub oaks and mountain laurel mixed in. The boy walked up to an oak tree with the sprawling limbs of a former pasture tree, stunted pines around it, and took a pocketknife out of his pants pocket. Carefully he pried out an irregular chunk of bark. Su'ranchingal looked over the boy's head and saw a handprint pad. The boy turned the pad twice, then put his left hand on it.

Su'ranchingal almost asked out loud, *What happens next?* But the boy laid a sweaty finger on Su'ranchingal's rigid lips. Su'ranchingal knew the sign for *quiet* and wiped the boy's sweat away.

They continued to walk through the woods, tall brush between the pines. Brambles scratched at Su'ranchingal, and he was so tense in the ears he heard the longer thorns screech against his scales, his heart pounding blood through all eight chambers, air hissing through his lungs and bones.

The boy dropped to the ground when they saw the cabin and slithered up to an old stump. The stump flipped to the side, revealing a tunnel, and the boy motioned for Su'ranchingal to crawl in.

"But it's dark there."

The boy hissed at him; Su'ranchingal went down into the hole, squeezing his closed eyes with all his ocular muscles to make light from nerve pressure. His fingers began to figure out this space, so he switched to an imagination of it well lit, then suddenly the boy was against his back and the whole visualization jumped beyond Su'ranchingal's body space . . .

. . . and turned yellow. Su'ranchingal opened his eyes, saw that the boy had turned on a light, and rolled his eyes to moisten them. The boy made a funny sound in his throat as though his back tongue flap had spasmed on a stop. But humans didn't have back tongue flaps, just a tiny protrusion that hung down from the far back of the throat.

"Sorry," Su'ranchingal said. His eyes had gotten dried out by the air-conditioning in the tractor cab.

The boy patted Su'ranchingal's shoulder as if to say eyeballs rolled into the head didn't bother him too much, then pushed more firmly to urge Su'ranchingal on down the tunnel. They followed a string of bare light bulbs wired along the ceiling. The tunnel was made of metal, iron and zinc tastes in the air. Underfoot was a wooden walk suspended about a foot off the rounded floor. Water trickled down under the walk, leaking from seams in the metal walls.

They went for twenty minutes underground, the tunnel sloping gradually up. The boy stopped at a barrier and opened another lock box and laid his hand on the palmplate, then stuck one eye against a rubber eyepiece. The barrier slid to the left with a greasy hiss.

"Who paid for this?" Su'ranchingal gasped, the *d* flipping down to the throat flap, strangling all resemblance to a human phoneme. Behind the door he saw a wrinkled skin woman, another young boy, and a grown human male with collapsed skin folds around the mouth and eyes, wrinkles. Su'ranchingal remembered that humans wrinkled with age.

The boy pointed to his vocal cord structure and moaned.

"Recorded your voice, Tommy?" the woman asked.

Tommy nodded vigorously. They all ran through a short broad stretch of tunnel, then climbed up into the kitchen.

Hu'rekhi sat in a chair, one leg bent, her ankle on the top of her thigh, but away from her distended belly. Su'ranchingal stared at the belly, skin white stretched between scales that seemed to float loosely over rigid internal organs. Distended, but not hugely as pregnant as the female humans got. Hu'rekhi said, "I'm pregnant, you asshole. They tried to abort me, but—"

Su'ranchingal interrupted her. "But what are we going to eat?"

"I smuggled out yeast. Bet you don't have any *ti'if*."

"*Ti'if*?" Su'ranchingal wondered why he felt hot.

"They addicted you to it, remember."

"You have some, then?"

"No. If it's a bad withdrawal, you're fucked."

The older woman came in and said, "We've got to do surgery on Tommy's voice."

"Didn't you get that transmitter out from under your ventral plate?" Hu'rekhi said, massaging the distended skin between her own scales.

"He said they got his voice before we threw it under a road steamer."

"Melter?"

"Yes, that." Su'ranchingal realized he didn't want an entire lifetime with Hu'rekhi. He didn't like her that much. "Will we stay here? Together?"

She flushed red between her scales. "How do we raise my babies? What kind of education?"

Su'ranchingal suspected their children would be sociologically human, as he was almost human, with his mind crystallized in Amerish. "I don't know. Did you ask the human scientists?"

"I have no nipples."

"Nipples, oh, yes. Perhaps their digestive systems will be more mature at birth."

"I don't have *any* idea." Hu'rekhi sounded hysterical. "I will have three babies, so the humans told me. It must hurt when they come out."

"Biologically, it would be inefficient if birth killed you for only three young."

"You idiot. What do we do?"

He withdrew from *ti'if,* hurting like a whipped child, wondering if he'd go mad before his nerves resheathed themselves.

Two months later, Su'ranchingal was with Hu'rekhi when she sighed and the skin stretched around her scales twitched as if she was trying to raise them. Su'ranchingal, almost revolted, watched her belly squirm more as the young inside it moved. He thought he could understand why the humans wanted to send the two of them back, away, out. Three at a time plus parental care was K plus Y reproductive strategy. Hu'rekhi finally tilted the scales on the sides of her swollen belly up and *humphed* like a human at him. "Su'ranchingal, we don't get along, do we?"

"No."

"Have you ever considered that the humans preferred that we not be a team? Two isolates are not as scary as a mated pair."

Su'ranchingal remembered how Culpepper had encouraged him to speak badly of Hu'rekhi, how the men got Hu'rekhi drunk on the isopropyls. "But we didn't have to like each other to breed. It was unconscious. The *zr'as* knew that."

"Yeah." She rolled her eyes back into her head convulsively, little strands of eye muscles visible at the bottom of her eyes when they rolled all the way up.

One of the space freaks came in and watched Hu'rekhi without looking away. The freak was a male, tall for a human, with black hair and brown and white eyes, white bordering the variable eye color as with all humans. He called, "Mary," and a woman came in with warm olive oil and began massaging Hu'rekhi's skin between the scales, pouring oil on her slightly haired human hands, then rubbing around Hu'rekhi's belly.

Hu'rekhi said, "My genitals need to be stretched."

A vague image rose in Su'ranchingal's visual center: *zr'a* hands loosening a belly sphincter, then one of the older *zr'as* laughing and moving him out of the room. "Yes," he said. *I'll have to do it for her.* His throat seemed heavy—something in it gave way and he felt thick matter rise, gulped and saw Hu'rekhi gulp at almost the same time. *One to two babies, one parent nurses; three babies, two parents feed.* "Hu'rekhi?" he said in human question tones—there seemed to be vague memories of a ritual for this, but that was fractured into only partial visuals and feelings, memories of electronic media, focus lost by a child who didn't understand what he witnessed.

Hu'rekhi's eyes fluttered back and up again—he felt her distress. "We'll never do it right," she said. Su'ranchingal bent his head and took the oil from the human woman, began massaging Hu'rekhi's belly, touched her sphincter gently with an oiled finger. When the Terran oil didn't seem to burn, he began working to loosen the sphincter muscle ring. "You're an idiot," Hu'rekhi told him, her eyes still rolled back blindly in her head, "but we have to try. If things go badly, get help."

"They'd send us out to space."

"I'd rather not die."

Digging his finger into Hu'rekhi's belly hole seemed right; being sent to the humans seemed right; everything seems right to Su'ranchingal now. *Earth aches for our biomasses.* He wondered vaguely if he'd been drugged. *No drugs now, it's just really right.* The humans left them alone as he worked on Hu'rekhi, and that was perfect.

"Personalities," Hu'rekhi mumbled, "don't matter now."

Su'ranchingal felt air tremble from speech apparatus to auditory organs, but her meaning seemed to coil out of his own brain. "I hope these humans will like lots of us." He drew the first fist-sized baby from her and thick matter rose to his tongue, which curled into a tube. The baby drank.

About the Authors

Octavia E. Butler began publishing science fiction in the 1970s. Among her highly regarded novels are *Patternmaster* (1976), *Mind of My Mind* (1977), *Survivor* (1978), *Kindred* (1979), *Wild Seed* (1980), and the volumes of her Xenogenesis trilogy, *Dawn* (1987), *Adulthood Rites* (1988), and *Imago* (1989). She has won the Hugo Award and the Nebula Award for her short fiction, and her recent novel *Parable of the Sower* (1993) was published to critical acclaim.

About herself, Octavia Butler has said:

> I'm a forty-seven-year-old writer who can remember being a ten-year-old writer and who expects someday to be an eighty-year old writer. I'm also comfortably asocial—a hermit in the middle of Los Angeles—a pessimist if I'm not careful, a feminist, an African-American, a former Baptist, and an oil-and-water combination of ambition, laziness, insecurity, certainty, and drive. (From "A Brief Conversation with Octavia E. Butler," a personal statement issued by the author)

Pat Cadigan has been honored with the Arthur C. Clarke Award for her novel *Synners* (1991) and with Locus Awards for her short fiction collection *Patterns* (1989) and her story "Angel" (1987). She has been a Nebula Award and Hugo Award finalist as well. Her other books include *Mindplayers* (1987), *Fools* (1992), and *Dirty Work* (1993). Her short fiction has appeared in *Omni, Asimov's Science Fiction, The Magazine of Fantasy & Science Fiction,* and in several best-of-the-year anthologies of science fiction. She has referred to herself, aptly, as a "technofeminist."

Pat Cadigan has said the following about childhood, a time that is a rich source of material for any writer:

If you're over the age of sixteen, you can relax now. The worst is over. You're never going to be as terrified again as you were in childhood. . . .

Take my word for it, childhood is a time of unrelenting terror. That many of us don't remember it that way lets us recover and go on with our lives. But if you carry with you a certain fear you are helpless in the face of, that you live with but will never overcome, you probably acquired it in childhood. You may deal with it like a champ, but inside you're cold water and you truly understand the phrase, "Fate worse than death." ("Introduction to 'Eenie, Meenie, Ipsateenie,' " in *Patterns* by Pat Cadigan [Kansas City, Mo.: Ursus, 1989])

Jayge Carr is a physicist who once worked for NASA. She published her first science fiction story in 1976 and has appeared in *Omni, Analog, Synergy, Amazing, Marion Zimmer Bradley's Fantasy Magazine,* and other magazines and anthologies. She is also the author of the novels *Leviathan's Deep* (1979), *Navigator's Sindrome* (1983), *The Treasure in the Heart of the Maze* (1985), and *Rabelaisian Reprise* (1988).

About her work, Jayge Carr has written:

I've . . . discovered quite a bit about myself by reading my own work. Many people, on the evidence of *Leviathan's Deep,* have labeled me a feminist. Well, maybe. I prefer to think of myself as a peoplist. Everyone should have equal opportunities and no one should be shoe-horned into a role unfitting or barred from a role desired because of sex—or age, creed, color, or what-have-you. . . . Sometimes . . . I try to show men what it feels like to have the shoe on the other foot, pinching. But women are not our only minority, just the most prevalent one. Prejudice, intolerance, bigotry; all of them are so cruel, and they cause so much tragedy—and they're so foolish. (From *Twentieth-Century Science-Fiction Writers,* Third Edition, edited by Noelle Watson and Paul E. Schellinger [Chicago: St. James Press, 1991])

Angela Carter, who died in 1992, was one of the major literary figures in British fantasy. She was honored with the John Llewelyn Rhys Memorial Prize for her novel *The Magic Toyshop* (1967) and won the Somerset Maugham Award for *Several Perceptions* (1968). Among her other books are *Heroes and Villains* (1969), *The Passion of New Eve* (1977), *The Bloody Chamber* (1979), *Nights at the Circus* (1984), and

American Ghosts and Old World Wonders (1993), as well as an anthology, *Strange Things Sometime Still Happen: Fairy Tales from around the World* (1993).

Angela Carter wrote the following on how she came to write short fiction:

> I started to write short pieces when I was living in a room too small to write a novel in. So the size of my room modified what I did inside it and it was the same with the pieces themselves. The limited trajectory of the short narrative concentrates its meaning. Sign and sense can fuse to an extent impossible to achieve among the multiplying ambiguities of an extended narrative. I found that, though the play of surfaces never ceased to fascinate me, I was not so much exploring them as making abstractions from them. I was writing, therefore, tales. (From the afterword in *Fireworks: Nine Stories in Various Disguises* [New York: Harper & Row, 1974])

Suzy McKee Charnas has a degree in economic history from Barnard and worked as a Peace Corps volunteer in Nigeria during the '60s. She has won a Nebula Award and a Hugo Award for her short fiction and writes both science fiction and fantasy. Her novels include *Walk to the End of the World* (1974), *Motherlines* (1978), *The Vampire Tapestry* (1980), and *Dorothea Dreams* (1986). She has also written several novels for young adults, among them *The Bronze King* (1985) and *The Golden Thread* (1989).

Suzy McKee Charnas wrote the following about how a writer's values can be reflected in her work:

> Whatever values an author claims to hold . . . her work invariably demonstrates her true convictions. The question for me is not, "Is there a strong woman character in this story?" It's easy to write a deeply sexist story around a female protagonist and not even know it. . . .
>
> No, my test is this: "Are there female characters of complexity, variety, and true importance to the protagonist of this story? Or is she or he *surrounded by and significantly connected only to males?*"
>
> In other words, does the protagonist have a mother? Or sisters, women friends and confidantes, aunts, daughters, a grandmother? Female colleagues, enemies, lovers, rivals, teachers, you name it—as well as brothers, fathers, and so on? Does being human include . . . important connections with *both* halves of the human race?

If not—okay. *Provided* there's a damn good reason in the story. (From "No-Road," in *Women of Vision,* edited by Denise Du Pont [New York: St. Martin's Press, 1988])

C. J. Cherryh taught Latin and ancient history before becoming a writer; she has become one of the most popular and prolific authors in science fiction. She was honored with the John W. Campbell Award for Best New Writer at the beginning of her career. Since then, she has won Hugo Awards for her novels *Downbelow Station* (1981) and *Cyteen* (1988), as well as for her short story "Cassandra" (1979). Her novels include *The Book of Morgaine* (1979); the Faded Sun trilogy *Kesrith* (1978), *Shon'jir* (1978), and *Kutath* (1979); *Serpent's Reach* (1980); *Merchanter's Luck* (1982); *The Pride of Chanur* (1982); *Voyager in Night* (1984); *Rimrunners* (1989); *Heavy Time* (1991); and *Hellburner* (1992).

C. J. Cherryh has said about science fiction:

Science fiction is the oldest sort of tale-telling . . . Homer; Sinbad's story; Gilgamesh; Beowulf; and up and up the line of history wherever mankind's scouts encounter the unknown. Not a military metaphor. It's peaceful progress. . . . Tale-telling is the most peaceful thing we do. It's investigatory. The best tale-telling has always been full of what-if. The old Greek peasant who laid down his tools of a hard day's labor to hear about Odysseus's trip beyond the rim of his world—he wasn't an escapist. He was dreaming. . . . He might not go. But his children's children might. *Someone* would. And that makes his day's hard work *worth* something to the future; it makes this farmer and his well-tilled field participant in the progress of his world, and his cabbages then have a cosmic importance. (From the introduction to *Visible Light* by C. J. Cherryh [New York: DAW Books, 1986])

Storm Constantine's short fiction has appeared in *Zenith: The Best in New British Science Fiction* (1989), *Zenith 2* (1990), and *New Worlds*. Her first published novels were *The Enchantments of Flesh and Spirit* (1987), *The Bewitchments of Love and Hate* (1988), and *The Fulfilments of Fate and Desire* (1989), all part of her Wraeththu trilogy. Among her other novels are *The Monstrous Regiment* (1990), *Aleph* (1991), *Hermetech* (1991), *Burying the Shadow* (1992), and *Calenture* (1994); most of her work is imaginatively concerned with sex and gender.

Storm Constantine has offered the following insight into how our world often seems:

> Most of us, at some time, get a feeling that there *just might be* another side to reality that exists alongside our own. Perhaps more than simply one other side—perhaps a great tangle of them! In paranoid moments—or moments of solitude in the dark—you might think that maybe the conspiracy freaks are right, and there really *are* weird people about, people who are unnervingly different to ourselves, who could be hiding within our society. People with Another Kind of Knowing. Sometimes we might even get what appears to be glimpses of these people and their other, "not our" worlds. You know those times. It's when coincidence aligns to alarming effect, invoking incredulity, bafflement, and a creepy feeling up the spine. (From the introduction to *Dirty Work: Stories by Pat Cadigan* [Shingletown, Calif.: Mark V. Ziesing, 1993])

Carol Emshwiller began writing during the '50s and is a respected and unique voice in both science fiction and literary circles. Her short fiction has appeared in *Orbit, The Magazine of Fantasy & Science Fiction, New Worlds, Dangerous Visions, Triquarterly, The Voice International Literary Supplement,* and *New Directions Annual.* Her first novel, *Carmen Dog,* was published in 1988. Her collections of short fiction are *Joy in Our Cause* (1974), *Verging on the Pertinent* (1989), and *The Start of the End of It All* (1991), which won a World Fantasy Award. She teaches writing at New York University.

In one of her stories, Carol Emshwiller playfully writes of women and art:

> Life, when seen as though through the eyes of small women or when looking at a small woman . . . the close attention to details, for instance, or the taking-pains-with of small women wherein even the monumental can be made, fundamentally, minute . . . the elegance of tiny women as they closely scrutinize, nearsighted, squinting over tiny stitches or tiny brush strokes . . . This is the essence of art, and, moreover, art within which the actual function of being a woman is similar (if not identical) to the function of art. . . .
>
> Large women, however, do not have the capacity for art. They are anti-art women. . . . But the potential of large women! The huge, unrealized potential! Their great longings, their colossal grudges, their long-term memories, their rage! No wonder they deny all art . . . deny all civilization and try to convince their tiny, more

discreet sisters to join them. (From "Queen Kong," in *Verging on the Pertinent* [Minneapolis, Minn.: Coffee House Press, 1989])

Sheila Finch was born in England but has lived in the United States since the '60s. She began publishing science fiction in 1977; her stories have been published in *The Magazine of Fantasy & Science Fiction, Amazing Stories,* and other magazines and anthologies. Among her novels are *Infinity's Web* (1985), *Triad* (1986), *The Garden of the Shaped* (1987), *Shaper's Legacy* (1988), and *Shaping the Dawn* (1989).

Sheila Finch, who began writing in midlife, comments about that experience:

> There are many advantages to starting late. Because I came into the field after many, many years as a wife, mother, reader, and teacher, I think I have a more coherent philosophy of life, a sharper eye for character, a finer sense of the ironies of our existence, a better ear for style, and a sounder grasp of the traditional values of plot and character. . . . I think I've learned a lot about being human in a difficult world—the grandest theme of all in science fiction. . . .
>
> But I've paid for it, too. I'm not an experimental writer. . . . Not for me the far-out exuberance of cyberpunk, the searing illuminations of painful and sometimes shocking subjects, the grand attempts to transform the field stylistically. That sort of risky business, like high-wire work, is best started in youth. It's as if when you don't exercise the talent for being outrageous when you're young, then the "window" closes. After that, you're always going to write with an accent. (From "Bulletin Symposium," in *The Bulletin of the Science Fiction Writers of America* [Vol. 23, No. 2, Summer 1989])

Karen Joy Fowler, after earning two degrees in Asian studies, teaching ballet and athletics, and bringing up two children, began publishing science fiction in 1986 and was immediately hailed as one of the finest new writers to enter the field. She won the John W. Campbell Award for Best New Writer and her stories have been finalists for several awards. She is the author of a short story collection, *Artificial Things* (1986), and a highly praised first novel, *Sarah Canary* (1991).

About her experience as a writer and mother, she has said:

> Having a son was enormously important to me in terms of my fiction. I am a feminist, deeply committed to feminism . . . but I believe that

> I'm more sympathetic to men now, because I've watched my son grow up. . . . I've seen up close what happens to men as they grow. You never saw such a limited life as an adolescent boy leads. The channel of acceptable behavior couldn't be more narrow. I think teenage girls have much more freedom. They can dress like a boy, that's OK. They can be masculine, to a certain extent, and it's kind of cute, or it's spunky, or it's admirable. A boy who's feminine is beyond discussion. (From "Karen Joy Fowler: A Question of Identity," in *Locus* [Vol. 31, No. 3, September 1993])

Mary Gentle published her first novel, *A Hawk in Silver* (1977), at the age of twenty one. Her short fiction has appeared in *Interzone, Despatches from the Frontiers of the Female Mind,* and *Isaac Asimov's Science Fiction Magazine;* she has also reviewed fiction for the British science fiction magazine *Interzone*. Among her richly detailed novels are *Golden Witchbreed* (1983), *Ancient Light* (1987), *Rats and Gargoyles* (1990), and *The Architecture of Desire* (1991); her most recent books are *Grunts!* (1992), a comedy-fantasy, and *Left to His Own Devices* (1994), an Elizabethan cyberpunk novel. A collection of her short fiction, *Scholars and Soldiers,* was published in 1989.

Mary Gentle has said the following about her profession:

> I actually think writers are quite disgusting people. A writer is a person who, in the middle of a most terrific emotional crisis, is mentally taking notes. You work out crises when you're writing fiction. . . . A work of fiction takes what has happened to you and uses it, irrespective of how you feel about it. Writers are users. (From "Mary Gentle: On the Borderline," in *Locus* [Vol. 22, No. 4, April 1989])

Lisa Goldstein won an American Book Award for her first novel, *The Red Magician* (1982). Since then, she has moved easily between science fiction, magic realism, and fantasy. Her novels include *The Dream Years* (1985), *A Mask for the General* (1987), *Tourists* (1989), *Strange Devices of the Sun and Moon* (1993), and *Summer King, Winter Fool* (1994). Some of her short fiction appears in the collection *Travellers in Magic* (1994).

In an interview, Lisa Goldstein commented:

> Magic realism is when magic is a part of everyday life and it's so commonplace you don't even talk about it, it just happens. . . . I saw that as a metaphor for the marvelous that exists in everyday life, which is something the surrealists were interested in too. In the

United States, there isn't really a sense of magic in everyday life. Everything is scientifically explained. So it's very difficult to write a North American magic realist novel. . . .

I get a certain feeling from magic realism, and . . . a certain feeling from science fiction, and they're not the same. The feeling I get from magic realism is closer to what the surrealists called the "marvelous," and from science fiction it's the old, overused "sense of wonder," which is different. (From "Lisa Goldstein: Astonishments and Strange Devices," in *Locus* [Vol 27, No. 6, December 1991])

Nancy Kress published her first novel, a fantasy titled *The Prince of Morning Bells,* in 1981 and has gone on to become one of the most versatile and rigorous writers of science fiction. She has been honored with two Nebula Awards, a Hugo Award, and several award nominations. Among her novels are *The Golden Grove* (1984), *The White Pipes* (1985), *An Alien Light* (1988), *Brain Rose* (1990), *Beggars in Spain* (1992), and *Beggars and Choosers* (1994). She has also published two collections of short fiction, *Trinity and Other Stories* (1985) and *The Aliens of Earth* (1993).

Nancy Kress has said the following about possible future societies:

The vision of a society that interests me is one where men and women have found a way to live together . . . found some sort of structures that integrate some very basic facts, such as that women get pregnant and bear children, and men don't. Ninety percent of women will have a child by the time they're forty. So it should be a society that looks sensibly and reasonably and practically at the necessity for raising children, integrating children, bearing children, and yet still allowing both sexes as much as possible to realize their own personal capabilities.

We all started out as children. This is the formative experience. And I think it's important to talk about children—even if you don't have any, you *were* one, and what you are was formed, to a large extent, by what you experienced as a child. . . . So discussions of future society that consider children irrelevant not only seem sexist, they seem insane. (From "Nancy Kress: The Children's Hour," in *Locus* [Vol. 29, No. 6, December 1992])

Tanith Lee began her career in the early '70s by publishing fantasy novels for younger readers. Soon she was writing both science fiction and fantasy for adult readers and has been honored with two World Fantasy Awards and the August Derleth Award for her novel *Death's*

Master (1979). Among her many science fiction and fantasy novels are *The Birthgrave* (1975), *Don't Bite the Sun* (1976), *Drinking Sapphire Wine* (1977), *Night's Master* (1978), *Electric Forest* (1979), *The Silver Metal Lover* (1981), *Days of Grass* (1985), and *A Heroine of the World* (1989). Her short story collections include *Red as Blood; or, Tales from the Sisters Grimmer* (1983), *The Gorgon and Other Beastly Tales* (1985), *Dreams of Dark and Light* (1986), and *Women as Demons* (1989).

Tanith Lee has said about her writing: "What I'm writing about always, because what fascinates me always, is people. That remains the same [for any genre or audience]." (From "The Many Faces of Tanith Lee," in *Locus* [Vol. 16, No. 11, November 1983])

Rosaleen Love was born in Sydney, Australia, and teaches professional writing at Victoria University of Technology in Melbourne. She has won several Australian literary awards for her short fiction and has published two collections, *The Total Devotion Machine and Other Stories* (1989) and *Evolution Annie* (1993).

In one of her stories, Rosaleen Love offers the following wry look at one future possibility:

> The children don't leave home any more, nor do the grandchildren, nor the great-grandchildren. . . . The children and descendants stay on, for it is no trouble now the housework problem has received the ultimate technological fix.
>
> Yes, one day there is an end to housework. Personal living tubes are set into the city walls in neat three deep layers. Each tube has its own self-shaking self-making bed, and all the in-tube life-maintenance and entertainment devices are superconductor charged and unbreakable. Electrostatic whizzers remove dust from all exposed surfaces within minutes of it settling and recycle it into the compost bin. Food still presents a problem, for though the quaint old-fashioned notion of a kitchen is gone for good, someone must still remember to recharge the Instamix and the Multiveg and the Compostacycle, and yes, you've guessed it, that still is women's work. (From "The Children Don't Leave Home Any More," in *The Total Devotion Love Machine and Other Stories* by Rosaleen Love [London: Women's Press, 1989])

Judith Moffett is a poet who has taught at the Iowa Writers' Workshop, the Bread Loaf Writers' Conference, and the University of Pennsylvania. She has published two volumes of her own poetry, *Keeping Time*

(1976) and *Whinny Moor Crossing* (1984), and one volume of translations from the Swedish. Her first science fiction story, "Surviving," won the Theodore Sturgeon Award in 1987; she was also honored with the John W. Campbell Award for Best New Writer in 1988. Her novels include *Pennterra* (1987), *The Ragged World: A Novel of the Hefn on Earth* (1991), and *Time, Like an Ever-Rolling Stream* (1992). She now lives in Salt Lake City, Utah.

Judith Moffett has commented on the experience of writing her first novel:

> For all my plotting and note-taking, there were a lot of unexpected developments. Particularly, I didn't know how the book was going to end. I knew that to make the story resonate in a deep enough key, one of the characters would have to die; I knew that the Sixers would be punished; but I didn't know which character or what punishment till the moments when I absolutely had to know. I've never had a more powerful experience of how the creative unconscious pulls things together than when I suddenly realized what the perfect punishment would be, and that I'd been setting it up unknowingly throughout the book. (From "My First Novel," in *The Bulletin of the Science Fiction Writers of America* [Vol. 25, No. 1, Spring 1991])

Pat Murphy has a degree in biology, lives in San Francisco, and works as an editor at the Exploratorium, a museum of science, art, and human perception. Her novels include *The Shadow Hunter* (1982) and *The City, Not Long After* (1989); a short story collection, *Points of Departure*, was published in 1990. She has won Nebula Awards for her novel *The Falling Woman* (1986) and her novelette "Rachel in Love" (1987); some of her other honors include a World Fantasy Award, a Locus Award, and a Philip K. Dick Award.

Pat Murphy writes about some of the childhood experiences that led her to become a writer:

> When I wasn't reading about secret places, I would look for secret places to call my own. . . . I cleared a patch of ground in a secluded corner of the backyard . . . and I planted crocuses and Johnny-jump-ups to make a secret garden. I couldn't go past a hole in a hedge or a cave or a culvert or a dark passageway without peering into the darkness and wondering if this were the one that led to a new world. In best junior scientist fashion, I learned to identify edible wild foods: young plantain leaves and such. I was, I think, planning

to live off the land when something happened. I didn't know what the event would be . . . but I knew that something momentous was going to happen. I might need to be able to recognize edible plants when I found the way through and ended up in Oz or Perelandra or Narnia or wherever it was I would finally end up. (From "Afterword—Why I Write," in *Points of Departure* by Pat Murphy [New York: Bantam, 1990])

Rebecca Ore began publishing science fiction in 1986 and won critical praise for her first novel, *Becoming Alien,* which was published in 1988. Among her other novels are *Being Alien* (1989); *Human to Human* (1990); *The Illegal Rebirth of Billy the Kid* (1991); a fantasy set in a present-day Appalachian community, *Slow Funeral* (1994); and *Gaia's Toys* (1995). Her short fiction has been collected in *Alien Bootlegger and Other Stories* (1993), and she has been nominated for the Philip K. Dick Award.

Rebecca Ore, who is particularly gifted at creating believable aliens, writes:

We have turned each other into our own aliens. . . .

We of the genus that includes humans and chimpanzees turn whole groups of conspecifics into artificial individuals, troop against troop. Our enemies are fry predators—baby killers—and must be slaughtered, not just dominated. . . . Humans seem to be the only ones who further turn conspecifics into aliens: the Cherokees, the Yanomamo, the primitive cultures that must be preserved as though they were endangered species. Otherwise, why do they seem to have lost their culture when they operate computers? Did we turn into an extension of Chinese culture when we borrowed the spinning wheel, the magnetic compass, and the horse collar? (From "Aliens and the Artificial Other," in *Alien Bootlegger and Other Stories* by Rebecca Ore [New York: TOR, 1993])

Sydney J. Van Scyoc published her first science fiction story in 1962; since then, several of her stories have been reprinted in various best-of-the-year anthologies. Her novels include *Saltflower* (1971), *Assignment Nor'Dyren* (1973), *Starmother* (1976), *Cloudcry* (1977), *Sunwaifs* (1981), *Darkchild* (1982), *Bluesong* (1983), *Starsilk* (1984), *Drowntide* (1987), *Feather Stroke* (1989), and *Deepwater Dreams* (1991). She lives in Northern California.

Sydney J. Van Scyoc comments about the path her writing has taken:

> My earlier short fiction was set on Earth in the not-too-distant future. . . . I took several years off from writing in the mid-1960s, while my children were very young. Soon after I began writing again, I found my focus had shifted to short fiction set on other planets and dealt primarily with communities struggling against inexplicable alien environments. I am increasingly intrigued now by the genetic and social changes which I believe will overtake the human race once we begin to colonize other planets. (From *Twentieth-Century Science-Fiction Writers,* Third Edition, edited by Noelle Watson and Paul E. Schellinger [Chicago: St. James Press, 1991])

Connie Willis has been writing science fiction since the '70s and began to win attention for her work in the '80s. She received a National Endowment for the Arts grant for her writing in 1982 and has gone on to win multiple Nebula and Hugo awards, becoming one of the most honored writers in the field. Her subtle yet accessible short fiction regularly appears in best-of-the-year anthologies and has been gathered into two collections, *Fire Watch* (1985) and *Impossible Things* (1993). Her first novel, *Lincoln's Dreams* (1987), won the John W. Campbell Award; her second, *Doomsday Book* (1992), won both a Hugo Award and a Nebula Award.

About the form in which she has most often chosen to write, Connie Willis has said:

> I love the short story. . . . I think I like the variety of moods, styles, and themes I can explore in the short story, which I have always felt was the most successful form of science fiction. It is necessary to work with only a few characters, to create worlds with only a few words and hints of background, and to make everything in the story do double duty. It's an exciting challenge. I have written everything from screwball comedies to mysteries to fairy tales and have found to my delight that science fiction welcomes them all. (From *Twentieth-Century Science-Fiction Writers,* Third Edition, edited by Noelle Watson and Paul E. Schellinger [Chicago: St. James Press, 1991])

About the Editor

Pamela Sargent sold her first science fiction story during her senior year at Binghamton University, where she earned a B.A. and M.A. in philosophy and also studied ancient history and Greek. Her novel *Venus of Dreams* (1986) was listed as one of the "100 Best Science Fiction Novels" by *Library Journal; Earthseed,* her first novel for younger readers, was named a 1983 Best Book for Young Adults by the American Library Association. Her other science fiction novels include *Cloned Lives* (1976), *The Sudden Star* (1979), *Watchstar* (1980), *The Golden Space* (1982), *The Shore of Women* (1986), and *Venus of Shadows* (1988); she has won a Nebula Award, a Locus Award, and has been a finalist for the Hugo Award. She also edited the anthologies *Bio-Futures* (1976) and, with Ian Watson, *Afterlives* (1986). Her most recent novel is *Ruler of the Sky* (1993), a historical novel about Genghis Khan, in which the Mongol conqueror's story is told largely from the points of view of women. She lives in upstate New York.

Recommended Reading

SCIENCE FICTION BY WOMEN, 1979–1993

The following list is intended to direct readers to science fiction written by women. Books and stories were included on the list because of their historical interest, their literary merit, their popularity, their worth as entertainment, or their importance to and influence on the genre. I have tried to make this list representative of all kinds of science fiction and to include as wide a variety of works as possible, but the list is not meant to be comprehensive.

An attempt was made to limit this list to works of science fiction and to exclude fantasy, horror, prehistorical fiction, historical fantasy, and other related categories of fiction; but some writers resist classification, and often it's hard to know where to draw the line. Many of the writers on this list are equally accomplished at other kinds of writing (a few have only occasionally ventured into science fiction), and some writers often claimed by science fiction do not appear here. I have tried to be as inclusive as possible, but had the list grown to encompass works that are, in my judgment, only marginally related to science fiction, the list would have been the size of a book.

Any such list is subject to the prejudices of the person making it, but I have tried not to let my personal tastes interfere with listing as many different kinds of works as possible. Even so, it seems impossible to escape a system for noting especially important books and stories for readers unfamiliar with the genre. Those works that I feel deserve more attention are marked with one star. Important works that, in my opinion, belong in any basic library of science fiction by women are marked with two stars. No ideological yardstick was used to measure these works; although they are all by women, some do not reflect a feminist sensibility.

The following books and publications were of great help in compiling this list:

Anatomy of Wonder: A Critical Guide to Science Fiction, edited by Neil Barron. 3rd ed. New York: R. R. Bowker, 1987.

The Encyclopedia of Science Fiction, edited by John Clute and Peter Nicholls. New York: St. Martin's Press, 1993.

Locus: The Newspaper of the Science Fiction Field, edited by Charles N. Brown, various issues. Oakland, Calif.: Locus Publications.

More Than 100 Women Science Fiction Writers: An Annotated Bibliography, edited by Sharon Yntema. Freedom, Calif.: Crossing Press, 1988.

Science Fiction Book Review Index, 1974–1979, edited by H. W. Hall. Detroit: Gale Research, 1981.

Science Fiction and Fantasy Book Review Index, 1980–1984, edited by H. W. Hall. Detroit: Gale Research, 1985.

Twentieth-Century Science-Fiction Writers, edited by Curtis C. Smith. 2nd ed. Chicago: St. James Press, 1986.

Twentieth-Century Science-Fiction Writers, edited by Noelle Watson and Paul E. Schellinger, et al. 3rd ed. Chicago: St. James Press, 1991.

I have listed only works published in English. Foreign-language science fiction in English translation is barely represented here for the following reasons. The genre has, throughout much of its history, been overwhelmingly dominated by English-speaking writers, and American science fiction publishers, with few exceptions, have not been that receptive to science fiction from other countries. Also, not many women in other lands write science fiction, although some do write what could be labeled fantastic literature. There are a few signs that the numbers of women writing science fiction in non-English-speaking nations may grow, especially in Russia and Ukraine, but at present little is available in English translation.

One of the difficulties in preserving science fiction's history is that so many science fiction books rapidly go out of print or are published in less durable paperback form; hardcovers are often printed only in small numbers. Today, the field has grown tremendously in size and diversity, but most books, both hardcover and paperback, seem to remain in print for increasingly brief periods of time. Publishers have also become even less receptive to quirky or highly original writing that doesn't seem to fit the market and do not often reprint older works of science fiction unless the author is extremely popular or still productive. A few specialty presses, happily, are reprinting some science fiction books in more enduring editions.

Preserving the genre's short fiction is a problem as well, since magazines and anthologies of new work rapidly disappear from newsstands and bookstores, and fewer trade publishers are willing to do collections of short fiction by individual authors, although some excellent small presses are publishing such collections. Many fine anthologies reprinting science fiction stories are available to interested readers, but most of these do not remain in print for as long as they merit.

This list includes novels, collections, anthologies, and short fiction. Some of the works listed were originally published for younger readers but are worthwhile reading for people of all ages. Novels are designated by [n], short fiction collections by [c], anthologies by [a], omnibuses by [o], and chapbooks by [ch]. Books for young adults are labeled [ya]. Titles of individual pieces of short fiction are in quotation marks; I have tried to avoid listing stories that can be found in story collections by their authors.

It is my hope that readers will find this list a useful tool in seeking out some of these works, and that renewed interest in them may help to bring some of them back into print.

Acker, Kathy. *Empire of the Senseless*. New York: Grove Press, 1988. [n]

Ames, Mildred. *Anna to the Infinite Power*. New York: Scribner's, 1981. [n-ya]

★Anthony, Patricia. *Cold Allies*. New York: Harcourt Brace, 1993. [n]

———. *Brother Termite*. New York: Harcourt Brace, 1993. [n]

Antieau, Kim. "Hauntings." *Isaac Asimov's Science Fiction Magazine*, February 1985.

★★Arnason, Eleanor. *A Woman of the Iron People*. New York: Morrow, 1991. [n]

★———. *Ring of Swords*. New York: TOR, 1993. [n]

★Ashwell, Pauline. [Paul Ash, pseud.] *Unwillingly to Earth*. New York: TOR, 1992. [c]

———. "Fatal Statistics." *Analog*, July 1988.

★★Atwood, Margaret. *The Handmaid's Tale*. Boston: Houghton Mifflin, 1986. [n]

Bailey, Hilary. "Everything Blowing Up: An Adventure of Una Persson, Heroine of Time and Space." *Interfaces*, edited by Ursula K. Le Guin and Virginia Kidd. New York: Ace, 1980.

Baird, Wilhelmina. *CrashCourse*. New York: Ace, 1993. [n]

Bell, Clare. *Ratha's Creature*. New York: Atheneum, 1983. [n-ya]
Bohnhoff, Maya Kaathryn. "Home Is Where . . ." *Analog*, November 1991.
Bradley, Marion Zimmer. *Hawkmistress*. New York: DAW Books, 1982. [n]
★———. *Thendara House*. New York: DAW Books, 1983. [n]
★★———. *The Best of Marion Zimmer Bradley*, edited by Martin H. Greenberg. Chicago: Academy Chicago, 1985. [c]
———, with Julian May and Andre Norton. *Black Trillium*. New York: Doubleday, 1990. [n]
Bujold, Lois McMaster. *Ethan of Athos*. New York: Baen, 1986. [n]
———. *Shards of Honor*. New York: Baen, 1986. [n]
★———. *Falling Free*. New York: Baen, 1988. [n]
★———. *Barrayar*. New York: Baen, 1991. [n]
Bull, Emma. *Bone Dance*. New York: Ace, 1991. [n]
★Burdekin, Katharine. [Murray Constantine, pseud.] *The End of This Day's Business*. New York: The Feminist Press of the City University of New York, 1990. [n]
★★Butler, Octavia E. *Kindred*. New York: Doubleday, 1979. [n]
★★———. *Wild Seed*. New York: Doubleday, 1980. [n]
★★———. "Speech Sounds." 1983. Reprinted in *The Norton Book of Science Fiction*, edited by Ursula K. Le Guin and Brian Attebery. New York: Norton, 1993.
★———. *Clay's Ark*. New York: St. Martin's Press, 1984. [n]
★———. *Dawn*. New York: Warner Books, 1987. [n]
★———. "The Evening and the Morning and the Night." *Omni Magazine*, May 1987.
★———. *Adulthood Rites*. New York: Warner Books, 1988. [n]
★———. *Imago*. New York: Warner Books, 1989. [n]
★★———. *Parable of the Sower*. New York: Four Walls Eight Windows, 1993. [n]
Cadigan, Pat. *Mindplayers*. New York: Bantam, 1987. [n]
★★———. *Patterns*. Kansas City, Mo.: Ursus, 1989. [c]
★★———. *Synners*. New York: Bantam, 1991. [n]
———. *Fools*. New York: Bantam, 1992. [n]
★———. *Dirty Work*. Shingletown, Calif.: Mark V. Ziesing, 1993. [c]
★Carr, Jayge. *Leviathan's Deep*. New York: Doubleday, 1979. [n]
★———. *Navigator's Sindrome*. New York: Doubleday, 1983. [n]
★———. *The Treasure in the Heart of the Maze*. New York: Doubleday, 1985. [n]
———. *Rabelaisian Reprise*. New York: Doubleday, 1988. [n]

———. "Blind Spot." 1981. Reprinted in *The 1982 Annual World's Best SF,* edited by Donald A. Wollheim. New York: DAW Books, 1982.

★———. "Chimera." *Synergy 4,* edited by George Zebrowski. San Diego: Harcourt Brace Jovanovich, 1989.

———. "Mourning Blue." *Analog,* February 1993.

Carter, Angela. *Saints and Strangers*. (Published in Britain under the title of *Black Venus*.) New York: Viking, 1986. [c]

Charnas, Suzy McKee. *Dorothea Dreams*. New York: Arbor House, 1986. [n]

★★———. "Listening to Brahms." 1986. Reprinted in *Nebula Awards 22,* edited by George Zebrowski. San Diego: Harcourt Brace Jovanovich, 1988.

★———. "Boobs." *Isaac Asimov's Science Fiction Magazine,* July 1989.

Cherryh, C. J. *Fires of Azeroth*. New York: DAW Books, 1979. [n]

★★———. *The Book of Morgaine* (includes *Gate of Ivrel, Well of Shiuan,* and *Fires of Azeroth*). New York: Nelson Doubleday/Science Fiction Book Club, 1979. [o]

★★———. *Downbelow Station*. New York: DAW Books, 1981. [n]

★———. *Visible Light*. New York: DAW Books, 1986. [c]

★★———. *Cyteen*. New York: Warner Books, 1988. [n]

★———. *Rimrunners*. New York: Warner Books, 1989. [n]

———. *Heavy Time*. New York: Warner Books, 1991. [n]

———. *Hellburner*. New York: Warner Books, 1992. [n]

Collins, Helen. *Mutagenesis*. New York: TOR, 1993. [n]

★Constantine, Storm. *Wraeththu* (includes *The Enchantments of Flesh and Spirit* [1987], *The Bewitchments of Love and Hate* [1988], and *The Fulfilments of Hate and Desire* [1989]). New York: Orb, 1993. [o]

Davis, Grania. "The Songs the Anemones Sing." *Universe 1,* edited by Robert Silverberg and Karen Haber. New York: Doubleday, 1990.

———. "Chroncorp." *The Magazine of Fantasy & Science Fiction,* August 1993.

Dorsey, Candas Jane. "(Learning About) Machine Sex." 1988. Reprinted in *The Norton Book of Science Fiction,* edited by Ursula K. Le Guin and Brian Attebery. New York: Norton, 1993.

Douglas, Carole Nelson. *Probe*. New York: TOR, 1985. [n]

Downing, Paula E. *Flare Star*. New York: Ballantine, Del Rey, 1992. [n]

———. *Fallway*. New York: Ballantine, Del Rey, 1993. [n]

★Dunn, Katherine. *Geek Love*. New York: Knopf, 1989. [n]

★Eakins, Patricia. *The Hungry Girls and Other Stories*. San Francisco: Cadmus, 1988. [c]

Ecklar, Julia. "Promised Lives." *The Magazine of Fantasy & Science Fiction,* September 1993.

★Eisenstein, Phyllis. *Shadow of Earth*. New York: Dell, 1979. [n]

———. "In the Western Tradition." *The Magazine of Fantasy & Science Fiction,* March 1981.

———. "Nightlife." *The Magazine of Fantasy & Science Fiction,* February 1982.

★———. "Sense of Duty." *Isaac Asimov's Science Fiction Magazine,* March 1985.

★Elgin, Suzette Haden. *Communipath Worlds* (includes *The Communipaths* [1970], *Furthest* [1971], and *At the Seventh Level* [1972]). New York: Pocket Books, 1980. [o]

★★———. *Native Tongue*. New York: DAW Books, 1984. [n]

★★———. *Native Tongue II: The Judas Rose*. New York: DAW Books, 1987. [n]

★Emshwiller, Carol. *Verging on the Pertinent*. Minneapolis, Minn.: Coffee House Press, 1989. [c]

★———. *Carmen Dog*. San Francisco: Mercury House, 1990. [n]

★★———. *The Start of the End of It All*. San Francisco: Mercury House, 1991. [c]

★———. *Venus Rising*. Cambridge, Mass.: Edgewood Press, 1992. [ch]

Engh, M. J. *Wheel of the Winds*. New York: TOR, 1988. [n]

★———. *Rainbow Man*. New York: TOR, 1993. [n]

———. "Moon Blood." *Universe 1,* edited by Robert Silverberg and Karen Haber. New York: Doubleday, 1990.

Etchemendy, Nancy. "Lunch at Etienne's." *The Magazine of Fantasy & Science Fiction,* November 1987.

———. "Shore Leave Blacks." *The Magazine of Fantasy & Science Fiction,* March 1990.

★Fairbairns, Zoë. *Benefits*. London: Virago, 1979. [n]

Fancher, Jane. *Groundties*. New York: Warner Books, 1991. [n]

Farber, Sharon N. "Passing as a Flower in the City of the Dead." *Universe 14,* edited by Terry Carr. New York: Doubleday, 1984.

———. "The Sixty-Five Million Year Sleep." *Isaac Asimov's Science Fiction Magazine,* June 1991.

Felice, Cynthia. *Double Nocturne*. New York: Bluejay Books, 1986. [n]

Felice, Cynthia, and Connie Willis. *Water Witch*. New York: Ace Books, 1982. [n]

———. *Light Raid*. New York: Ace Books. 1989. [n]

★Finch, Sheila. *Infinity's Web*. New York: Bantam, 1985. [n]

★———. *Triad*. New York: Bantam, 1986. [n]

★———. *The Garden of the Shaped*. New York: Bantam, 1987. [n]

———. *Shaper's Legacy*. New York: Bantam, 1989. [n]

———. *Shaping the Dawn*. New York: Bantam, 1989. [n]

★———. "The Old Man and C." 1989. Reprinted in *What Might Have Been, Volume 2*, edited by Gregory Benford and Martin H. Greenberg. New York: Bantam, 1990.

★★Fowler, Karen Joy. *Artificial Things*. New York: Bantam, 1986. [c]

★★———. "Lieserl." 1990. Reprinted in *Nebula Awards 26*, edited by James Morrow. San Diego: Harcourt Brace Jovanovich, 1992.

★———. *Sarah Canary*. New York: Holt, 1991. [n]

★———. "The Dark." 1991. Reprinted in *Nebula Awards 27*, edited by James Morrow. San Diego: Harcourt Brace, 1993.

———. "Black Glass." *Full Spectrum 3*, edited by Lou Aronica, Amy Stout, and Betsy Mitchell. New York: Doubleday, 1991.

Friesner, Esther M. "Such a Deal." *What Might Have Been, Volume 4*, edited by Gregory Benford and Martin H. Greenberg. New York: Bantam, 1992.

———. "All Vows." *Asimov's Science Fiction Magazine*, November 1992.

Geary, Patricia. *Strange Toys*. New York: Bantam, 1988. [n]

Gedge, Pauline. *Stargate*. New York: Dial Press, 1982. [n]

★Gentle, Mary. *Golden Witchbreed*. New York: Morrow, 1984. [n]

———. *Ancient Light*. New York: New American Library, 1989. [n]

★★———. *The Architecture of Desire*. New York: ROC, 1991. [n]

Gloss, Molly. "Interlocking Pieces." 1984. Reprinted in *The Norton Book of Science Fiction*, edited by Ursula K. Le Guin and Brian Attebery. New York: Norton, 1993.

———. "Personal Silence." *Isaac Asimov's Science Fiction Magazine*, January 1990.

★Goldstein, Lisa. *The Dream Years*. New York: Bantam, 1985. [n]

★———. *A Mask for the General*. New York: Bantam, 1987. [n]

———. "Cassandra's Photographs." *Isaac Asimov's Science Fiction Magazine*, August 1987.

★———. *Tourists*. New York: Simon & Schuster, 1989. [n]

★★Gotlieb, Phyllis. *Son of the Morning and Other Stories*. New York: Ace, 1983. [c]

———. *Heart of Red Iron*. New York: St. Martin's Press, 1989. [n]

★Green, Jen, and Sarah Lefanu, editors. *Despatches from the Frontiers of the Female Mind*. London: The Women's Press, 1985. [a]

★Griffith, Nicola. *Ammonite*. New York: Ballantine, Del Rey, 1993. [n]
★Gunn, Eileen. "Stable Strategies for Middle Management." 1988. Reprinted in *The Norton Book of Science Fiction*, edited by Ursula K. Le Guin and Brian Attebery. New York: Norton, 1993.
Haber, Karen. *Thieves Carnival*. New York: TOR, 1990. Published with *The Jewel of Bas* by Leigh Brackett as a TOR Books Double. [a]
———. "Madre de Dios." *The Magazine of Fantasy & Science Fiction*, May 1988.
Hall, Sandi. *The Godmothers*. London: The Women's Press, 1982. [n]
★Hamilton, Virginia. *Dustland*. New York: Greenwillow Books, 1980. [n-ya]
★———. *The Gathering*. New York: Greenwillow Books, 1981. [n-ya]
Hand, Elizabeth. *Winterlong*. New York: Bantam, 1990. [n]
———. *Aestival Tide*. New York: Bantam, 1992. [n]
———. *Icarus Descending*. New York: Bantam, 1993. [n]
Henneberg, N. C. *The Green Gods*. Translated from the French by C. J. Cherryh. New York: DAW Books, 1980. [n]
Hoffman, Nina Kiriki. *Unmasking*. Eugene, Oreg.: Axolotl Press, 1992. [ch]
Jones, Gwyneth. *Escape Plans*. London: Allen & Unwin, 1986. [n]
★★———. *Divine Endurance*. New York: Arbor House, 1987. [n]
★★———. *White Queen*. New York: TOR, 1993. [n]
Kagan, Janet. *Hellspark*. New York: TOR, 1988. [n]
———. *Mirabile*. New York: TOR, 1991. [c]
———. "The Nutcracker Coup." *Asimov's Science Fiction*, December 1992.
Karl, Jean E. *But We Are Not of Earth*. New York: Dutton, 1981. [n-ya]
★Kavan, Anna. *My Madness: The Selected Writings of Anna Kavan*, edited by Brian Aldiss. London: Pan Books, 1990. [c]
★Kennedy, Leigh. *The Journal of Nicholas the American*. Boston: Atlantic Monthly Press, 1986. [n]
★———. *Faces*. New York: Atlantic Monthly Press, 1987. [c]
———. *Saint Hiroshima*. San Diego: Harcourt Brace Jovanovich, 1990. [n]
Kerr, Katharine. *Polar City Blues*. New York: Bantam, 1990. [n]
Killough, Lee. *A Voice Out of Ramah*. New York: Ballantine, Del Rey, 1979. [n]
★———. *Aventine*. New York: Ballantine, Del Rey, 1982. [c]
———. *Liberty's World*. New York: DAW Books, 1985. [n]
Koja, Kathe. "Distances." *Isaac Asimov's Science Fiction Magazine*, Mid-December 1988.

★Kress, Nancy. *Trinity and Other Stories*. New York: Bluejay Books, 1985. [c]

★———. *An Alien Light*. New York: Arbor House, 1988. [n]

★———. *Brain Rose*. New York: Morrow, 1990. [n]

★★———. *Beggars in Spain*. New York: Morrow/AvoNova, 1993. [n]

★★———. *The Aliens of Earth*. Sauk City, Wis.: Arkham House, 1993. [c]

★★———. "Dancing on Air." *Asimov's Science Fiction*, July 1993.

★★Lee, Tanith. *The Silver Metal Lover*. New York: DAW Books, 1982. [n]

———. *Days of Grass*. New York: DAW Books, 1985. [n]

———. *A Heroine of the World*. New York: DAW Books, 1989. [n]

★★———. *Women as Demons*. London: The Women's Press, 1989. [c]

★———. *Forests of the Night*. London: Unwin, 1989. [c]

★★Le Guin, Ursula K. *The Compass Rose*. New York: Harper & Row, 1982. [c]

★———. *The Eye of the Heron*. New York: Harper & Row, 1983. [n]

★★———. *Always Coming Home*. New York: Harper & Row, 1985. [n]

★———. *Buffalo Gals and Other Animal Presences*. Santa Barbara, Calif.: Capra Press, 1987. [c]

★Lessing, Doris. *Shikasta*. New York: Knopf, 1979. [n]

★———. *The Marriages Between Zones Three, Four, and Five*. New York: Knopf, 1980. [n]

———. *The Sirian Experiments*. New York: Knopf, 1981. [n]

———. *The Making of the Representative for Planet 8*. New York: Knopf, 1982. [n]

———. *The Sentimental Agents*. New York: Knopf, 1983. [n]

Lichtenberg, Jacqueline. *Mahogany Trinrose*. New York: Doubleday, 1981. [n]

———. *RenSime*. New York: Doubleday, 1984. [n]

———. *Dushau*. New York: Warner Books, 1985. [n]

Lindholm, Megan. *Alien Earth*. New York: Bantam, 1992. [n]

★Love, Rosaleen. *The Total Devotion Machine and Other Stories*. London: The Women's Press, 1989. [c]

———. *Evolution Annie*. London: The Women's Press, 1993. [c]

Lynn, Elizabeth A. *The Woman Who Loved the Moon and Other Stories*. New York: Berkley Books, 1981. [c]

★———. *The Sardonyx Net*. New York: Putnam, 1981. [n]

★———. "At the Embassy Club." *Omni Magazine*, June 1984.

Lyris, Sonia Orin. "Motherhood." *Asimov's Science Fiction*, November 1993.

MacAvoy, R. A. *The Book of Kells*. New York: Bantam, 1985. [n]

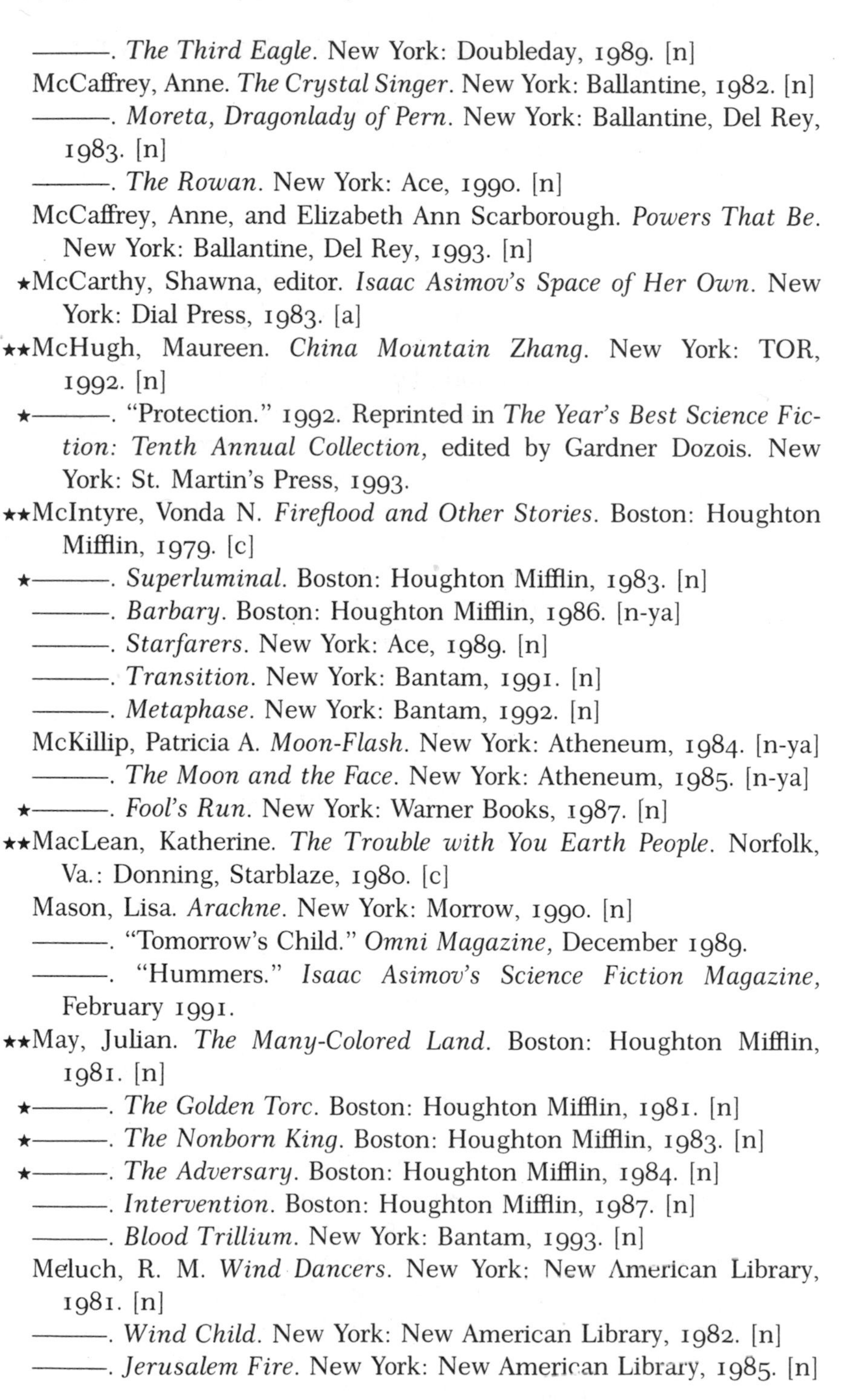

———. *The Third Eagle*. New York: Doubleday, 1989. [n]

McCaffrey, Anne. *The Crystal Singer*. New York: Ballantine, 1982. [n]

———. *Moreta, Dragonlady of Pern*. New York: Ballantine, Del Rey, 1983. [n]

———. *The Rowan*. New York: Ace, 1990. [n]

McCaffrey, Anne, and Elizabeth Ann Scarborough. *Powers That Be*. New York: Ballantine, Del Rey, 1993. [n]

★McCarthy, Shawna, editor. *Isaac Asimov's Space of Her Own*. New York: Dial Press, 1983. [a]

★★McHugh, Maureen. *China Mountain Zhang*. New York: TOR, 1992. [n]

★———. "Protection." 1992. Reprinted in *The Year's Best Science Fiction: Tenth Annual Collection,* edited by Gardner Dozois. New York: St. Martin's Press, 1993.

★★McIntyre, Vonda N. *Fireflood and Other Stories*. Boston: Houghton Mifflin, 1979. [c]

★———. *Superluminal*. Boston: Houghton Mifflin, 1983. [n]

———. *Barbary*. Boston: Houghton Mifflin, 1986. [n-ya]

———. *Starfarers*. New York: Ace, 1989. [n]

———. *Transition*. New York: Bantam, 1991. [n]

———. *Metaphase*. New York: Bantam, 1992. [n]

McKillip, Patricia A. *Moon-Flash*. New York: Atheneum, 1984. [n-ya]

———. *The Moon and the Face*. New York: Atheneum, 1985. [n-ya]

★———. *Fool's Run*. New York: Warner Books, 1987. [n]

★★MacLean, Katherine. *The Trouble with You Earth People*. Norfolk, Va.: Donning, Starblaze, 1980. [c]

Mason, Lisa. *Arachne*. New York: Morrow, 1990. [n]

———. "Tomorrow's Child." *Omni Magazine,* December 1989.

———. "Hummers." *Isaac Asimov's Science Fiction Magazine,* February 1991.

★★May, Julian. *The Many-Colored Land*. Boston: Houghton Mifflin, 1981. [n]

★———. *The Golden Torc*. Boston: Houghton Mifflin, 1981. [n]

★———. *The Nonborn King*. Boston: Houghton Mifflin, 1983. [n]

★———. *The Adversary*. Boston: Houghton Mifflin, 1984. [n]

———. *Intervention*. Boston: Houghton Mifflin, 1987. [n]

———. *Blood Trillium*. New York: Bantam, 1993. [n]

Meluch, R. M. *Wind Dancers*. New York: New American Library, 1981. [n]

———. *Wind Child*. New York: New American Library, 1982. [n]

———. *Jerusalem Fire*. New York: New American Library, 1985. [n]

★Mitchison, Naomi. *A Girl Must Live: Stories and Poems*. Glasgow: R. Drew, 1990. [c]

Mixon, Laura J. *Glass Houses*. New York: TOR, 1992. [n]

★★Moffett, Judith. "Surviving." 1986. Reprinted in *Nebula Awards 22*, edited by George Zebrowski. San Diego: Harcourt Brace Jovanovich, 1988.

★———. *Pennterra*. New York: Congdon & Weed, 1987. [n]

★★———. *The Ragged World: A Novel of the Hefn on Earth*. New York: St. Martin's Press, 1991. [n]

★———. *Time, Like an Ever-Rolling Stream*. New York: St. Martin's Press, 1992. [n]

★Moore, C. L. *Northwest Smith*. New York: Ace, 1982. [c]

Moroz, Anne. *No Safe Place*. New York: Warner Books, 1986. [n]

Morris, Janet. *Dream Dancer*. New York: Berkley Books, 1980. [n]

———. *Cruiser Dreams*. New York: Berkley Books, 1980. [n]

———. *Earth Dreams*. New York: Berkley Books, 1982. [n]

★Murphy, Pat. *The Falling Woman*. New York: TOR, 1986. [n]

———. *The City, Not Long After*. New York: Doubleday, 1989. [n]

★★———. *Points of Departure*. New York: Bantam, 1990. [c]

———. "Traveling West." *Isaac Asimov's Science Fiction Magazine*, February 1991.

———. "An American Childhood." *Asimov's Science Fiction*, April 1993.

★———. "A Cartographic Analysis of the Dream State." *Omni Best Science Fiction Three*, edited by Ellen Datlow. Greensboro, N.C.: Omni Books, 1993.

O'Neal, Kathleen M. [Kathleen O'Neal Gear.] *An Abyss of Light*. New York: DAW Books, 1990. [n]

★Ore, Rebecca. *Becoming Alien*. New York: TOR, 1988. [n]

★———. *Being Alien*. New York: TOR, 1989. [n]

★———. *Human to Human*. New York: TOR, 1990. [n]

★★———. *The Illegal Rebirth of Billy the Kid*. New York: TOR, 1991. [n]

★★———. *Alien Bootlegger and Other Stories*. New York: TOR, 1993. [c]

Palmer, Jane. *The Watcher*. London: The Women's Press, 1986. [n]

Palwick, Susan. *Flying in Place*. New York: TOR, 1992.

★Piercy, Marge. *He, She, and It*. New York: Knopf, 1991. [n]

★Piserchia, Doris. *Earth in Twilight*. New York: DAW Books, 1981.

Plowright, Teresa. *Dreams of an Unseen Planet*. New York: Arbor House, 1986. [n]

★Pollack, Rachel. *Unquenchable Fire*. Woodstock, N.Y.: Overlook Press, 1992. [n]

Randall, Marta. *Dangerous Games*. New York: Pocket Books, 1980.

———. "Lapidary Nights." *Universe 17*, edited by Terry Carr. New York: Doubleday, 1987.

Reed, Kit. [Kit Craig.] *Magic Time*. New York: Berkley Books, 1979. [n]

★★———. *Other Stories, and The Attack of the Giant Baby*. New York: Berkley Books, 1981. [c]

★———. *Fort Privilege*. New York: Doubleday, 1985. [n]

★———. *The Revenge of the Senior Citizens*. New York: Doubleday, 1986. [c]

Roessner, Michaela. *Walkabout Woman*. New York: Bantam, 1988. [n]

★———. *Vanishing Point*. New York: TOR, 1993. [n]

Rosenblum, Mary. "Synthesis." *Isaac Asimov's Science Fiction Magazine*, March 1992.

———. *The Drylands*. New York: Ballantine, Del Rey, 1993. [n]

———. *Chimera*. New York: Ballantine, 1993. [n]

———. "The Rain Stone." *Asimov's Science Fiction*, July 1993.

Rusch, Kristine Kathryn. "Skin Deep." *Amazing Stories*, January 1988.

———. "Fast Cars." *Isaac Asimov's Science Fiction Magazine*, October 1989.

★———. "The Gallery of His Dreams." 1991. Reprinted in *The Year's Best Science Fiction: Ninth Annual Collection*, edited by Gardner Dozois. New York: St. Martin's Press, 1992.

———. "Sinner-Saints." *The Magazine of Fantasy & Science Fiction*, May 1993.

Russ, Joanna. *On Strike Against God*. New York: Out and Out Books, 1980. [n]

★★———. *The Adventures of Alyx*. New York: Pocket Books, Timescape, 1983. [c]

★★———. *The Zanzibar Cat*. Sauk City, Wis.: Arkham House, 1983. [c]

★★———. *Extra (Ordinary) People*. New York: St. Martin's Press, 1984. [c]

★★———. *The Hidden Side of the Moon*. New York: St. Martin's Press, 1987. [c]

★★———. *Souls*. New York: TOR, 1989. Published with *Houston, Houston, Do You Read?* by James Tiptree, Jr., as a TOR Books Double. [a]

★★St. Clair, Margaret. [Idris Seabright, pseud.] *The Best of Margaret St.*

Clair, edited by Martin H. Greenberg. Chicago: Academy Chicago, 1985.

Salmonson, Jessica Amanda. *Tomoe Gozen.* New York: Ace, 1981. [n]

———. *The Golden Naginata.* New York: Ace, 1982. [n]

———. *The Swordswoman.* New York: TOR, 1982. [n]

★Salmonson, Jessica Amanda, editor. *Amazons!* New York: DAW Books, 1979. [a]

★———. *What Did Miss Darrington See? An Anthology of Feminist Supernatural Fiction.* New York: The Feminist Press at the City University of New York, 1989.

Sargent, Pamela. *Earthseed.* New York: Harper & Row, 1983. [n-ya]

———. *Venus of Dreams.* New York: Bantam, 1986. [n]

———. *The Shore of Women.* New York: Crown, 1986. [n]

———. *The Best of Pamela Sargent,* edited by Martin H. Greenberg. Chicago: Academy Chicago, 1987. [c]

———. *Venus of Shadows.* New York: Doubleday, 1988. [n]

★★Saxton, Josephine. *The Power of Time.* London: Chatto & Windus, 1985. [c]

———. *Queen of the States.* London: The Women's Press, 1986. [n]

★———. *The Travails of Jane Saint and Other Stories.* London: The Women's Press, 1986. [c]

★———. *Jane Saint and the Backlash: The Further Travails of Jane Saint* and *The Consciousness Machine.* London: The Women's Press, 1989. [n]

Scarborough, Elizabeth Ann. *The Healer's War.* New York: Doubleday, 1988. [n]

Scott, Jody. "The American Book of the Dead." *Afterlives,* edited by Pamela Sargent and Ian Watson. New York: Vintage, 1986.

Scott, Melissa. *Five-Twelfths of Heaven.* New York: Baen, 1985. [n]

———. *Silence in Solitude.* New York: Baen, 1986. [n]

———. *The Kindly Ones.* New York: Baen, 1987. [n]

———. *The Empress of Earth.* New York: Baen, 1988. [n]

———. *Dreamships.* New York: TOR, 1992. [n]

Shwartz, Susan. *Heritage of Flight.* New York: TOR, 1989. [n]

———. "Getting Real." 1991. Reprinted in *Nebula Awards 27,* edited by James Morrow. San Diego: Harcourt Brace, 1993.

★———. "Suppose They Gave a Peace." *Alternate Presidents,* edited by Mike Resnick. New York: TOR, 1992.

Slonczewski, Joan. *Still Forms on Foxfield.* New York: Ballantine, Del Rey, 1980. [n]

★★———. *A Door into Ocean.* New York: Arbor House, 1986. [n]

★———. *The Wall around Eden*. New York: Morrow, 1989. [n]
★★———. *Daughter of Elysium*. New York: Morrow/AvoNova, 1993. [n]
★Soukup, Martha. "Over the Long Haul." 1990. Reprinted in *Nebula Awards 26*, edited by James Morrow. San Diego: Harcourt Brace Jovanovich, 1992.
———. "The Arbitrary Placement of Walls." *Isaac Asimov's Science Fiction Magazine*, April 1992.
———. "The Story So Far." *Full Spectrum 4*, edited by Lou Aronica, Amy Stout, and Betsy Mitchell. New York: Bantam, 1993.
Springer, Nancy. *Ap♀calypse*. New York: Baen, 1989. [n]
Steele, Linda. *Ibis*. New York: DAW Books, 1985. [n]
Sturgis, Susanna J., editor. *Memories and Visions*. Vol. 1 of *Women's Fantasy & Science Fiction*. Freedom, Calif.: Crossing Press, 1989. [a]
———. *The Women Who Walk Through Fire*. Vol. 2 of *Women's Fantasy & Science Fiction*. Freedom, Calif.: Crossing Press, 1990. [a]
Sykes, S. C. "Rockabye Baby." *Analog*, Mid-December 1985.
Tepper, Sheri S. *The Gate to Women's Country*. New York: Bantam, 1988. [n]
★———. *Grass*. New York: Doubleday, 1989. [n]
★———. *Raising the Stones*. New York: Doubleday, 1991. [n]
★———. *Sideshow*. New York: Bantam, 1992. [n]
———. *A Plague of Angels*. New York: Bantam, 1993. [n]
Thomas, Sue. *Correspondence*. Woodstock, N.Y.: Overlook Press, 1993. [n]
★Thompson, Joyce. *Conscience Place*. New York: Doubleday, 1984. [n]
Thomson, Amy. *Virtual Girl*. New York: Ace, 1993. [n]
★★Tiptree, James, Jr. [Raccoona Sheldon, pseud.] *Out of the Everywhere and Other Extraordinary Visions*. New York: Ballantine, Del Rey, 1981. [c]
★———. *Brightness Falls from the Air*. New York: TOR, 1985. [n]
———. *Byte Beautiful*. New York: Doubleday, 1985. [c]
———. *The Starry Rift*. New York: TOR, 1986. [c]
★———. *Tales of the Quintana Roo*. Sauk City, Wis.: Arkham House, 1986. [c]
———. *Crown of Stars*. New York: TOR, 1988. [c]
★★———. *Her Smoke Rose Up Forever*. Sauk City, Wis.: Arkham House, 1990. [c]
★Tuttle, Lisa. *A Spaceship Built of Stone*. London: The Women's Press, 1987. [c]
★———. *Memories of the Body*. New York: Severn House, 1992. [c]

———. *Lost Futures.* New York: Dell, 1992. [n]
Tuttle, Lisa, editor. *Skin of the Soul.* London: The Women's Press, 1990. [a]
Van Scyoc, Sydney. *Darkchild.* New York: Berkley Books, 1982. [n]
———. *Bluesong.* New York: Berkley Books, 1983. [n]
———. "Fire-Caller." 1983. Reprinted in *Isaac Asimov's Space of Her Own,* edited by Shawna McCarthy. New York: Dial Press, 1983.
———. *Starsilk.* New York: Berkley Books, 1984. [n]
———. *Drowntide.* New York: Berkley Books, 1987. [n]
———. *Feather Stroke.* New York: Avon, 1989. [n]
Vinge, Joan D. *Eyes of Amber and Other Stories.* New York: New American Library, 1979. [c]
★★———. *The Snow Queen.* New York: Dial Press, 1980. [n]
★———. *Psion.* New York: Delacorte, 1982. [n-ya]
★———. *World's End.* New York: Bluejay Books, 1984. [n]
———. *Phoenix in the Ashes.* New York: Bluejay Books, 1985. [c]
★———. *The Summer Queen.* New York: Warner Books, 1991. [n]
Vonarburg, Elisabeth. *The Silent City.* Translated from the French by Jane Brierley. New York: Bantam, 1992. [n]
★———. *In the Mothers' Land.* Translated from the French by Jane Brierley. New York: Bantam, 1992. [n]
Webb, Sharon. *Earthchild.* New York: Atheneum, 1982. [n-ya]
———. *Earth Song.* New York: Atheneum, 1983. [n-ya]
———. *Ram Song.* New York: Atheneum, 1984. [n-ya]
———. *The Adventures of Terra Tarkington.* New York: Bantam, 1985. [c]
Weldon, Fay. *The Cloning of Joanna May.* New York: Viking, 1990. [n]
Wheeler, Deborah. "Madrelita." *The Magazine of Fantasy & Science Fiction,* February 1992.
Wilder, Cherry. *Second Nature.* New York: Pocket Books, Timescape, 1982. [n]
★Wilhelm, Kate. *Juniper Time.* New York: Harper & Row, 1979. [n]
★★———. *Listen, Listen.* Boston: Houghton Mifflin, 1981. [n]
★★———. *Welcome, Chaos.* Boston: Houghton Mifflin, 1983. [n]
———. *Huysman's Pets.* New York: Bluejay Books, 1986. [n]
★★———. *Children of the Wind.* New York: St. Martin's Press, 1989. [c]
———. *Cambio Bay.* New York: St. Martin's Press, 1990. [n]
★———. *Death Qualified: A Mystery of Chaos.* New York: St. Martin's Press, 1991. [n]
★★———. *And the Angels Sing.* New York: St. Martin's Press, 1992. [c]

★Williams, A. Susan. *The Lifted Veil: The Book of Fantastic Literature by Women*. New York: Carroll & Graf, 1992. [a]

★★Willis, Connie. *Fire Watch*. New York: Bluejay Books, 1985. [c]

★———. *Lincoln's Dreams*. New York: Bantam, 1987. [n]

★———. *Doomsday Book*. New York: Bantam, 1992. [n]

★★———. *Impossible Things*. New York: Bantam, 1993. [c]

Wood, N. Lee. "Memories That Dance Like Dust in the Summer Heat." *Amazing*, March 1990.

★Yarbro, Chelsea Quinn. *Ariosto*. New York: Pocket Books, 1980. [n]

———. *Hyacinths*. New York: Doubleday, 1983. [n]

★———. *Signs and Portents*. Santa Cruz, Calif.: Dream Press, 1984. [c]

Yolen, Jane. *Tales of Wonder*. New York: Schocken, 1983. [c]

———. *Cards of Grief*. New York: Ace, 1984. [n]

★———. *Sister Light, Sister Dark*. New York: TOR, 1988. [n]

★———. *The Devil's Arithmetic*. New York: Viking, 1988. [n-ya]

———. *White Jenna*. New York: TOR, 1989. [n]

———. "Feast of Souls." *Isaac Asimov's Science Fiction Magazine*, January 1989.

★★Zoline, Pamela. *The Heat Death of the Universe and Other Stories*. (Published in Britain under the title of *Busy about the Tree of Life*.) Kingston, N.Y.: McPherson & Co., 1988. [c]

PERMISSIONS ACKNOWLEDGMENTS

"Cassandra" by C. J. Cherryh. Copyright © 1978 by Mercury Press, Inc. First appeared in *The Magazine of Fantasy and Science Fiction*, 1978. Reprinted by permission of the author.

"The Thaw" by Tanith Lee. Copyright © 1979 by Tanith Lee. Reprinted by permission of the author.

"Scorched Supper on New Niger" by Suzy McKee Charnas. Copyright © 1980 by Suzy McKee Charnas. First published in *New Voices III* (Berkley Books, 1980). Reprinted by permission of the author.

"Abominable" by Carol Emshwiller. Copyright © 1980 by Carol Emshwiller. First appeared in *Orbit 21;* reprinted by permission of the author and Virginia Kidd, Literary Agent.

"Bluewater Dreams" by Sydney J. Van Scyoc. Copyright © 1981 by Sydney J. Van Scyoc. Reprinted by permission of the author.

"The Cabinet of Edgar Allan Poe" by Angela Carter. Copyright © 1982 by Angela Carter. Reprinted by permission of Rogers, Coleridge & White Ltd.

"The Harvest of Wolves" by Mary Gentle. Copyright © 1984 by Mary Gentle. Reprinted by permission of the author.

"Bloodchild" by Octavia E. Butler. Copyright © 1984 by Davis Publications, Inc. First published in *Isaac Asimov's Science Fiction Magazine*. Reprinted by permission of the author.

"Fears" by Pamela Sargent. Copyright © 1984 by Pamela Sargent. Originally published in *Light Years and Dark* (Berkley Books). Reprinted by permission of the author and her agent, Richard Curtis Associates, Inc.

"Webrider" by Jayge Carr. Copyright © 1985 by Jayge Carr. Reprinted from *The Third Omni Book of Science Fiction* by permission of the author.

"Alexia and Graham Bell" by Rosaleen Love. Copyright © Rosaleen Love 1986. Originally published in *Aphelion* 5, 1986–87. From *The*

Total Devotion Machine by Rosaleen Love, published 1989 by The Women's Press Ltd. Used by permission of The Women's Press, 34 Great Sutton Street, London EC1V ODX.

"Reichs-Peace" by Sheila Finch. Copyright © 1986 by Sheila Finch. Reprinted by permission of the author.

"Angel" by Pat Cadigan. Copyright © 1987 by Davis Publications, Inc. First published in *Isaac Asimov's Science Fiction Magazine* (June 1987). Reprinted by permission of the author.

"Rachel in Love" by Pat Murphy. Copyright © 1987 by Davis Publications, Inc. First published in *Isaac Asimov's Science Fiction Magazine* (April 1987). Reprinted by permission of the author.

"Game Night at the Fox and Goose" by Karen Joy Fowler. Copyright © Karen Joy Fowler, 1989. First appeared in *Interzone* 29 (May/June 1989). Reprinted by permission of the author.

"Tiny Tango" by Judith Moffett. Copyright © 1989 by Davis Publications, Inc. First published in *Isaac Asimov's Science Fiction Magazine*. Reprinted by permission of the author.

"At the Rialto" by Connie Willis. Copyright © 1989 by *Omni*. Reprinted by permission of the author.

"Midnight News" by Lisa Goldstein. Copyright © Lisa Goldstein, 1990. Reprinted by permission of the author.

"And Wild for to Hold" by Nancy Kress. Copyright © 1991 by Davis Publications, Inc. First published in *Isaac Asimov's Science Fiction Magazine* (July 1991). Reprinted by permission of the author.

"Immaculate" by Storm Constantine. Copyright © 1991 by Storm Constantine. Reprinted by permission of the author.

"Farming in Virginia" by Rebecca Ore. Copyright © 1993 by Rebecca Ore. Reprinted by permission of St. Martin's Press, Inc., New York, NY; the author; and the author's agents, Scovil Chichak Galen Literary Agency, Inc., New York, NY.

Passages from *Women of Vision*, edited by Denise Du Pont (St. Martin's Press, 1988), are quoted here by permission of Ms. Du Pont and her agent, Richard Curtis Associates, Inc.

WITHDRAWN